*for*

Beth Baughman DuPree, M.D., F.A.C.S.,
who wages this war with a velvet sword
and the healing spirit of Mother Nature

IN MEMORY OF THE COURAGEOUS WOMEN I LOVE
AND WILL NEVER FORGET. . .

Christina Duess,
my brave and beautiful sister-in-law.

Marie Murphy Purcell,
my aunt who tried to spare us always.

and

Katherine Kilgannon,
my cousin whose courage surpassed all.

# TEARS
## *of the*
# WILLOW

# TEARS
## *of the*
# WILLOW

# Tears of the Willow

For more information, visit
www.MarieDuess.com

Cover photo: iStockphoto.com/davetownsend
Willow tree on inside pages: iStockphoto.com/marinamariya
Author's photo: Dave Austria Photography

Printing History: First Printing 2013

WATERFALL
PUBLISHING
™

Printed in the United States of America
10 9 8 7 6 5 4 3 2 1

# ACKNOWLEDGEMENTS

As always, I thank my husband, Edward Duess, who has proven that men are just as courageous as women. I love him with all my heart. He always believes in me, even when I don't. He still makes all my dreams come true.

So do my children—my cheerleaders—they are my oxygen, as are my nephews, Tommy and Christian, and my niece Jessica. All of them should see a little of themselves in Joey, Philip and Suzy. I borrowed a little from their childhoods—their sweetness, their sassiness, their good common sense, and even from their wounds and sadness. What a privilege it has been to walk with all of them on their journeys in life so far. I hope they'll always welcome me to walk with them.

The same is true of my sister Joyce. We've walked many miles together through happiness and heartache, and always with love. She read the earliest version of the manuscript, and she told me she laughed, she cried, and she loved all of it. She has asked me ceaselessly, "When is that book going to be published?" If she likes it, I figure it has to be good. That's how much I trust and respect her opinion.

Most importantly, I would like to thank Ann LaFarge, editor extraordinaire, who took the time to edit the manuscript—not once, but twice.

Ann's expertise was invaluable. Her comments in the margins of the manuscript, "You've got a winner here" and "…beautifully written" allowed me to be courageous and to believe in this book. I join all the writers who were mentored and guided by Ann in thanking her for being the gentle yet tough editor she is.

And Emily DiBala, my great friend, who came to the rescue at the last minute to line edit the proof copy of the book. What a lifesaver she is!

# Willow Wood Farm

## 1846

"We'll bury it here... here under the willow," the girl in a yellow and black shawl whispered. Her voice was shrill, verging on hysteria. She held crumpled linens against her chest, and the corners of the sheet fell in all directions as though it had been taken up in haste and rolled into her arms. She turned her face to another girl who was slightly shorter than she was and who walked a few paces behind. "Hurry!

"We can't. We don't have enough time to dig a hole deep enough to keep it from washing up if the river floods. It can't be done here. This is too close to the river and the canal." She reached out to take the wrappings from the taller girl's arms. "Please don't do this!"

"No, it will be here!" the taller girl replied, hugging the linens to her chest protectively. "This is where I will bury it."

The damp ground on the berm that ran along the silent canal stained the hems of their skirts and their bare feet were muddy. A light drizzle lay over the land and the water of the canal, and the night was so dark that it was difficult for the girls to see each other's faces. They could hear the shad jumping in the river, but they couldn't see the water through the inky night. Their breathing was labored, and the smaller girl grunted when her bare sole landed on a small jagged stone.

"This is a mistake, I tell you," she said as she balanced on one foot and pulled the stone from her flesh.

"It's not a mistake. Don't you see, I will always know where it is. I can watch from the house to make sure no one finds it." The girl pulled her shawl back from her face a little and looked up at the soft branches of the willow. "And if no one else will weep for it, the tree will," she added in a sad whisper.

"It's so dark out here we don't even know if a canal boat is tied up nearby for the night. Someone could see us or hear us."

"If we can't see them, they can't see us. Just be quick and quiet."

They reached a soft spot of ground behind the willow tree and the girl in the yellow and black shawl, the sheet still pulled close to her, indicated with her head that the other girl should begin to dig.

They stood across from each other looking down at the spot of grass under the tree. A sob escaped from the smaller girl as she slowly swung the shovel she had been holding at her side and pushed it down into the earth. The grass and dirt gave reluctantly, and she tried to use her bare foot to push the tip of the shovel deeper into the ground. "I can't," she whined.

"Do it! Will you just do it! Quickly! Don't make me do it. I can feel the blood running down my legs and my belly is cramping. I'm not strong enough tonight." Her voice softened. "Please do this for me."

The plea propelled the other girl, and she pushed harder and the shovel moved the earth. She dug again and this time it moved more easily. She sliced the ground once more…and again…and the hole grew, but her movements were strained and she was tiring. The taller girl laid the sheet down on the ground gently and fell to her knees. She used her hands to help dig the hole. She could feel the dirt become embedded under her nails; her fingers ached with the effort of clawing and pulling the dirt out of the hole.

"Hurry," she said. "Hurry…before I become too weak."

Together they broke up earth, pushed it to the side, and then broke more. The hole wasn't large, nor was it deep. The yellow and black shawl fell off the girl's head and then her left shoulder, showing a white linen sleeve beneath. She stopped digging with her hands and laid her palms flat against the ground, her fingers dangling over the shallow hole, her back arched, her head down. The mist surrounded her, dampening her fine red hair, and she breathed in the cool wet air with a jagged breath that made her cough. She grabbed her stomach with a hand that was black with muck and braced herself against falling over with her other hand.

"I can't do more," she said. "I must get back to the house…to my bed. This has to do."

The other girl dropped the shovel and ran to her sister's side. Falling on her knees, she placed her arm over the sick girl's back. "Will you faint, do you think? If you do, I'll never get you back to the house without anyone knowing. You mustn't faint."

The older girl shook her head slowly. She reached up and wiped her nose with her muddy fingers, then reached for the sheet, pulling it close to her chest again. Her fingers stained the white linen as she pulled it up and buried her face in it, crying for the first time. She shrugged the other girl off and started to put the sheet into the hole.

"It's not deep enough, I tell you. You can't bury it like this. It is too shallow a grave. The dogs will dig it up," and with those final words, she, too, began to sob. "This won't be good."

"We'll come back when I'm stronger and dig a deeper hole. I can't go on tonight. Just help me press it down as far into the grave as we can and cover it."

They reached over the hole they had dug and placed the sheet down into it. Then as an afterthought, the older girl took off her shawl and placed it on top of the sheet. Together with shovel and hands they pushed the mound of dirt over the sheet. When the girls finished, they stayed beside the tiny grave for a long silent moment, each in her own thoughts.

"Was it a girl or a boy?" the older girl asked her sister.

"Don't ask me that. It will be harder for you if you know." The younger girl quickly pushed more dirt over the sheet with her shovel. "I won't tell you."

"Will you tell me this, then? Will you tell me what color was its skin?"

# Part One

*It is one of the most beautiful compensations of this life that no man can seriously help another without helping himself.*

Charles Dudley Warner, 1873

# *One*

| | |
|---|---|
| From: | Lillian Phelan [lpfreelncrwrtr@aol.com] |
| To: | Dan Paulsen [dpaulsen1@msn.com] |
| Subject: | I did it again |
| Sent: | 6/13 2:47 PM |

Stupid … stupid … forgetful idiot that I am. You won't be hearing from me until I find a place to live. Poor Mrs. Snyder sold the house while I was away and didn't know how to reach me. Today is moving day. No place to plug in the computer after this email. Just got home from Oklahoma half an hour ago to find the moving men on the doorstep. Gotta go … don't worry. Don't bother calling – the cell phone battery is dead and I can't find the charger (probably in Oklahoma or plane). When in God's name will I get my act together?

| | |
|---|---|
| From: | Dan Paulsen [dpaulsen1@msn.com] |
| To: | Lillian Phelan [lpfreelncrwrtr@aol.com] |
| Subject: | Wait! |
| Sent: | 6/13 2:55 PM |

Are you still there? Lillian, I can't believe you're homeless … again. Come here to me – get the 4:30 to Penn Station and I'll meet you there. My darling, Lillian, you are a calamity! I'm worried now. For all I know you'll be sleeping on a park bench. Don't leave me hanging too long. Call me and let me know where you are.

| | |
|---|---|
| From: | T. Darryl Worthington |
| To: | BJohnson @ BendersonJohnsonEsq.com |
| Subject: | Closing 12379 State Street |
| Sent: | 6/13 3:50 PM |

Ben, just wanted to tell you that Eleanor Snyder is about moved out (I can see the brownstone from my office window), and her tenant has returned from her business trip. It's easy telling that she didn't know we decided to close on the house early, which explains why poor Mrs. Snyder was so upset at the closing this morning.

By my estimation, the tenant should be heading to Starbucks on the corner in about ten minutes. She can't do anything without a cup of coffee in her hand.

We'll follow up tomorrow. As always, it was a pleasure. I hope your client enjoys her lovely historical home. Please, I beg of you, don't let your client turn it into another restaurant. We've got too many of them in town as it is.

Sincerely,
Darryl

| | |
|---|---|
| From: | Lillian Phelan [lpfreelncrwrtr@aol.com] |
| To: | Dan Paulsen [dpaulsen1@msn.com] |
| Subject: | Okay, I'm not on the street |
| Sent: | 6/13 2:00 AM |

I have a propensity for being stupid and forgetful, as you know, and stop smirking, Danny boy. Sorry for my earlier panicked email. I have found a home, temporarily anyway. I have a charger now, so I'll call when my phone is completely charged and fill you in. BTW, thanks for the invitation (which I got too late, obviously). I knew I could come to you, but then that would have been too easy, and I never do anything easy. I'll call.

| | |
|---|---|
| From: | Fourforlife@comcast.net |
| To: | BJohnson @ BendersonJohnsonEsq.com |
| Subject: | mission accomplished |
| Sent: | 6/13 2:35 AM |

Thanks for your help. Everything worked out perfect so far. I'll keep you informed, and you keep me in your prayers.

# Two

Lillian hit the "send" button, waited to make sure her email to Dan went through, and started to work on an article she was writing. Her cell phone rang. It was plugged into the charger and resting on the floor near the outlet. She smiled. He just couldn't wait until she called him. She wasn't certain if she liked the fact that Dan was so worried about her or resented it a little. Probably both, she thought as she put the laptop aside and grabbed the cell phone.

"Yes, you impatient pest," she answered, sitting on the bed and leaning back against the headboard. "You do know it is two o'clock in the morning, right?"

"You can't do that to me," Dan responded. "You can't email me to tell me you don't have place to live, then email me to tell me you have a place and you'll call me later. I've had my Blackberry in my bed this whole time waiting for your next email or call. For all I know, you've taken up residence with a traveling circus."

Lillian smiled. "Would that surprise you?"

"Not at all, but I'd just like to know what's going on."

"Okay, here's my sad story. I left for Oklahoma last week to interview a holistic veterinarian for my article, and I left for the airport early in the morning and didn't have a chance to say a word to poor Mrs. Snyder about where I was going. I thought I had plenty of time to find another apartment and move out when I got back from Oklahoma, but it turns out that the buyer for her house wanted to close earlier and Mrs. Snyder couldn't reach me to tell me."

Lillian took a quick swallow from a bottle of water before finishing. "When I got back to Newtown, I thought that I'd have the rest of the afternoon to finish the story, and then I saw the moving van parked outside and two large smelly, sweaty men carrying Mrs. Snyder's lovely antiques out the door."

"Large, smelly sweaty men...you always paint such a pretty picture."

"At first I thought she had died. I was relieved when she came out of the house. The poor old thing was so upset. It's bad enough she has to leave that gorgeous old house to live in the assisted living place, then I wasn't there and she didn't know what she was going to do with my things—meager as they are—and most of all, bless her ancient old heart, she was worried sick about where I was going to stay when I got home and the place was empty. I reassured her that I would be fine, and she felt better by the time her son came and drove her off to the Quakers, but I must have put ten years on her life."

"Living with you has put more than ten years on her life," Dan offered. "But let's get to the point, where the hell are you staying?"

"Here's the weird part of the story. I went to Starbucks on the corner to get my usual plain old ordinary coffee, which always makes them smirk because nobody around here orders plain coffee anymore. The truth is, I didn't have enough cash to take the train to New York to stay with you, and my checking account has about twelve dollars in it, barely enough for my coffee. Where does my money go? Anyway, there's this blond woman sitting in the corner smiling at me. It took me a good twenty seconds to realize she's my cousin, Ann, whom I haven't seen in about twenty years. She's moved back to Bucks County and is living in at the old farm."

"Your grandparents' old house?" he asked.

"The same. Remember I told you about four years ago that Ann's husband had died? A heart attack or something and he was only 28. She's got two kids, a boy and a girl. Well, anyway, I told her my story and she asked me to stay with her. She drove me over to a car rental service and we got a utility van. She helped me move my stuff from Mrs. Snyder's and then into her house, or rather her garage at this point."

"I always say you have unbelievable luck. How did the interview go with the holistic vet?"

"A little weird, but kind of interesting. She makes herbal potions for sick cattle and claims to communicate with them through mental telepathy...stop laughing, Dan. I was getting some really strong vibes that she's for real, but that's another story."

"Why are you so broke?"

"You have to ask? You know I'm horrible with money. And I had to pay for my flight to Oklahoma and the hotel there. It'll take a few weeks before I get my check for the story."

Lillian stretched her leg out and winced when the muscles in her hips and back protested. "I'm exhausted and I ache all over from moving my things. It's a weird feeling being in this old house again after such a long time, Dan. After my grandparents moved to Florida, my Aunt Helen—Ann's mom—and her husband continued to live in it for a few years before they, too, moved to Florida."

"Are you going to be all right staying there?" Dan asked, his voice softer now.

"I don't know," she answered honestly.

"Bad memories?" he asked.

"Not the worst memories here in this house. I loved my grandparents and my aunt was always my favorite person in the whole world. I could never understand how she could be my mother's sister. Ann said she's in a place down in Florida near where my uncle lives. They take care of Alzheimer's patients."

"It sounds like Ann has had a tough time," Dan said. "How are her kids?"

Lillian thought the question over. She had just met them for the first time that evening and spent only a few minutes with them before coming up to her room to settle in and work on her article. She couldn't even remember their names.

"Her kids seem okay, but you know I'm not crazy about kids—except your gorgeous, brilliant daughter, of course. I'll have to put up with them temporarily until I can find my own place. First I need to email my article to my editor, get a check for it, and then..."

"You know you can..." Dan started to reiterate that she should come to his apartment, but she interrupted.

"I know, I know," she said. She was too tired for that argument.

He was silent for a long moment, then started, "Lillian..."

"No, please, Dan," she groaned, "not tonight. We'll talk about my plans tomorrow."

"I was going to say that maybe it's good that you're there. Maybe you could get rid of those bad memories."

"You mean exorcise my demons, don't you?"

"And then move on with your life," he continued.

"I'm forty-four, Danny boy; if I haven't exorcised those demons by now, I never will."

He was silent then.

"Hey," she said.

"Hey," he answered quietly.

"My demons go away when I'm around you."

"You *are* a demon when you're around me," he answered, his voice lighter now, suggestive.

"All right, that's enough of that. You can stop worrying about me tonight. I have a roof over my head, I haven't become the first and only homeless person to sleep in the park in Newtown, and I'm fed and fine. Luckily, Ann has the same type of cell phone, and she's letting me use her charger. She's also got a tablet, an iPhone, and God only knows what else. I think she's rich."

"You don't have to be rich to own up-to-date technology. Let her give you a lesson in how to use it."

"I don't need it. A laptop with Wi-Fi, a cell phone, and a good cup of coffee—that's all I need in life."

"Be a good girl, Lillian," Dan said, "be nice to your cousin and her kids."

"I'm always good, am I not?" she answered, huffing. "Haven't I always been nice?"

"No."

She chuckled, "Tomorrow, Dan."

"Tomorrow…but call my office. I'm meeting with a new author and I'll have my cell turned off."

Lillian agreed but neither one of them hit the end button on their cell phones. They sat in silence, connected by the satellite. He always refused to be the first to hang up, and she always protested, yet it made her feel safe…loved.

"You first," she said at last.

"No … you."

"You're such a child!" she laughed. "All right, good night." She hit the end button.

She looked around the room. Except for the curtains, everything in the room was exactly as it had been when she was a child and came to visit. It was the room she'd always slept in when she stayed with her grandparents and later when she visited her aunt. It was the room her mother and aunt had shared as little girls growing up.

Lillian spent many nights sleeping in this room when her aunt asked her to baby sit for Ann who was five years younger than she. Ann would beg to sleep in the wrought iron bed with her and then nag Lillian to tell her elaborate ghost stories, which Lillian would do, but always after feigning great annoyance.

She would make the stories very scary until Ann would start to whimper in fear and pull her sheet all the way up to her round terrified blue eyes, and then Lillian would give the story a silly ending, and Ann would giggle with relief and complain all at the same time that it really wasn't the right ending.

They would snuggle down under the luxurious lavender satin feather-filled comforter that was always on that bed, light as air yet offering a luscious warmth on chilly nights.

Ann would fall asleep with her little blond head on Lillian's shoulder. Lillian always felt tenderness and contentment when tucked down beside her sleeping little cousin.

She always slept well in that room. The loneliness that was such a constant companion for most of her childhood—most of her life in general—would always seem very far away in that room with her little cousin snuggled down next to her. Aunt Helen would come in when she and Uncle Tim came home and would kiss each of the girls on their foreheads, the scent of her Arpege lingering around the bed. "I love you, Aunt Helen," Lillian would say if she was awake, or just think it if she was too sleepy to speak.

"Sleep well, my precious girls," Aunt Helen would say before closing the door.

But that was a million years ago, in a life Lillian had escaped as soon as she could—leaving behind the good as well as the bad.

Lillian sat on the edge of the bed now and gazed into the oil painting on the wall above the headboard. It was an inexpensive old pastoral that some unknown Bucks County artist had painted early in the 1900s. Her grandmother had bought it at an art fair when her daughters were little girls.

*If I've ever really been happy, it was here in this room...in this house.*

She heard a very tentative knock on the door. "I'm up, come on in," she said.

Ann opened the door a little. "Can't you sleep?"

"I haven't tried. I still have to finish my article and email it to my editor. Thank God you have wireless. This house is so old I didn't think it was possible to have cable."

Ann smiled. "It may seem like it's the only change I've made, but there are some others."

"Yeah, I noticed the high-definition televisions, too."

"Gotta have the technology along with the antiques or I'd go crazy," Ann said, her blue eyes shining. Her short blond hair lay in soft shiny ringlets all over her head and it gave her a waiflike appearance. Lillian remembered Ann's natural blond hair was always thick and long, but never curly, which was probably why Lillian didn't recognize her in Starbucks at first.

An awkward silence fell in the room. They started to speak at the same time, then stopped, then laughed a little nervously. Ann spoke again. "It's a little noisy here in the mornings when I'm getting the kids ready for camp. We'll try to stay as quiet as possible, but I can't make you any promises."

"Don't worry about me," Lillian smiled.

"Well, I just wanted you to be forewarned."

"Thanks, I'll sleep with the pillow over my ears. I'm sorry I didn't have much time to get to know your kids this evening. It was nice of your friend to keep them for dinner so you could help me move out of my apartment."

Ann grinned and leaned against the antique dresser. "You'll have more time with them tomorrow when they get home from camp."

Lillian could tell that Ann wanted to say more but was hesitating. Ann had a very serious look on her face, as though she was struggling with what she wanted to say or what she wanted to ask. Lillian wished she wouldn't try. She wasn't up for any weighty conversations.

She got off the bed, sat at the desk and started to tap on the keyboard of her laptop, hoping it would give Ann a hint. It worked. Ann stood up straight and said, "Well, I'll let you finish your work. Have a good night's sleep."

"Thanks."

Ann turned back when she reached the door. "Lilly..."

Lillian closed her eyes thinking *here it comes...all the questions.*

"Lilly, I just wanted to tell you that you're welcome to stay here as long as you want."

"Thanks," Lillian said again.

"I'm not just saying it. I'd love to have you stay...indefinitely."

"Thanks...really. I appreciate your saying that, but," Lillian shrugged, "I need my own place. I keep weird hours. Sometimes I write all night long, then sleep all day, then write again all night. I'd wear out my welcome fast. I actually couldn't even keep a roommate. I drove them all nuts."

Ann looked down at the floor. "You won't drive me nuts, Lilly. I can't tell you how much I've missed you all these years."

Lillian yawned. "God, I'm tired. And I have so much to write yet."

Ann pulled her bottom lip in with her teeth, and looked away. "Right. I'll see you in the morning. Good night."

Lillian didn't answer, afraid that saying good night would perpetuate the conversation. A few seconds later she heard the door close.

She sighed and leaned forward until her head almost touched the laptop.

*I have to find a place tomorrow,* she thought. *This is not good. This is definitely not good for me. She's bound to start conversations I don't want to have.*

She finished her article and then climbed between the sheets on the bed and pulled the pillow under her neck. She looked around the room again. She could almost hear her aunt's sweet, husky voice…her grandfather's laugh…her mother's footstep on the stairs. "God, no," she whispered aloud, closing her eyes as her heart pounded in her chest. "I can't stay here."

ॐ

True to what Ann had said the night before, Lillian was awakened by the voices of children trying to be quiet yet whispering loudly back and forth through the hallway outside Lillian's room. Toilets flushed…water ran through the ancient pipes…a glass clanged in a sink… a door closed …a shoe dropped…footsteps sounded on the staircase then disappeared as little feet rushed down to the lower floor.

Lillian stretched and arched her back then turned on her side, slipping back to sleep until she heard a car motor and tires on the long gravel driveway leaving a half an hour later.

She had slept quite well considering it was her first night in a strange bed. Not so strange, she thought, looking down at the bed. New mattress and box spring, of course, but very familiar all the same. The whole room was familiar. It worried her. She wanted to feel out of place…not at home.

Perhaps she hadn't moved forward much, but backward was not an option. No reminiscing for her. Her past was not a place that gave her comfort; she never longed for her childhood. On the contrary, she dreaded remembering it.

After using the bathroom and washing quickly, she pulled her unruly red hair up into a clip, threw on shorts and a tee shirt and went down to the kitchen. The coffeemaker was on and the carafe was full, and she smiled when she saw that Ann had left an oversized mug beside the coffee maker—a message that she was welcome to help herself to as much as she wanted.

She poured the strong fragrant coffee into the mug and took a long drink, throwing her head back as she swallowed. It's good, she thought happily. *Thank God ... a good cup of coffee. Is there anything better than that first sip of coffee in the morning?*

She opened the door of the kitchen and stepped out onto the path that led to an herb garden surrounded by well-groomed boxwood hedges. The day was already hot and the late June sun was just peeking through the lower leaves of the trees surrounding the property. The insects were loud— always a sign of a hot summer day.

Lillian looked out at the back lawn which hadn't changed much at all since her grandparents owned the house. At the very end of the property, down at the bottom of a long graceful slope, stood an ancient willow tree, its soft drooping branches just barely touching the still waters of the Delaware Canal.

A green film had formed over the dark water at a spot just beneath a gazebo that overlooked the quiet ribbon of water, which had been a "highway" of commerce for coal in the 1800s.

Her grandfather had built the gazebo with his own hands when he was still a young man and a newlywed. It was his contribution to the property, which was his through marriage. The farm had been in his wife's family for generations, dating back to the American Revolution, and although he could afford to build a new home for himself and his wife, he agreed that it should remain in the family. But from the very start of their marriage, he made the property his own by adding the gazebo first, then an addition to the old stone building, and a three car garage in what had been the carriage house. Seventy years later, the gazebo remained, overlooking the canal and the river beyond it.

Tears suddenly flooded Lillian's eyes. "Granddad's gazebo," she said aloud. She had loved that gazebo when she was a child—playing with her dolls, pretending to have tea parties with her grandmother and Aunt Helen, who wasn't married yet and had always made Lillian feel as though she was the light of her aunt's life. And Granddad would fuss in the garden around the structure, which was painted white and green, pulling weeds and swearing quietly under his breath whenever he found anything awry. His silver hair would stick out in all directions from under his baseball cap as though he always needed a haircut, and his old jeans were way too baggy around his backside.

Seeing the gazebo now made Lillian feel lightheaded and breathless.

She wanted to turn back into the house, but her eyes stayed on the gazebo while she remembered a summer day when she was a little older. Her aunt had been married and had given birth to Ann by then. Lillian was rocking Ann in her baby carriage while her aunt sat in an lawn chair reading a book, tanning her legs and arms, and smiling up at Lillian and Ann from behind her sunglasses.

"Do you still love me, Aunt Helen, now that you have Annie?" Lillian had asked.

"I love you more than ever, darling Lilly," her aunt called back. "You were my first baby, remember that."

"I thought that I was my mommy's first baby," Lillian corrected her.

Aunt Helen laughed in that throaty way of hers. "You were all of our first baby–the first one of the next generation is always the most special forever."

Lillian thought it over before her aunt said, "And on top of that you are Annie's much older, much wiser cousin. She'll look up to you, and she'll want to be just like you. I want her to be just like you."

Satisfied that she hadn't been displaced by her little cousin, Lillian went back to rocking the carriage and feeling very special that she was the first one of the next generation as well as the very older, very wiser big cousin. Lillian remembered that this scenario had played out often the summer after Ann was born, because Lilly just wanted to make sure it was true, she wanted to hear it again and again, and Aunt Helen never tired of answering.

On those summer days, Grandma would bring out blueberry pie, vanilla ice cream and Coca Cola and they would eat and drink the sweet dark syrupy soda, shaded from the sun by the roof of the gazebo, listening to Aunt Helen's transistor radio. Sometimes they would dance to the songs, which were now classic golden oldies.

They bounced and gyrated and did the Mashed Potato and the Bristol Stomp—Grandma, Aunt Helen, and Lillian—while Granddad would watch from the gazebo step, the cola bottle in his hand, shaking his head with amusement as though all his women had gone crazy.

Then Grandma would gather up the purple stained dishes and empty glasses and say she had to go into the house to get dinner started. Uncle Tim would be home from work soon and expect his dinner ready.

Aunt Helen would agree, pick up baby Ann from the carriage, kiss her round little cheek, and carry her into the house following behind Grandma to change her baby and dress her in a pretty little dress for when her daddy would come home.

Then Grandma would call out, "Come on, Lillian, your parents will be here soon to pick you up."

Dreaded words that would make the magic disappear; for Granddad, too, it seemed.

He always looked as disappointed as Lillian felt, and she'd go and sit on the step next to him. He would put his arm around her shoulders and pull her close to his side. He smelled of sweat and earth after working in the garden, and she loved the way the scent clung to him like perfume. She liked it much more than her mother's cologne.

Lillian closed her eyes now almost feeling the weight of her grandfather's arm on her shoulders, his huge freckled hand holding her tight against him, protectively.

"Granddad," she whispered now, longing for that arm around her. Her throat ached and she swallowed hard.

Lillian heard Ann's car drive up to the front of the house. The sweet memory was gone, just as the magic would disappear all those years ago when she would hear her parents' Impala pull into the driveway. She turned away from the gazebo and went back into the kitchen.

Ann was there and smiled. "You found the coffee."

"I did, and thanks. I can't function without it first thing in the morning."

"Did we wake you this morning?" Ann asked, pouring herself coffee.

"Yeah, but I fell back to sleep. I'm going out to the van to get some more clothes."

"Need help?"

Lillian looked at Ann again and realized that she looked even thinner today in her light running suit. "No, thanks, you don't look strong enough to carry anything."

"Hey," Ann protested, sitting down at the kitchen table, "I did a good job yesterday, didn't I? I'm wiry."

More like a pipe cleaner, Lillian thought, wondering if Ann had an eating disorder. She walked out the front door toward the small moving van. There were only a few pieces of furniture in there as most of the furniture in her apartment at Mrs. Snyder's belonged to the house.

Lillian had a desk, some file cabinets, two chairs, three lamps, and boxes of office supplies. She also had an antique set of china that had belonged to her grandmother, a beautiful porcelain tea set she had purchased on one of her writing trips in Europe.

Lillian reached into the back of the van and pulled out a box of clothing, thinking that she'd keep the van another day in case she found another place right away. If she did, she could borrow the money from Dan.

She dropped the box in the foyer at the bottom of the staircase and looked around more carefully than she had the evening before.

The house was the same; and it was different. Her grandparents' furniture had been replaced with newer period reproductions that matched the character of the old house, yet they were more comfortable and updated.

Deep emerald greens, mixed with light shaded earth tones, decorated the large living room. An expensive oil painting depicting the canal hung over the stone fireplace and the raised stone hearth looked as if it had been repaired very recently. But the old pumpkin pine floors were covered with the huge oval braided rugs she remembered so well from her childhood, and some of the lamps and tables—a little scarred and seeming smaller than she remembered them—were scattered about the room.

"Some of these older pieces were in the attic," Ann explained, coming into the room, her coffee mug in her hand. She had noticed that Lillian was fingering one of the tables. "I think they belonged to Grandma. I found them in the carriage house."

"Your mother used them, too," Lillian confirmed, remembering them well.

"Until my wedding, then she bought all new furniture to spruce the place up. I was married at St. Andrew's and we had the reception in a tent out on the lawn. Even though we lived in Florida then, this was still home for us."

"Oh…" Lillian answered, feeling guilty at the mention of Ann's wedding. Ann had written to her in California where she was working at the time, asking her to be her Maid of Honor.

The day after receiving the letter, Lillian bought an airline ticket to South Korea and left the next day. She waited a week, then answered the letter, saying she had been assigned to Korea by a news magazine and would be over there for more than a year.

"Sorry I can't make the wedding. Have an extra glass of champagne for me," she had written, "and send me a picture."

She had sent the bride and groom a port wine set—a green glass carafe and tiny glasses hand-painted with gold leaf.

Then she never contacted Ann again—no Christmas cards, no birthday cards, no letters or phone calls. She never answered any of Ann's correspondence, and finally Ann stopped writing.

Lillian had no idea if any of her family ever wondered if the article she was supposed to have written was ever published, or if they even looked for it. She lived in South Korea for a short time, flew to London from there, and lived from hand to mouth from small freelance writing assignments. She saved just enough to fly back to New York, where she lived with a friend briefly until she could manage her own apartment in Queens and lived there for several years.

In all that time she never tried to contact Ann. She didn't come home for funerals or birthdays or anniversaries. Family stopped sending invitations.

Lillian looked back at Ann now. Ann's face was still as sweet as it was when Lillian had last seen her cousin all those years ago. Ann was about seventeen then; she'd be about thirty-nine now. There were fine lines around her cousin's eyes, and a sadness that had faded the blue lights that had always shone in Ann's eyes.

These were not the eyes of the innocent, friendly young girl Lillian remembered. These were old eyes in a still young face, a little thinner, delicately lined, but still a very pretty face.

"So many things have happened since the last time we saw each other," Lillian began. "I'm sorry about your husband, Ann. Your father wrote me about it after the funeral. . . I should have sent a sympathy card or something, but I'm . . . well . . ."

Ann smiled. "Don't worry about it."

"He died of a heart attack, right?" Lillian asked.

Ann shook her head no. "A pulmonary embolism—sudden, quick, and deadly."

"You were going to tell me how you ended up back here in this house," Lillian said.

Ann sipped her coffee. "I missed my home, that's all. Right after Billy died, I wanted to come back, but I felt I had to stay in New Jersey to keep things as much the same as possible for the children. Then I wasn't well myself for a while and had to get over that. But I really couldn't wait to come home."

"How were you able to get back into this house? I thought it was rented."

Ann hesitated, seemed to search for just the right words, then said "One morning I woke up, decided what I wanted to do, drove from Jersey directly to this old house, walked up to the front door, rang the bell, and told them who I was. I offered them cash if they would allow me to break the lease. My parents had given me the deed years ago. I kept this old place as an income property; I couldn't let it go. As luck would have it—and believe me it was pure unadulterated luck—the husband was being transferred to Des Plaines, Illinois, and they took the money and ran. They have no kids. She's a pharmaceutical sales rep and didn't seem to care about moving, and within a month I was back at Willow Wood Farm."

Lillian shook her head. "Amazing," she said. "This is a pretty big place for just the three of you. How many bedrooms? Five?"

"And five bathrooms," Ann added with a grimace. "But I don't care. The kids love running around in it. It's a grand place, Lillian."

Now Lillian smiled. *It is a grand place*, she thought, *a grand place that had sheltered many grand families—most of whom were their grandmother's ancestors.* And once again, Lillian wondered how her mother could have been raised in this beautiful house, with such loving parents, and a saint for a sister, and turn out to be such a hateful human being.

The sisters had been close, though Lillian could never understand why. Aunt Helen was the antithesis of Lillian's mother Regina, who was bitter, cold, and always dissatisfied with everything around her. Regina could turn angry and mean in a second, while Helen was patient and slow to anger.

Lillian wondered now, as she had over and over again as an adult, what her life would have been like if her aunt, or her grandparents, had rescued her from her mother and had kept her here. She wondered if they fully understood that she was an abused child. If they did, how could they allow it? They said they loved her. You don't let someone you love be hurt.

"I always loved this house," Ann said, interrupting Lillian's dark thoughts.

"You're lucky to be living in it now, though it's probably not quite the same without Aunt Helen and Uncle Tim, is it?"

The sadness returned to Ann's eyes. "No, it isn't."

"How is Aunt Helen?" Lillian asked, suspecting that she really didn't want to know the answer.

"Worse," Ann answered. "She doesn't know who I am at all, let alone my children. She thinks I'm one of her nurses or sometimes she thinks I'm an old neighbor. If I'm very lucky, she thinks I'm her mother and she wants me to rock her, which I love doing. I miss her terribly. I long for her gentleness, her sage advice. She was always such a gentle woman with good common sense." She managed a weak smile and tried to sound a little lighter when she said, "Alzheimer's is the pits."

The news made Lillian feel angry and depressed. "How come the nice guys always have to suffer?"

"She's not suffering—not really," Ann said. "We who love her are. But she is not, though at the beginning she railed against it. Daddy takes wonderful care of her. He visits every day for hours. I'm so proud of him for it, yet I worry about his mental health. It can't be easy for him. I haven't been able to visit lately. As I said, I hadn't been well, and then with the kids it's hard to travel. Joey goes down whenever he has a break at school."

"Joey . . ." Lillian said.

"Yes, my brother. He's is in graduate school in Boston now. He'd like to be an architect, but first he's thinking he'd like to teach, maybe be an assistant professor next year when he gets his Master's degree."

"That's great," Lillian said, lowering her eyes.

She grabbed the box she had dropped earlier. "I have to take this upstairs," she said, then quickly followed with, "but not for long."

When Ann looked confused, Lillian added, "I'm going to look for an apartment today."

Ann frowned. "You don't have to."

"Yeah, well, you won't think that after a day or two. I'm impossible. A friend of mine says I'm self-absorbed and self-centered, and I can't see beyond my own nose."

"Oh? Is this a good friend?" Ann asked, smiling.

"Yeah, actually, he is my best friend." Lillian turned and started up the steps with the box. "I'm glad you live here, Annie. I hope you're happy."

"I would love it if you'd stay. As I said last night, you can stay as long as you like. Actually, Lillian, you're welcome to move in with me permanently. As you, yourself, mentioned, there's plenty of room, the kids would love having someone other than me around, and it would be fun to reminisce about the old days."

"No, but thank you," Lillian said, knowing that she sounded too sharp and her smile was too forced. "I'll probably see you in town all the time, though. We'll meet for coffee. I'll let you know where I wind up."

Ann followed her and persisted. "Lillian, please. I mean it. I need you."

Lillian turned back, puzzled, and the box slipped a little from her arm.

"I mean, I'm a little lonely in the house," Ann told her. "I have no family close by. It would be nice to have you here, too; it would be so nice to get to know you again. We only have each other, Lillian … and Joey. No other siblings or cousins. Couldn't we become reacquainted?"

Living in this house could be an answer for Lillian. She didn't want to move back to New York yet. She wasn't ready to move in with Dan. And she struggled with rent money. She'd never find another apartment as nice and as cheap as she had at Mrs. Snyder's. She had nowhere else to go. And although she tried hard not to, she felt at home here. The problem was that there were unsafe memories all around her in this house, memories just hiding beneath the surface, ready to grab at her.

Still she was drawn to the house…to this cousin.

"You're sure I wouldn't be a …"

Ann smiled warmly. "Oh, no, you would only be welcome, Lilly; I'm serious."

Lillian leaned the box against the rail and looked down at her cousin again. "I guess I could stay for a little while."

Lillian was certain she was misreading the look in her cousin's blue eyes, but she could have sworn she saw relief in them, relief and happiness.

"I'm thrilled, Lilly. I really am. We'll celebrate tonight. I'll have a pot roast with gravy and mashed potatoes and carrots."

Ann turned quickly and walked back into the kitchen leaving Lillian standing and wondering how her cousin, whom she hadn't seen in more than twenty years, would remember that pot roast with mashed potatoes and carrots were Lillian's very favorite dinner.

# Three

Lillian put the box down in a corner of her bedroom. She took some of her makeup and toiletries out of the box and brought them into the bathroom. Although the fixtures were old, they were in perfect condition. There was a white sturdy looking pedestal sink, and a clawed bathtub where a shower had been added. And of course, a commode, which Lillian was happy to see was new.

When she came out of the bathroom and looked around the room in the early morning light, she smiled just as Ann entered the room with a box she'd taken from the van.

"Why are you smiling like that?" Ann asked her.

"I'm remembering an annoying little brat who always wanted to stay up all night but could never make it past midnight."

"I did too!" Ann frowned, and placed the carton on the bed. "I always stayed awake. You were the one who used to drowse."

"Taking care of you was exhausting," Lillian threw back, smiling and walking to the front window of the bedroom. It looked out over the circular drive, down at a magnolia tree and garden beneath it.

"Nothing's the same, yet everything's the same," she mused as she had earlier. The magnolia tree was ancient, but the garden beneath was different. The driveway that was once gravel was paved now, but it followed the same exact route—up from the road, around in front of the door, back to another driveway where one could turn right to leave, or left to go to the garage."

"Can I help you unpack?" Ann asked her.

"No, I'll take care of it."

"Good, because I have some food shopping to do. Will you make a list of the things you like to eat and drink and whatever else you need?"

"I can go with you," Lillian offered.

"No, that's not necessary," Ann answered. "I have another appointment first. I'll just stop on my way back."

Lillian shrugged and bent over the box. "Okay, I'll think about what I want. Ann, I don't have any money right now to give you for my share of the food. I should receive a check for the article I sent last night, but in the meantime…"

"Lillian, please don't worry about it. I'm just so happy to have you here with me."

"Well, I'll have to give you…"

"Sure, later on. We'll work all that out later on," Ann said and backed out of the room and started down the staircase.

"Ann," Lillian called coming to the doorway. "I haven't said thank you. It isn't that I'm not grateful, I am. Just a little surprised to be here I guess. I do want to thank you, though."

"Well, I can't have my cousin be the only homeless person walking the streets of Newtown now, can I?"

∽ℯↄ

| | |
|---|---|
| From: | Lillian Phelan [lpfreelncrwrtr@aol.com] |
| To: | Dan Paulsen [dpaulsen1@msn.com] |
| Subject: | Still safe |
| Sent: | 6/14 10:00 AM |

Okay, here's the story. I'm going to stay here with my cousin a little while. I didn't want to, but she's talked me into it. I'll probably run screaming out of here in a week. But I told her I'd give it a try. I like her, Danny. I always did, even when she was an annoying little girl who always wanted to wear my clothes and makeup and go with me wherever I went. She was always a sweet kid. I confess that I was a little jealous of her—she got to be my aunt's daughter and I couldn't be. I got the wicked mean sister for a mother. Anyway, I agreed to stay awhile, so I will.

| | |
|---|---|
| From: | Dan Paulsen [dpaulsen1@msn.com] |
| To: | Lillian Phelan [lpfreelncrwrtr@aol.com] |
| Subject: | Re: Still safe |
| Sent: | 6/14 10:05 AM |

You could live with me.

❦

When Ann came home later that day, Lillian looked down from her bedroom window to see that Ann had her children with her. Each one carried a backpack and a pool towel rolled up under their arms. She heard Ann say, "Put your towels in the laundry room," as they came through the front door.

Lillian waited a little while, then walked down the main staircase to the living room. Ann and the kids were in there. The boy stood aside and stared at Lillian, while the little girl put her arms around her mother's hips and studied Lillian. She looked as if she was going to giggle any second, but was controlling it.

Lillian's heart froze as she realized suddenly that she was going to be sharing a house with two kids, something she had never done and had never intended to do. She had no idea how to talk to them or act around them.

"Lillian," Ann said, touching her daughter's blond head. "I know you met them very briefly last night, but in case you didn't remember their names, this is Suzy, she's six, and that's Philip, who is ten." Then looking at Philip, Ann said, "And I know that Lillian is our cousin, but I'd like you to call her Aunt Lillian."

"Oh, Christ, no…" Lillian said. "Not 'aunt.' Please."

Ann was taken aback. "What should they call you?"

"Lillian is fine."

Ann was not comfortable with that. "I think they should address you with respect."

"Then let them call me Lillian with great respect."

The kids laughed then. "That's a long name," Suzy said with a gap-toothed smile.

Both women looked at them, puzzled.

"Okay, *Lillianwithgreatrespect*, let's go into the dining room so we can eat," Philip said, smirking slightly, sharing the joke with his little sister.

The women laughed now, too.

"Smart or smart aleck?" Lillian asked her cousin, glancing at Philip.

Ann raised her eyebrows, "A little of both, I think." Then turning to the children, she said, "It's not ready yet, Philip. Go and read your books for a little while."

The kids settled onto the couch after taking a book from the coffee table. Lillian followed Ann into the kitchen. It was the one room that had changed drastically. Lillian wouldn't have recognized it, with its modern cabinets and stainless steel appliances. It even had a new sunroom built off the back of the kitchen, beyond where a walk-in fireplace, which had once been against a wall, now stood as a room divider. The back staircase was tucked behind the fireplace. "Now, this room has changed."

Ann nodded, "For the better, I'd say." She walked to the double oven and opened one of the doors. The scent of beef cooking in its own juices wafted through the room.

"Mm," Lillian said, closing her eyes. "I must be hungrier than I thought. My stomach just growled. God, that smells good."

Just then, the potato water sputtered and boiled over onto the cook top.

"I'll get it," Lillian said, moving swiftly to the stove and turning the heat down under the pot. She stirred the potatoes, and then sat down at the kitchen table in the middle of the room to watch Ann carve the beef.

"I'm sorry about your husband," Lillian said again, watching her cousin's slender back as her arms moved deftly over the roast.

"Yeah, me too," Ann said, without stopping.

"From what I remember, Bill was a really nice kid. He was about two years behind me in school, and he was a star on the football field. Right?"

When Ann nodded, Lillian continued, "When I heard that you two had hooked up and were getting married, I was happy for you. I always thought that it was romantic that you grew up in the same town, hardly knew each other, and then met at Christmas when you were home on break from college. He was the love of your life, I gather."

Ann said quietly, "He was...always will be." Then she asked, "How did you know all that?"

"Your mother wrote to me from time to time," Lillian answered. "The potatoes are done. Do you want me to drain them?"

Ann indicated the strainer already in the sink. They worked in silence as they finished getting dinner ready. Lillian helped carry the food into the dining room while Ann called the children.

Lillian smiled when she saw the kids bless themselves and silently say grace over their empty plates. Ann didn't join them, but Lillian could see she was pleased that the kids didn't need to be told to do it.

"Wow," Lillian said to them. "You do that at every meal?"

"Of course," Suzy said, surprised by the question.

"I mean, you don't all say it out loud?"

The children looked at their mother, who looked away. "Mom stopped saying prayers when she went bald," Philip told her.

Lillian saw that Ann was startled by the boy's answer and she looked at him sharply. "Philip," she said quietly to quiet him.

"You went bald?" Lillian asked, surprised. "Is that why your hair is so short?"

"It grew back," Suzy said, glowering at her brother.

Lillian went on, "You always had the longest, thickest, most beautiful natural blond hair. I wondered why you cut it so short when I saw you yesterday."

"It's hard to take care of two kids and a house and yourself, too. I had a little problem after Bill died...you know...from nerves...and I lost some of my hair. But as Suzy said, it grew back. I just keep it short now."

"Twice," Philip said. "She went bald twice."

"Shut up," Suzy told him.

"Suzy don't say 'shut up.' It isn't polite. And, Philip, Lillian doesn't want to hear any more about my hair." Ann rolled her eyes at Lillian as much as to say *boys*.

Lillian decided not to pursue the conversation further. Obviously it wasn't a favorite topic.

Lillian admitted to herself that these kids seemed pretty tolerable.

"You know, you probably go to the same grammar school I went to," Lillian said to them, changing the subject.

"Elementary school," Ann corrected Lillian. "They call it elementary school now."

"Sorry...elementary school...anyway, how do you guys like it? At least that old bitch principal, Mrs. Horseshit, must be retired by now."

The kids' mouths dropped open.

"Mrs. Hors*chtvelt*," Ann said, opening her eyes wide at Lillian, "and yes, I believe she did retire and move away many years ago."

The kids were still wide-eyed, looking first at Lillian, then at Ann, then at Lillian again.

Lillian realized that she had shocked them with her language. *Here goes*, she thought. Ann and her kids were going to have to get used to Lillian's language because she wasn't going to change. Not even to live in a house and not a homeless shelter. So here was their first challenge. Well, at least Ann would realize asking Lillian to stay wasn't such a great idea after all.

Ann surprised all of them when she laughed and shook her head. "Okay, this is probably a good time for all of us to get the rules and regulations set."

She looked at her children and laughed again at expressions.

"Lillian has never had children," she explained. "She's independent and she has led a rather...well...different life than I have. But this is her home now, too. She's welcome to do whatever she wants and speak however she is used to speaking."

Ann became serious then. "That said, you are never to mimic her. You're both smart enough to know that calling a teacher 'Mrs. Horseshit' or using that sort of word at all is just not accepted in children. It's not that it is 'right' or 'wrong,' it's just not what kids are supposed to say. Your friends' parents would not be pleased, though your friends would think you're cool, I'm sure. And if you used that sort of language in school, you'd get into trouble."

Lillian tried to find some scolding in her direction from Ann's words, but she couldn't.

Ann looked at Lillian then. "I mean it. I want you to feel like this is your home, and I'm not going to put restrictions on you. I will ask, though, that you think a little before you speak. The kids are new in that school and in the neighborhood. They're just getting to know people. I'd hate for them to be considered misfits because they get used to hearing unsuitable language and it pops out of their mouths unexpectedly. I want them to make friends and be happy here in Newtown. Does that sound reasonable, Lilly?"

Again, there was no scolding in her manner, only a mother's request and Lillian did understand.

"Of course," she said, smiling. "I can't guarantee that certain words won't slip out from time to time but I promise to try."

Looking at the faces of her cousin's children, she knew they were astonished at what had just transpired.

"You guys are going to have to try to correct me when I forget . . . in a nice way, of course, because remember that you have to address me with great respect and all that." Lillian smiled at her cousin then, "but try to keep me on the straight and narrow when I'm in the house. Okay?"

"Okay, Lilly, we'll do that," Suzy said with great intensity and seriousness.

"Is it all right if she calls you 'Lilly'?" Ann asked, surprised that her daughter had picked up on the nickname. Before today, Ann had rarely mentioned her cousin to them, and had always used her full name when she did.

Lillian sighed before answering, thinking it over. "I like it, I think. Yeah, she can call me that. You too," Lillian said to Philip, "if you want."

He shrugged, not committed to calling her anything yet. "Whatever," he mumbled. Lillian saw a dimple in his cheek deepening with a suppressed smile before he added, "I kind of liked *Lillianwithgreatrespect*."

The rest of their conversation that first meal together focused on the kind of work Lillian did—her writing assignments, how some of those assignments had taken her around the world, and the types of magazines for which she freelanced.

The kids loved it, and Lillian knew that the stories she told made her seem very glamorous and exotic to them. That suited her. Most of the stories she wrote were benign, fluffy and anything but journalism—like following a house-call-making veterinarian who did Reiki over cattle—but, hell, the kids didn't have to know that. She liked playing the role of idol for a change.

And she knew that it wouldn't last long. She'd be found out eventually.

"I loved the article about Monarch butterflies that you wrote for Women's World," Ann said.

Lillian was surprised and pleased that her cousin had read it and remembered it. It was barely 350 words…a little blurb. "You saw that?"

"Of course . . ."

"I'm impressed."

"I wish I could find more of your articles. You jump around so much, I never know what magazine to subscribe to. One time you've written an article about makeovers, and the next your work is in a healthcare journal. I can't always find you."

"I didn't know you were looking," Lillian said, taking a last forkful of lemon cake.

"Always," Ann answered, standing and picking up the dishes. "I Google your name and usually a new article by you will pop up. You are the famous person in the family."

The children were looking at Lillian with renewed interest.

"Are you rich?" Philip asked.

Lillian laughed, and decided that being here with these kids wouldn't necessarily be such an awful thing. "Your mother says I'm famous, and that's got to be good enough 'cause God knows I'm not rich."

Philip wasn't as interested after hearing that, but Suzy was still wide-eyed. "Will you write stories while you're living here with us?"

"I had better. That's how I earn money—as little as it is."

"So, that means," Ann said to her children, "that when we tell you that Lilly is writing, you have to be quiet and leave her alone."

"I promise," Suzy said, her face serious.

"Whatever," Philip shrugged again.

"Writing runs in the family, I think," said Ann from the kitchen where she was stacking dishes near the dishwasher.

"It does?" Lillian asked. "I don't remember anyone else in the family who wrote."

"Ah, but there were," Ann corrected her, coming back into the dining room to gather more dishes. Lillian stood up to help, while the kids ran outside into the yard. "When I was in the attic looking for antiques, I found an old blanket chest filled with hand-written papers, several are tied together like separate manuscripts, and there are lots of journals and letters that date to the late 1700s."

"Get out of here!" Lillian said wide-eyed.

Ann laughed. "I thought that would pique your interest. When I moved into the house, I went to Doylestown—to the Spruance Library where all the historical papers and records are kept—and I looked up all sorts of information about the house. The main part, here where the kitchen is, this is the oldest part of the house. It was built before the Revolution. There's a book called the History of Bucks County, Pennsylvania, written by a General Davis—I think he was a general during the Civil War—and our family name is mentioned all over the place. We had ancestors that fought in the Revolution, the French and Indian War, the War of 1812, and the Civil War."

"Okay, now *that's* amazing," Lillian said, looking around the room with renewed interest.

"I haven't had time to read the papers and letters in the chest, but I'm sure they fill in the gaps about the house."

"Well, *yeah*, I guess so…is there a lot in there?"

Ann was very pleased to have her cousin's complete attention and she smiled slyly when she turned from the dishwasher to answer. "You bet there is; lots. Journals, letters, sketches, photos…it would take months to read them all."

Lillian walked over to the screen door to watch the kids running around in the yard catching fireflies, but her mind was on the attic.

"Can I go up to look?"

"Lilly, this is your house now, too. It's our ancestral home so don't ask me what you can and can't do in it. However, I suggest that you do it in daylight because there's this one bulb that doesn't give off much light, and I think there may be things up there."

"What kind of things?"

"Spiders at the very least...but I suspect that there are bats. I think I hear them sometimes when I'm in bed. I know I hear scratching...mice, maybe?"

"Oh, come on, you'd know if there were bats. Right?" Ann shrugged again and made a face. "Go up in the morning, that's all I'm saying. It's really creepy up there at night."

There were bats. Lillian couldn't wait until morning. She grabbed a flashlight and ran up the first flight of steps, down the hall past the bedrooms, and up five more steps to the attic door. Just as she opened the old oak door to the third story of the house, one of the "things" opened its wings and flew at her flashlight. She slammed the door shut with a scream and fell back, slipped down three steps, landing with one leg up the steps and one against the wall. She didn't breathe for a moment, and she then looked around to make sure the bat hadn't escaped through the door.

That took care of exploring the attic until the exterminator arrived.

# *Four*

The first few weeks that Lillian lived with her cousin were tolerable, if not perfect. There were adjustments to be made in all their lives and attitudes. The first week could be called a "honeymoon," with everyone on their best behavior and tiptoeing around each other. But by the end of the second week that had worn thin.

Lillian slept late in the morning because she sat up late into the night researching and writing another article her editor had assigned to her. She found the noise of children getting ready for camp in the morning annoying, and although she tried not to show it and said nothing, she knew her mood was dark when she entered the kitchen at noon each day, looking for coffee rather than lunch. At first, Ann would greet her with a big, happy grin, but before long, she just let Lillian come down, pour herself a cup of coffee, and sit alone at the table while Ann cleaned and straightened up the rest of the house.

After the second cup of coffee, Lillian would help Ann dust, vacuum, and whatever else needed to be done. She never mentioned the noise in the morning, and Ann never mentioned it either. Ann tried hushing the children as they rushed around in the morning, but it was useless.

Ann came down late one night to make herself a cup of tea while Lillian was still working on her computer in the library on the first floor. It was nearly two o'clock in the morning.

"Don't you get tired?" Ann asked from the doorway.

Lillian shrugged.

"Do you want a cup of tea?"

"No," Lillian answered, clicking away on the keyboard.

"Why don't you write during the day and sleep at night?"

"You mean like normal people?" Lillian asked, knowing that there was an edge to her voice but unable to soften it.

It took a long time for Ann to answer, but when she did, her tone was gentle. "I'm just asking, Lilly. I was just curious."

"Because I don't do anything else all day, so why don't I write then? This way, your kids wouldn't bother me in the morning, because I'd be awake like the rest of the world. Oh, and by the way, when you try to shush them, you make more noise than they do. I don't know which is more annoying."

Ann backed away from the doorway. "Good night."

Lillian didn't answer. She heard Ann moving around the kitchen and then listened to her footsteps on the back staircase. She knew that Ann would check on each of the kids in their rooms, before going back to her own bedroom. Lillian wondered why Ann did that all the time. If she put them to bed herself, why did she have to check them in the middle of the night?

It was during the third week that Ann asked Lillian to babysit. "If you could just get them off the bus at the end of the driveway, give them their snack, and watch while they play in the back yard, I'd really appreciate it."

"Where are you going?" Lillian asked. This was not part of the deal, and she didn't want to start a precedent by saying yes. They weren't her kids and she didn't want to be stuck with them.

"Philadelphia . . . I have an appointment there and I'm afraid I won't be home in time."

Lillian thought it over a long minute. "All right …this time. But Ann, I really don't want to be saddled with babysitting on a regular basis. Your kids are great—really they are—but I'm not…I don't know…into the kid thing."

Ann just looked at her and Lillian shrugged a little. "They bore the hell out of me. Not yours only; *all* kids. They just don't have anything to say that I care to listen to."

Ann smiled at Lillian. It was a small, sad smile.

"Is this going to be a problem?" Lillian pursued. "I mean, have I offended you now?"

Ann shook her head. "No, Lilly, it's okay. Just for today…all right?"

"Sure, no problem. Bus … snack … play outside … I can handle it today. Are you driving to Phili?"

"I'll get the train in Yardley," Ann answered, pulling an old sweater closer around her. "I hate driving on I-95."

Lillian watched Ann as she placed her coffee mug in the dishwasher and wiped the counter top.

"You're losing weight … no wonder you're always cold. Are you feeling all right?"

Ann smiled over her shoulder, "I'm good."

They looked into each other's eyes for a moment, and Lillian thought Ann's eyes were a little too bright, tearful almost. "You're sure?" she asked her cousin, sorry now that she had given Ann a hard time about taking care of the kids.

Ann laughed a little, turning her face away. "I'm sure, Lilly." She finished wiping the counter and put the sponge in the sink. "But I'm late. I've got to go get dressed."

Lillian detected an uncharacteristic moodiness in Ann, but she shrugged it off after Ann left the kitchen. She's been through a lot, Lillian thought. It only stands to reason that she'd get into moods. Yet it bothered Lillian.

She had come to rely on Ann's perpetual optimism in contrast to her own lack of cheerfulness.

*We love having you here with us, Lilly ... it's an honor to have you set up your office in the library and write your masterpieces there ... the kids adore you, you know ... they look up to you the way I always did as a kid ... you're a brilliant writer ... you're wonderful with the children ... you make me laugh, and I never thought I'd laugh again—not really laugh ...remember when Grandma ...remember when Granddad ...remember when my mother...remember when your father ...*

At first, Lillian was wary of Ann's reminiscences. She waited for Ann to move into dangerous waters, but Ann always spoke of the gentler memories—the ones that didn't hit Lillian in the gut. Ann rarely mentioned Lillian's mother, in fact she didn't mention Lillian's parents much at all. If she did, it was always in generalities or just to place everyone in the memory of an event or party.

*I should let her know one of these days*, Lillian thought, *that I'm starting to like living here. I have to stop being a bitch. She doesn't deserve it. I have to start acting like a nice person.*

She passed the rest of the day on Granddad's gazebo, drinking diet cola and listening to the frogs jumping into the canal. She brought her laptop out with her and worked on her novel—the one she'd been writing for seven years but could never seem to finish. She put it on the wrought iron table, double clicked on the "My Documents" icon, and then again on the non-title "the novel." She worked for two hours, then the battery died, and since there was no electricity in the gazebo, she closed the laptop, leaned back on her chair, and put her head back until she could look up at the gazebo's ceiling.

The ceiling was an intricate pattern of boards, juxtaposing at odd corners to form a hexagon, the joints covered with perpendicular beams. At one time the inside had been a beautiful golden color, but now it was a silvery gray.

Granddad had never painted the inside of the gazebo; just the outside was painted white. The interior always looked a little shabby to Lillian, but no one else seemed to notice. It sat on the edge of the canal berm, opposite the graceful willow tree, gray inside and whitewashed out, surrounded by day lilies, Shasta daisies, and black eyed Susans. There were even more plants on the banks of the canal—hostas and ferns and others, the names of which Lillian couldn't remember, and wild vegetation grew along the thin ribbon of canal water.

Insects would land on the vegetation, hover a moment, then whiz away. The area was home to frogs of all sizes, whose calls at night could drive people crazy, but Lillian didn't mind. She watched the canal's world in silence, wishing her laptop hadn't died, and feeling the same melancholy she thought she'd seen in Ann earlier in the day.

Then a hummingbird appeared from nowhere. It hovered just beside her head as it explored the bright colored flowers in the basket that hung in the open window of the gazebo—Ann's touch in making the gazebo inviting during the summer months. The hummingbird's wings were invisible because of their rapid movement, and it hummed from one side of the basket to the other side, its long beak sipping on the nectar inside each flower.

Lillian was breathless as she watched the pretty little bird—she believed it was a bird—and she didn't move. Then the hummingbird moved from the flower basket closer to her to cheek, then near to her bright red tank top. Its beak pointed at her heart, and Lillian held her breath as it hovered in front of her. Then it darted up higher, eye to eye with her.

It repositioned itself so quickly, it was dizzying. It came so close Lillian could hear the hum and then felt the tiniest movement of air from its whirling wings.

She held her breath and sat so perfectly still that the muscles in her back started to ache.

*I told my aunt right here in this spot. I cried. And she cried.*

The humming bird came eye to eye with Lillian again. She stared back at it while remembering Aunt Helen's pale face, her eyebrows drawn together in anguish, her eyes overflowing with tears, at first showing shock, maybe even revulsion, then compassion and sorrow.

Lillian drew in air with a sob now and the hummingbird started away, turned back for a second, as though it didn't want to leave her, and then disappeared. Lillian's chest constricted with another sob, then another...deep, stomach-wrenching sobs that she hadn't experienced in more than 22 years.

She covered her face with her hands, turned her body to the side in the hard metal chair, and pulled her knees up to her chest.

"Aunt Helen," she sobbed, "Oh, God, Aunt Helen."

∾

The kids didn't get off the bus as Ann had told Lillian they would. She hadn't quite made it up to the end of the driveway when the school bus carrying the campers slowed, then kept going. Lillian panicked and started to run after it. A black Lexus SUV pulled into the driveway, but Lillian ignored it, still running after the bus, trying to remember exactly what Ann had told her about the kids getting off the bus. Then she heard Suzy's voice calling from the car.

"Lilly … it's us. We're in here!"

The car stopped beside her. The automatic window at the driver's side opened and a woman with brightly streaked hair and a bright white toothy smile called out to her.

"Hello, there, you must be Ann's cousin. The kids were just telling me all about you."

Lillian nodded, relieved as she watched Philip and Suzy jump out of the car, followed by four more children.

"I'm Monica Handel?" The statement sounded more like a question.

An up-talker, Lillian thought, and tried to hide her frown.

"Ann's friend?" Monica tried again.

Lillian had all she could do not to ask "are you sure?" Instead she held out her hand and said, "I'm Lillian Phelan."

"It's so nice to meet you. I hope you don't mind, but I thought I'd bring the kids home from camp myself. I know Ann had an appointment in Philadelphia today, so I wanted to make sure the kids got home okay."

"Don't they usually take the bus?" Lillian asked.

"Well, yes, but …"

"Were you afraid Ann wouldn't have me meet them?"

"No, of course not, she's so protective of them, but I…"

"You thought I might forget?"

"No…" Now the sunny smile slipped a little from Monica's face.

Lillian felt a little guilty for enjoying Monica's discomfort. She just didn't like this woman, and for no reason at all. Quick to make amends, in case it got back to Ann, she said, "Monica, would you like a cold drink?"

The sunny smile was back. "I would love one."

Lillian led the way into the kitchen, noticing with a glance that the six children were playing in the side yard.

"Ann's and my kids became fast friends in the spring when she first moved into the area," Monica explained, "especially Suzy and my Montana."

"Montana?"

"My daughter? … her name is Montana?"

"Oh," Lillian said, intent on pouring a diet coke over ice and putting it on the kitchen table where Monica had seated herself.

"You're a writer, I hear," Monica said.

"I freelance."

"I hear you're famous."

"Who did you hear that from?"

"Oh, Suzy's all abuzz about you. Even Philip talks about you once in a while and you know how quiet Philip is."

*I didn't even think Philip knew I existed,* Lillian thought. He barely spoke to her. "Well, they're exaggerating. I'm anything but famous," she said, pouring herself a diet soda.

"It's awful about Ann's husband, isn't it? It's really nice of you to move in with her to help her raise the kids."

Lillian put her glass down and looked carefully at Monica to make sure she understood her meaning. "I'm not here to help Ann with her children. In fact, Ann helped me out when the house I was living in was sold. I'm just here until I can find a place of my own."

"Oh," Monica was clearly disappointed. She was looking for more drama in the story of the beautiful young widow and her writer cousin.

"Well, it's nice she has some company, some family living nearby."

The children stormed in, Philip leading the way.

"Can we have ice pops?"

Lillian shrugged, "I don't know, can you? Do we have any?"

"They're in the freezer–we have them every day when we get home."

"Then I guess you can have some today."

Everyone stood still and stared at her, and Lillian suddenly realized she was supposed to get up and get the ice pops, which she did.

"I want blue."

"I want orange."

"I like the raspberry."

Little hands were all reaching out at her and she backed up against the fridge, hitting her head on the shelf of the open freezer door. One of Monica's kids grabbed the box from her hands and started to hand out the frozen juice sticks, then threw the box back into Lillian's hands and they all ran back out into the garden. All except Suzy, who was looking at Lillian with a serious expression on her face.

"Is your head all right?" she asked.

Lillian rubbed the back of her head, feeling for blood. "Yeah, I'm all right."

"Thank you, Lilly...for the pop," Suzy said holding it out as she ripped the cover off before turning to run back outside. She left the white paper, stained and sticky with the remnants of sweet red ice, on the counter.

Lillian left it there but Monica, who obviously couldn't stand the paper being left, stood up, grabbed it, and threw it in the trash can.

*Mommy Lesson Number 1—throw sticky ice pop papers in garbage*, Lillian thought, rolling her eyes.

"Where do you suppose the other kids put their papers?" She asked mockingly, knowing that they were probably strewn in the grass in the yard.

Monica ignored the question. "So, are you originally from here?"

"Born and bred."

"But you haven't lived here all this time?"

"Actually, I've lived in Newtown for the last four years. I left when I went to college, moved around the world for quite a number of years, lived in New York, then in Boston and Philadelphia. Four years ago I rented an apartment in an ancient brick house in Newtown."

"The one catty-corner to Starbucks?"

"Yes, that one."

"I saw that it was sold. Who bought it?"

"I have no idea."

"Are they going to turn it into another restaurant?"

"I have no idea."

"I hope not," Monica said, trying to frown but her brow didn't move.

It fascinated Lillian to see how smooth and unexpressive that brow was. Botox, Lillian thought, frowning, satisfied when she felt her own skin move.

"We agree on that," Lillian said, smiling for the first time.

"My husband and I moved here with the kids about a year ago. He was transferred to Princeton and Bucks County seemed like a nice place to raise the children. It's close enough to where he works."

*What in my expression gives you the idea that I care*, Lillian thought. "That's nice. How do you like it here?" When the hell is she going to leave?

"We love it. We came from the Chicago area, which was great, too. But this is a wonderful place. We love the schools. Our oldest son—Dakota?— it was a little hard on him. He had to leave all his friends, but the others were young enough to be flexible. Dakota has settled in nicely now."

"Are you guys originally from the West?"

Monica tried to raise her eyebrows, but again nothing happened to her brow. "No, why do you ask that?"

"The names of your children…they're a little, um, Western."

Monica laughed. "Oh, that, we just like unusual names. There's Dakota?…Steele…Montana…and Malory." Monica counted the names off on her French-manicured fingers. "I wanted the girls to have my initials."

Lillian moved her head at the mention of each name, pretending to take them in. Monica seemed to be expecting a reply, so Lillian said, "Well, they're probably the only kids in the school with those names. There's something to be said for that, right?"

"I like the names," Monica said, sounding a little defensive.

"Oh, yes, I don't blame you. Very nice names." Please make this woman go home.

They heard Ann's car in the drive and her car door closing quickly. She came in the front door, which surprised Lillian as she usually used the kitchen door. They heard her go right into the powder room.

Monica looked at Lillian, and Lillian smiled, saying, "I guess she had to go."

Monica smiled back, "I guess so."

A few minutes later, Ann called from the foyer. "Hey," she said, "I'll be right in. I just have to run up to my room for a minute."

*Oh great, make me socialize even longer with this brainless wonder*, Lillian thought, getting up from the table. "More soda?" she asked Monica.

"No, thank you. So what are you writing now?" she asked, looking at the closed laptop on the counter.

"Nothing."

"No articles for a magazine?" Monica persisted.

"No."

"Oh, I get it, you keep it to yourself until it's published," she said, and she pressed her lips together and pretended to lock them up.

Lillian stared at her. *Who does that anymore? Who does that! I don't know anyone who does that under the age of five.* "No, I'm just not writing anything right now. I'm between jobs, which is why I'm living off my cousin's kindness."

Ann walked in then, and Lillian could tell she had heard. She was pale and tired looking, but she laughed as she stepped into the kitchen. "You aren't living off my kindness," she said, leaning over to kiss Monica's cheek. "What are you doing here?"

"I brought the kids home," Monica answered. "I picked up my own and thought I'd give yours a lift, too. I was going to take them all for ice cream but then realized Lillian might worry if they didn't get off the bus."

"I *was* worried when they didn't get off the bus," Lillian said. "I almost had a coronary when the bus didn't stop."

"I'm sorry, but I was right behind the bus. It wasn't a minute…"

"Thank you for thinking of them," Ann said with a warm smile.

"You look so worn out, Ann," Monica said.

"It's the train, I hate taking it almost as much as I hate driving on I-95. It exhausts me. And I think I'm getting a migraine."

"Where did you have to go?" Lillian asked.

"Center City," was all she said, then looked into the refrigerator. "I don't know what to make for dinner tonight."

"How about we get a pizza?" Lillian asked. "I'll drive into town to get it. I haven't had pizza since I moved in with you and I'm craving it."

Ann straightened and closed the door of the fridge. "Now that's a good idea."

Monica stood and put her glass in the sink. "Well, I'd better get the kids and go. You're reminding me that I have to figure out what to do for dinner myself." She turned to embrace Ann. "I'll see you soon."

Lillian noticed that the hug was genuine and warm, and for the tiniest moment, Lillian was almost jealous that Ann seemed so close to this stranger. It occurred to her that she and Ann hadn't embraced at all, not even when they first met in Starbucks.

Monica called out to her kids and they all piled into her Lexus. As she drove away everyone waved—everyone but Lillian.

She left the kitchen and carried her laptop into the library, plugged it into the surge protector, and made sure that the charging light went on. Then she returned to the kitchen. Ann jumped when Lillian entered the room. She had been sitting at the table, her forehead in her left hand, her right hand over her mouth.

"You look green," Lillian said concerned now. "You're sick, aren't you?"

"I think I have a stomach bug. Maybe I've been drinking too many cold drinks."

"Go to bed right now," Lillian said, taking Ann's arm and pulling her up from the chair gently.

"I can't, that's not fair to you. It's bad enough that I asked you to watch the kids after camp today…"

"Forget that. I'm sorry I made an issue of it, Annie. I'll take care of them. I'll take them into town for the pizza."

"I feel terrible that I'm …"

"You feel terrible, but it shouldn't be about me and my sulkiness."

"I'm taking you up on it, then. I have to get to bed."

As she was leaving the kitchen, she squeezed Lillian's arm. "Thanks…*really*. Just for tonight. It's just a migraine."

"All right. Let me know if you need anything," Lillian said.

❧

Lillian's favorite pizza place was packed with the summer crowd. "Don't they know families don't go out in the middle of the week?" she mumbled, giving her name to a hostess and leading the kids against a wall to wait.

"That's not true," Suzy told her. "Families go out in the middle of the week all the time, especially in the summer."

"They do?" Lillian asked.

"All the time," Philip joined in. "When Dad was alive, we went for pizza every Wednesday."

"Yes, and then on one Friday a month we went to a nice restaurant, and we'd each get a turn to pick which one. Sometimes Mommy would pick, sometimes I would…"

"And I would sometimes," Philip told Lillian.

"Well, I stand corrected then," Lillian said. "Do you guys like anything on your pizza?"

"Plain," said Suzy.

"Pepperoni," said Philip.

"I hate pepperoni," said Suzy, pushing at her brother's arm.

"I like it."

"I hate it, too," said Lillian.

"Two against one," Suzy said smugly.

"Mom likes pepperoni," Philip said, just as smugly. "We have to bring some home to her."

Lillian grimaced, "Oh, I don't think your mother wants any pizza at all tonight, let alone pepperoni."

"Why not?"

"She's not feeling well. She's got a little stomach bug."

The children looked at each other, their eyes meeting a long time, their entire demeanor changed.

"Is that what she said? A little stomach bug?" Philip asked.

"Yes. She's just a little sick to her stomach."

"But did she say 'a little stomach bug?'"

The teenaged girl who was acting as hostess called Lillian's name. Lillian took the kids by the shoulders to lead them to their table, saying, "For crying out loud, she's fine, guys. Don't make a federal case of it."

They didn't say anything more, but they were very quiet during their meal.

Philip didn't make an issue about not getting pepperoni on his pizza, and Suzy picked at one piece and wasn't as gabby as she usually was.

"Look," Lillian said half way through eating the pizza, "I know I'm not as much fun as your mom, but …"

"Will she lose her hair again?" Philip asked.

Lillian was surprised by his question. "No…no …that was from nerves. Really, kids, this is nothing. Everyone gets sick from time to time. You can't expect bad things to happen just because they did in the past."

For the first time since meeting them, Lillian felt genuinely sorry for them. On some conscious level she knew they had gone through a lot with their father's death and having to move to a new home, but only now did it strike her how much they had faced at so young an age. Ann must have been grieving hard and this, too, would have had an impact on them. Their faces pulled at her heart as she looked at them over the tray of pizza.

"How about we go for Rita's Italian ice after this? It's right across the street."

"I like Rita's Italian ice," said Suzy, brightening a little.

"Good! But you have to finish that piece of pizza."

Suzy lifted it and took a bite. Philip wasn't as easily comforted and his large blue eyes, so like Ann's, studied Lillian. She was compelled to reach out to touch the dimple in his right cheek but half way to getting there, she pulled her hand back.

"What's your favorite flavor, Philip?" she asked him quietly.

He shrugged and looked down at the plate. "I like the vanilla gelato with the orange ice on top," he answered finally.

"Yeah, me too, that's my favorite," Lillian said smiling. "We've got something in common!"

He smiled this time when he shrugged and the dimple deepened. Suzy finished her slice of pizza. "I ate it all!"

"You did. I'm impressed. Well, all right then, it's Rita's for us!"

∽

Ann was in the kitchen on the phone when they returned home. Lillian and the kids were laughing and telling one another silly jokes, the sillier the better. Ann looked up, pleasantly surprised to see how much fun they were having together. Suzy ran to her, giggling, throwing her arms around her mother's waist, and Ann put one arm around her little girl's head. Lillian noticed that Ann looked a little better; some color had returned to her cheeks.

"They're home now." She listened to the person on the other end and answered, "I will. I promise. Next week, same time. No, I don't want that." Ann's voice was insistent. "No, Joey, you stay there and finish the semester. Love you, too. Be good."

She hit the "off" button on the cordless phone and smiled at Lillian. "That was Joey."

Lillian didn't say anything.

"My brother, Joey," Ann repeated.

"Yes, I know who Joey is," Lillian answered, putting her purse and the box with the leftover pizza on the counter.

"You guys looked like you were having a good time," Ann said, pulling Suzy close to her again and smiling down into the little girl's face.

"Lillian took us to Rita's and guess what?"

"What?" Ann asked, placing her cheek on the little girl's blond hair.

"She likes the same flavor that Philip likes!"

"Wow," Ann said, laughing a little. "What a coincidence!"

"And she doesn't like pepperoni on her pizza just like me!"

Ann chuckled again, "Well, you know, she is our relative. She's bound to be slightly normal."

Lillian groaned, "Don't make it worse. They already think I'm an ogre."

"No, that's not true, they don't," Ann said smiling at Lillian.

"What's an ogre?" Suzy asked.

"Not me!" Lillian answered.

"Shrek," Philip answered.

"Who's Shrek?" asked Lillian, which made them all laugh.

Ann told them it was bedtime and they balked. "We want to catch fireflies," Suzy said. "Lillian said we could."

"Oh she did, did she? Well, two minutes of firefly catching and then bed," Ann told them.

The kids ran outside and Ann flipped on an outdoor light in order to be able to see them in the dark. She stood at one of the windows in the sunroom watching them.

Lillian sat down heavily on a chair in the sunroom overlooking the lawn and the children. "I'm exhausted."

"From going for pizza and ice?" Ann teased her. "You must be getting old."

They were quiet a few minutes, sitting in each other's company without feeling the need for small talk, watching the children in the yard. Then Lillian said, "I like them, Annie." She looked across the room at her cousin. "I like your kids."

Ann smiled. She still looked tired and pale. "I like them, too...so much that I sometimes think it will split my heart into a million pieces. When you're first in love you kind of feel that way, but then love settles down and becomes less intense, just as beautiful, of course, but not so extreme. But the love you feel as a mother never cools down." She looked a little embarrassed then. "Listen to me talking to you as though you've never been in love." She waited for a response, and when none came, she asked Lillian, "Have you?"

"No...yeah...well...yeah I guess I have...am."

"Don't be so certain," Ann said laughing, and Lillian joined in the laughter.

"There's this guy in New York," Lillian explained. "He's a little older than I am. He's a senior editor at one of the largest publishing companies. I worked for him a few years ago, and he's just such a great person that the next thing I knew, I was crazy about him. He is divorced. He has a beautiful daughter who is a senior in high school now. She's a doll, and we really get along—more like good friends. He also lives with his twin sister, Louise, who has never been married. She's an editor, too, for a fashion magazine. She's a lot of fun … I don't know why she never married, except that it's just not for some people. Like me."

"How do you know?"

"What?"

"That marriage isn't for you?"

"It isn't."

"How do you know that?"

"I don't want to get married. Even when I first fell for Dan, I never even thought about marrying him. When he broaches the subject, I find myself running away for weeks. That's how I ended up back here in Newtown four years ago. I left his apartment after we argued about getting married, and drove straight here, although I can't imagine why to this day. There was a sign that said 'vacant apartment' in Mrs. Snyder's window, and I took it on the spot."

"He understands?"

"He understands about everything that concerns me. He's my very dearest friend in the whole world. But I won't marry him. It's been a source of contention from time to time, but now he just accepts it. He lives his life and I live mine. We talk every day—sometimes two times a day—and when I can't stand being apart from him, we get together, and then we part again. I adore him for allowing me to be this way. I adore him, period. I just won't marry him."

Ann sighed and pulled her sweater closer around her. "That's the most you've told me about yourself in three weeks."

"I've been a royal bitch, haven't I?"

Ann was surprised by the statement, but she didn't deny it.

"Maybe there's a lot more of my mother in me than I ever want to admit."

No comment from Ann.

"Hmm?" Lillian prodded a response.

Still no comment, Ann just looked down at her hands.

"She was a bitch, Ann. You won't offend me if you admit it. So am I."

"You aren't a bitch. And your mother was mentally ill. She was unhappy and her whole life was a disappointment to her. That does awful things to a person."

"I was the biggest disappointment…from birth on."

"I don't think that's true, Lilly. You were her only child. Think about what I said before about a mother's love."

"Oh, Annie, come on. I received more love from your mother than I did from my own. The kind of love you were talking about before doesn't sound like the kind I ever got. She'd slap my face so hard that it would knock me off a chair, and that was on a *good* day. Does that sound like a mother's love? I wouldn't even know how to be a mother myself. I detested my own mother, why in God's name would I want to be one?"

"And that's why you won't marry?"

"I won't marry because I don't want to be tied down to any one person or any one home or any one thing."

They were quiet again, each lost in her own thoughts.

Remembering her mother—remembering those slaps that were for nothing more than the fact that Lillian might forget and chew with her mouth open, or that her mother could hear her chewing with her mouth closed, or that Lillian made noise with the fork against the plate—made Lillian's stomach tighten and bile creep up into her throat now. Noise of any kind could enrage her mother, the slightest noise. Not every day, maybe not every week, but always when her mother was in one of her moods. And Lillian never knew when one of those *moods* would show up, at least not until she was old enough to learn the signs.

Her father would pick her up off the floor and say, *Lillian, honey, when will you learn? Please, honey, don't make noise at the table. Just eat quietly so your mother doesn't hear.*

"Tell me something," Lillian said after a long while. "Did my mother commit suicide?"

Ann didn't answer her.

"Annie, look, I never really wanted to know—I never cared how she died—so if you don't tell me, then fine. But sometimes I wonder… if she …"

"Yes."

There it was, the conversation neither of them really wanted to have, and an answer Lillian really never wanted to hear..a one-word answer she dreaded for years.

The humidity from the summer night permeated the sunroom. Lillian felt almost unable to breathe.

Ann inhaled, ready to speak again, but Lillian held her hand up to stop her.

"Good night," Lillian whispered, getting up from the chair and walking toward the back door of the kitchen. She opened it and stepped out.

"I'm sorry," Ann whispered.

# *Five*

The pair of exterminators arrived early the next morning, and Lillian let them in since Ann had decided to drive the kids to camp. She showed them to the stairs leading to the attic, and then escaped into her room with her door closed. She turned the lock with a shiver—just in case bats knew how to open doors. She listened to the noise above her...men's voices...footsteps... faster footsteps...a strangely high-pitched scream for a man...a thwack...another thwack...another scream...laughter...a crash...and then the slam of the attic door.

"Lady?" one of them called.

She turned the lock and pulled the door open a sliver. "All gone?" she asked, peeking out at the exterminators.

"All gone...but you have to call someone to close up some holes. You can see daylight through them. It's an old house, you know."

Lillian opened the door wider. "Yes, we know that."

"Call a contractor or a handyman. It's not the roof, the roof is sealed good, no holes there. It's the siding and under the eaves."

"But the bats are gone now, right?"

"For now, right," he said, handing her a paper to sign.

"And I can go up there without worrying?"

"I can't see why not...but call a handyman or a siding company so they don't come back. Bats are one thing, but you get a squirrel up there and you could get some real damage. We put some poison pellets around so don't let your pets go up there."

He was holding a black garbage bag.

"What's in that?" Lillian asked him, eyeing the bag, backing away.

The men looked at each other and grinned.

"What do you think it is?"

"Where are you going to put it?" Lillian asked.

"We're taking it, don't worry."

She signed the paper and escorted them to the door, watching carefully that they threw the bag in the back of their pickup. When they drove away, Lillian looked at the ceiling. There was nothing between her and the blanket chest filled with letters and hand-written journals now, yet she couldn't bring herself to go up alone.

She decided to wait for Ann…just in case there was bat blood around, or something else that might be gross.

But when Ann returned, she was feeling ill again. She couldn't seem to get over the stomach bug. She'd be feeling better, then it would hit her again, then she'd be all right for a few days. Lillian suggested she go to her doctor, which Ann did, and the medicine the doctor gave her seemed to help a little. After a few days, she perked up but she still looked pallid.

Ann complained about the way she looked. She even went to the most exclusive hair salon in the area and got what she called a "makeover," although to Lillian it looked as though she just shortened her hair even more and darkened the color just slightly. She bought some new makeup, which did improve her color a little, and Lillian noticed she was using new mascara, the lengthening kind, because her eyelashes were suddenly longer and thicker.

There was no further mention of Lillian's mother—no mention of the conversation they had that night at all.

Talking about Dan with Ann had made Lillian lonesome for him.

"Is it time for a conjugal visit?" he asked her during one of their calls when she told him she missed him. His voice warm and amused.

"I'm horny, so I guess it is," she answered.

"I'm only good for a lay, then?" he teased.

"That and a back rub. You give the best back rubs, you know."

"So I've been told," he answered.

"By me only, right?" she asked, laughing a little.

"What do you think I am, a eunuch?"

"You are totally devoted to me, Danny boy, and the only relief you get is me in your bed or choking the chicken."

He laughed heartily then, and a warm feeling of contentment coursed through Lillian. She loved his cackle.

"I do have to come soon, Dan. I really miss you."

He grew serious, just as she had. "I'm here, babe…anytime and on your terms."

"Forever, Dan?" she asked him. "You won't feel that way forever."

"Forever, Lillian. It won't be forever, anyway. One of these days you're going to let yourself love me the way I want you to. Until then, I'll love you the way I want to."

"Okay. I'll come soon. I promise."

"In the meantime, I'll be choking the chicken, so have some mercy on me and come soon."

They both laughed. As she slid her cell phone closed, Ann walked into the library where Lillian had been working at her laptop. "Hey," she said, "wanna go up to the attic and see what's in the chest? I'm dying for you to see it, and you've been really patient."

The holes in the attic had just been closed up by the local handyman. He was on his third day of filling in holes, checking for rotting wood around the windows, and replacing that, and now doing anything else that the old house needed. Lillian felt confident enough that they wouldn't be attacked by a ferocious animal. She leaned into Ann, "Yeah, let's go."

Like children, they rushed up the stairs and then to the attic landing. Ann reached the door first and turned the knob slowly and pushed at the heavy oak door just enough to peek in and make sure the exterminators had left nothing behind.

"Coast is clear," she said and pushed the door open all the way.

They walked into the hot dusty attic. It was still early morning, but the room held the heat of the summer. It smelled of dust and old wood. Slashes of sunlight from the dormer windows gave them just enough light to look around. Except for the blanket chest, some wicker baskets, broken pottery, and a box of old books, the attic was empty. It was decorated with some pretty serious spider webs, however. Worn ruffled blue checked curtains hung on the four windows.

"A little creepy, no?" Ann asked looking at the intricate webs.

"Nah," Lillian answered, "just an attic." She walked to the blanket chest. It was plain and thick with dust, and it looked like cherry wood. It was taller than most she had seen, about three feet tall and four feet wide. The lid was slightly larger than the rest of the box; its edges were carved in clean lines, the corners rounded. The likeness of a bird sitting on a magnolia branch, surrounded by double oval lines, was carved lightly into the top, and an intricate brass keyhole, dark with age, was the only adornment on the front of the chest. "It's beautiful, isn't it?" she said aloud. She pulled on the top and it opened easily.

"There was no key in it," Ann said as Lillian pushed it open until the hinges locked.

Inside there was a wool blanket that looked as though it had been used just the winter before, it was so pristine. "Is this your blanket?" Lillian asked, picking it up.

Ann shook her head no. "It was there. The cedar protected it, I guess. There's not a moth hole in it."

The strong scent of cedar did surprise Lillian, since the chest must be more than a hundred years old. Wouldn't the cedar have faded a little over the years, she wondered?

"They knew how to build things in the old days, didn't they?" She handed the blanket to Ann and bent over the chest. On the small shelf attached to the inside of the lid were two pins, a hair clip made of silver and pearls, and some old photos. There were also pencil renderings of two young women, probably sisters. The rest of the chest was filled with papers of all colors, some tied with satin ribbons, most very yellowed. The papers at the bottom were ready to crumble under Lillian's fingers.

"Wow," Lillian breathed in a whisper. "This is so cool."

Ann chuckled. "I knew you'd be impressed. We can't really read up here, it's much too dark…and hot. How do you want to handle it? We can't carry it all downstairs."

Lillian thought for a few minutes. "Let's get the handyman to help us carry the chest down to the library," she said rushing toward the attic door, leaving Ann standing alone before she could even respond. Within minutes, Lillian was leading the tall lanky handyman named Larry up the attic steps. "It's going to be heavy," she was telling him. "It's a huge chest."

He was a quiet man, in his late forties, tall and graying at the temples. He was wearing work clothes, and he had taken his cap off and stuck it in his belt.

"Mornin'," he said to Ann, who greeted him with a smile. Then he walked around the chest, eyeing it carefully, measuring its weight in his mind. "This is a beautiful piece of furniture," he said as he pulled it up at one end and grunted with the strain. "And it's pretty heavy."

"I can handle it with you," Lillian insisted. "Believe me, I'm a work horse. I've lifted heavier than this."

Larry pursed his lips, debating whether he should encourage it, but Lillian went over to the chest, closed it, and placed her hands under it without waiting for him to protest. "Come on, let's do it," she said.

The tall man went to the other side of the chest and they lifted it up together. Ann flew to Lillian's side to help lighten the load. Lillian would have protested except that she couldn't speak under of the strain of the chest's weight in her hands.

"I'll go first," Larry said and he led them to the attic steps, taking the brunt of the weight as they lowered it down to the next floor where the bedrooms were. The three of them put the chest down on the hallway floor, panting with the effort.

"New idea," Lillian said, breathing heavily and leaning on her thighs, while Ann sat down on the second step, suddenly very pale. "Let's just put it in my room. I don't think I could carry it all the way to the library."

"Thank you," said a relieved Larry, his face and hair soaked with sweat.

When they had rested a minute, Larry and Lillian moved the chest into her room and placed it against an empty wall. Now that it was in brighter light, they could see just how grimy it was from being in the attic for an unknown number of years. They could also see that it was even lovelier than they had originally thought.

Larry wiped the sweat from his face with his handkerchief. Ann patted the man's arm, "Come on, I'll get you a bottle of water. You need it." Lillian closed the door behind them and pulled off her white T-shirt which was smeared with filth.

She washed her hands and face in the bathroom and quickly put on an old sleeveless shirt.

Walking past the chest, she drew her finger over the top, leaving a track in the dust and grime. She felt more exhilarated and excited than she had in a very long time; she had come across a great treasure. She wanted to dive right into the papers in the chest, but she knew that it would be more prudent to clean the piece. She hunched down in front of it, looking at the elaborate brass keyhole.

"What stories have you to tell us, lovely old chest?" she asked out loud. "What secrets to reveal? What heartaches? What skeletons do we have here?" She chuckled at herself. She was much too gleeful. It wasn't like her to be this keyed up. Just then someone knocked at her door and she called, "Come in."

Larry entered with a drop cloth and some cleaning materials. "Let's put this under the chest so that when you clean it, the floor doesn't get ruined," he said. "And I brought these from my truck," he added, putting some cans of liquids and rags on the floor near the chest.

He held up yellow rubber gloves. "Wear these when you use this stuff. It's a homemade recipe to clean old wood furniture—just some linseed oil and turpentine and some other stuff. It'll help clean off that muck without hurting the wood. The other can is a really good furniture moisturizer. Once you get it all cleaned off and moisturized, I'd like to see it again. I have a strong hunch it's worth a lot of money. It looks Quaker to me and really old—eighteenth century, maybe pre-Revolutionary. It was probably built right here in Bucks County…maybe Philadelphia…but like I said, I have a hunch. Take care you don't damage it when you're cleaning it."

Lillian looked down at the chest with surprise. The treasure for her was what was inside it. She hadn't even thought of the value of the chest itself.

Larry lifted the front while Lillian pushed the tarp under it, then he lifted the back so that she could pull it through. Together they spread the floor covering wide so there was enough room for Lillian to work.

"Thanks, Larry," Lillian said smiling at him. "You're a real pal."

The quiet man just smiled shyly and left the room without saying anything else. A few minutes later Ann appeared.

"So, have you gone through it yet?" she asked.

"No, I think I better clean it first."

"Let's do it," Ann said, holding up another pair of rubber gloves. She picked up the cleaning fluids that Larry had left. They each took a side and started to wipe the chest down, and Ann was glad that Larry had put the drop cloth under it. Years of dust, grime, and even bird droppings—or were they bat droppings, she wondered with a shudder—came off the large cherry wood trunk. They were still working on it when the children's camp bus stopped at the end of the driveway.

Ann dropped her rag and ran down to meet them, and Lillian could hear the kids laughing at seeing dirt all over the front of their mother's shirt and sleeves. Lillian sat back on her heels and looked it over. It was starting to look much better, just a little dry. She would begin the moisturizing process the next morning. It was certainly clean enough for her to open it now and rummage inside a little.

There were so many papers—letters without envelopes, letters in envelopes, and what looked like hand-written manuscripts.

She didn't know what to pick up first. Then she noticed a large tan envelope with type face in a single line: *It is better to know some of the questions than all of the answers*—James Thurber (I think).

Lillian turned the manila envelope over and saw that it had been sealed but the dry air in the attic had loosened the glue at each corner. It opened with just a gentle movement of her thumb. Inside were about a hundred single spaced typed sheets.

She pulled them out and smiled at the old fashioned typewriter print. The "t" must have been bent as it didn't print completely. She glanced through and could tell when the typewriter was just about out of ink and when the ink ribbon had been replaced.

It was familiar to her but she couldn't figure out why.

The first page contained a title of sorts: *Our Mothers and Daughters, Our Life Beside the River*. There was no author's name. Lillian sat on the edge of her bed before turning to the next page. There were no page numbers, and she made a mental note not to get the pages mixed up. "God help me if I drop this," she murmured to herself.

The first sentences read:

"I don't know why I'm writing this. I'm not one to record history and although I have played with the idea of being a writer my whole life, I have no talent for it. However, all the letters and papers in Great-great-grandmama's chest are in a hodgepodge, and it's hard to understand who's who. I at least have the benefit of having had the stories handed down verbally.

For some reason, I never really passed many of them on to my girls. It seemed so old fashioned to do it. Helen might have liked hearing some of it, but my Regina would have thought it boring and 'old news.' She wouldn't have had the patience, I'm sure."

Lillian gasped; these pages had been written by her own grandmother! Now she knew why she recognized the typeface—her grandmother had started to type her letters to Lillian right before she died. Her arthritis was crippling her hands by then and she couldn't hold a pen. Lillian continued to read the sheets.

"Now that I'm at the end of my years, I realize how important it is to keep the history of our mothers and our mothers' mothers preserved, and the stories of their lives as women who worked and dreamed and cried beside this beautiful Delaware River. Their whole lives—our whole lives— revolved around this river and the canal. Both gave life, both took life, and both just kept moving along while the women in this family suffered and rejoiced. Perhaps Helen and Regina's girls will want to know these stories someday. My beautiful Lillian seems to like stories. She's always got her nose in a book and she's kept busy for hours when we give her a notebook to write in. Her little stories were so adorable when she was little. Sometimes they were very disturbing, though. She's hurt and angry; I can tell that by some of what she writes. I ache for her. But there is nothing I can do to change her mother. God knows, I have tried for many years, and I'm old and weaker now than I was when Regina was a child. I can't do this, or I will crumble up and blow away. Or wish I had."

Lillian put the page down on the bed. *So, my grandmother knew what my mother was. She knew I was abused. No one to my rescue, then, even among those who knew and claimed to love me? What kind of power did my mother have over everyone that no one could stand up to her? Including me. I left, but I never confronted her.*

Suzy appeared at the bedroom door.

"Hi, Lilly," she said, sounding tentative as though she wasn't certain how Lillian would respond to the interruption.

"Hey, gorgeous," Lillian answered smiling.

Suzy took that as an invitation and ran into the room and jumped on the bed.

"Easy, bucko," Lillian said, grabbing at the typewritten sheets. "You're rambunctious today."

"I rode a horse today," Suzy said. "We had equestrian day at camp. He was big and brown and had a black mane."

"Sounds like my kind of guy," Lillian answered, lying back on the pillows beside the little girl who sat with her sandaled feet on the bedspread. "So did you fall off?"

"Nope," Suzy said, shaking her blond head from side to side. "I wore a helmet just in case."

"That's a good thing, I guess," Lillian yawned against the back of her hand.

"I couldn't wait to come home to tell you," Suzy told Lillian, as though they'd been friends for her entire life.

*I can't be all that bad if this little person wants to share her stories with me.*

"What's that?" Suzy asked pointing to the chest.

"That, my little urchin, is a treasure chest of information and if I'm right, it will give us all the answers to our ancestors and maybe why I'm so fucked up… I mean messed up." She caught herself; at least now she was starting to realize when she said something wrong. Suzy looked at her and shook her head. It wasn't the first time she slipped with the "f bomb" in front of the kids. "I really mean messed up," Lillian corrected herself again.

"You *are* messed up," Suzy agreed, looking at the dust and grime on Lillian's shirt. "You are *filthy* today—and not just your language." The little girl made a face when she said it. "Mommy is too."

Lillian laughed so hard it startled Suzy. When she stopped laughing, she asked, "Did your brother ride a horse today, too?"

"No, he's in the 'Tigers' because he's older and a boy. I'm in the 'Chipmunks' this year. We do different things on different days."

"Oh, I see."

"No, you don't, but that's all right. You'll get the hang of it someday," Suzy pulled herself to the edge of the bed and jumped off. "You better get washed up and changed before you come down for dinner, Lilly." She threw the order back over her shoulder as she moved toward the door.

"You're a bossy little imp, aren't you?" Lillian, who was still lying on the bed, called after the little girl but received no reply.

With a sigh, she pulled herself up off the bed and put the typed pages back in their envelope.

She closed the lid of the chest and placed the envelope on top, over the carved bird, and as she did, she whispered, "I don't care that you knew and did nothing, Grandma. I love you anyway."

# Six

For three days after finding the chest, both Lillian and Ann read pages from their grandmother's typewritten journal. Much of it was very dry reading, and even though it was their grandmother's attempt to help clarify which person was which in their ancestral line, they were still confused. It didn't help that a lot of the names were repeated from one generation to another. "Which Hannah was that?" Ann would ask Lillian, confused.

They were enthralled with the numerous cards, letters, old photographs and daguerreotypes they found as they dug deeper into the chest. There were old graduation autograph books from the twenties and thirties and poetry written by courting gentlemen and lovelorn young girls.

"The things in this chest will help to introduce my granddaughters and their children, and perhaps the many generations to come, to the women who were born to and lived in this house," their grandmother had written. Ann and Lillian chose not to rush and open all of them at once. Instead, they decided to take a few at a time and read them when the house was quiet and they weren't pressured to do anything else. This way they could absorb them, laugh at them, and sometimes cry over them.

Ann took three of the letters from the chest to read aloud one afternoon when they sat in the gazebo waiting for the kids to come home from camp. It was one of those surprising July afternoons that had turned cool and dry after a long heat spell, and they each had a glass of iced tea with a lemon wedge and sprig of mint from Ann's herb garden.

The sky was cloudless and a breeze off the river moved through the open windows of the gazebo, gently playing with the corner of one of the old letters Ann had just taken out of its envelope.

"This one was written on the 22nd of April in 1905," Ann said, steadying the thin paper against the breeze by splaying her long delicate fingers out at the top and bottom.

*Dearest brother,*

*I hope this note finds you much improved. Tom tells me that you may be coming home soon and I can't express just how happy I am. Please know that I have readied a room for you at Willow Wood and so you must not worry about where to go. I insist that you come here to us.*

*This house is so full of life with the laughter of the children and I know how much you love them. The spring peepers are singing in the canal already, and the breeze from the river has been delightful. Until you are ready to work again, I will set a fine rocker on the back porch and you can while away the days watching your little nephews and niece at play and call to the mule drivers and boat captains as they go by. You must start a list of your favorite meals, so that I will know what to prepare for you.*

*Your Godson is learning his letters, you know, and quite well. PJ is six, and a big boy who helps me with his little brothers and sister. Tom-tom is also trying to learn to write. He's always imitating his big brother. Anna is a quiet little girl most of the time, but I find that even at two years old, she can hold her own with the boys. She's very sweet and I'm so happy that God saw fit to give me a girl before sending me another boy. Teddy, our baby, is just about ready to get up and walk. He gets so excited when his brothers start running around, he jumps up and down in his crib, and I know he can't wait to join them, bless his baby's heart.*

*My prayers and thoughts are with you every day, Patrick. Although you are my husband's brother, you are the brother of my heart, the older brother I never had, and I only wish the best for you. I know you will soon be well enough to come home, and when you do, there will be great rejoicing at Willow Wood. You mustn't fret about coming home. You will be here with us who love you, and I will do everything in my power to protect you from any sadness or worry as will your loving brother. Take care, my dear Patrick. I will write again next week.*

*Your sister,*

*Kate"*

Ann passed the letter across the wrought iron table to Lillian who glanced down at it. The note paper was very fine and had been well preserved. The woman's handwriting was typical of the day, scrolling and elegant, yet not oversized. "She must have been very fond of him," Lillian said.

"Let's figure out who they are," Ann said, picking up the typewritten guide their grandmother Julia had prepared before she died. "Let's see, 1905…Katherine…okay, this was her own grandmother, Katherine Ginley Fitzpatrick. She was born in 1882 and died in 1906 and had six children.

Good Lord, she was so young."

"She really was," Lillian agreed. "Who was the man she wrote to? I wonder where he was when she wrote this to him…prison, do you think?"

"No," Ann said, "she mentions his health. He must have been sick…tuberculosis maybe." Ann read silently for a minute then said, "Katherine was married to Thomas Fitzpatrick, who was a boat builder in Uhlerstown. Patrick was his younger brother…he was 'put away,' as our grandmother states it, in a mental hospital in the Poconos. He had a nervous breakdown when the girl he was in love with rejected him.

She actually did more than that, she and her friends went to the store where he worked and apparently scorned him publicly. I guess she means ridiculed him…and treated him terribly. He was so mortified and bereft he tried to drown himself in the canal. His brother saved his life and the family doctor advised them to put him in a mental institution until he recovered."

"I wonder if he did. Read the next letter and see."

Ann opened the envelope and unfolded the same notepaper the first letter had been written on. "This one was written a few weeks later," she told Lillian. "It basically says the same things, just chit chat, but very encouraging and supportive. She doesn't mention his coming home this time though, so he must not have been ready. She mentions that she's enclosing two pictures drawn by her sons for him to display in his room to cheer him."

Ann leaned forward and said, "Listen to the end of her letter, Lilly."

*I do not mean to bring anything to your attention that will hurt you or upset you, dear brother, but I would prefer you hear this from me than from anyone else.*

*They read the banns in the Church today and Eileen is engaged to be married to Bolton Johns in September. I don't know how many of your friends continue to correspond with you, and since most go to St. Andrew's as we do, I am certain that someone will let you know. I wanted it to be me, who loves you as a sister.*

*And since I haven't mentioned it before, and intend never to do so again, I feel it is a good opportunity for me to say that Eileen never felt worthy of you, Patrick. She felt that she was never good enough, kind enough, intelligent enough for a man of your keen intellect and true compassion. I believe that was the reason for her profound abuse of you that night.*

*She didn't hate you, Patrick, she hated herself. She was frightened that you would marry her and come to think of her as she has always thought of herself.*

*Having come from a poor family, she didn't have the fortitude to realize that had she embraced your goodness, learned from you and your gentle ways, she herself could have embraced the goodness that you seemed to have found in her.*

*It's a complicated matter. It's a complicated and harsh world, Patrick. Sometimes Tom says to me that he always felt that you were too fine to be able to understand the harshness of this life, even as a child. I don't know if that's true, but I do know that there are others like you in this world, and you will find someone who will adore you and cherish you.*

*Let this news of Eileen help you to let her go so that you can live again and come back to us."*

Ann stopped reading. "Do you think he bought it?"

"Who knows? But what a sweet person Katherine was," Lillian said, carefully folding the letter. "I mean, it was so nice of her to take the time to write to him with four babies under foot. He wasn't even her brother." She smiled at Ann, "That's like something you would do."

Ann shook her head no. "That's not true, Lillian. I'd be nervous about what to say and what not to say; afraid I'd say the wrong thing. I'd avoid writing to him, but you wouldn't."

"Me?" Lillian asked surprised.

"Look at how you write a note or send a card to your old landlady every week. You visit her as much as you can. I think that is so thoughtful."

Lillian brushed the compliment off with a wave of the folded letter. "That's different, she was my friend for four years. I feel sorry that she's in that assisted living place. She liked her own home and now she has to do what they tell her."

"It's a wonderful facility and you're wrong—it's not a prison, for goodness's sake. They will take wonderful care of her. But that's not the point," Ann continued. "You haven't deserted her. You write to her, send her lovely little cards with flowers. You are more like Katherine."

Lillian laughed. "Minus all the brats," she said off-handedly. "Okay, read the last one."

*Dearest Patrick,*

*At last, you will be coming home! Tom is elated. As you know, he never felt you should be there in the first place. But that is behind us now. You are well and we can't wait for your arrival next week. Your mother gave us a little bit of a hard time about your not going back to her house, but Tom has explained the situation to her satisfaction, at least for now. Once you are home and you discern when the time is right, you can decide what to do and where you want to live.*

*PJ and Tom-Tom spend their days drawing pictures for you. They intend to decorate your room with them, and I'm enclosing a little note that PJ wrote to you. He is most excited about your coming.*

*Well, then, we will see you next week. Tom will pick you up bright and early on Sunday. Until then I pray that you are happy and looking forward to coming here to us.*

*Your loving sister,*

*Kate*

Lillian raised her eyebrows. "I wonder how it all worked out. How sad that she died the year after. Does Grandma say what she died from?'

Ann studied several of the typewritten pages, looking for the answer. Red blotches appeared on her fair, almost lucid, neck and face before she said, "It must have been breast cancer. She found some lumps in her breast just after her sixth baby was born. She died eight months later." Ann put the papers down and looked out toward the river. "It must have been a very aggressive cancer."

Lillian saw her cousin swallow hard a few times and knew that Ann was holding back tears.

"You're such a softie," Lillian said, shaking her head.

Ann was trying to control her emotions. "It's sad; just very sad," she said. She picked up their grandmother's manuscript again and told Lillian, "Grandma says that Katherine's husband remarried within a month and the new wife came into the house to raise the children. Apparently she didn't give birth to any of her own. She died young, too, and eventually the daughter Anna—Grandma's own mother—took over running the house. Grandma writes, 'My mother always said that her stepmother was stern and a little cold, but kind enough.' Two of the boys got jobs out of state and moved away, PJ eloped with a local girl and moved in with her family, and Anna and her husband inherited Willow Wood and the care of her youngest brother when her father died."

Ann flipped to another page.

"Grandmother notes that Patrick was devastated by Katherine's death and after her funeral—on the very day of her funeral—he took a train west to Colorado. He was killed waiting for a train at a Chicago train station during a robbery twelve years later. He was on his way home to Pennsylvania when it happened."

Ann sat up straight in her chair then, still reading. "Oh my God, Lilly,

56

he was on his way home to marry the woman who had originally rejected him, that Eileen person, who caused his nervous breakdown. They had been corresponding through letters and she agreed to marry him after all those years. She was widowed by then. He had made a lot of money in silver mines in Colorado, and he left half of his fortune to his Godson—that would be the PJ who is mentioned in Katherine's letters I guess—and the other half to this woman he had always been in love with."

"Wow," Lillian breathed, "what a freakin' love story that is!"

"It's tragic, Lilly. It's absolutely heartbreakingly tragic...the whole story." Ann started to weep. She tried to stop, but the harder she tried, the harder she cried. She put her face into her hands and choked on the tears that flooded her eyes and throat.

Lillian was alarmed and jumped out of her chair. "Ann, for God's sake, stop," she demanded. "Why are you so upset?" But Ann put her head down on her arms at the edge of the table and continued to sob.

Lillian put her hand on her cousin and stroked her back. "Stop, Annie, don't do this to yourself. It was so long ago."

Ann shook her head against her arms and couldn't speak, so deep was this sudden sorrow. Lillian put her cheek down on the back of Ann's head, "Hey, kiddo. Please calm down. I know it's been hard for you, too, with Bill dying and all, but don't make yourself sick over it, Annie. This isn't good for you. And I'm not much comfort, as much as I wish I could be. I don't handle other people crying very well."

Ann continued to cry and Lillian knelt beside her. "Aw, don't, Annie, don't cry like this. Enough already...what the hell is wrong with you?"

Lillian could see Ann was trying to stop sobbing; she just couldn't succeed.

"God damn it I wish I was more like Aunt Helen," Lillian said in exasperation. "She'd be able to help you. She wasn't a worthless piece of shit like I am."

Ann lifted her head and looked at Lillian then, her eyes still flooding over. Lillian put her hands on each side of Ann's red, tear-stained face. "Just ...a...worthless...piece...of..."

Ann smiled a little. "You aren't a piece of shit," she said before Lillian could finish.

"Yah*hunh*," Lillian answered in exactly the way she'd heard Suzy say it when telling Philip she was right and he was wrong. She wiped Ann's face with her thumbs. "Cow dung...no worse, elephant dung...no, wait, I'm no better than what comes out of a man who's been on a beer binge for seven—no, ten—days and has the beer runs!"

Ann burst out laughing now. She fell back in her chair. She pushed at Lillian. "That's disgusting!"

"It's true, and he had beans…lots of beans… and kielbasa, too!" Lillian added, smiling herself now as she relished playing the comedian.

Ann pulled her knees to her chest. "No more," she begged, "just shut up."

"Okay, as long as you'll stop crying."

"I've stopped." Ann grabbed the condensation soaked napkin from under her iced tea to wipe her face and blow her nose.

Lillian went back to her chair and sat down again, satisfied that she had somehow pulled her cousin out of near hysteria.

Then Ann jumped to her feet, her hand gripping her stomach. "I'm going to be sick," she said, and ran to the edge of the berm and vomited into the canal. Lillian followed her, saying, "I *told* you that you were going to make yourself sick! And since when am I ever right?"

She helped ease Ann onto the grassy bank, handed her a napkin she had grabbed from the table, and they sat there quietly until Ann's stomach settled.

"I'm sorry I made such a fool out of myself," Ann said. "It's just thinking about that poor young woman, how she must have been agonizing over leaving her children when she died." She raised her eyes to Lillian's. "Who would love her little guys? Who would know what to do when they were afraid in the night and how to comfort each one when they were sick? Kids are so different, they each have different needs. Katherine went through an awful hell, Lillian, before she died; an indescribable kind of hell."

"Well, her husband was there. He would know how to take care of them. And his brother was there."

Ann pulled her knees up and hugged them against her chest, looking out at the river beyond the canal. "The brother left them to go to Colorado—and the husband might not have known how to care for them. Men don't always have the same intuition about children that women do."

"That's ridiculous. My friend, Dan, is absolutely wonderful with his daughter Jessica. He's this sensitive, caring man, and she shares everything with him. She even talks to him about her boyfriends."

Lillian saw Ann wasn't convinced and insisted, "Men can be as intuitive and loving as women can."

Ann leaned her mouth against her knees and Lillian could see that although she didn't want to argue, she wasn't convinced.

Lillian got to her feet and pulled at Ann's long sleeved T-shirt. "Come on, let's forget it. It was all a long time ago and doesn't have anything to do with us. The kids will be getting off the bus in a few minutes and they shouldn't see you looking like you just fought a bunch of insurgents."

Ann let Lillian help her up and they started to walk back toward the house after gathering their tea glasses and the old letters. They didn't rush but strolled slowly across the lawn as the three o'clock sun rays slanted from the west in patterns under their feet.

When they reached the kitchen door, Ann took Lillian's arm. "I like you, Lillian," she said. "I always loved you, but now I really like you. The truth is, you're not the shit…I am."

"Yeah, right," Lillian said, pushing against her cousin's shoulder playfully with her own as they entered the house at the same time.

# *Seven*

Lillian had decided to go to New York that weekend to be with Dan. There was so much to tell him. She would bring some of the very old letters in hopes that he'd be able to decipher the old English that she and Ann found difficult to understand. And she had two very old, first edition books from the attic that she knew he'd love.

She packed them in her suitcase and set the alarm on her cell phone to wake her at six o'clock so she'd get an early start. She wanted to get up before Ann and the kids did and try to catch the train from Trenton before the rush of commuters. When she turned the shower on, she realized she didn't have any shampoo, so she threw on her robe and ran down the hall to see if Ann had any.

At one time Ann's bathroom was the only bathroom in the house, and there was still a door to it from the hallway. She pushed the door open and started to enter when she realized Ann was in the bathroom. She started to back out, but was stunned by what she saw reflected in the mirror. Ann stood before it, her robe pulled aside, and she was touching a scar on her collar bone; there was a bump beneath the scar. And where her arm crossed her chest, Lillian could see that her breasts were gone. Most startling of all in that split second was the fact that Ann was completely bald.

Ann pulled her robe around herself quickly and spun around when she realized Lillian was standing there. Now Lillian could see the short wig stretched over a head form on a shelf beside the sink. Ann's mouth was open wide, as though she was about to scream.

"What in the name of God ..." Lillian started.

"I ..." Ann croaked, unable to speak, unable to say a word.

Lillian backed out of the bathroom and walked down the hall to her own room, shaking and struggling to understand what she'd just witnessed. She closed her bedroom door behind her and sat down on her bed, holding her robe close around her in the same manner Ann usually did with her sweater.

She heard the tap on her door, but ignored it. She was trying to take it all in, trying to make sense of what she'd just seen. There was a tap again, and again she ignored it, but this time the door opened.

"Lillian, we have to talk." And just as Ann said this, the whole situation became clear.

"You have cancer. You have breast cancer. You're sick to your stomach all the time because you have been going for chemotherapy. You didn't get a makeover, you got a wig!" She stopped speaking and stood to pace from the bed to the window, understanding even more as she talked it out. "And the last time you went bald wasn't from nerves or grief, or whatever you told me...you had cancer then, too." Lillian turned from the window and looked at Ann. "This is a recurrence?"

Ann's bald head nodded twice. Her eyes looked sunken in her head, dark circles outlined them.

"You didn't think to mention this to me?" Lillian asked, outraged. "You let me come and live here, let me take care of the kids every Wednesday and cook for them every night when you couldn't because you had 'a little stomach bug' that wouldn't go away, but you never thought to mention that you have cancer?"

"You would have left," Ann said.

Lillian just stared at Ann now, confused.

"You would have left, Lillian," Ann said again.

Lillian took a deep breath and brushed her hair off her forehead letting her hand stay against the top of her head. She stared at Ann a long moment and then said, "You're goddamned right I would have left!"

"There's more, Lilly."

"What do you mean there's more?"

"The cancer is stage four. I'm not going for chemo anymore because it won't work. I decided that this past Wednesday. So, here it is...I'm going to die. And you also should know that I was the person who bought the house you were living in, and I arranged to have the closing a week earlier than we originally agreed hoping that when you got home you'd have no place else to go. And I arranged to be in Starbucks when you came home that day."

Lillian sat down on the edge of the bed trying to comprehend everything Ann was telling her. "You manipulated all of that?"

Ann nodded.

Lillian shook her head and looked at the bald woman. "Why?"

"I wanted you to love my children."

Lillian continued to stare at her cousin, but it was painful to see her so frail, so frightened looking, her scalp shiny, her eyelashes missing completely.

"You wanted me to love your children? You wanted me to love..." and then it was completely clear, and Lillian recoiled against the headboard. "Are you serious? Oh, my God, you manipulative bitch," she whispered at first, then more loudly, "you fucking manipulative bitch."

"I want you to take care of them when I die."

"You picked the wrong person," Lillian said getting off the bed and throwing her suitcase on it. She didn't even bother to hold her robe closed now. She opened the dresser drawer and threw clothes into the suitcase she'd gotten out the night before. "You *tricked* the wrong person."

"Lillian..."

"Who do you think you are? My God, Ann, what right have you to plan someone else's life like this?"

"I'm desperate. Someone has to love them. Someone has to take care of them."

"Maybe that's true, but it doesn't have to be me," Lillian said, pointing to her own chest, enraged. "Not this someone. I don't want to take care of your children, Ann. I don't want to be their substitute mother; I don't want to live here with them anymore."

"Sh," Ann said, closing the bedroom door. "Please don't wake them."

Lillian threw more clothes into the suitcase, then put on her underpants and a bra. She pulled on jeans and a T-shirt, grabbed her suitcase and left the room, brushing past Ann.

Ann followed her down the front stairs and into the library where Lillian went to get her laptop, but she didn't say anything. There was no begging, no trying to defend herself. She just kept following Lillian around the house, still holding her robe closed, her hands shaking.

But she stood in front of the door, barring Lillian's way. Her blue eyes were larger than Lillian had ever seen them in her pale bald head. There were no tears in them now—just fear.

"Get out of my way," Lillian ordered.

"I need you."

"Get out of my way."

"They need you."

"Find...someone...else," Lillian said slowly and deliberately.

"I'm dying, Lillian," Ann said, "we need you. Please don't leave."

"Pretend that I don't exist. Pretend that I have never been here. Okay? Get someone else."

"There is no one else. My husband hasn't any family either, he was an only child, and his parents are too old, too frail. They live in Colorado. My mother has Alzheimer's, my father has all he can do to take care of her, and my brother is still in graduate school. My children need a mother, Lillian. They need you. There is no one else."

"No! No! No!" Lillian shouted at her, getting louder with each word. "Do you hear me? Now get the hell out of my way."

Lillian pushed Ann aside, and even in her anger, she was astounded at how easy it was, how light and frail Ann was, and she felt a pang of remorse and fear. She walked to the garage, opened it, threw her things into the car, and drove out of the garage and down the driveway, spitting gravel behind her when she veered off the macadam. She didn't dare look in her rearview mirror.

She didn't get a train in Trenton. She drove directly to Manhattan, parked in the five level garage three blocks from Dan's apartment building between First and Second Avenue. He was in the lobby leaving the building when she bolted through the door, ignoring the doorman who was about to greet her.

Dan stepped back, surprised to see her, and when she saw him, she fell forward into his arms, sobbing.

"Oh, boy," he said above her head, his hands finding her arms and pushing her away so he could look down into her face. "This can't be good," he said.

He took her suitcase, and led her to the elevator without saying anything else. He shrugged a little at the doorman who was still watching them. The doorman shrugged in response, pulling both palms up in a familiar New York gesture with the universal message of "whatever."

They didn't speak in the elevator. Lillian turned away from him and faced the corner, trying to control her sobs. When they entered his apartment, Dan took her in his arms.

"What's up, kid?" he asked. She just shook her head, her face buried in his suit jacket. "I've known you for twelve years, and I have never seen you cry. I've never even seen you well up! Not even when you found out about your father's death and then your mother's...not a tear."

"I need to sleep, Danny. I'm so freakin' tired."

"What has happened to you?"

"Later…please. I'll tell you later. Now I just need a bed."

He led her into his daughter's bedroom and closed the blinds against the summer sun and heat. She was exhausted, he could see that, but he knew that she wanted more to escape than to sleep. "Darling, please tell me…"

"Go to work," she said to him. "We'll talk when you get home."

"I'm not leaving you like this…"

"Go to work, damn it!" she shouted. "Go to work, Dan. Let me alone for awhile. I need to sleep and I need to think…alone."

She crawled into the bed onto his daughter's lavender sheets and turned toward the wall. He left her then.

When he arrived in his office, Dan called his sister, Louise, to warn her about Lillian in case she got home before he did.

"When did she get here?" Louise asked.

"Before I left this morning. I've never seen her this way."

"Well, whatever it is…we'll take care of her," his sister told him.

Dan tried to call Lillian once, but she didn't answer her cell phone. He couldn't concentrate on the work on his desk, and half way through a meeting in the middle of the day, he excused himself and left the office.

When he entered the apartment, Lillian was sitting on the sofa in his daughter's pajamas. Her red hair was uncombed. The television was on, but she was looking in another direction, staring out of the window. He stood silently at the doorway of his living room and she turned to look up at him.

"I'm the meanest bitch you've ever known," she said.

"Yeah, I know," he answered, moving into the room, dropping his keys on the coffee table as he sat down next to her.

She put her head on his chest. "You have no idea, Dan. I'm going straight to hell, and I don't even care."

Just then they heard the apartment door open. "I came home early," Louise said.

"I'm the meanest bitch you've ever known," Lillian said looking at Louise with her head still on Dan's chest.

Louise raised her eyebrows and looked at her brother. Paternal twins, they still looked very much alike. They were natural blondes, complete with pale brows and eyelashes. Now almost 52, Louise was leaning toward plump, but she dressed in designer clothes, her fair hair was always cut in a classic bob, and she wore subtle but effective makeup.

"Tell me something I don't already know," Louise said with a grin, moving across the room and sitting on the sofa on the other side of Lillian. She rubbed the younger woman's back with her perfectly manicured hand.

Dan relinquished Lillian to his sister and stood up, "I'll get us all a drink."

Dan was taller than Louise, but only by an inch, which put him over six feet. He always wore his shirt sleeves rolled up casually, and never wore a tie, which was typical in the publishing business. He had a full head of curly hair that he kept short, and his and Louise's eyes were a deep shade of blue.

They had a tender relationship—siblings first, friends always. The only time they had a falling out was when Dan married his first wife, who Louise detested, but when Dan's daughter was born, they made amends. Louise couldn't live without her niece in her life. And when the marriage ended, Dan moved back into the same apartment Louise and he had shared with their parents all their lives.

Louise slept in their parents' bedroom now that they were gone, Dan slept in the same bedroom he'd always slept in except when he was married, and they fixed up the extra bedroom for Jessica, who visited every other weekend, and often during the week since Dan had joint custody with his first wife.

When she first met Lillian, Louise liked her, but with reservations. She was afraid her brother would be hurt again, and she never wanted to see him as sad and unhappy as he had been with his wife and then after his divorce. But in time she learned to trust Lillian. She realized Lillian wasn't out to hurt Dan. Louise wondered why they weren't married, but she minded her own business. The truth was, all three of them—Dan, Louise, and Jessica—had fallen in love with the elusive Lillian, with her devil may care attitude, her wit, and the way she could bring fun and excitement to the apartment the moment she walked into it.

They all accepted her wandering in and out of their lives because they knew that when Lillian was with them, she was with them heart and soul. Then she'd leave. She always emailed, or called, and each time she visited, they hoped it would be the time she'd finally stay forever, but they harbored no expectations.

Louise realized that she needed to leave the two of them alone that night. She knew that Dan was the only person Lillian ever opened up to, and Louise didn't want to be in the way. When Dan came back with three vodka tonics, Louise took hers, kissed Lillian's forehead, and left them on the couch to go into her own room.

She made a few phone calls, planned a get-together at a restaurant with her friends, walked into the living room and kissed Lillian on the forehead again, bade her brother goodbye, and left them alone—all within ten minutes.

Dan turned to Lillian in the now silent apartment. "Time to talk yet?" he asked, not waiting for her to initiate the conversation.

"I have never been angrier in my life."

"I doubt that," he said, "but what's happened and who are you mad at?"

"I've been completely manipulated, duped, lied to…"

"Duped means the same thing as lied to…"

Lillian looked at him and groaned, "Oh, please, leave the editor at the office…"

"Sorry, go ahead," he motioned with his glass.

"My cousin is dying of cancer."

Dan brought his lips together and let out a long, slow whistle. "That's a tough one."

"You're immediately feeling sorry for her, aren't you?" Lillian said, putting her drink down on the coffee table in an angry gesture.

"Tell me the rest," he said, putting his arm around her and pulling her against his chest again.

"Apparently she is the one who bought Mrs. Snyder's house. She was waiting for me in Starbucks when I got back that day from Oklahoma, though I don't know how she knew that I was away or that I'd go to Starbucks. She brought me into our grandparents' house, made me feel comfortable and content, made the bad memories seem insignificant compared to all the good memories she reminded me about, and then she made me love …"

She picked her glass up again and drank deeply of the clear potent liquid.

"Made you love…?" Dan prodded.

"Her kids…"

Dan leaned back against the couch while Lillian rested her elbows on her knees and held her head between her hands, the cold glass to her cheek. "And her," she finished.

"You mean Ann?" Dan asked.

"Yes, I mean Ann. She orchestrated the whole thing so that I'd be hooked and I'd take care of her while she is dying and then the kids after she is gone. I can't believe her duplicity, Dan. I can't believe how cunning she's been. Like I have no right to my own life because she's dying and needs a mother for her children? I haven't seen her in years. What would make her think I'd even consider it?"

Dan didn't say anything, and when Lillian looked back at him, he had tears in his eyes. She jumped up from the sofa, angry at him now. "I should have known you'd take her side."

"I haven't taken anyone's side, baby. I'm just moved by how desperate she must feel."

"Oh, yes, she used that same word."

"Desperate people do des…"

"Please," she stopped him by holding up the palm of her hand. "Don't even."

He took a long sip of his drink. "It was wrong of her to do what she did, Lillian. It was very wrong of her."

"Thank you," Lillian said, waving her arm in satisfaction. "Thank you."

"It was manipulative and deceitful."

"Yes, it was."

"Thank God you found out when you did, before the children grew even fonder of you. That would have been cruel for them."

"Exactly! Imagine how that would have been! And those kids are complicated…you know? Well, Suzy's not complicated really, she's just a ball of sunshine. But that Philip…now he's complicated. He's deep…so deep. He's got this old soul. He doesn't look you in the eye that often, he's self-conscious and awkward, but when he does, it's as if he's looking into your heart. And he's got this dimple that deepens whenever he smiles, so you want to stand on your head to make him smile…you know what I mean? And he worries; he worries all the time, especially about his mother and his little sister, like the earth is going to fall to pieces at any minute and he's going to be responsible for it."

Lillian took a deep breath and another pull on her drink. "Like I said, they're complicated, and I couldn't handle that."

"What will you do now, darling?" he asked.

She walked back to the couch and took his hand. "I'll make love to you, first. Then we'll go for our license and plan a nice, sweet little wedding at City Hall."

His eyes met hers. "You want to marry me?" Dan asked her, his voice flat.

"It has been too long in coming, Danny boy."

"But first we make love?"

"Yep."

"Nope."

"What?"

He pulled her down to her knees in front of him and put his hands on each side of her face. "Look, I love you more than there are words to express how much. Making love with you has given me the most spiritual and tremendous moments of my life. I'll be yours for the rest of my life, even if it means being alone for the rest of my life. That's how in love I am with you, Lil. But tonight I won't make love to you, and don't think it won't bother me."

She was completely perplexed. "I'm sorry, Danny, I don't get it."

"Well, when we make love, it's so special—and so infrequent—that I won't have it tainted with what's going on in your mind. You're feeling anger, betrayal, and you're also feeling selfish and self-centered. You won't be in my bed with me alone; there will be three additional people in there with us. I deserve better than that."

"Dan…"

"Get your head together; we'll talk about marriage and sex later."

"Are you impotent suddenly, is that what this is about?"

"No," he chuckled, despite being annoyed. "I'm not impotent."

She lowered her rear end down to the floor, and ran her tongue over her lips. "Is it because you are disgusted with me—disappointed in me because I won't stay and take care of her and her brats? Is that it? I disgust you because I'm so selfish and self-centered?"

"You worry me, but no, Lil, you could never disgust me. Lillian, you are who you are and I've always known that."

"A selfish bitch, right?"

"A beautiful, deeply wounded woman, who hasn't come to terms with being a victim of abuse…"

"Don't bring that up."

"I don't want to, but I'm telling the truth. If nothing else, kiddo, you've always been able to tell the truth about yourself to me."

She looked at the floor for a long time before she said, "Look, Dan, I know you think I want to marry you to save me from Ann—from all that crap—but the truth is, I really want to be with you."

"I won't put myself in a situation where you're half the time with me and half the time pining away over them, feeling guilty and hating yourself, while pretending to feel righteous. I won't marry you right now. It'll happen, but not now. Not this way."

"Are you telling me to go back there? To do this thing she wants? Are you out of your mind?"

"No, I'm sane." He stood up from the couch and pulled her to her feet with him. "Sleep in Jessica's room tonight…stay here as long as you want, but eventually, you've got to work this out with your cousin, even if it's just to explain to her your reasons for not wanting to help her. Otherwise, you'll always feel that you are The Meanest Bitch We've Ever Known." He smiled then, "And you aren't, darling. Not even close."

Lillian pushed him away and walked into the kitchen to pour more vodka into her glass.

"You want me to help her. I know you. You want me to help her because you're such a bleeding heart. The hell with what *I* want.    The hell with what's good for me or right for me."

"No, Lillian, and stop throwing a temper tantrum. That may not be what's right for you or for them, but it has to be resolved one way or another before we get married. You're much too upset over it. Not now, not tomorrow, but eventually you have to go back and get rid of all the shit you've been carrying around all these years. I think this may be your way of doing it."

"What Ann was trying to do to me is supposed to scare away all my 'demons' as you've always called them? Are you crazy? Taking on a dying woman and her two children will not erase the past. It will just add more crap to my life. I will not do this. I will not do this. Do you understand?"

He didn't answer her.

"Marry me," she challenged him. He raked his hand over his hair before shaking his head no.

"Dan, don't do this to us," she threatened.

"Lillian, don't *you* do this to us. Give us half a chance, for God's sake."

She swore under her breath. "Did it occur to you that if I go back to Ann and the kids, I'll come back to you all used up…do you know what I'll have to face…what I'll go through? I won't have any emotion left in me. I barely have any as it is."

He kissed her forehead, then her eyes, and her cheeks, and lightly brushed her lips with his. As he pulled her against him, the customary longing he felt whenever he touched her surged through his body. How many times had he asked her to marry him? How many times had he dreamed about her saying yes? And now he was telling her no. Life was really bizarre.

"That didn't occur to me," he said holding her closer to him, thinking what a child this independent, feisty, beautiful woman really was when all was said and done. What a wounded and complex person he loved.

"What has occurred to me is that you may come back to me all *filled* up."

# Eight

Ann sat under the willow tree watching the children playing in the yard. The wig was uncomfortable in the heat, her scalp itched, but she refused to allow the children to know that she was bald again. It seemed to deeply upset Philip. She wondered if he suspected the real reason why she'd been bald the last time. He was too young to be told the truth, and she didn't think his friends from their old neighborhood had known about her illness, so there was no reason to think that he knew she had cancer. Nonetheless, it had upset him before when she lost her hair, and she didn't want them to know this time no matter how hot and uncomfortable the wig felt.

She was feeling desperately guilty about what she had tried to do to Lillian. She knew at the time it was wrong. Now she felt foolish. In fact, it was a foolish thing to do. She hadn't been around Lillian in years. For all she knew, Lillian could have become like her mother, and was that the type of person Ann wanted raising her children? What was she thinking? She wasn't thinking, obviously. She was appalled that she could be so dishonest and ruthless, and so careless with her children's future.

Ann looked over at the kids trying to play badminton. She had put up the net herself earlier and it was already falling over. She had no strength in her arms, although she felt a little stronger since she had stopped the chemo. What a difference even a week made. She wondered how long it would last before the cancer sapped her strength.

She watched them playing and thought, who will love them? A sentence that played through her head every day, every night, since finding out that the cancer had spread to her lungs and bone.

Joey already loved them, but he was so young. His own life hadn't even begun yet, and to saddle him with two kids just didn't seem fair. Not that he would not do it with all the love he had in his heart, Ann knew that, and he had begged her to let him come home from school to help out when she told him what was going on. It looked like that was going to have to happen now. Joey was the only person she could turn to now with Lillian gone.

She closed her eyes and dropped her head back against her lawn chair thinking of—longing for—her mother. *Oh, Mom, if only you weren't sick. God how I need you; how my babies need you.*

In the seven days since Lillian had left, Ann asked herself a hundred times a day why she hadn't told Lillian the whole story before that morning. Perhaps if she had, Lillian would have stayed, or at the very least, helped her figure out a solution before she left.

She heard a car in the driveway and she wanted to get up to see who it was, but she was too weary. The motor stopped and she waited. Soon, coming from the other side of the house, she saw a figure in black with just a little square of white showing at his neck. Ann smiled.

"Could you find a prettier place to sit?" asked Father John Murray as he approached the willow tree.

"Actually, Father, I can't," Ann answered, "it *is* the prettiest place to sit."

He followed her gaze to the canal, and the willow's leaves danced in an unusually cool breeze off the river. "Isn't it buggy under here?"

She laughed, "Sometimes, but I love the feel of the tendrils on my cheeks." She took his arm and said, "Come over here, I'll show you."

She motioned for him to sit on the wide flat arm, which he did. The breeze lifted the sweeping branches and they swung gently around them. Then, since it was early in the morning and the dew was still clinging inside the flowing branches, Ann reached up, grabbed a handful of the leaves, and tugged. The dew rained down on them, and she laughed when Father Murray jumped up.

"It's weeping, Father," she said, smiling up into the branches.

"Well, its tears are drenching my cassock," he said, laughing now.

The kids ran over to them.

"Hi, Father," said Suzy.

"Hi," said Philip not looking directly at the priest, but aside as he usually did when speaking to an adult.

He touched them both on their heads. "You're good badminton players," he told them.

They smiled shyly. "Mommy's making the willow tree cry again," Suzy said, moving over to the chair to hoist herself onto her mother's lap.

"I see that," he said, laughing when Ann pulled again and the dew trickled down on all of them.

Father Murray looked up into the tree, allowing a few sprinkles to touch his face. "The tears of the willow," he said quietly. His eyes met Ann's.

They were a sparkling hazel color, surrounded by dark lashes, and crow's feet spread out from the corners of his eyes to his graying temples.

"Go play," Ann told Suzy and Philip. "Father Murray and I have to talk."

They ran back to grab their racquets and started to hit the birdie again. Ann turned her face up to the priest. "Making a sick call?"

"It's called the sacrament of the sick, Ann, and it's to sustain you. But I came more to talk, or rather to listen if you want to talk."

Ann had met Father Murray sitting in the waiting room at the cancer center where she had been getting her infusions. Father Murray was being treated there, too, and they had started talking one day. Ann hadn't been to church since her husband's funeral Mass, but she considered herself a Catholic still, albeit a non-practicing one.

Father Murray had been so accessible, and although he himself was going through radiation treatment for prostate cancer, he said very comforting things to her, always taking the time to show concern. She'd been back to see him a few times at the rectory where he worked, taking comfort from his gentle demeanor, his wit and his belief in God and an afterlife. She desperately wanted to believe in an afterlife. She wanted to be reunited with her children one day…and to be with Billy. It was a comfort to think she'd be in her husband's arms again.

Although she didn't know why, she had called the priest when Lillian left and cried on the phone with him for an hour. He begged her to come to the church to see him and talk to him. She had agreed, but she didn't go. She imagined that was the reason for his visit days later. He was worried, and she appreciated it.

"How are you feeling?" she asked him.

"Treatments are over," he said, almost with pride in his voice.

"Good, you'll get stronger now."

"And you?"

"No more treatments for me. It's futile."

"There is always hope, Ann."

"I've got to be well enough to take care of the kids now that my cousin has left. I can't afford to be sick from chemotherapy right now."

"You've got to fight this cancer for them. That's more important. I was thinking that I might be able to find someone to come in to help out, Ann. I can certainly have meals brought to you. And if you can't afford…"

Ann laughed gently. "That's definitely not a problem for me, Father. I have more money than I need. Between my husband's life insurance and the sale of my house in New Jersey, we're all right financially. But I'm afraid to bring a stranger in to take care of us. Besides, I want to take care of them myself for as long as I can."

He looked out at the canal again and sat on the grass at her feet. He stretched his legs out beneath his cassock and leaned back on his arms. "I guess I can understand that," he said. He seemed deflated.

She reached forward and put her hand on his arm. "Now you're depressed, Father. Don't be. I'm all right. I'm too happy *for you* that your treatments are finished to allow you to be worried about me. I'll work this all out somehow. My brother is coming home this weekend so we can discuss it."

The priest looked at her again. "You're a strong lady, Ann, and you're young. I can't believe that there's nothing else that can be done."

He thought a moment, then said, "I know of a doctor at St. Margaret Medical Center. She's a brilliant oncologist. She believes in combining naturopathic remedies and holistic therapies with whatever medical science has to offer. She's had some wonderful outcomes, and she's full of life. Her patients adore her. I'm one of them, so I should know."

Ann looked away and didn't answer him.

"You've given up, Ann?" he asked after a long silence.

"Your God—or the universe—has given up on me."

Before he could protest, they heard another car come up the driveway and he turned to her. "Were you expecting company?"

She shook her head no. They watched for a minute. The back door of the kitchen opened, and Ann sat up, surprised. She thought she'd locked the front of the house when she came out back with the children. Lillian appeared at the kitchen doorway and stepped out. She was wearing a yellow sun dress, and her long red hair was loose around her shoulders. As she walked toward them, Ann couldn't help notice how much Lillian looked like Ann's mother.

She had never noticed just how alike they looked until this moment. It took her breath away.

"Who is it?" Father Murray asked.

"My cousin," she whispered.

"Really?" Ann saw him studying Lillian before he jumped to his feet.

Lillian walked halfway to Ann, but stopped to look at the children. They

74

were standing near the fallen net silently staring at her, racquets at their sides. "Well?" she said. "No hello?"

They both said hello at the same time, and Suzy dropped her racquet and ran over to Lillian and took her hand. She kissed it twice with a delicate touch of her lips and then looked up into Lillian's face with a huge smile—another tooth missing since Lillian had last seen her.

Suzy led Lillian toward her mother. "She came back, Mommy. She's back."

"I see, Suzy," Ann said, smiling at her little girl, but looking nervously at Lillian.

Suzy looked up at Lillian again, her eyes bright and happy as she pulled Lillian toward Ann and the priest. "I told Mommy you'd come back. I told her that you would miss us as much as we missed you."

Lillian smiled at the little girl. "You missed me, did you? What did you miss most, my cranky face or my bitchy personality?"

Suzy leaned into her and whispered, "Language ... there's a priest around."

Lillian covered her mouth, "Oops."

"It's okay, though, he's a cool priest. He won't yell."

Lillian was overcome with delight in seeing this child again, hearing her silly chatter, seeing her gap-toothed smile, and she scooped Suzy up, laughing, and carried her across the yard until they reached the willow tree. "You were right Suzy Q, I did miss you," Lillian whispered in the little girl's ear before putting her down so that she could run over to play with her brother again.

Ann was still smiling, but she felt cautious...nervous.

"Hi," was all she said at first.

"Hey," Lillian answered.

"This is Father John Murray," Ann said. "Father, this is my cousin Lillian."

Lillian shook the priest's hand. "I'm very glad to meet you," he told her. "Ann has told me a lot about you."

Lillian grimaced. "I bet she has."

"All good," he reassured Lillian, but letting her know by his eyes and his sheepish smile that he knew the whole story.

"We met at the hospital," Ann told Lillian, "weeks ago when we were both waiting for treatments."

Lillian looked at him. He was thin and a little pale, but looked healthier than Ann.

"I'm finished with my radiation, and those treatments don't take as much out of us as chemo does," he explained, as though reading her mind.

Lillian nodded, not knowing what to say. Then she looked at Ann.

"I'm feeling better, too," Ann said without being asked.

"Good."

"She stopped going to chemotherapy, though, and she had several more treatments to go," Father Murray blurted out, turning slightly red when Ann looked at him sharply.

"You did?" Lillian asked Ann. "Why would you do that?"

Ann just shrugged and looked over at the canal away from both of them.

"I've just been trying to talk her into seeing another oncologist I know who is remarkable."

"Father…" Ann said, trying to silence him.

"I'm sorry. You're right. I've said too much and minded your business beyond the limits." He took Ann's hand in both of his. "Will you forgive me?"

Ann smiled despite being annoyed. "Will you have me give you absolution and penance? Then say six decades of the rosary and an act of contrition."

He stood back, feigning surprise, "But there are only five decades of the beads!"

"Go the extra mile, Father."

They all laughed. "All right, I'll be off. I've got a lot of Hail Marys to say tonight it seems."

He shook Lillian's hand again and covered it with his other hand. "I'm happy to have met you, Lillian."

"Thank you," she answered.

He leaned down and kissed Ann's cheek. "If there's anything, you just…" he let the sentence hang. Ann nodded.

He bade them goodbye and walked away, waving to the children as he passed.

The two women watched him leave, neither of them knowing how to speak to each other at that moment. Then Ann asked, "Lillian, why are you here?"

Lillian went over to sit on the broad arm of the Adirondack chair, and she leaned back so that her shoulder was just touching Ann's head.

Now they were both looking out in the same direction toward Philip and Suzy.

"Because I want to be, Annie."

"I don't believe you," Ann said sadly. "I think it's out of pity or shame and guilt."

"That would have been true four days ago. Maybe three days ago. But today it isn't true, which is why I'm back. I wouldn't come back until it was right in my head."

"You forgive me for manipulating you that way?"

"No, I do not! Let's not ask for the impossible, here, kiddo." Lillian sighed. "Do you forgive me for being a selfish bitch?"

Ann sat up and turned to look at her cousin. "I'm serious, Lillian. What I did was horrendous. I tried to trick you into how I wanted you to live the rest of your life. I had no right to do that, and you had every right to be angry with me."

Lillian pulled her bottom lip in with her top teeth. She took a long while and a deep breath before saying. "I do resent it, Ann. I don't know what to tell you. I was furious with you, but I was also scared to death to think you would want me to raise your kids. I have been the most irresponsible human being who ever walked the earth for most of my life. I'm not mother material, and you should know that."

Ann sat back again in the chair, and this time *she* sighed heavily. She leaned her head on Lillian's shoulder, wrapped her arm through Lillian's, and held her cousin's hand. "I don't care, Lilly. I need someone to love my children. You might turn out to be a horrible mother, I don't know, but I saw you starting to love them. I saw you coming around, and you were kind to them."

After a long silence, when Lillian didn't comment, Ann continued, "When my mother was starting to become forgetful and the doctor told us that she probably had early onset Alzheimer's, she told me that if I ever needed anyone once she couldn't help me anymore, to get a hold of you. She told me that I could trust you. I argued with her, Lilly, I won't lie. I actually laughed at her, but she was dead serious."

Lillian whispered, "Pay back."

"What does that mean?"

"You don't know?"

"No, I don't know."

Lillian took a deep breath, thought a minute, and then said, "It's stupid.

Never mind that I said that."

Ann squeezed Lillian's hand; her head was still resting on Lillian's arm. "I need you, Lillian. You can hate that as much as you want, and you can hate me for it, but the truth is I need you."

"I know. Annie, I'll try. Can that be enough? Can I try and if it doesn't work, we'll figure out what will? That's all I've got ... that and the fact that you are right, I have grown to love your children, and I realize that I have always loved you like a little sister. I'm telling you that because you have to realize that even if you were my sister, I'd be afraid of all of this. I'd still want to run away from it. I'm being honest with you; I want to jump right back in my car and escape. I don't think I've ever been more afraid of anything in my life—except learning the truth about my mother's death."

They were quiet a long time, and then Ann asked, "Should I have lied about that? Should I have told you what my mother told you when she called you all those years ago—what she told everyone about your mother? That she had an allergic reaction to some medication?"

"No. I asked because I wanted to know. Hell, I knew anyway or I wouldn't have asked."

"She was very ill, Lilly, truly mentally ill. She never meant anything she had ever done. It was all because of her illness."

"I hated her, Ann. There was no love between us."

"There was always love, Lilly, never hate. Hurt...it was hurt and pain, but it was never hate."

"No fairytales, Annie. Life is what it is, and life with my mother was hell and I hated it."

"Okay, I'll give you that—you hated it, *life* with her, but not her."

"Listen, Pollyanna, I think we've had enough of this conversation," Lillian tried to sound lighter. "So, do you take me back or not? Cause if it's not, I finally get to sleep on the park bench in Newtown."

"The room is exactly the same as it was when you left. In fact, the bed still isn't made. I couldn't bring myself to go in the room."

"Wouldn't be the first time I slept on dirty sheets. Now about this oncologist the priest mentioned..."

Ann stood up and pulled Lillian with her. "Tomorrow, okay? We'll talk about it tomorrow. Today we celebrate, let's go ride on the carousel at Peddler's Village. I want to have fun today."

She put her arms around her cousin and hugged her tightly. And her cousin hugged back.

# *Nine*

Lillian heard the key in the lock of the front door early that Saturday morning, and she heard Ann bolt down the stairs and shriek, "Joey!"

She heard the entire commotion from her bed and lay staring at the ceiling, dreading the rest of the weekend, wishing that she had decided to stay with Dan a few extra days.

Dan. She suddenly remembered she had to email him. She had called him the night she arrived back at Ann's, and in usual fashion he reassured her that she was doing the right thing, not only for Ann, but for herself—and for them as a couple.

His resolution not to make love with her had failed, and by the second night she shared his bed and their lovemaking was better than she could ever recall. She had teased him, of course.

"And you said you wouldn't make love until after I went back to my cousin's house," she chided him, placing her cheek against his chest. He always pushed the right buttons, but this time there was so much more to their passion, something deeper, almost spiritual as he liked to say.

"I will never stop loving you," he told her, stroking her head.

"And I will never let you," she told him, and meant it. "What's with us, anyway? Why is this so damn good, yet so few and far between?"

She felt him shrug.

"We've been doing the dirty monkey dance for more than ten years now," she said. "It's always good … it's always hot … it's always for such a short period of time. I must be nuts."

"Yeah, that could explain it," he said with a crooked smile.

She loved his smile. His face, which was always a little tanned even though he was fair, and lined in all the right places, and his eyes were so light brown they were almost yellow. He was in his fifties, yet he looked so darn good, so strong…so built. She loved his mind, too. They could talk for hours on end about literature, books he was editing, books he hated, books they both loved. And they could argue for hours about the fact that she wasn't finishing her own book. It seemed to frustrate him to distraction, so she usually avoided the topic.

"What am I going to do, Dan?" she had asked him that night. "I can't go back."

He didn't answer her, just stroked her arm.

"I don't want to take care of her while she's dying or her kids when she dies."

"I don't know anyone who would *want* to do this." he answered. "It's going to be very difficult. Don't make a decision tonight. Stay a few more days, think it over, enjoy New York…you'll know what to do in the end, baby."

How could he know that? Knowing her as he did, how could he even think there was a possibility that she'd figure out what to do?

"And you won't marry me?" she had asked him.

"Not tonight," he answered.

"You know what I mean," she smacked his belly.

He laughed and grabbed her hand. "You don't want to marry me, you just want to escape from Ann's problems."

She had stayed a few days as he suggested, and he took some time off from work to be with her. She gave him the first edition books that she'd found in the attic of Ann's house, and she showed him the ancient letters that were difficult for her and Ann to decipher because of the script and the old fashioned "ye's" and "thy's and thou's." They spent hours pouring over them, and Dan interpreted them the best he could.

They saw a show, walked through Central Park, ate in their favorite Italian restaurant near the United Nations, and on the last night, she told him. "I'm leaving in the morning."

"Yep," he had answered. He hadn't even asked her where she was going or what her decision had been. He just kissed her lips lightly and said again, "yep."

Now, lying in her bed in her grandparents' old house, she could almost feel the brush of his early morning whiskers on her cheek. She didn't recall ever missing him quite this much after what he called one of their "sessions." It didn't matter if she stayed with him a day, a week, or a month; he still called them "sessions."

She needed him now, today more than ever. She dreaded the day ahead.

Lillian heard Philip walk outside her door and down the steps, and seconds later his voice cried out, "Uncle Joey!"

That's the most animated Lillian had heard the boy since she met him. He was always so quiet. He wasn't always easy to love, and she admitted only to herself that she was drawn more to the open chatty Suzy. Yet something about Philip touched her heart. She wanted him to like her. She actually wanted to earn his love.

The hum of voices in the kitchen must have awakened Suzy, because all of a sudden Lillian's door burst open and Suzy rushed in and jumped on her bed. The little girl had a serious case of bed head and it made Lillian smile. "Lilly, Uncle Joey is here. Let's go down."

"You go, Suze. I'll be down soon. It's too early in the morning for me."

"Oh please come meet him," the little girl pleaded.

"I don't have to meet him. I met him—years ago."

"He was only nine years old the last time you saw him," Suzy argued, still pulling on Lillian's hand.

"How do you know that?"

"Mommy told me; now come on, let's go down."

"I need to take a shower first, and comb my hair. Do you want him to think I smell and have bad breath?"

That made a lot of sense to Suzy, and she thought it over. "Well, no…so okay. Get up and into the shower, then come down. Mommy's made coffee, can you smell it? She'll make bacon and eggs, too. She always makes bacon and eggs for Uncle Joey, and fried potatoes, too."

"Hurry down," Lillian said pointing to the bedroom door. "He's probably waiting for you. I'll be down soon."

Suzy jumped off the bed, then turned back and said, "Wear green—you look good in green," and closed the bedroom door behind her. Lillian heard her bare feet on the stairs, and then a great deal of squealing and noise coming from the kitchen.

Lillian thought about the last time she saw Joey. He was only nine, a serious boy with the family's red hair and large round green eyes. It was Granddad's 85th birthday party, and it was right in this house. Aunt Helen and Uncle Tim had moved to Florida already with Grandma and Granddad, but they hadn't started to rent this house to strangers yet and always returned in the summer for a month and celebrated Granddad's birthdays here. Lillian had avoided several before that, but that year her parents were in Europe and she took advantage of it. She had been so lonesome for her grandparents and aunt she couldn't resist.

The boy had been drawn to her all day. He showed her his bike, and then brought her a hand-held game to show her.

And always those round green eyes looked up into hers. She remembered thinking that he was a nice boy, not bashful and awkward like most nine-year-old boys can be with strangers. He was very personable, with a slight southern drawl from living most of the time in Florida.

The memory hurt too much. Lillian pulled herself out of bed and walked into the bathroom. She let the water from the shower fall on her far longer than she needed, and she took much too long washing her hair, then blowing it dry, which she usually didn't bother to do.

She dressed in white shorts and a green T-shirt and sat on the edge of the bed for a long time before leaving her room.

The aroma of bacon hit her squarely in the nose, just as it had when her grandmother cooked breakfast when she was a child staying in the house.

Lillian used the back staircase which landed in the sunroom off the kitchen. Ann was at the stove cooking, Suzy sat on the young man's lap, while Philip sat next to him, his face leaning against Joey's arm, listening to every word the young man was saying. Seeing his face broke Lillian's heart into a hundred pieces and she froze on the last step.

"Lillian?" Ann called, peeking around the wall to the sunroom. "My brother's here."

Lillian cleared her throat. "I heard."

She walked fully into the room, trying not to look at him, but it was unavoidable. He stood up and put Suzy on the chair he'd just abandoned. "Hi, Lillian" he said, holding out his hand to shake hers, "I'm Joe."

Lillian knew her smile was too quick, too bright, too fake, and she knew that her eyes must be shining a little too brightly.

"How are you?" she asked, taking his extended hand. It was warm and hard and so large that it covered all of hers. The contact left her breathless.

"Isn't he handsome?" Ann asked from around Lillian's shoulder, beaming at her brother. Lillian hadn't seen Ann this energetic since she had moved in with them.

"Yep, he is that!" Lillian agreed, quickly moving away and pouring herself a cup of coffee.

"It's great that you're living here, Lillian," he said, picking Suzy up again and sitting down with the little girl planted on one of his long thighs.

She smiled but didn't answer.

"This is the first chance I've been able to get here since Ann moved in. What a great house. I forgot how nice it is. We used to come up from

Florida in the summers."

"Yes, I recall," Lillian answered, looking down into her mug of coffee.

"I love this house," he said again.

"From what your sister tells me, it has been in our family since the 1700s."

"Sweet," he said, looking up at the beams in the kitchen.

"We have a badminton net," Suzy told him, grabbing his chin with her little hand and pulling his face around to look into hers. "Will you play with us?"

Ann laughed, "Well, you'll have to fix the net first. I put it up and half of it fell down within five minutes."

"I can do that," Joey said, rubbing noses with Suzy.

"Can we play catch with the baseball, too?" Philip wanted to know, more excited than Lillian had ever seen him.

"Yeah, why not? I'm here for the weekend, so we can have a blast." He looked at Lillian again. "I'd like to get to know you better, too. Maybe we'll have time to talk."

"Sure."

Ann made a great ceremony out of putting the bacon and eggs on Joey's plate from an iron frying pan that had belonged to their grandparents. "Try that on for size," she said putting it in front of him, while shooing Suzy off his lap with her spatula.

"I want some, too," Philip whined. He stole a piece of bacon from Joey's plate, and Joey made a pretense of slapping his hand.

"It's coming …" Ann said, her voice singing with joy at having her brother there with them.

He was twelve years younger than she, and eighteen years younger than Lillian. Aunt Helen was always faithful in writing to Lillian, and told her stories about Joey growing up. Lillian never answered the letters, but she kept them; she hadn't thrown one out.

Helen had written about his first day of school, his first kiss in kindergarten, his first fist fight in second grade.

She wrote about his grades—good and bad—and his growing pains throughout elementary school. Lillian read in her aunt's letters about his first date, his swim team accomplishments, his lacrosse skills. Then the letters stopped sometime during his junior year of high school. There were no accounts about his prom, his graduation, his entry into college.

Aunt Helen's mind had faded away around then, and Ann didn't really know where to write Lillian, so looking at him now Lillian felt she'd missed a whole piece of his life.

The day was festive because Joey was there. Too festive for Lillian, who excused herself mid-afternoon to take a nap. Ann didn't even look tired, and as Lillian climbed the stairs to the second floor, she stopped at the window on the landing and could see brother and sister walking together out to the gazebo, Ann's thin arm in his, the kids bouncing around them. Ann threw her head back and laughed at something he said, and then put her cheek against his arm.

Lillian was overcome with melancholy. She lowered herself to the step next to the window and put her forehead on the pane.

*Don't let her die*, she begged. *Please don't let her die.*

Eventually, she climbed the rest of the stairs, fell across her bed, and slept until it was dark outside.

When she awakened, she was starving. She went down to the kitchen. No one seemed to be around so she looked in the fridge and found some chicken salad and plums. She made a sandwich, grabbed an iced tea, and walked out the back door toward the gazebo.

The night was still warm, lightning bugs flickered in the yard, and the sky was filled with stars. She stepped up into the wooden structure and was surprised to find Joey sitting there. He was holding his cell phone between his hands, thumbing on the keys, obviously communicating with someone through a text message.

"Hi, Lilly," he said to her looking up.

"I didn't mean to disturb you. I'll leave you…"

"No, sit down. Eat your sandwich," he told her. He put the phone down.

"Where is everyone?" she asked him, putting the paper plate with her sandwich on the wrought iron table.

"Ann was exhausted, so I told her to go to bed. The kids are watching TV in the living room."

Lillian nodded and took a bite of her sandwich.

"Ann's dying, right?" he said directly.

Lillian put the sandwich down again, and wiped the corner of her mouth, wondering how much Ann had told him and how much she should say.

"She said she's finished with the chemo," he told Lillian.

Lillian thought it over a few minutes, and then said, "She wasn't

84

finished with the chemo. She stopped before the course was done."

"Why would she do that?"

"Because I acted like an asshole, left the house, and she thought she couldn't handle the chemo and the kids alone. I came back two days ago."

"Why'd you leave in the first place?"

"Because I don't want to take care of a dying cousin and her two children. Because I'm afraid I won't do it right. Because I'm selfish and self-centered."

"You ran away." There was no accusation in his voice, just a declaration.

"I ran away."

"But you came back?"

"I'm here, aren't I?"

"And will Ann go back for chemo now?"

"Don't know the answer to that, but I want her to. Maybe between us, we can talk her into it. She has a priest friend who was starting to tell me about an oncologist he wants her to see, but Ann wouldn't let him finish."

They were quiet a long time, and Lillian started eating her sandwich again. The insects were noisy, and the bull frogs in the canal were vociferous in the warm July night.

"I know everything," Joey said to her.

Lillian froze.

"I know the whole story," he said again.

She took a mouthful of the cold tea and forced the bite of sandwich down. She waited awhile until she could find her voice.

"You know what?" she asked him.

"I know that you are my birth mother, Lillian."

She put her napkin to her mouth.

"When my mother's Alzheimer's started getting real bad, she would say weird things. My father took me out fishing one day, and he explained everything to me. He was afraid my mother would tell me in a way I wouldn't understand and he didn't want me to be hurt. I know the whole story pretty from beginning to end."

Lillian still couldn't speak. Her body throbbed with tension.

He leaned forward in his chair. "Lillian, I don't care. Helen and Tim are my parents. They will always be my parents...until the day I die. It was weird, you know, when I first found out. But then I came to terms with it. You chose to give me away, and the choice you made was a good one. I've been happy my whole life. I still am, except for my sister's illness. I'm only telling you so it doesn't have to be this…this… gorilla in the room. Let's establish a relationship now—cousins…friends—anything that would make you feel comfortable, because I don't give a flying you-know-what. We have to join forces to help Ann and the kids. Right?" He waited a moment for her to answer and then asked again, "Okay?"

Lillian pushed the sandwich away from her. This too, she asked herself, staring at the black wrought iron grid of the table top. I have to deal with this, too? Then she looked up at him. He was sitting slouched and leaning over his arms on the table, his fingers splayed on the wrought iron. He looked exactly like her—a masculine version of her.

"I told Aunt Helen right here on this gazebo," she said to him. "I was eighteen, getting ready for graduation from high school, and had missed three periods. I knew. I'd been an idiot that whole senior year. I was wild and stupid.

I couldn't tell my mother…good God, I couldn't ever tell my mother. I knew she would have beaten me to a bloody pulp, literally. And she would have made me feel as though I was …I can't even think of the words to describe how she'd make me feel."

Lillian sat back in her chair then. "I had gotten into Boston College, the only college, by the way, that my mother wanted me to go to. A Catholic college in the early 80s would not have taken a pregnant coed, not that I would have lived that long if my mother knew."

"You didn't consider an abortion?"

"Of course, I did. A thousand times every day for three months. That's why I came to Aunt Helen. I asked her for the money."

He whistled through his teeth. "That must have been something. She's such a devout Catholic. I can't believe you asked her that."

"I was desperate. And she knew that I couldn't tell my mother. Even she wouldn't have been able to protect me. She looked at me, right here, on this gazebo on a late May night, and she asked me, 'Do you want to abort this little child?'" Lillian stared at the pattern of the wrought iron table.

"Here I was, sitting here, asking for money for an abortion, and she asks me that. Yeah, okay, I knew what she was thinking and why she phrased it that way, but it still…like, floored me, you know? The question…the words…*little child*…it just brought it home to me." Lillian closed her eyes, not wanting to look at his face.

"Then she asks, 'If you want an abortion, I'll take you and I'll pay for it.

I just need you to look me in the eye and tell me that's what you want. If you had other options, would you take them? Because I have to tell you that it will kill me to help you with this, but I'll do it.'" She repeated her aunt's words verbatim. She would never forget them.

Lillian stood up now and walked to the window of the gazebo and looked away from Joseph into the night.

"What did you say?" he asked, his voice very soft.

"I said that I believed with all my heart that it was the only way and I would probably kill myself after the abortion, but at least my mother wouldn't know that I was pregnant."

They were both silent while Joey absorbed what she said. Then he asked, "What did Mom say?"

"She came up with a better solution—or so we thought. She had always wanted more children, but couldn't conceive after Ann. She had just started designing for the people in New York. They wanted her to go to their place in Europe and it was going to take a few months." Lillian stopped, lost in the memory again.

Lillian sighed and continued. "So she proposed that as a graduation gift, she'd take me to Europe and I would work for her as her personal assistant. I could defer starting BC for a year, which was permissible, and live in Europe with her until her work there was finished. While in Europe, I'd have the baby, she'd say that she had left not knowing she was pregnant because, after all, she couldn't get pregnant again, and tell everyone the baby was hers. We'd come home with a new brother for Ann, a cousin for me, and a son or daughter for Uncle Tim."

"Dad told me the story, but not in as much detail."

"Yeah, well, here's the rest, since you know so much already." Lillian turned back to look at him. The moon was high in the sky now, and it cast some light into the gazebo, but not much. She could make out his silhouette, but not his face. She imagined that he couldn't see hers either. She hoped he couldn't.

"You were born in St. Elizabeth's hospital in a little hamlet outside of Paris. Aunt Helen held my hands during fifteen hours of labor. She rubbed my back, fed me ice chips, put salve on my lips, and kissed my forehead and cheek every five minutes. She sang, told jokes, let me yell at her. And then you came out. The nurse wrapped you in a receiving blanket and put you on my stomach and Aunt Helen and I cried together. Then she left me alone with you."

Lillian pressed her hands against her thighs and closed her eyes again. "I unwrapped the blanket and looked at your little face and counted your fingers and toes and put you to my breast just as the nurse had told me to do because she didn't know I was giving you away. I have never known such peace and contentment...not before that moment and not since then. You were the most precious little being I had ever seen or touched or held."

Lillian sat down again and leaned toward him. "So here it is, Joey, something that I never wanted to have to admit, but here it is. You were an inconvenience for a brief few months, but you were worth it. If you have ever thought that I rejected you at birth, you are sadly mistaken. You say that I chose to give you away, but it was not an easy choice. No baby had ever been loved by a mother as much as you were the night you were born. And at that moment, I had changed my mind about giving you up. You were mine and Aunt Helen couldn't have you. And the hell with my mother, too."

Lillian willed herself not to break down and cry. She had more to tell him.

"Then Aunt Helen came back into the room, and she asked me if she could hold you. She whispered sweetly to you; rocked you, sang to you. Her beautiful face was so soft, so loving, when she looked down at you. I didn't know how I was going to tell her that I had changed my mind and I wasn't giving you to her. Then she looked at me and said, 'I love him, but I know he's yours. You don't have to give him up to me. I'll fight for you when we get home. You can live with me and Uncle Tim. I won't let your mother near you, darling. I promise. I'll protect both of you.'"

Lillian's throat ached painfully as she told this story to her son.

"At that moment, I knew you were as much hers as you were mine. She had gone to so much trouble for me. She left her own daughter home—a daughter who was really angry about it, by the way—to do this for me. She could give you so much.

I could give you nothing. I was emotionally immature, and I was so beaten down by my mother that I realized that I'd be the worst thing for you. Before I got pregnant with you, I was like a zombie, going through the motions of living. I fucked every guy who asked me during my senior year just to feel something, but I never did. I don't even know who your father is. Oh, God, that is so mortifying to say to you, it kills me. I only felt like a human being the night you were born. You made me human again."

"Shit," he breathed into the night. "This is tough."

"You have no idea."

"So if my mother told you she'd protect you from your mother, why didn't you just take her up on it?" he asked like the innocent he was.

Lillian sat heavily in her chair again.

"No one, not even my beautiful loving aunt, could have protected me once my mother went on the warpath. That just wasn't an option, and Aunt Helen knew it as much as I did. So you became her son to save me from my mother."

"The story worked? Everyone believed it?"

Lillian smiled. "Everyone. Except my mother…"

"Uh, oh," he whispered.

"Yeah … uh, oh." Lillian remembered it so vividly that she could still feel the burn of the strap on her scalp and back; the lamp crashing over her head. That was the least of it. The words were much, much worse.

"We got home on a Thursday afternoon. Everyone met us at the airport. Everyone wanted to hold the baby, especially my mother. She was so thrilled and delighted for my aunt. Aunt Helen and I dared to glance at each other in relief. It was a wonderful homecoming. We told everyone stories about our work at the fashion designer in France, and our trips to London, Ireland, Italy, and Great Britain—and then about Aunt Helen finding out she was seven months pregnant, and how the doctor said it would be too dangerous for her to fly home because she was bleeding on and off and was put to bed for the remainder of the pregnancy. Uncle Tim even flew to France, pretending to want to see her. And then we went into great detail about her going into labor, and we described the delivery—exactly as it was—only we put Aunt Helen in my place and me in hers." It took a while before she could continue. Joey waited patiently to hear the rest.

Then she told Joey, "Ann was head over heels about you. She took you into her arms, and after that no one could get a hold of you. When it was time for me to leave to go home with my parents, I had to ask Ann if I could kiss you goodbye and she was very begrudging. She allowed me a quick kiss on your forehead, which was probably best because if I had taken you in my arms…" Lillian didn't want to continue with the story, but Joey was staring at her, waiting for the rest.

"My parents took me home. My mother made such a fuss over me, told me how much she missed me while we were away. She actually tucked me in bed that night, and she told me she was worried about how jet lagged I was going to be the next day. I knew she was in a manic state, but she was being so nice to me and I needed it that night. My father was in such high spirits when he kissed me good night. For one instant in time, everything seemed all right...except that you weren't in my arms."

Lillian stopped talking and listened to the bull frogs for awhile. After about three minutes, Joey prompted, "Lillian?"

"My mother figured it out in the middle of the night. She was so smart. We were idiots to think we could fool her. When she figured it out, she raided the liquor closet. Then she used everything she could get her hands on to beat me. She fractured my skull that night. She broke my father's arm in two places when he tried to pull me away from her. I had to have surgery to relieve the bleeding on my brain. Daddy had to have two surgeries on his arm and wore a cast for sixteen weeks, and my mother was committed for several months—just long enough for me to get up to Boston and away from her. I had a restraining order against her.

"I never came home again. Daddy paid for my education. He visited me in Boston whenever I'd let him, but he knew to never let my mother come with him. I wouldn't have met with her anyway. I never saw her again. Then Daddy had a heart attack."

"So your father knew the truth about me then?"

"No, he didn't believe it. You see, Mother was given to paranoia. She was schizophrenic, a manic-depressive, a psychopath—absolutely insane. She would make things up in order to abuse us. The things she had accused him of were enough to keep him from believing anything she said about me."

"How could he let her treat you that way?"

"Beats me ... sorry about the pun," she said without humor in her voice. "In truth, he tried. He tried in his own way, always while trying to keep peace with *her*. I actually loved my father. Go figure."

He was very quiet for a long time. Then he said, his voice heavy with emotion, "I'm so sorry, Lillian, that I was the cause of such a horrible experience for you."

"No ... no, no, Joey ... *you* weren't. I had caused it. I believed I deserved it. Then I realized that my mother, and only my mother, was the cause of it. She was the perpetrator, not me...not Daddy...and God knows, not you, Joey. But imagine what kind of mother I would have been at that time. Everything Aunt Helen and I did, we did right. You were safe, loved, cared for."

"Yes, that's absolutely true," Joey told her. "Just so you know, I have no resentment toward anyone. I never wonder what it would have been like if I got to stay with you. I love them, both of them. They were the best parents."

He leaned over toward her then. "That doesn't mean that I don't want to love you."

Lillian cringed at how vulnerable he sounded, and at how vulnerable she felt. She would have given her life to avoid this conversation, but here it was and there was no escape from it.

"Look, Joey, when I gave you to Aunt Helen I somehow cut out something inside me that allowed me to feel anything for you. I felt it would betray Aunt Helen if I longed for you. I had to survive, Joe. Do you think you can understand that?"

"I think...maybe. Like I said, I'm cool with it all..."

Lillian realized that what she had just told him must have been extremely hard for him to hear, and she hated herself for saying it. Yet, she was telling him the truth, or at least she thought it was the truth. After the reaction she had at seeing him that morning, she wondered if she really had cut that part of her life out. She wanted to tell him that now, but she was afraid. They were quiet for a long time.

"Does Ann know?" Lillian asked him.

"No, Dad and I never felt like she had to. She's my sister; she'll always be my sister, just like they'll always be my parents."

Lillian nodded. "You're a good guy, Joey. Do I have the right to say that I'm proud of you?"

"Do I have the right to say I'm proud of you?" he asked Lillian

"For?" she asked him.

"For reaching down deep inside to find that part of you that you think you cut out a long time ago but that's got you here taking care of my sister and niece and nephew."

She smiled a genuine smile now. "We'll see how that works out."

"I trust you, Lillian. I really do."

Lillian found no comfort in his words. Then she said, "Let's not tell her about this, Joe—ever. No need to add to whatever may be going through her head right now."

"I didn't intend to tell her, Lillian. Like I said, she's my sister, Helen and Tim are my parents, and you....you're a person who has come out of the past to take care of her and her family, and I'm very grateful."

They sat a long time in the gazebo, saying nothing, just living with the words they'd just exchanged. Then he said, "The bugs are biting."

And she answered, "Yeah, let's go in."

Together they left the gazebo and started walking toward the house. Joey reached over and flung his arm around her shoulders. Lillian let him.

∼∾

| | |
|---|---|
| From: | Lillian Phelan [lpfreelncrwrtr@aol.com] |
| To: | Dan Paulsen [dpaulsen1@msn.com] |
| Subject: | I got through it |
| Sent: | 7/27 2:50 AM |

He's here, Dan. And he knows the whole story. He has for a long time. I feel light as air. Good night, Danny boy.

# *Ten*

Joey left for Boston early Sunday morning. Ann was all smiles and sunshine when he was getting ready to leave. She had washed his laundry and put his folded clothes in his gym bag, and then threw the bag in the back seat of his car, laughing. She gave him a big hug, then stood and waved until the car disappeared from the road.

Lillian watched from the window of her bedroom. She hadn't gone down for breakfast that morning. She didn't want to intrude on their last few hours of the weekend. And she didn't want to say goodbye to him. She felt sad knowing that he was leaving, and it surprised her and worried her.

For twenty-two years, Lillian thought she had divorced herself from the child to whom she had given birth, yet within seconds of seeing him, she had known it wasn't true. She *had* loved him all those years. Like the secret stories that were hidden up in the attic in the blanket chest, Joey was a secret she had kept locked up in her heart like a treasure she didn't want to lose. Yet she still thought it was wrong to feel that way. She had no right to feel that way...he was Aunt Helen's and Uncle Tim's.

The truth was, she was afraid that when she said goodbye this time, she wouldn't be able to let go of him and would make a complete fool of herself. And it would be cruel to confuse him...to tell him she "cut him out" of her heart, and then let him see she never did that at all. So she watched from her bedroom window where she felt safe.

When the car disappeared, Philip and Suzy ran around the house to the backyard. Ann stood alone in the driveway, still looking toward where Joey had driven away. Lillian saw her shoulders droop over. Ann covered her face, and Lillian could see she was crying.

*She thinks that's the last time she'll ever see him*, Lillian thought and realized that Ann believed she was going to die soon, that her death was imminent. *Did the doctors tell her that?*

She leaned against the windowsill, watching Ann compose herself. A car pulled into the driveway, and Lillian recognized it as Monica's.

*Oh, great timing. Here comes the Botox queen just when life is at its worst.*

Ann brushed her eyes with the palms of her hands and straightened her shoulders. When Ann turned toward the car, Lillian saw that she was trying to smile.

Monica embraced Ann when she got out of the car, while three of her brood lunged from the SUV and ran around to the back where Suzy and Philip were playing. Lillian sat on her bed, wondering how long it would be before Monica left.

She had no intention of going down to the kitchen while Ann was entertaining the up-talker.

Monica's visit was longer than Lillian thought it would be, and sheer boredom and a rumbling stomach brought her downstairs to the kitchen.

When she entered the kitchen, Monica and Ann were drinking coffee.

Monica's eyes were red and wet and she didn't try to hide it from Lillian.

"Where are you having treatments?' she was asking Ann.

*So, Ann just told Monica*, Lillian thought.

Before letting Ann answer, Monica said, "There's a doctor right here in the county—she's something special. She's an oncologist, and everyone who goes to her loves her. You'd think she walks on water the way people talk about her. She's everybody's girlfriend, you know, that type of physician."

"I have an oncologist," Ann told Monica.

They both looked up at Lillian then, as though they hadn't heard her enter, and Monica said, "Hi, Lillian," then looked back at Ann. "But she's different."

"Maybe," Ann said, "but there's nothing she can do for me."

"Don't say that. Just go to her, consult with her. I have several friends who either have cancer or had family members with it, and they think she's wonderful. Her kids go to our kids' school."

Lillian poured herself a cup of coffee and then turned to lean against the counter. "Do you think that's the same doctor that priest friend of yours told us about?"

"I don't know," Ann answered in a weary voice.

"What's her name?" Lillian asked Monica.

"Dr. Meg Raphael. She's wonderful."

"It can't hurt just to talk to her," Lillian said, looking at Ann.

Monica smiled at Lillian then, "Of course it can't ... please, Ann, just go see her."

"No," Ann said, gently but firmly, leaving no room for further argument.

The next day, Lillian called Dr. Raphael's office and made an appointment for the following week. She had lucked out, the voice on the other line told her, it usually takes months to get in to see Dr. Raphael for a consultation, but she'd just had a cancellation.

Lillian never mentioned it to Ann, thinking she'd just go see the doctor herself and explain the situation. Monica stopped by two days before the appointment, while Ann was napping, and Lillian told her about the appointment.

"I think you have to bring all her medical records with you, and there's something called HIPAA, which means they can't talk about a patient without the patient's permission. Unless the doctor knows exactly what kind of cancer Ann has, you know, what grade and what stage and all that, she won't be able to advise you."

Lillian thought it over and then said to Monica, "So what do I do, cancel? Ann is adamant about not going."

Monica leaned over the table and took Lillian's hand. "Don't cancel. Do whatever you have to do to talk her into it, Lillian. It may be her only chance."

Lillian nodded, then despite her aversion to Monica, smiled at the concerned woman. "You really care about Ann, don't you?"

"Of course I do. She's so gentle and sweet, and beautiful, and the kids…" with that, Monica's voice caught in her throat and she couldn't finish the sentence.

Lillian was embarrassed. She wasn't used to people falling apart on her this way. She got up to get Monica a tissue, but Monica grabbed her hand again. "I'm sorry. I know I must look like a fool, but this is really killing me."

Lillian handed her a napkin from the holder on the table. "It's all right. I'm upset too. I just don't show it."

"Thank God she has you."

Lillian grimaced inwardly. "That remains to be seen."

❧

Ann was particularly quiet that evening as the four of them watched television in the living room. Ann was lying on her side on the couch, her knees pulled up; Suzy's head was resting on her hip. Ann would stroke her little girl's hair for awhile, and then stop to pull a light cotton throw closer around her, even though the late summer night was warm.

There were dark circles under her eyes, and her skin was very pale. Philip kept glancing up from his spot on the floor to look at her. "You all right, Mom?" he'd ask, and she'd smile and answer "I'm great, Phil." But she wasn't fooling him. She wasn't fooling Lillian either.

Lillian offered to put the kids to bed so Ann could rest on the couch. They ran up ahead of her and she offered a challenge that the first one who was washed, teeth brushed, in pajamas and in bed would get to go with her to Rita's for gelato and Italian ice the next day. She made a huge scene out of the fact that they were both in bed at the same moment and that meant that they both won and now she'd go broke because she had to pay for two instead of for one. She tucked Suzy in first with a quick brush of her lips against the little girl's forehead.

"Goodnight, Suzy Q," she said as she turned out the light.

"I want cherry ice and vanilla gelato," the little girl announced.

"You got it," Lillian told her.

She walked to Philip's door. He was sitting on the side of his bed, in his pajamas, his bare feet and ankles showing as they dangled just above the floor. A lock of his gold-brown hair hung in his eyes. "Get a good night's sleep, old boy," Lillian said to him. She knew better than to go in to tuck him under the covers the way she had Suzy. He was more independent and seemed to want less affection—especially from her.

She started to close his door, when she heard him call, "Lilly?" Lillian opened it again and stepped just inside his room. It was the first time he'd ever really addressed her. "Yes?"

"Is my mom all right?" he asked her.

"Sure," Lillian lied. "She's great. A little tired, I think. That's all." He didn't believe her. She saw it in his eyes, heard it in the impatient way he sighed, and she walked quietly across the room to sit beside him on the bed. "You worried?" she asked him.

"She was sick once before, you know."

Lillian nodded but didn't say anything else. She didn't know how much he knew about Ann's illness the first time.

"I just was wondering if that's…like…what's going on with her again. She looks sicker this time."

Lillian studied him a little while before answering, "She's not herself but she doesn't want you to worry." Then she touched his shoulder and added, "And neither do I. I'm here now, Philip. You let me do all the worrying, okay?"

He nodded and Lillian pulled the covers away from his pillows and he got under them. She pushed his hair from his eyes. Neither of them said anything more but their eyes met. Lillian felt a lump form in her throat. His eyes looked years older than they should have.

"Thanks, Lilly," he said before turning away from her.

Lillian went down to the living room where Ann was drowsing. She sat crossed leg on the floor in front of the couch, took a deep breath, and said, "I made an appointment for you to go see this Dr. Raphael."

Ann opened her eyes. "You what? You did *what*?"

"And we're going. It's at the end of the week."

"No."

"Yes, and that's that," Lillian said, but she knew by the look in Ann's eyes that it wasn't.

"Okay, I'm going to explain this one more time, Lillian, and then never again. I have stage four breast cancer. It's in my lungs, my liver, my spine and my lymph nodes. I tried chemo for eight weeks and my numbers didn't change at all—that means my blood showed that the cancer was still floating around in me. The MRIs showed that the two lesions in my liver are a little larger, and my lungs have several tumors." Ann lifted her palms and said matter-of-factly, "I'm done for. It's just a fact."

"No..." Lillian said shaking her head, "no you aren't. Give it another shot."

"No, Lillian."

"Just one more...just talk to her...maybe, just maybe, there's some kind of trial or protocol or something."

"No, Lillian."

Lillian stood up then. "All right then do me a favor, go upstairs and tell your son that you're dying and you are too much of a coward to fight any longer."

Ann jumped from the couch and grabbed Lillian's arm. "What did you say to him?" Her face was red and her eyes black with anger. "I swear to God, Lillian, if you told him I have..."

"He knows," Lillian said, pulling her arm out of Ann's grasp. "He doesn't know exactly what...but he sure as shootin' knows you are sick and he's worried about you. He's afraid, Annie. You can see it in his eyes."

"What did you tell him?"

"Nothing! I told him you're all right—so thanks for making a liar out of me."

Ann sat on the couch again, her energy depleted. "What will I say to him?"

Lillian took a few seconds before answering her. "You'll tell him that, yes, you are sick but that you're going to a really good doctor to see what she can do to help you and that as long as you have an ounce of strength left in you, you will fight this illness until you're well again. You will tell him that he and Suzy are worth it...you'll tell him that you won't go down without a fight."

Ann let out a choked sound. "You are such a pompous ass, Lillian; you really are! Do you think I haven't fought...that I haven't given it my all, you idiot?"

Her anger silenced Lillian.

"The first time around, I did everything—*everything*—surgery, chemo, radiation—all of it. I even had them do a prophylactic mastectomy on my other breast 'just for insurance.' And the second time around, I did the chemo and once again was told that it was fine—it looked good—the numbers were great. Then this time I let them drip that poison in my veins again, every week, and for what? I don't have the strength to do it anymore. Don't talk to me about fighting, Lillian. I've had the shit knocked out of me in the ring!"

"I wasn't there then. I couldn't help. I can this time. I'll get you through it. Just give this doctor a chance. I promise you that if you meet with her and she tells you she can't help, I'll leave you alone and we'll take a different path. I just want to see what tricks she's got in her little black bag."

Ann let herself fall back on the couch and shook her head. "I'm so weary of it all, Lilly."

"I know. But you have to do this for me. I came back, right? I'm here, right? You owe me something for that, don't you?"

Ann started to protest, but stopped. There was silence in the room now. Ann's eyes were closed and Lillian combed her hand over her hair and let it stay at the back of her neck as she waited for Ann to say something more.

Finally, Ann let out a long breath. "All right, I'll go see her. You come with me and you listen to everything she says so that you hear it with your own ears. And then you'll accept whatever she says, right?"

Lillian raised her right arm. "I swear."

A thin, weary smile crossed Ann's lips. "You're such a nudge…"

# Eleven

In the morning, Lillian asked Ann if they could go through more of the papers in the chest. She thought that the busier they were until their appointment with Dr. Raphael, the less anxiety Ann would feel and the less likely she'd be to cancel the appointment.

Ann wasn't enthusiastic, but she agreed. Lillian had read through their grandmother's guide to the family the night before when she couldn't sleep, and identifying which ancestor was which was becoming a little easier. While she read her grandmother's typewritten pages, Lillian took a red pen and made notations in the margins. She even designed a makeshift family tree and a timeline.

Dan's "translations" of some of the oldest letters indicated that the original family members came from Ireland in the mid-1600s, even before William Penn himself arrived. He also discerned that they were Quaker, escaping persecution from the Church of England.

A one-page, wrinkled and greatly compromised sheet of paper indicated that their ancestor was actually friends with Penn and had been sent ahead of the first Governor of Penn's Woods to assist others in establishing the city of Philadelphia. There was no explanation as to how they ended up in the neighboring county of Bucks, but back in the 1600s there were no counties.

"You know," Dan had told her, seriously fascinated by the papers she had shown him, "you really should give these to a museum or a historical society."

She had frowned when he said it.

"I'm serious, Lil. Do your own research first, but handle these with care—great care—and then for God's sake, put them where they will be preserved and saved."

Two of the people Grandma Julia wrote about seemed particularly interesting—Hannah Smythe Ginley and her daughter Selina Ginley Deitz. They lived during the establishment of the Delaware Canal, the same channel of water that flowed—or used to flow—along Willow Wood property. She was also intrigued by the mention of Juliana-Alma Emory— who was born in 1762 and lived until 1892. The thought that there was more information in the chest about this eight-times-great-grandmother who lived during the American Revolution was fascinating to Lillian.

"So, all right, what exactly am I looking for in here?" Ann asked, sitting on a chair in front of the chest and bending over it.

"Find anything that has one or all three names—Juliana-Alma, Hannah, or Selina," Lillian answered, rifling through her own stack of papers on the bed.

Ann pulled neatly stacked sheets of paper wrapped in cord from the chest. They were old, the paper was very yellowed, and some of the pages had been eaten away by age. "This is like looking for a needle in a haystack," Ann complained. She took a tissue and wiped dust off the stack of pages.

Selina Ginley Deitz, she read aloud from the first page.

"Bingo!" Lillian said, putting down the papers she was holding and grabbing the corded stack from Ann. She laid it down on the bed.

"You're getting your bedspread filthy, Lilly," Ann protested, then sneezed three times. Dust spread throughout the room, and Ann noticed that a patina of fine dust lay on all the pieces of furniture. "What a mess," she added, blowing her nose and wiping her hands on a tissue.

"I'll wash it later," Lillian said as she carefully untied the cord. She flipped the cover sheet over and read the first sentence to Ann.

"I don't know if this is prudent or not, but I have taken on the unenviable task of recording for history the events that have taken place in my family in the last one hundred or more years. They are exciting in some cases, but they are shameful in others. In writing them down, it is my hope that I will be able to diminish the horrifying dreams I live with, come to terms with my mistakes—nay, my sins—and that I will not be condemned to the fires of hell for the role I played in some of the happenings I will record. I would confess my sins to my priest, but I cannot bring myself to do so, and so I live in mortal fear of them. Yet in writing these stories down, I also live in fear of the harm they will do to my reputation, present and future. I can only ask that the reader stand not in judgment of me or mine, but instead offer understanding and perhaps even pity."

Lillian stopped reading and looked up at Ann, whose eyes were wide with what looked like amusement. "What melodrama," Ann said with a smile.

"Whatever she's talking about is probably nothing that would shock us," Lillian said. "Life was pretty innocent in those days…what years would it be…if she died in 1892 and she's writing about the past one hundred, it brings us back to 1792 or earlier. Life was pretty bland back then, no?"

Ann shrugged, "I guess we'll find out. How many pages are there in her text?"

"About 100."

Ann went back to the chest and pulled out some more papers, then reached all the way down to the bottom where she found a fold of wax paper. She opened it carefully and inside was a drawing of a young woman holding a rifle in one hand and a ladle in the other. Her face was serene and in Ann's opinion very beautiful, surrounded by the ruffle of a mop cap. Her eyes were large and sad, her lips turned down slightly. Her clothing was 18th Century.

She wore a full skirt topped with a vertical striped short jacket that was longer in the back than in the front, and she had an accentuated narrow waist, but the hem of her skirt was tattered and another rip was drawn at the seam where the sleeve met the shoulder. At the bottom of the paper were two names: Juliana-Alma and the other, written small and to the right of the sketch was the name Peale and under that the date January 1777.

"Juliana-Alma," Ann whispered, looking closely at the woman's face.

Lillian looked up quickly, "Really?"

"There's a sketch here of a woman holding a rifle and a ladle and it seems her name was Juliana-Alma," Ann told Lillian, holding out the wax paper with the drawing on it.

"Here she is…oh my God, she's the one who lived during the Revolution. See if there's anything else about her."

Ann looked deeper into the chest and found some letters, but the paper didn't look old enough to be from that time period. "I don't see anything…wait," she said, pulling out two small almanac-type books, one of which was falling apart. Both had yellow, faded papers.

"Damn, these are old," said Lillian. "I'll go to the library in Newtown tomorrow and see if I can find anything about these and Juliana-Alma in the history books. I'll see if there's a mention of her in one of them or if I can find anything else." Lillian looked carefully at the drawing again. "I wonder why she's holding a rifle. She was a Quaker; the whole family was Quaker then. The Quakers don't fight in wars, do they?"

"I wouldn't think so," Ann said. "Maybe she hunted the food that she was cooking in the pot?"

"She's pretty, isn't she?" Lillian said, looking at the image on the fragile paper.

"Yes, in a way, except for the tattered clothing."

"Her cheek bones are very high and her neck is so long and slender, or does it seem that way because her cheeks are so hollow? If this was drawn during the war, she may have been starving. There wasn't much food during the winter months."

Ann nodded but didn't say anything.

She reached into the chest again and pulled out an intricately woven grass basket that held a bulky fold of wool. It was tied with satin ribbon.

She took the wool out and untied the ribbon and unfolded the piece. It was a yellow and green wool shawl. It smelled of cedar and although almost pristine, it did have a few holes in it.

"This is beautiful," Ann said. "I wonder who it belonged to."

Lillian looked up at her. There were dark circles under Ann's large blue eyes and she had no color in her face at all. Lillian didn't acknowledge the shawl Ann was holding. Instead she said to Ann, "Go rest awhile. The kids won't be home for hours. You look exhausted. Are you feeling ill again?"

"Just tired," Ann got up from her chair slowly. She put the shawl on Lillian's bed as she walked to door. "I do need a nap. I haven't slept well the last few nights. Wake me if I'm not up when it's time for the kids."

She left the room and Lillian reached over to finger the shawl. It was soft even after all these years. She got up from her bed and picked up the basket. It was discolored, but in perfect condition. It looked very much like the baskets that are woven from the marsh grasses in South Carolina. Was it possible that one of her ancestors had lived there at one time? She smiled to herself as she often did when going through the chest. It contained so many mysteries. Every question answered led to another question to be asked.

∽

The next day, Lillian took some of the old letters, her grandmother's text, the ancient looking books and the sketch of the beautiful Juliana-Alma to the local historic society library and did some research on the surname

Emory. There was some information in the two most important historic tomes recording the history of the county. Lillian discovered that Juliana-Alma was indeed the great granddaughter of a couple who traveled to America on the ship John and Sarah in 1681, and disembarked in Pennsylvania among those who were to become called the "first landers."

Even before William Penn was able to come to his newly acquired land and begin what he called his "Holy Experiment" in the new world, he had offered land to English, Irish, German, and Dutch—in fact, anyone—who wanted to live in a place that offered religious freedom and economic opportunity. Several ships left England carrying the takers of his offer that same year, mainly Quakers. They sailed directly to Pennsylvania.

The "first landers" settled near the mouth of the Delaware River, then moved upriver and settled on the land that was to become Philadelphia, Bristol, Morrisville, and all points above and inland where the tributaries brought them to lush, fertile land.

Jonathan and Irene Ward took their three children and settled one home in the city of Philadelphia and a country home a few miles upriver from Pennsbury Manor, where Governor Penn had arranged to build his own country manor. A few years later, they decided the country life was more to their tastes, especially after three more children were born, and they packed their belongings on a barge that brought them beyond Bristol to the area called Falls.

In one of the letters Lillian had brought to Dan, Jonathan had written to someone named Samuel, "The fruit in the orchards are beyond compare and the trees bend with their heaviness. There is fowl for the taking and more venison than we could eat in a lifetime. And the fish jump from the river into our boats. It is a plentiful land, with rich soil and green meadows. And the land is cheap to purchase."

Either the letter was never sent because it was never finished, or Samuel brought it back from Europe when he came to live in what Jonathan described as the land of milk and honey.

Lillian showed the letters and some of her notes to the volunteer librarian, a woman in her eighties, and the woman jumped out of her chair. "Yes, yes, we know who this is," she said. "We have another letter here from this same family—the wife I suppose it is." She walked around the desk and led Lillian to a second story and started to pull out large leather-bound books with neatly printed dates on each. "Here it is," she said, taking one of them off a shelf and placing it on a long table.

She flipped through the pages carefully, then stopped and said again, "It was written by Irene Ward to Governor Penn as testimony for one of the natives that he was to meet in his home at Pennsbury Manor. The Lenape was to become a messenger, and Irene wanted Penn to know what the man had done for her family a few years before. All of these old papers are preserved in these books. You can't take it out, but please feel free to read it."

The librarian stood aside and Lillian leaned over the book. Her first thought was that Irene must have been fairly well educated as her script was clear and her sentences well formed. The woman started the letter in a familiar way, mentioned the "Meeting," perhaps she and William Penn attended the same Quaker Meeting House when he was at Pennsbury. Irene told the Governor that due to the lack of roads and the hardships of the winters her twelve year old granddaughter, who had been tending the cattle, was lost for three nights in the early autumn rainy season.

The men in the family had searched with no success, and Irene wrote of the sadness that had overcome her when they returned on the third day without the girl Germaine.

"Though I have six children and ten grandchildren," she wrote, "each is precious to me. Yet these youngsters who came with us to this new colony are a blessing from the Almighty and closer to my heart."

She goes on to say that on the fourth morning, as she carried her pail to the well to get ready to prepare the morning meal, one of the local "savages" appeared in the early morning light from the line of trees.

"I held my breath," she wrote, "for although we've never had any trouble from those who call themselves Lenape, we have heard terrible bad stories about other colonies where whole families were massacred. We believe that it is due to thy great friendship with them, and thy honest dealings with them, that we haven't had the problems that the Puritans of Massachusetts have had. Yet, it is always with trepidation that we see them approaching us and our plantations.

"On this morning, this native walked steadily toward me, and just as I was ready to call for my son, I saw the native was carrying a child and I knew in my heart that it was our child, our Germaine. I dropped the pail and ran toward him and took the girl into my arms. She was cold and could barely keep her eyes open. He was a powerful big man. I wondered had he hurt her, but I could see no damage on her or on her clothes except that they were wet and dirty. He said not a word, nor did I. He touched

Germaine's hair with his brown hand and smiled gently at her, bowed to me, and left us in the meadow.

"I carried the girl to our cabin, calling the entire time to my husband that she was home. When she could speak, she told us of how she had gone to the swamp along the river to find some of the cattle that had wandered away, and walking farther than usual to find them she became lost and wandered for hours, cold and crying out for her father and brothers, but none came. She slept beneath a tree, then tried again the next day and the day after to find our plantation. She fell on the third night and could not get to her feet so tired she was.

Then she felt hands move her onto her back and saw a native's face. He picked her up, covered her with his own blanket, and smiled at her and she fell asleep in his arms. When she woke, she was home.

"Friend Ward and the boys loaded the horse with breads and meat pies I had baked the day before and a side of beef and some pork and found the place where the Indians live to thank them.

It was a meager offering since they do their own hunting, but they seemed to enjoy the bread I had sent.

"Since that day, every end of week when the weather is fine, the native comes to the meadow and our Germaine and her sisters walk out to meet with him and they sit always where I can watch them. They teach him our language, and he teaches them his tongue, though I can't imagine what good that will ever do them. But we allow it, for it is little enough a price for having him save our girl.

"There have been other kindnesses this native has shown us. When Friend Ward fell and was injured one deep winter, we found fowl and meat on our porch every week. Almost grown now, our Germaine remains friends with this Lenape and he with her. He is good."

Lillian sat down on a chair next to the table. "What a lovely story," she said aloud. She thought she was alone, but the librarian was still standing behind her.

"It was like that back in the early days of this Commonwealth. The Native Americans and the colonists were good friends. No one stole from the Native Americans. The newcomers paid for their land. Under order from William Penn, and perhaps because they were Quaker, the settlers made good and kept their promises. That changed once William was dead. His sons didn't have the integrity that he had, perhaps."

Lillian looked down at the ancient letter and read it again. She thought of the dates and calculated that the woman in the sketch, Juliana-Alma, would have been the great-granddaughter of Irene and Jonathan Ward, who knew William Penn and who came to the colonies even before he did.

Now she understood why her mother would say to her father with a great deal of haughtiness, "I'm an eighth generation American, you know," as though she had a much better standing with the universe than he did because of it.

Until this moment, it hadn't meant anything to Lillian. Suddenly, it meant a lot.

# Twelve

Dr. Raphael's waiting room was decorated more like a comfortable living room than a physician's office. Beautiful toile paper in pale green and white covered the walls. The furniture was upholstered, soft and inviting, in pale camel-colored plaids and soft greens that complemented the wallpaper. The hardwood floors were covered with an oriental rug and the artwork was interesting and eclectic. Lillian handed Ann's paperwork, test results, and x-ray films, which filled up two canvas tote bags, to a woman they assumed was the receptionist while Ann wrote her name on the sign-in sheet.

The woman, who was very tall and slender, with skin the color and texture of brown satin, and dark eyes that took up most of her beautiful face, shook Ann's hand then and said with a bright smile, "I'm so happy to meet you. I'm Millicent Jacob, Dr. Raphael's Physician's Assistant; our receptionist is out today. I work closely with Dr. Raphael. I'm going to take these back and study them while she meets with you. She will only be a minute, so just have a seat. There's some ice water with lemons on the table near the couch; please help yourself."

Lillian smiled and thanked Millicent, but Ann just nodded and sat down.

"She seems really nice, doesn't she?" Lillian asked Ann, taking on the role of optimist.

"Yeah…nice."

"It's a beautiful office, don't you think?"

"Mm hmm."

"You're being negative. I can sense it."

"I'm here, Lilly. Don't ask for peppy, happy, hopeful. Been there, done that before."

True to her word, Millicent opened a door a moment later and said with a brilliant smile that lit up the room, "Come on in, ladies."

Lillian stood up and started toward the door, then realized Ann continued to sit, her face set and hard.

"Annie..." Lillian pled in a whisper.

Ann looked up at her, sighed, and pushed herself out of the chair with both arms. As she passed Lillian, she whispered, "And away we go ... again...and again...and again."

Millicent heard her, smiled, and put her arm through Ann's in a gesture of support as they walked to an office at the end of a hallway which was graced with original oil paintings and looked more like a gallery than a doctor's office.

Dr. Margaret Raphael was sitting behind a French provincial desk with the sunlight streaming in from a large window that overlooked a park. She stood up as soon as Ann and Lillian approached and took Ann's hand in both of hers.

She wore several bracelets and they jangled when she reached out. Her long curly hair was a beautiful shade of gold, and Lillian could see that it was natural—both the color and the curl. She had a broad open face, blue eyes, and she showed just the hint of one crooked tooth in a bright, warm smile. She wore a soft white blouse tucked into a light camel pencil skirt and bone high heels that were at least three inches in height. The typical white coat was missing. Lillian estimated that she was around 45, but she looked younger.

"I'm Meg," she said, sitting down in a chair on their side of the desk and motioning for them to sit in either the other chair or on a rose colored silk settee.

She moved her chair around so that she was right next to Ann and just slightly turned from Lillian who was on the settee.

"You're Ann," she said, and looking at Lillian added, "and you are her cousin, right?"

"Good guess," Ann said. "I don't suppose the fact that I weigh 100 pounds soaking wet and am wearing a wig gave me away, did it?"

Dr. Meg laughed, and Lillian was surprised to find that it wasn't forced or fake in any way. "You know my tricks, I see," she said with sparkling eyes.

"Funny you should mention tricks," Ann said with sarcasm in her usually warm voice. "My cousin was mentioning just the other night that she'd like to see what kinds of tricks you have in your medical bag."

Dr. Meg shook her head when she looked at Lillian. "Sorry to say, I haven't got a single trick in there. I wish I did. Magic would make my profession a hell of a lot easier. Oh, to have a magic wand…but if you ask my husband and family, they'd tell you the closest I have is a broomstick on which I fly once every month."

Ann had to chuckle despite her dark mood.

Dr. Meg's smile turned a little softer as did her voice when she looked at Ann again. "You're a pretty sick lady, aren't you?"

Ann nodded.

"Millicent and I looked at your most recent reports but didn't have much of a chance to look at everything in that file yet. It's pretty extensive, I have to admit. You've been to the brightest and the best in my opinion. So, I guess I need to know what you want from me."

Ann looked directly into Meg's eyes. "I want to survive. I want you to tell me it was all a mistake and I'm just ding-dong dandy. I want to watch my babies grow up. I want to dance at their weddings…in other words, I want…"

"Magic…" Meg finished for her.

"Or a miracle," Ann added.

"Would you settle for peace of mind? Would you settle for a good appetite, some weight gain, less nausea, and a different cocktail of chemo that won't completely compromise your quality of life…what's left of it?"

Lillian was not comfortable with how this was going. She didn't like the words *what's left of it*. It was hard to follow what this doctor was asking, but Ann seemed to understand.

"Maybe," Ann said with a shrug. "What were the outcomes?"

Dr. Meg pushed the left side of her hair behind her ear and cocked her head as she addressed Ann. "Sometimes an extra six months…sometimes an extra six years. I don't have a crystal ball, and I won't lie to you or try to convince you that I do. And although we doctors like to play God and some of us think we actually are him—her—we aren't. We're just healers—or at least that's what we're supposed to be, and that means doing whatever we can to help our patients heal inside, outside, and upside down. Healing doesn't always mean curing. It's a concept a lot of doctors just can't get their arms around. But the truth is, we can't cure everyone who comes to us, but we can try to help them heal, to come to terms emotionally, all while fighting like warriors against whatever disease exists in our patients."

Ann sighed again. "So, what you're saying is that I'm going to die, but you can help me depart this life ten pounds heavier and with a smile on my lips?"

Meg nodded. "Yeah, I guess that's it in a nutshell, but maybe I can offer a little more time. Complementary treatment used in conjunction with the best medical science can offer does seem to help—if not cure—some people in stage four. In some people—*some* people, Ann, but not all—we're able to contain the cancer and treat it as a chronic disease for years."

"Tell me about this cocktail," Ann said.

"It's a mixture of chemos that are considered experimental when mixed together."

"This is a trial?"

"No, not really. These are reliable chemo treatments. But we integrate them with vitamins, protein shakes, massage therapy, Reiki, and when needed, pain killers. Some things will work for you, others won't. But it's another shot. And I do know that the integrated therapies will help you cope and improve the quality of your life…for awhile if not for a long time."

"Not forever?"

"Not forever," Dr. Meg said, reaching over and taking Ann's hand again.

Ann told the doctor, "I have two kids who are six and ten. My husband died two years ago. My mother has Alzheimer's. I have a brother still in college."

This was all said in a matter-of-fact tone, but Lillian knew that Ann was pleading her case.

Meg grew very serious. Three little creases appeared between her eyebrows, and her mouth turned down a little. She nodded. "No promises, Ann, but I want to try to help you."

"All my doctors wanted to help me. I even had one of them break down and cry in front of me when he told me the last round of chemo didn't work. *I* had to comfort *him*. No, I've never had a shortage of caring doctors."

"You're a very special person." Meg said.

Ann shrugged. "The way I see it, if I'm going to die anyway, I want to live the rest of my life without kneeling in front of a toilet vomiting poison that's not going to save me. Do you understand that?"

"Absolutely," Meg answered.

"Yet you want to fill up my veins with poison anyway?"

"One more time, yes, but my way this time. Do you have a port?"

"Yes, I didn't have it taken out yet." Ann opened the first three buttons on her shirt and Dr. Meg stood up to examine the little bump that Lillian had seen in the mirror the morning she discovered Ann in the bathroom. It was just under Ann's collar bone, near her left shoulder.

"It feels okay. We could still use that and you wouldn't have to worry about collapsing veins or more surgery to put a new one in."

Ann said nothing while Meg sat back down in her chair. Lillian could feel the pulse in her temples while she waited for Ann to speak—to agree or not.

Finally, Ann looked over at Lillian, a smile on her lips. "My cousin thinks I owe it to her."

"Is that right?" Meg asked, raising one eyebrow as she looked at Lillian, a small smile playing on her lips.

Lillian felt the heat of a blush rise from her chest to her cheeks. She wanted to protest that it wasn't that Ann owed it to her, that she really didn't mean it that way, but at the same time Lillian knew she had meant it.

Ann looked back at the well-dressed, bejeweled blond who could have been a big city interior decorator or real estate mogul for all she looked like a physician and said. "I guess this one's for Lillian. Let's do it."

# Thirteen

"Stop, Lillian. Stop reading it."

Lillian put down Juliana-Alma's journal and looked up at Ann in surprise. They were sitting in the sunroom because the air in the yard had turned unusually chilly for the middle of August. Camp was finished and the children were at Monica's for the day. Ann had received her first infusion of the chemo cocktail that morning and so far, she was handling it well. She didn't complain of nausea. She did have a headache, but she thought it was more from fatigue than from the chemo.

"I don't want you to read it to me. I want you to put it all in a book and I want to read your manuscript."

"Why?" Lillian wanted to know.

"I want you to write a book, Lilly, about these women…all these women. Start from the beginning—from this Juliana-Alma—and make some sense of it. I don't like getting it all piecemeal like this. And then, after you write each chapter, you can read it to me when I'm receiving my infusions. It will pass the time for me…for both of us."

Lillian put the papers down on the table next to her. "I don't know…I don't have a great track record with finishing books. I've got a manuscript in my laptop that I've been so-called writing for years now. It makes Dan crazy that I don't finish it."

"You'll finish this one."

"And you know this how?"

"You never had me supervising you before," Ann said smiling. "Besides, we have a brief window of time in which you have to complete it…so I won't let you procrastinate."

Lillian looked away from her cousin. She knew what Ann meant.

"Put Katherine's story in it and our mothers should be in it, too—change everyone's name, of course."

"If I put my mother into it, it will read like a horror story."

"In every family's life there is a horror story…many horror stories, probably."

"Nah, I don't think it's…"

"Please." Ann stated the word so strongly it took Lillian by surprise. It sounded more like a declaration than a plea.

Lillian didn't answer at first. She thought about it for a long while, formed the first paragraph in her mind—the hook—then started to plan the outline. It would require so much research, from the Revolution, through the building of the Delaware Canal, and the Civil War, and the World Wars. And would she put her own story in there? And Ann's? Would anyone believe all the tragedies in one family—schizophrenia, giving up babies, Alzheimer's, suicide, breast cancer…and all of that in the last twenty years alone? "It's outrageous," she said aloud.

"It's the way it is, Lilly. People relate to shocking family sagas. They either relate or feel elated that it isn't their family. We all have stories to tell, we just don't know how to tell them the way writers like you do."

Lillian didn't answer. She had already given up the idea of writing the book. "Ann, this journal is written by Juliana-Alma…it would be difficult to rewrite it as though I were the narrator. This is an important story she's telling, and I like the way she tells it. It just wouldn't work if I…"

Ann interrupted Lillian, "Let *her* be the narrator of her own story. Make all of them the narrators of their own stories—just as they are in these journals and letters. Give each generation a voice, her own voice. Be creative, for crying out loud, Lilly. Just put it all in one place—one book— like Grandma wrote in her paper, the story of the women of Willow Wood." Ann was annoyed by Lillian's arguments.

Lillian huffed, already defeated by the idea.

"I dare you," Ann said before bringing a glass of ice water to her lips. "I double dare you. I think you can do it even if you don't. So let's see who is right. Do you have the balls or not?"

Lillian laughed then. "You're such a jerk…I don't have balls at all."

"Oh? You only act like it?"

"I do not."

"Well, do you have the courage, then? The stamina? The moxie?"

"No, and I never said I did."

"You do too, you stupid, stubborn woman."

"Annie…"

"Shut up. Go start writing that book. It's got to be finished soon, so just stop yapping about not doing it and go do it."

"What about my other book? The one I never finished?"

"I don't like that one."

Lillian laughed again. "You never read it."

"I know, but I won't like it."

"How do you know?"

"Because you don't like it. That's why you never finish it...you're bored by it. And if you're bored by it, I'll hate it. Put it to bed and start this one."

Lillian frowned. She wondered if Ann was right about that...was she bored by the story she started years ago? Did she not like it?

"I want you to write this one," Ann said, pointing to the journal on the table at Lillian's elbow. "And I'm sick and dying so that trumps your laziness and stubbornness and I better get my own way in this. Damn it, I've got to get my own way in something, don't I?"

Lillian wasn't certain if Ann was serious or kidding. She studied her cousin a long while before she spoke. "Yeah, I guess you do deserve to get your own way in something."

"Finally..." Ann said with a frown, putting both her palms up.

"I'll start tomorrow."

"No, go in and start now. I'm going to nap right here in this chair and you're bothering me."

"God, you've become feisty. What the hell was in that chemo cocktail of Raphael's?"

"Truth serum."

Lillian chuckled. "Okay, I'll leave. You don't have to tell me twice."

"I want to fall asleep to the tap, tap, tapping of your fingers on the keyboard," Ann called after her.

Lillian walked into the library and turned on her laptop. While it was loading, she called Dan on her cell.

"Hey, beautiful," he answered.

"She wants me to write a book about our ancestors and she wants it finished before she dies."

"Good for her."

"She's pulling the cancer card on me, too." She mimicked Ann, "*I have cancer so you better do what I want you to do...*"

He laughed. "I think I love her..."

"Yeah, you *would.*"

"So what are you waiting for?" Dan asked her.

"Talent…ability…intelligence…the mood…"

"Oh, give me a break."

Lillian took a deep breath as she rested her head on her free hand and stared at the monitor. "So you think I should then?"

There was silence on the other end of the line.

"Danny boy, are you there or do you just not know how to answer that question?"

"You write it, I'll publish it. How's that for an answer?"

"Sight unseen?"

"I've seen your work. We will buy the rights and publish the book. Don't make me wait too long or the deal is off the table."

"What deal? How much?" she asked, chuckling.

"Much…"

"Will it pay the electric bill?"

"I have a feeling that with royalties, it will pay for the electric company."

"You have that much faith in me?"

"You have to ask me that?"

She smiled but didn't answer. Then she said, "Well, you'll have to discuss it all with my new agent, and she's tough. She'll take you to the cleaners."

"I have to meet Ann first," he said laughing.

"Yeah, you're right, you do."

"Lillian, baby" he said, his voice low as he said her name sensually.

"Oooo, I love it when you say my name that way. What is it you want, lover boy?"

"A manuscript. You've got two months to get me the first five chapters."

She rolled her eyes, disappointed that he wasn't going to say something sexy and romantic. "I have two words for you and they ain't happy birthday."

"Get to work."

# *Fourteen*

The kids, dressed in their new back-to-school outfits, descended the back staircase into the kitchen on the first day of school. Philip wore khaki shorts and a green and white striped polo shirt and Suzy was in long navy blue pants and a light blue shirt trimmed in white lace at the neck and cuffs. Her long hair was pulled back with heart shaped barrettes. Philip's hair was gelled and stood up in the front and top. They both had on new sneakers; Suzy's lit up when she walked.

Lillian was still in her pajamas and robe, nursing a mug of coffee when they bounded into the kitchen. She looked at Ann who entered just behind them. "Is this how they dress for school?" Lillian asked her cousin.

Ann laughed at Lillian, "Well, of course. Haven't you noticed that we aren't living in the 1960s anymore?"

Ann had gained some weight, and her lovely face had filled out again. She had color in her cheeks, and Lillian noticed that she wasn't wearing false eyelashes; there was a hint of fringe around her eyes that matched the color of her fair hair under her wig. She rushed around the kitchen getting the kids' breakfast, while Lillian packed their lunches and placed them in brand new backpacks filled with all new school supplies.

Lillian noticed that Philip's eyes were bright with excitement. He'd been looking that way a lot lately, and he was much less morose than he'd been for most of the summer. She knew his good mood had less to do with going back to school than it did with the fact that his mother was looking and feeling better. Her energy level was up, she sang when she cooked, she took the kids on long walks along the canal towpath every day, going farther every week and needing to stop less to rest as the summer months came to an end.

"I'm done!" Philip declared as he pushed his cereal dish away and leaned over to zip up his backpack.

"You're *finished*," Ann corrected him, leaning over the table to wipe a drop of milk from Suzy's chin. "You aren't a roast in the oven that's 'done';

117

you're a little boy who has finished eating."

"I'm finished," Suzy said very deliberately, smiling at her mother.

"No, you have to eat two more spoonsful, my love, you've hardly eaten any of the cereal in that bowl."

"I can't, Mommy," she said, holding her stomach and dramatically throwing her head back. "I'm soooo full."

"Two more," Ann said, pushing the dish closer to the little girl.

Philip pulled on his backpack and Lillian could see he was doing a mental check of what he needed, and then, seeming satisfied, he threw his arms around Ann in a bear hug and just as quickly, started to run from the house through the kitchen door. "See you later."

"Hey," Lillian shouted after him.

He stopped dead in his tracks, turned to run back into the kitchen, hugged her, too, just as he had his mother, and ran out again. She was surprised. She was soliciting a "good bye" not a hug, but it pleased her.

"Wait!" Suzy screamed, "wait for me, Philip…Mommy, he's not waiting for me."

Ann smiled, "It's okay, Suzy. You have time."

But Suzy was already pulling at her backpack and Lillian reached out to help seat it on her little back. "Thanks, Lilly, I love you," she said, kissing Lillian's hand. Then she grabbed Ann's hand and said, "Come on, Mommy, we'll miss the bus."

Lillian leaned against the door jamb of the kitchen and watched Ann walk with the kids to the end of the driveway to wait for the school bus. It was a typical early September morning, with just a hint of autumn coolness in the breeze, yet the world was still green and lush.

She looked up at the leaves in the surrounding trees as a breeze filtered through the branches, making them sway as though in slow motion, and adding a rustling sound to the song of the birds. Lillian loved this time of year. She always had. School was her escape as a child, and the first day of school always gave her some hope that things might be better at home. If she got good grades, maybe her mother would be happier with her. Sometimes it worked. Mostly it didn't, but Lillian still hoped, every September.

Her eyes drifted back to Ann and the children. Suzy had her arm around Ann's hips and Ann stroked the little girl's head, obviously listening to some story Suzy was telling her. The bus pulled up, stopped, and the kids kissed Ann again before stepping up into the bus. Ann exchanged a few words with the bus driver, then waved as the doors closed and the bus gears groaned in protest as it pulled away. Ann threw kisses, and Lillian knew that Philip must be grimacing in embarrassment sitting with his buddies while his mother threw kisses at him. Suzy, however, would be responding with her own kiss throwing.

Lillian watched Ann walk up the drive. She looked so well, although Lillian knew that she was still fatigued every afternoon and had to rest.

*The new meds are working* she thought as she had numerous times during the last two weeks, although Ann would not let her say it out loud. "Don't' jinx me," she'd scold Lillian. But there was no mistaking that even though Ann had started receiving infusions again—this time in the beautifully appointed private treatment rooms of Dr. Meg Raphael—she was not violently sick afterward and not as weak.

She drank the shakes and took the vitamins faithfully, exercised every day whether she felt like it or not, and attended weekly support group sessions and gentle massage therapy twice a week.

She had joined the same gym that Dr. Meg went to and they exercised together, becoming fast friends. Lillian agreed to walk the canal with her, but a gym was beyond what she was willing to do for the love of her cousin.

The word exercise wasn't in Lillian's vocabulary.

"What are you standing there looking so smug about?" Ann asked as she came closer to the door where Lillian stood.

"I'm not smug," Lillian said.

"Don't jinx me," Ann warned, moving past Lillian with a warning look.

Lillian frowned and lifted her arms in a shrug, "I didn't say a word…"

"You were thinking it."

"Oh, you read my mind now? You know what I'm thinking all the time?"

Ann changed the subject. "Did I mention that Father Murray is coming over for lunch today?"

"Three times," Lillian said, pouring more coffee into her mug.

Father Murray hadn't been to Willow Wood for a few weeks, and Lillian was secretly happy that she'd get to see him.

He was a pleasant man, easy to talk to and be around, and she enjoyed his company. And he put up with her questions—arguments, really—about the sex abuse scandal in the Church, the Church's stand on women priests, celibacy, and homosexuality. He always listened to her position, and she had to admit, sometimes his arguments made sense.

They always seemed to agree to disagree, but in a good-natured way.

Ann told Lillian that he was helping her spiritually. Lillian wasn't sure how, or whether that was a good thing for Ann, but it did seem to be making a difference in Ann's moods and her outlook. Lillian noticed that Ann took her Rosary Beads to the infusions with her every week now, and Lillian often saw her sitting beneath the willow tree with them, her lips moving to the rhythmic prayers.

"Have you ever noticed that he's handsome?" Lillian asked Ann when she sat down at the table to finish her coffee.

Ann stopped preparing her protein shake and turned to look at Lillian with a serious frown.

"Oh, for God's sake, I'm not *into* him," Lillian told her, annoyed. "Can't I just observe that he's nice looking?"

"No, you can't."

"Annie, stop being so provincial. I know he's a priest. He's also a man."

"He's a good priest, a truly dedicated priest. He's one of the most spiritual men I've ever known."

"And he's handsome, too," Lillian persisted.

Ann shook her head but laughed a little. "And he's handsome, too, I guess." She went back to the shake. The blender squealed and stopped, and Ann poured out the tan liquid into a large glass. "It wouldn't hurt you to drink this, too," she said, sitting across from Lillian.

"Put some ice cream into it, and a little chocolate syrup, with a jigger of Stoli and I just might."

"That would be defeating the purpose, no?"

"No."

They both laughed. Then Ann's smile faded and she looked around the kitchen. "I hate the first day of school. I hate when they get on that bus."

Lillian was perplexed. "Why? They went to camp all summer and were gone the same amount of time during the day."

"It's different, Lilly. School days are different, but I can't explain why." She turned her head to look at the door. "They are growing up so quickly."

Lillian didn't like the melancholy mood Ann was sinking into and decided to change the subject. "Next weekend is Labor Day and I was wondering if I could..." she stopped, not sure if she really wanted to do what she was proposing to Ann. She'd thought about it for days, but couldn't decide if it was really a good idea or not.

"What?" Ann asked.

"Can I invite some friends for the weekend?" There, it was out of her mouth, so now she was committed to doing it.

"Of course, this is your home as much as it is mine. I've told you that a thousand times. Who?" Ann asked, very interested.

"I thought I'd ask Dan and his sister and daughter. Dan's been hounding me about meeting you and the kids, and it would be nice for them to get out of the city for the long weekend."

Ann's eyes lit up. "I'd love it! Suzy can sleep with me and Jessica can have her room. Louise can sleep in the guest room, I'll get some fresh flowers from the Farmer's Market to dress it up a little, and Dan...well, of course, we know where Dan will stay..."

"Dan will sleep on the couch in the library," Lillian said. "How would we explain his staying in my room to the kids? Besides, I've never slept with him when Jessica is around."

Ann laughed, "Who's being provincial now?" She leaned toward Lillian, "I'm excited about this. I wish you had invited them sooner."

"Yeah, well, you weren't really up to it," Lillian said, without mentioning that she was the one who wasn't up to what might turn out to be uncomfortable and awkward, though she couldn't put a finger on why she felt that way.

Later that morning, they put a colorful floral tablecloth on the table in the gazebo and set it with white ironstone dishes for Father Murray's visit. Ann cut some mums from the garden and made a tiny arrangement in the center of the table.

"Wow," he said when they brought him out to the gazebo, all of them carrying serving dishes filled with salads and cold chicken and salmon. "To what do I owe all this fuss?"

"Just because we like you," Ann said lightly.

"And because you're handsome," Lillian added.

The crow's feet crinkled at his temples. "I am, aren't I?" he said to her, pretending to be serious. "I've been told that before. I can't stop looking at myself in the mirror. I even put one on the altar so I can watch myself offering the Mass." His laugh was hearty and deep. It was contagious.

They served themselves and chatted easily. Lillian and Father Murray bantered back and forth, but didn't get into their usual serious and philosophical conversations about the Church, errant priests, mean nuns, and the Vatican.

Ann was serving slices of lemon meringue pie when they heard a voice call out. They looked back at the house and Dr. Meg appeared from the side of the house.

"We're back here," Ann called to her. Meg saw them and waved.

Meg walked across the lawn to the gazebo. When she got to them, she noticed Father Murray and let out a delighted squeal. "Hey, Priest!" she said, reaching over and planting a big kiss on his cheek.

"How are you doing, Rafe?" he said to her, returning her hug.

"What are you doing here alone with these two gorgeous women?"

"Enjoying every minute of it, and now with your arrival, I'm even happier."

"Yeah, I bet you are, you flirt."

He pulled a chair from the table and Meg sat down.

"Are you hungry?" Ann asked her.

"I'm starved, what have you got?"

They took the almost empty platter of chicken, added salads to it, and placed it in front of Meg. There were extra forks on the table and Lillian gave her the cloth napkin from her own lap saying, "It's clean, I didn't use it."

"How do you know each other?" Lillian asked the priest and doctor.

"We serve on the hospital board. We're on the ethics committee together," Father Murray answered. "And she's my oncologist, too... *was* my oncologist."

"He's trying to convert me," Meg said between bites.

"I'm not at all trying to convert her," he said. "She drives me crazy! All I said to her was that her last name is the same as the Archangel Raphael who is the patron saint of healing and that she should pray to him. You'd think that I was dragging her by the hair to the baptismal font. Not that I wouldn't love her to join the Church."

Lillian asked the doctor, "What do you think of women priests?"

"I think you need a few in your church."

Lillian looked at him with a grin. "She's my kind of woman...let's convert her."

"Listen to who's talking about conversion," he said playfully. "You haven't been to Mass once with Ann and the children. I have to convert you first."

"If you do, can I enter the seminary?"

"Leave him alone," Ann said to both women. "You're ganging up on him."

"Aren't you curious as to why I'm here?" Meg asked when she finished eating lunch, and motioned for a slice of pie.

Ann stiffened a little; her face looked tight when she said, "No." Then when everyone looked at her in surprise, she added, "We're just glad you're visiting. You don't need a reason."

"Well, *I'm* curious, now" Lillian said.

Meg put a piece of lemon meringue pie in    her mouth to make them wait for her answer. She closed her eyes and moaned, "Mm, good pie." Then she swallowed and looked at Ann.

Ann sat back in her chair, no smile on her face now at all. It was obvious that she did indeed know why Meg was there. "Okay, go ahead...there are no secrets between me and Father Murray and my curious cousin. Let's hear it."

Lillian was alarmed now. "What's going on?"

Ann said, "I went for my scans and blood tests the other day. She's here to give me the results. Isn't that right, Meg?"

Lillian was angry. "You went for your scans alone? You told me you were going shopping for the kids' clothes. Why didn't you tell me the truth? Why didn't you let me go with you?"

Ann shrugged and didn't answer.

"I do have the results," Meg said, ignoring the interchange between the cousins. "Want them?" she asked Ann.

Ann barely nodded and stared at the colorful tablecloth.

"The lesions in the liver have shrunk and there are remarkably fewer in your lungs—barely visible—the markers in your blood are good, too. All the counts are good."

There was silence in the gazebo as each of them took the information in. Finally, Ann moved.

"It's working," she breathed.

Meg smiled, "It's working for now."

"It's working," Ann said again, louder this time. "Lilly," she said, excitement rising in her although she was trying not to let it, "it's working."

Lillian let her breath out slowly, careful not to let them see that she'd been holding it. "I knew that," she said nonchalantly. "I told you..."

"It's working," Ann interrupted her, saying the words to no one in particular.

Lillian looked at Father Murray and his eyes were shining with tears. His smile took up half his face. Then she looked at Meg, who just kept eating her piece of pie.

Ann jumped up from the table and ran to the house without saying a word, but she danced and skipped as she ran.

Lillian put her hand on Meg's wrist preventing her from lifting the fork. "This is great news, right?"

Meg answered, "Cautious optimism, we call it. No promises, though, right? You remember that?"

Ann was returning already, a bottle of champagne in one hand and four flutes dangling from their stems in the fingers of her other hand.

"We're celebrating, people," she said.

"You're not supposed to drink," Meg reminded her, but laughed. "Oh, what the heck, just a sip…and only a sip for me, because I have patients to see this afternoon."

"Fill the glass up for me," Lillian said, holding it out, feeling dizzy with joy.

"And Father Krauser is taking care of the parish the rest of the day, so fill me up, too!" the priest said.

Ann finished pouring and the four of them clinked glasses.

"To life!" Ann said, still standing, her face flushed and her eyes shining.

Father Murray agreed whole-heartedly. "To life!"

Lillian chimed in, her glass lifted high, "To life!"

Meg smiled, clinked her glass against theirs, and sipped without saying it.

# Part Two

*What lies behind us and what lies before us are tiny matters compared to what lies within us.*

Ralph Waldo Emerson

# *Fifteen*

*The Women of Willow Wood*
*Author's Note*

*There is an ancient weeping willow tree that sits on the berm of the Delaware Canal in Bucks County, which runs parallel to Pennsylvania's Delaware River. The elongated, feathery leaves and graceful branches hold fast to the secrets of the women of Willow Wood Farm, from the time when those leaves were used for medicinal purposes for injured soldiers during the Revolutionary War, through the tree's location as a gravesite for a seemingly stillborn baby, and until a dying young mother sits beneath it and allows the tree's tears to stream down her face along with her own.*

*The willow has stood silent, guarding these stories, until now when the newest generation of women of Willow Wood, myself and my cousin, Ann, have come along to unveil the willow's mysteries.*

*For reasons that will unfold later in this book—when it is time for me to tell our story—Ann and I are living in our ancestral home, which has been handed down from one generation of women of Willow Wood to the next since the 1700s.*

*We have found a beautiful blanket chest in the attic—I like to call it a treasure chest—filled with letters, journals, autograph books, and very old photos that have been carefully preserved and secreted for each new generation to find. The people who have lived in this beautiful old house for more than two hundred years come to life again in their writings. They tell stories of great love, heartwarming beginnings, tragic endings, and in all cases, they remind my cousin and me that nothing is ever new…circumstances change, people change, but the happiness and tragedies of life are constant.*

*We have found these stories to be compelling, not because they are of our ancestors, but because they are lessons in history, persistence, strength of character, and endurance.*

Lillian hit the period key, the enter key, and tab and then sat back in her desk chair. *Now what?*

She pushed her wireless keyboard with the back of her fingers and it hit the edge of her laptop.

"Where the hell do I begin?" she asked aloud, looking across her desk, through the window and toward the willow tree.

"Which one, good old willow tree? Which woman do you want me to undress for the world to see? The revolutionary, Juliana-Alma? Her poor mother Germaine, who was rescued by the Indian when she was a young girl?"

Germaine, came the answer; the girl who was found by the Native American in the swamp and carried in his arms back to her parents' plantation. Germaine began a journal in 1776, when her children were almost grown, and wrote in it faithfully for a short time during the War for Independence. According to Dan it was very unusual for a woman to write at all at that time. Most people were taught to read the bible and understand it, but in the 18th Century no one seemed to feel women needed to know how to write. Germaine and her daughter, Juliana-Alma, did know how to write and were prolific.

Lillian found that trying to read what Germaine wrote was labor intensive. She wrote with flourishes and in the Italianate style of penmanship and spelled many words phonetically—hors for horse, pees for peace, independnse and revolushun. There were words Lillian had never heard before and there was also the problem of the decaying pages, some of which fell apart when she handled them.

Yet, there was a gentle, compelling prose to the writings. Lillian had to admit that the woman's story was captivating, and in many cases, very sad. Each journal entry began with an address to "my beloved," as though she were writing to a lover, yet most of the entries were about her husband and children. Dan told Lillian that once he deciphered the writing, he realized she was writing to the Indian who had found her when she was a child.

Lillian dug into a shopping bag where she had placed some of the papers from the chest, rifled through them, and found Germaine Bournes' journal. Some of the pages were falling apart, but mostly the hand-bound book was intact, and each page was carefully ruled, apparently by Germaine herself.

Lillian sighed deeply at the work it would take to interpret the journal, then she pulled the keyboard closer to her again.

"All right," she murmured as she began the first page of her own book, "for what it's worth."

### Germaine Bournes—1712 to 1802

*9 November evening*
*Sixth day of the week*

*My beloved, my heart is heavy. I have great fear. I cannot help but wonder what will become of my family, my home. What a resolute man I have married. James says he cares not whether they confiscate our land because he will not fight and will not allow our sons to fight in this war for independence. He detests the King and his taxes as much as any man, and I know that his heart is on the side of those who fight with General Washington, yet he is loyal to his Quaker faith. He is a Friend. He will not kill. He says that it would make him like the rest that his own father came to this colony to get away from. He will not sign a writ of assistance in any circumstance. There are stories everywhere about beatings that good Quakers are receiving because they won't fight. Their land is being confiscated, Friends are sent to camps in Virginia for punishment. Many from our meeting are leaving Pennsylvania and heading back to England for protection, forsaking all they have built and worked for. Others pretend to be on the side of Independence in front of patriots, but spy and report to the Tories.*

*There is much for me to worry about with this, yet the worst, and may God forgive me for it, is the shame that I feel. They will call my husband, my brothers, and my sons traitors and cowards. It burns deep in my very being, for my heart yearns for independence; not for me, but for my children. This is their land, their country. My heart is as divided as this county of Bucks is. I want freedom, yet I cannot bear the thought of any of my sons going to war to fight for it. I want freedom, yet I am torn by my faith. Is it not God's prerogative, and only His, in the setting up and pulling down of kings and governments? At least it says so in the Ancient Testimony and Principles of the People called Quakers that the elders have issued to all Meeting Houses.*

*You above all know that I have always believed in the Society of Friends. In all my years—thirty-six in all—I have never drifted from what I consider the goodness and fairness of the Society. It is woven into the fabric of my life, not what but who I am. I could never be anything else.*

*Have I not proven it? I gave up my beloved Lenu…my Indian, my dearly loved…because of this faith. I will never be over my love for you for as long as I live, but I will not allow myself regret. I am a Quaker and you an Indian and it could not have been. I knew it then. I know it still.*

*How I long to sit on the banks of the river in your presence and speak with you about this pain I suffer now. O beloved.*

*13 November evening*
*Fourth day of the week*

My beloved, he wants to send Jonathan, the son of our slaves, barely old enough to work the fields let alone fight in a war. I cannot bear it. When he mentioned it to me at his morning meal, I wanted to scream Hypocrite! He thinks it will appease them…he thinks that if he sends his slave to fight on his behalf it will save Willow Wood from being confiscated.

He is right, of course. They will accept a slave to fight from the accounts we've heard, but I cannot face this newest shame. How do I look at Jonathan's mother in the eyes? How can James work side-by-side with Jonathan's father, yet send his young son in harm's way but not his own sons? We should not even own these people.

It is an abomination; one that so many Quaker abolitionists want to eliminate. James is a leader in our meeting. He should be at the forefront of setting our slaves free as an example to the others. Yet now, because of the convenience of it, he wants to put a rifle in poor, sweet young Jonathan's hands and march him off to kill even though James himself will not nor allow our sons to go. O beloved, these are wretched, wretched times. Wretched, weary days.

*14 November late night*
*Second day of the week*

My beloved, Willie wants to join the Free Quakers. I knew it in my heart, but Juliana-Alma confirmed it for me this day when she was reading Common Sense to me while I sew near the fire. She, too, is burning with the flame of independence. I see it in her eyes when she speaks of the revolution.

It doesn't help that Willie comes home from town full of stories he has heard about George Washington's army, told to him by travelers, peddlers, and even by the members of the Continental Congress themselves as they pass through the county seat in Newtown where Willie works in our carpentry shop.

My Willie. My Willie will go and his father will disown him. My eldest child; he is the most intelligent of all six of my children, the most searching, and the most honest.

Do you remember, o beloved, when I brought him to see you when he was first born? And do you remember when he was just a small boy and I brought him with me to meet with you and you told us exactly where to build our home on Willow Wood? You drew a map for us to show us where to place the foundation so that the floods from the Delaware would never sweep our home away as it did my family's so many times.

Oh, what happiness I felt whenever I was with you, and what comfort it was for me to know that my Willie would never tell. He would only listen, and believe in your words and advice.

You knew and your people knew everything about this land and I trusted you—my native friends—especially my own beloved—who James would just dismiss as unknowing heathens if we asked him to seek your counsel.

Since the day that my Lenu found me spent and on the verge of dying in the swamps, I knew that you and your people could be trusted, believed…and yes, even loved.

James was more willing to listen to a boy of ten than he would have been to the men who had lived along the shores of the Delaware River for hundreds of years.

Willie committed your map to memory and advised his father, and he led the horse that pulled the stones that James dug up from the earth to build the foundation of our home, and he had helped me, heavy with my third child, lift and place them as high as possible until he was too short to help any longer.

He worked beside his father clearing the farm, sowing seeds, and harvesting. This is his land as much as it is his father's. This country will be his, and I know he will fight for it. He said as much to me in a veiled warning, and Juliana-Alma confirmed it today.

He will be excommunicated from meeting. Perhaps we all will be. He is a man now of eighteen. We cannot stop him. Not true, not true, I could and I know it. If I were to implore him, lay guilt upon him, he would reconsider; but I will not do it. I will not do that to the son I love so dearly.

He could be hurt. Dare I think it, he could be killed, and following General Washington into battle against the British will not be easy. Nay, it will be harder than any life he's ever known.

*18 November morn*

*Sabbath*

My beloved, my thoughts are difficult. It is the Sabbath, and all are sleeping still. The cock has not crowed and the moon is still high. I dream such maddening dreams. I have lived in peace for so long, why now, when there is so much else to be worried about do I long for you, for your voice, for your quiet presence and advice? I must stop thinking of you. I must concentrate only on my children and the threat that is looming over us every day since the fourth day of this July past. I have not had peace since the Declaration. O that I can only find peace in the scriptures as I used to. But they, too, fail me. All fails me.

I am wretched from fear.

*4 December evening*

*Fourth day of the week*

*My beloved, they are coming. We can hear the cannons from across the river. If they cross the Delaware into Pennsylvania, nothing will ever be the same at Willow Wood Farm. I try to pray, but nothing comes, just empty words that I recite, but nothing comes from my heart; it is so filled with fear and even grief. Once my prayers were heartfelt and pure; now they are just cymbals—noise only. I do not know what to pray for.*

*My sons, yes, most of all my sons; and for my country. I read the psalms, hoping for comfort, for guidance; but my mind will not stay on them. We will be branded as cowards and traitors if James remains firm. He is a good man, a righteous Quaker, and I know that he is also pained and worried, because if he sides with those who cry for freedom, we will be considered cowards and traitors by those who remain loyal to the King and we will be excommunicated from meeting. And so, this is our family's moment of truth.*

*I see the flame of liberty in my son's eyes. I understand it; I share it.*

*Yet, if he goes, I know that I will lose him forever. James will disown him if Willie goes against him and his faith. That is the least of my fears for Willie. How can I allow my son to go to war, to take up arms against his fellow man, when I have educated him to avoid violence at all costs? Yet how do I stop him? How do I say he cannot fight for his freedom from tyranny? How do I force him to stay, knowing that for the remainder of his life, he will feel that he was a coward and did not follow his heart? If the patriots lose this war, will Willie always wonder if he had joined the Continental Army, would it have made a difference? If they win, will he always feel that he has no share in the victory— in the freedom—if he did not fight for it with his own hands? Would he ever really be free?*

*7 December night*

*Seventh day*

*My beloved, they have arrived. All boats have been destroyed or hidden along the river to prevent the British from coming to Pennsylvania. The war has come to divide us.*

Lillian glanced at the clock on the fireplace mantel in her office. It was nearly three in the morning. The night was still black beyond the window frame. She picked the journal up and thumbed through it gingerly. Once she started reading and writing about Germaine's journal, she lost all track of time. She became surprised when the journal ended abruptly. It almost seemed as though Germaine stopped writing anything of importance during the weeks after writing about the arrival of the Continental Army. Was it because she was too busy? Too worried?

Then Germaine resumed writing in the journal after the troops left Bucks County, but those passages had a very different voice. Germaine stopped addressing them to "her beloved." She noted only mundane details of the days and weeks. Very little was personal or poignant. She wrote down her recipes, her medicinal potions, the days and times of neighbors' visits. It seemed to Lillian that Germaine had lost her desire to record anything important in her life or to try to connect with her long lost Leni Lenape brave—even through her imagination and memory. Just as suddenly as the entries had started in November of 1776, the entries ended. The last half of the journal was filled with empty pages except for one surprising abbreviated passage that read:

*3 April 1777 evening*

*James, my husband, the father of my children, was found floating in the river early this morning.*

Lillian put aside Germaine's journal and searched in the shopping bag for more papers until she found Juliana-Alma's journal. Obviously, Germaine's daughter had taken up the same habit of writing about her life as her mother had—more than likely encouraged to do so by her mother.

The writing in this journal was different. It had the ramblings of a young girl, boring little tidbits about life on Willow Wood Farm, school, the local Quaker meeting, and much about her brothers. Lillian turned to the passages that were written during the Revolution. There were more details about what went on during that Christmas of 1776 than there were in Germaine's journal.

Although she was exhausted, Lillian needed to know how it all turned out. Did Willie go to war? Was the family torn apart? And why the hell was James floating in the Delaware?

She decided to stay up just one more hour to find out. She opened Juliana-Alma's journal, much like Germaine's in that it was hand bound and still intact, but slightly easier to read. Each page was filled and crowded with script until the very last page. She searched for the entries in 1776. The dates were not as specific as Germaine's journal, but entries were clearly written and after reading the first three pages that began in December of 1776, she knew that the end of the story was in her hand.

Lillian took the journal to the cushiony leather chair near the fireplace, turned on the lamp that hung over it, and started to read. Before getting to the end of the first page, she fell asleep.

She awakened with a start. She had been covered by a soft chenille throw and a pillow from the couch in the living room was tucked between her cheek and the side of the chair. The sun shone brightly through the windows. Lillian unfolded her legs from under her with a wince. Her knees and hips ached after being cramped in the chair for hours. She looked around the room, getting her bearings, and found Ann sitting on the desk chair.

"Hey," she said, stretching her back first one way and then the other.

When Ann didn't answer Lillian looked over at her cousin and noticed a track of tears on Ann's cheek.

"Oh, God, now what?"

Ann shook her head slowly. "Nothing…it's just this journal. I picked it up from the floor when I found you this morning. I've been sitting here reading it for more than an hour."

Lillian sighed, relieved that the journal was the reason for Ann's tears. "Ann, you are such a freakin' bleeding heart. *Really*? A journal that was written two hundred years ago? You're sitting there crying over *that*?"

Ann smiled despite the tears. "You give birth, you nurture and kiss and tuck them safely into their beds at night, you make sure they're dressed, they're warm, they're fed…you teach them not to hurt other people…you forbid any toy guns in the house…you'd take a bullet yourself to protect them, and then some strangers decide to start a war and you're expected to send them off into harm's way."

Lillian sat back in the chair again. "So, okay, what happened to them?"

"You'll have to read it yourself," Ann said.

Ann stood and dropped the journal into Lillian's lap as she left the room.

"Did the American patriots lose the war? I knew it! The British won and they just forgot to tell us." Lillian called out as Ann disappeared through the doorway; there was no answer but she was gratified when she heard Ann chuckle.

### Juliana-Alma Bournes Smythe (1760–1812)

*4 December*

*It is very late as I write, but I must enter on this most important of all days before I hasten to bed. General Washington and his army are coming. Willie came home from a tavern across the river in New Jersey where he was selling some of the furniture he made and came into the barn where I was tending to the stock and he shouted, "They are on the run, they are heading this way, to Bucks County."*

*When I heard it, I was certain they were losing and I asked Willie if it was true.*

*"It wasn't said outright, but it sounds dire. The British have chased them out of New York and they are losing almost every battle in New Jersey. You can hear the cannons when across the river. They are close, Sister."*

*O, how his eyes shown with excitement. I have never seen our Willie this excited. Then he said to me, "I want to go, Juliana. I need to go. They need all the soldiers they can get. I have to tell Papa tonight."*

*"Take me with you," I begged. I told him that there must be something women can do in the war, something we can do to help. But he will not hear of it. He is worried enough about what Papa will do when he announces his decision and how desolate Mother will be. I reminded him that our mother will be overcome by his leaving anyway whether I should go or not.*

*"Thy life would be in danger, Sister. I cannot allow it," he told me.*

*"As will thine," I answered him, for it is as much my desire for liberty as it is his.*

*Willie became very serious then and almost in a whisper and with great sadness in his voice he told me, "Papa will disown me."*

*I could not disagree. But I told him that Mother would defend him. He smiled but shook his head no. "I fear not…she will be afraid for me and afraid of Papa's anger. She is a Quaker through to her bones."*

*It is true. I know that the war for independence is causing her great misery. She is worried that if we follow our faith and the edicts of the meeting, we will be branded traitors and our land will be taken from us. Yet, I know in her heart that she is not a traitor and that she yearns for our freedom almost as much as we do. Willie must know this too, for he said, "If I go, and Papa lets them know that he is not a loyalist, they will leave us alone. I know that he was hoping to send Jonathan, but I cannot allow it."*

*As if he'd already heard his name, Jonathan walked into the barn. He stopped short when he saw Willie and me and apologized for intruding. He is the same age as I and two years younger than Willie.*

*He excused himself and started to leave us, but Willie stopped him.*

*"We were just talking about the war. Come in and tell us what you think, Jonathan."*

*"My pa tells me it ain't much of my business," Jonathan said.*

*"But it will be," Willie told him. "Thou may have to join the army…and*

*fight the British so that our country will be free. Doesn't that mean anything to you? Doesn't it excite you?"*

*I could see that it didn't, for Jonathan looked down at his boots and touched the scarf my mother had made for him which was wrapped tightly around his neck. "Freedom is a good thing, I s'pose. But my pa still says I should mind my own business about it. I'm too young to join the army anyways." He looked at me then. "My father fought when the Indians rose up, and he says that it ain't a good thing to fight a war. But he believes in liberty—liberty for all Americans—free men or slaves."*

*He is honest in this thinking. There should be freedom for everyone. I have been reading about the abolitionist movement among the Quakers in Philadelphia and in our own meeting, but it has become a quiet rumbling.*

*Mother believes slavery to be wrong, as do I, for we truly believe to do to all men as we will have done ourselves. In fact, some of the local Friends in the county and in Philadelphia have already released their slaves, have given them wages and even granted them land they could farm and earn a living.*

*I know Mother longs to do this for Jonathan and his parents, but Father tells her he is not ready. He needs them to work the land and help in the shop in Newtown. He promises her often that the time will come, but it is not now.*

*Willie argued that it will be hard to get freedom for everyone unless we obtain our freedom from the King.*

*"Certainly thy father must understand that?" I asked Jonathan.*

*"I don' know, Miss Juliana, I jus' don' know how my father thinks except to tell me it's none of my business jus' yet."*

*Willie moved away from his horse and patted Jonathan on the shoulder. "Never mind, Jonathan; the time will come when thou will need to think about it. But not today surely."*

*But it was all Willie and I could think about when we entered the house. Jonathan's mother, Selma, was in the kitchen with our own mother. They were preparing the meal. Papa had returned home from the shop, and he was in the parlor reading as he usually did before the late supper.*

*Willie did not go into the parlor as he normally would have. He hung near the fireplace where the rabbit stew was cooking over the open fire and bread was baking in the brick oven, sending forth an aroma that made both our stomachs growl with hunger.*

*Selma shooed him away. "Young Willie, you in the way of our cookin'. Look sharp 'fore I burn you with the kettle."*

*Willie took several steps away but continued to hover near them, watching our mother as she moved around the room. She wore a petticoat of blue over her white gown and a large kerchief over her neck and shoulders. Poor Mother, she always tries to keep her unruly red curly hair carefully tied back and secured, but it always loosens from beneath her white cap, and tendrils hang around her face. There was high color in her cheeks from the warmth in the room and from her hurried activities, but her skin always seems so white. As I tied my apron around my waist, I could see Willie studying her.*

*I know that he was thinking that he would break our mother's heart tonight, and he regretted it deeply. I know, too, that he wishes her Indian friend was still alive so that she could meet the tall strange looking man secretly and receive comfort from him after tonight.*

*Willie and I know that the man had saved her when she was a young girl, and we know that they remained friends, but what we never understood was why it always had to be kept a secret. It always disturbed us, yet we have always kept the meetings to ourselves, though Mother never asked us to.*

*If meeting the Indian made our mother look as happy as it did, then it could not be a bad thing and we could never do anything to jeopardize that friendship. Willie and I knew that the man had died, Willie had heard it from another farmer, and Willie was the one to tell our mother. It is the only time in our lives that Mother took to her bed sick for three days.*

*We know in our hearts that the only thing that would create such sickness and sadness in our mother like that again would be the death of one of her children.*

*And now Willie will be putting himself in danger, and I know that it bothers him to think that our mother will be so ill again, like she was that time, if he were to be killed in battle.*

*He did not wait long to speak his peace. Willie cleared his throat several times and looked directly at Papa who had just finished saying the blessing over the food.*

*"Papa, I heard today when I was across the river that the Continental Army is headed here. They will be here within a day or so."*

*Papa looked up for a second, then back down at his food. "So, they bring the war directly to us. It was only a matter of time."*

*There was a long silent pause at the table. I looked at Mother and she had stopped eating and was staring at the center of the table. Her hands were folded on her lap.*

*O, it was terrible to see the color that had been in her face was gone.*

*She was so pale. My younger brothers continued to eat heartily. I tried to pretend to eat, but I was holding my breath.*

*"I will enlist when they arrive," Willie said quickly then. "Many of the soldiers' enlistments are due to expire, and they will need new men to take their places. I will be one of them."*

*What terrible silence. I pray that I will never hear such silence again. Papa stopped eating but didn't look up at Willie.*

*"Mother," Papa said after a long time, "control thy son."*

*"No, Mother will not control me, Papa. I am a man now, and I must do the right thing." I could not believe Willie would speak so to Papa. My heart beat so hard I thought everyone would hear it.*

*Papa slammed his fist on the table and everyone jumped except Mother; she knew it was coming. It was his way when he was thwarted. The only violence Papa would ever show.*

*"Woman," Papa said again, his voice very sharp now. "Thou will control thy boy. Thou will tell him why he cannot go to war. Thou will remind him that he is a member of the Society of Friends and thereby a pacifist and that no good comes from violence against thy neighbors."*

*Willie looked at our mother, but she could not speak. Her eyes shone in the candlelight and I knew she wanted to cry but would not allow herself to do so.*

*"Mother!" Papa said more demanding this time.*

*I could not bear it any longer. I stood up to Papa. "He wants to go, Papa…he is a man…an American…and it's his duty to fight for the cause of liberty! It is all of our duty."*

*Very quietly, almost in a whisper, Papa said to me, "Sit down, child." I did. My hands and legs were shaking and I couldn't hold my knees together because of the way I trembled.*

*Papa looked at Willie and said, "Thou needn't do it. I will be sending Jonathan in our family's stead."*

*"Jonathan is too young, and it is not fair to send a slave to do our work," Willie argued.*

*"Thou shalt not speak to me in that tone of voice…"*

*"Papa, I love you and I love my mother, sister and brothers. I want to cause no harm to this family. I am not going to enlist because I fear they'll take our land and send us away. I want to fight because I believe in what we are doing. I believe in a new nation. I believe that we should be independent to make our own laws and tax ourselves…"*

*"Thou knowest God?" our father asked him.*

"Yes, of course, but…"

"Thou knowest thy faith?"

"I am a Quaker and always will be. But I am not a pacifist."

"Thou cannot be one and not the other," Father told him, waving his fork in Willie's face.

"I can…I am!" O, Willie, how brave you were. How I long to be as brave as you are, my brother.

And then it happened just as Willie knew it would.

Father looked down at his plate and said, "Then get thy things and get out of my sight. I want nothing to do with thee again. If thou will be excommunicated from our Meeting, then thou will be excommunicated from this family as well."

I looked at Mother. She was barely breathing and she swayed slightly on her chair.

Papa said then, "And if thy mother will not control thee, then she can suffer the shame and bear the disgrace of a son who would kill, and receive no comfort from me if thou art to die." Papa's voice was very strange when he finished his sentence, and his own hands shook now. I could bear no more.

"No, Papa," I said to him. "No, thou cannot do this to thine eldest son."

"Will thou leave the room this moment," Papa said to me. "We have no need of your thoughts or thou may also find thyself without a family."

I stood up again and told him, "That would be fine. I will leave with Willie. I will also join in the revolution."

Mother finally found her voice and her tone silenced all of us when she said, "No!"

She looked at my brother and said, "Willie, it is forbidden that a Friend take up arms. However, as thou hast said, thou art a man. If thou will forsake all that thou hast been taught for what thou believeth is the truth, then thou must bear the consequences."

She looked at Papa then. "We have raised our children to be intelligent and honest. I will not disown my child for wanting what most men—and women, I feel I must add—want, and this is liberty. Our parents and grandparents came to this colony for just that reason—the right to believe, to think, and to worship as they wish. It is all they longed for, and they gave up everything to come here for that liberty. Sometimes we must fight for what we believe or we will lose the one thing our ancestors cherished most."

Mother looked at Willie then and said to him, "If this be thine own desire, and thou art willing to give up thy faith with a clear conscience because it is *what thou believeth in the depths of thy heart must be done, I will remain thy loyal and loving mother despite excommunication."*

*Dearest mother looked so old suddenly. "I do not know what the future will hold for any of us because of this war, but if thou shall join the army and survive, this will always be thy home if our land remains unscathed and still in our proprietorship. You must live with thine own conscience, son, as must I, and as must your dear father." She looked at Papa when she said the last, her voice was very quiet.*

*I ran from my place at the table and fell on my knees beside my dear Mother. I put my arm around her and rested my head on her arm, overcome by my feelings of gratitude, but also by sadness for her, knowing that she is suffering greatly because of the quarrel between her eldest son and her husband, and her own fear for my brother.*

*Papa stood and left the table…the room… and the house.*

*Believe me, yours faithfully, Juliana-Alma*

*7 December*

*They are here! They are quartering at many of the homes and lands across Bucks County, from north to south and east to west, almost five thousand in all.*

*Believe me, yours faithfully, Juliana-Alma*

*9 December*

*Willie told me today that the army is setting up a military hospital at Thompson's. General Washington hasn't heard from two divisions and they don't know what has happened to them. Willie said that the men who are here are low. They are sick, cold, hungry and unhappy. They need help, but what can we do? Willie told Mother that some of the troops will be coming this way and will need a place to camp. Since they stay close to the river, they will encamp at Willow Wood Farm, he is sure of it.*

*He told us that they need food and clothing as many of the men are in shirts and breeches with only tattered old blankets wrapped around them. And some wear rags on their feet; nothing but rags.*

*"I heard some of them saying that the army is done for and that we can't win," Willie told us.*

*There was anguish and disappointment on Willie's face. Mother saw it and touched his cheek with such tenderness and with tears in her eyes. "It is in God's hands, William," she told him. "He will guide General Washington. The Lord will lead and we must follow His will."*

*Believe me, yours faithfully, Juliana-Alma*

*10 December*

*Just as Willie told us, five hundred men have come to camp at Willow Wood. They have set up tents, those that have them, or they sleep on the frozen ground in the open on these cold December nights. They are pitiful to see. Some don't look any older than my youngest brother, and others are very much older than Papa.*

*Mother and Selma have gathered whatever materials they can find to make clothing for the men who are camped on our farm. They have even used some of their own gowns to make into shirts. They have taken whatever old clothes and boots that no longer fit my brothers out to the campsite to distribute to those who have the most need.*

*Selma and I help Mother bake all day and we are using all of the wheat and flour that we have. There will be none left shortly and there is no more to be found in Bucks County. Mother brews the leaves and bark from the willow tree to ease the pain of some of the wounded soldiers who aren't ill enough to be kept in the military hospital. She has become even more quiet than usual, and she sleeps only two or three hours each night. I hear her moving through the house and sometimes I can even hear her praying aloud.*

*Believe me, faithfully yours, Juliana-Alma*

*15 December*

*Almost all of our food is gone. The smoke house is bare, the root cellar holds but a handful of vegetables. Papa and the boys have gone up into the mountains and deep into the woods to hunt for game, and I have seen the soldiers in camp eating rats they have caught near the river.*

*I heard Papa telling Mother that he is disgusted with many of the loyalists around us who are hoarding their food, hiding it from the soldiers, while pretending that they themselves are starving. He even spoke aloud of it at Meeting, knowing there are even Quakers who are hiding food, but it is difficult to know which are patriots and which are Tories. Some of the loyalists even invite the officers to their homes and taverns, feed them and give them drink, pretending to be patriots, then in the dark of night they slink away to give information to the Tories and the British. The Doan boys and their gang are the worst offenders, and using the situation for their own advantage. They aren't much more than outlaws.*

*Late in the night, when they thought we were all abed, I heard Papa say to Mother that he won't fight, but he won't be a traitor to the cause. He declared that we are Americans and he vows to support the army in whatever way he can except to fight or allow his sons to fight. I am so proud of my Papa.*

*Believe me, faithfully yours, Juliana-Alma*

*17 December*

*We had nothing but fish soup without bread today. Our ale is so thin it is not much more than boiled water. Mother's medicinal herbs are used up and it pains her when she must turn away men who come to the door for help. We have done all that we can do for them now. My bother Mark pushed his dish away and was angry that we are hungry, but Mother told him, "It is the least we can do. These men will give their lives to obtain freedom for us, and we must do whatever we can to help them."*

*I know she is thinking of Willie. I know she is thinking that if he does enlist, perhaps some other family will help him when the time comes and he will need it.*

*Selma helps as much as Mother. She mends soldiers' clothing, tends to their wounds or illnesses, and when there is food, she cooks and bakes, but she says nothing for or against the war. She and Dorand don't think this is their war, but it will be in the end. Freedom must come for all of us. If we win this war, it will mean freedom for all slaves as well. Mother told her as much this noon, but Selma just raised her eyebrows in answer and said nothing.*

*Mother must be correct. The abolitionists will win their war, just as General Washington will win this other war. I long to see freedom for all God's children.*

*23 December*

*Selma came into our kitchen early in the morning, and she was smiling and her eyes were brighter than I've seen them in a long time. She was hiding something under her cape. When Mother and I looked at her, she opened the bundle over the table and a large piece of ham, potatoes, onions, carrots, nuts and a head of cabbage tumbled out. Mother and I could not speak we were so surprised.*

*"An officer came to my cabin and told me to bring all this to you, but to do it quietly so that no one saw. He said that seein' how kind your family has been to his men, he wanted your family to have a good Christmas, Mistress Bournes."*

*Mother sat on a chair as though her legs couldn't hold her.*

*"There's more," Selma told us laughing. "There's a jug of ale and wheat flour for bread still in my cabin. I couldn't carry all that he gave me."*

*Mother covered her face and I heard her sob, but when she stood again, she was composed. "Did he say his name?" she asked Selma. Selma told her that his name is Greene and he's staying at the Merrick's.*

165

*Mother looked out the window toward the camp, and for a moment I thought she was going to say that we must share all of the food with the soldiers, but instead she said, "We'll put it all in the root cellar and surprise everyone on Christmas Day. We may not celebrate Christmas the way the other Christians do, but at least we shall eat a proper meal."*

*O, how my stomach burned with the desire to eat the food right then. I have never known what it is like to be hungry before. I don't like it.*

*Believe me, faithfully yours, Juliana-Alma*

*23 December late night*

*The moon is high, but I cannot sleep. I borrowed the candle from the parlor so that I can write about the happenings of today. The joy of being given the food for a feast was soon gone. It was I who had to tell Mother the news, and I would have rather pulled my tongue from my head. Willie left this morning to enlist. And my brother Mark followed him. They went together, and all I could say to comfort her was that they will protect each other.*

*Willie told me that there is something afoot, that he was hearing rumors that General Washington is planning something but the officers are telling no one. He wanted to be a part of whatever is about to happen, and Mark decided that he didn't want to be left behind, although he had never shown any interest in the war before now.*

*All Mother said was, "Two sons...I must give two?"*

*I took her hand in mine and said, "Mother, they are doing what they must do. Thou hast to know that."*

*Then Selma came into the room, and she was crying. "My Jonathan," she said to Mother. "He's going to war. He went with your boys."*

*Mother was aggrieved. She said that wasn't possible, that Papa promised that he wouldn't send him in our stead, but Selma shook her head. "Friend James didn't send him. He joined himself."*

*"He's too young," Mother told Selma. "We will not send a third boy from this house. I don't care if we have to tell them that he is our slave and has no right to enlist of his own will without our permission. Two sons of Willow Wood are enough to sacrifice. I will fight to keep Jonathan home in a way that I cannot fight for my own sons."*

*Mother has never called Selma or Dorand our slaves before this day. But somehow I don't think Selma minded.*

*I am very tired. Suddenly the war does not seem as thrilling as it did before the Continental Army arrived. I feel weary in my soul and in my heart. Weary and worried for my brothers. I want to cry, but no tears come. I must read the scriptures and pray as I never have before. I fear that nothing will ever be the same at Willow Wood and I am deeply unhappy.*

*24 December*

*The men in camp are preparing for a cold and dreary feast day. They all appear to be in high spirits despite the wretchedness of their situation, and some even sing hymns that are familiar to me because I have heard these songs coming from the Anglican services that are held in Newtown and that I have heard my classmates sing when I was still in school. I feel sorry for those soldiers who are used to a festive holy day back when they were with their families. It has never bothered me that we do not celebrate Christmas Day as they do, but I feel for them now for they would be used to getting a gift or two and enjoy a table laden with meat or fowl. Perhaps some would come from a home that decorated their hearths and doors with fruit and holly.*

*But not today. Today they will sit around fires on the freezing ground and long for their mothers and fathers or their wives and children.*

*There are stories that the British are nearby and that the Hessians are encamped in Trenton. They are so close to us here. I wonder if that should have something to do with all the activity among the soldiers. Are they preparing for enemy troops to arrive?*

*We have not seen or heard from Willie or Mark since they left to enlist. We long to hear their voices and see their faces. The house is very quiet. Papa doesn't speak at all, and Mother keeps very busy, barely speaking to anyone. Even my little brothers are gloomy. They have taken to doing the work that Willie and Mark normally do as well as their own.*

*This morning General Greene came to speak to the soldiers at Willow Wood and when he saw Mother walking from the barn, he stopped to speak with her. I listened from the kitchen door and I heard her thank him for the food he had given Selma for our family.*

*"It is I who want to thank thee for your kindness to my men these past weeks," he told her.*

*Mother just smiled at him and together they walked toward the house. He had a limp and I was surprised that he spoke in the Quaker dialect. "Thou hast given us two new members of our army, as well," General Greene said then, "and I know that must have cost you dearly, especially because of your faith."*

*"You are a Quaker, sir?" Mother asked him.*

*"I am, I come from Rhode Island and I know that taking up arms is a difficult thing to do when reared in a Quaker family."*

Mother told him, "My boys know nothing of war—of fighting—and I fear they will misstep. For me it is not the fact that they want to fight for liberty, but more that I feel we never prepared them properly to defend themselves."

"Yes, I understand thy fear. I myself had to acquire books on the art of war and military strategy and study them carefully. I still have them, and if there is time, I will share them with thy sons. But I fear that time is scarce at this stage of the war."

Mother did not look comforted by this, and she began to walk toward the house again, with the General in step beside her.

"Is he a good general?" Mother asked him. "George Washington?"

"He is indeed."

"And is he a Godly man?"

"Yes, deeply devout, although not Quaker."

She smiled then. It was a sad smile, but I have not seen her smile for so long that it lightened my heart. "Then I must leave my sons in his—and thy—capable hands, and most of all, in the hands of our Creator."

General Greene nodded and touched Mother's shoulder. "If at all possible, I will watch over them for thou. If it will help, I want you to know that they will fight beside the bravest of men. This army looks ragged and weary, my dear lady, but there is a solid resolve and strength of character in each man who fights with us."

Mother looked out at the fields where the soldiers sat huddled around fires. "And my sons are two such men," she said. "Be safe, sir. I pray God will watch over all of you."

The bravest of men, the General called them. O, to be brave and to fight for what one believes to be right and just. I long to be counted as just such a person.

Believe me, faithfully yours, Juliana-Alma

27 December

How shall I begin? What I have done and what has been done to me in the last days are beyond any words that will explain. I have been impulsive and now I must do penance. Papa looks at me with great pain and yet also with great surprise in his eyes. Mother sighs and closes her eyes whenever I enter the room, although she has been kindly and forgives. My younger brothers think that I am a hero, even though they can never say it in front of Papa and Mother. I have been raised up in their esteem it seems by my foolishness. I must sleep and mayhaps on the morrow I will be able to write of my experiences.

Believe me, faithfully yours, Juliana-Alma

*28 December*

"*Keep your heads down and your rifles up,*" *I heard an older man call out to the soldiers around him. "It's as simple as that.*"

Until the day that I die, I will remember that man's voice and his words. I can only think that it was my great fortune to have heard them as I ran through the soldiers camped near McKonkey's Tavern. Most of the soldiers had left Willow Wood early on the morning of 25 December. Mother and I watched them march away and we both knew, although we said nothing to each other, that there was something afoot. Mother's hands shook violently as she prepared the morning meal, and she dropped Papa's dish when she took it away to clean it.

The food that we had secreted away for our special meal for Christmas was taken from the root cellar, but Mother, Selma, and I had not the excitement of when we first saw and planned our surprise. Three of Willow Wood's people would be missing, and we knew that they would certainly not have a warm and filling meal this day. Food was scarce among the soldiers, and my throat felt tight every time I thought of Willie, Mark and Jonathan hungry and cold while we ate in the warmth of our kitchen.

That was when the thought came to me, and I could do nothing to push it away. So I went into the barn, taking Mother's knife with me, and in the shelter of one of the stables, I cut off my hair as close to my scalp as I could without cutting myself. Then I put on the clothes I had taken from my little brothers' room. Dressed in britches and a blue flannel shirt, I took an old jacket from a hook near the door and a hat that was too large for my head and covered my ears almost to my shoulders.

I put the kerchiefs filled with slices of ham and bread, nuts and fruit that we shared at table that morning in the jacket's pocket and, sliding out of the barn carefully so that no one would see me, I ran as quickly as I could to the forest to make my way toward McKonkey's where I knew the soldiers were heading. When I arrived at the edge of the trees, I was amazed by all the soldiers gathered there along the river. Every soldier in the Continental Army must have been there. They had made new fires, and some cooked over them. Mostly they appeared to be sitting and waiting for orders.

I rubbed dirt on my face and then I searched until I saw the bright red hair that I knew could be no one else's but Willie's, so much like my own and Mother's. Then I noticed Mark sitting beside him. They looked lost and ill at ease there among all the other soldiers, some in torn and ragged uniforms. I called to Willie, but he didn't hear me at first. Then I called again, and Mark *looked up. I saw him touch Willie's shoulder and point toward me. I hastened toward them, and when I moved closer they both stood and I knew they were very surprised to see me—especially the way I was dressed. Before either of them could speak, I held my finger to my lips to silence them and not give me away.*

*"I had to find you," I told them in a whisper.*

*"Did Mother send you?" Mark asked me.*

*"She doesn't know. I slipped out right after our meal."*

*Willie pulled me down by the shoulder of my jacket and we sat huddled together. "What are you thinking? What mischief are you up to?"*

*"Whatever is happening, I am going with you," I told my brothers.*

*"No, sister, thou cannot." Willie hissed at me, but just as he started to say more, we were ordered to stand at attention. We got to our feet and stood shoulder to shoulder, both of my brothers' shoulders against my own.*

*General Washington came out of the tavern dressed in his uniform. It took my breath away to see him.*

*He addressed us, though I can barely remember anything he said, so taken was I with the scene before me. Then he ordered that the pamphlet "The American Crisis" be read aloud to all of us. A bitter wind had started to blow minutes before and a cold mist covered the land. I looked up at my brothers and they looked as much in awe as I felt.*

*"These are the times that try men's souls," the General's secretary read out. I held my breath as I listened and tears sprung to my eyes despite how hard I tried not to allow them when I heard him finish. "Tyranny, like hell, is not easily conquered, yet we have this consolation with us, that the harder the conflict, the more glorious the triumph."*

*Nothing would keep me from joining my brothers in this war now. If they tried to send me back, I would hide amongst the other soldiers, but I would not return to Willow Wood.*

*We sat again as the day grew colder, wetter, and dark, waiting for our turn in the Durham boats that would take us across the river to New Jersey. Hour after hour, the large, solid boats rowed across the river, dodging the ice flows, with the snow and sleet covering all of our backs and heads.*

*While we awaited our turn, Willie and Mark begged me to change my mind and return to Willow Wood, but I was resolute. Sleet and snow stung our faces, and Willie and Mark moved closer to me to protect me from the weather. When it was our turn to step into line to board a boat, Willie held each of our arms so that we would not be separated and he pushed us to the center of the boat so there would be less of a chance that we would fall overboard if the currents of the raging river took hold of the boat. We could barely see in the dark, brutal night.*

*An ice floe hit the side, and we were ordered to push it off. Several men reached over, almost capsizing the boat, and yet another ice floe hit the bow, changing our direction and forcing the men who were rowing to move more quickly and with greater effort to steer the boat in the right direction. What would have normally taken us but a few minutes to cross the Delaware from McKonkey's took more than an hour. This went on all evening and throughout the night, boats moving across and unloading the soldiers, then back again to the Bucks County side to board more.*

*O, what a night it was. O, what cold, what wetness enveloped us. Once we were on the other side of the river, there was more waiting until the last of the soldiers had been transported to New Jersey. We could hear the officers shouting orders, we could hear the horses whinnying and complaining about getting on the ferry for the crossing, we heard it even through the wind and the rush of the river.*

*And when all the soldiers, artillery and horses were finally together again, we realized that it had taken the entire night, for dawn was about to break. Thousands of men had crossed the black, turbulent waters in the boats that General Washington did not destroy when he first arrived on the shores of Bucks County but had hidden until this night.*

*We were split into two columns, with General Washington and General Greene in command of ours and the other under General Sullivan's command.*

*This way we would approach by the only two roads leading to the Hessian barracks in Trenton.*

*We followed one another through the snow and I noticed that there were smears and drops of blood from the feet of those men who had no boots or shoes. It was by that bloody path that my brothers and I followed toward the battlefield.*

*General Washington rode on his horse up and down the column encouraging us, urging us forward, and we followed him.*

*I slipped twice but was quick to get up so that no one saw. My heart pounded in my chest and my damp clothes clung to my skin. As we marched along, some men fell back, exhausted or in pain because of their feet. Before long, we met up with Jonathan who walked with another boy about Willie's age.*

*He looked familiar and smiled at me.*

*Suddenly, we heard shouts from the officers again, and then there were blasts of gunfire and cannons. I ran forward, propelled by my brothers and the other soldiers behind us. I felt myself being pushed onto my stomach by Willie, who handed me a musket and told me to shoot in the same direction he was shooting. I shot the gun. Willie handed me gun powder and told me how to reload just as he was doing with his own gun.*

*Willie had a much better aim, and I thought it would take much less time if I were to load one gun while he shot the other. And that is what I did for both Mark and Willie. They would shoot, hand me their guns, I would reload and hand it back to them, all three guns moving quickly from one set of hands to another.*

*We ran farther into the enemy camp and I closed my eyes when a man in a dark blue uniform fell directly in front of me, felled by Willie's bullet. Then I heard another man scream and looked up to see him lose his footing when Willie shot him.*

*We ran from spot to spot, and I was forced to shoot one of the guns I had just loaded when a Hessian carrying a bayonet lunged toward Mark. I saw him stop and grab his stomach and fall to his knees. I could not breathe. And then I saw him fall over onto Mark, and his bayonet pierced Mark's leg.*

*I lay on the ground unable to move, knowing I had just taken someone's life. I dropped the musket and looked at my hands and began to cry. Cracks and blasts surrounded me until I could no longer hear. Mark cried out in pain. I crawled to my brother's side and pulled the kerchief that had held our food from my pocket and wiped his leg. His pant leg was turning scarlet and I kept wiping at it.*

*"Juliana, there's no time," Willie shouted at me. "Take your gun and come with me." Then he said to Mark, "We'll be back to get you. Can you reload your gun?"*

*Mark nodded and using his elbows, he pulled himself closer to a tree for protection. "Go!" he shouted at me. "Go with Willie."*

*Jonathan and the boy who had been following him took Mark's place beside us. We ran together through the brush and into the open, then fell against the back of a building. Just as we finished reloading our weapons, three soldiers burst from the door on the side of the building and we all pulled our triggers at the same time. Two of the Hessians fell but a third turned his weapon on us.*

*Willie moved in front of me and a bullet hit his shoulder. I grabbed my musket and swung it against the side of the man's head. He staggered and looked at me with surprise, then closed his eyes and slumped down.*

*The boy with us helped Willie get to his feet and reload his rifle. A red stain spread from Willie's shoulder but there was nothing I could do. Then of a sudden all the shooting stopped and there was a great silence. We could see Hessian soldiers being taken prisoners by our own soldiers. General Washington sat upon his horse and watched, Generals Greene and Sullivan on each side of him.*

*Willie thrust his gun into my free hand and grabbed my jacket with his uninjured hand and pulled me back into the brush to where we had left our brother. We ran quickly and found him still leaning on the tree trunk, holding his leg.*

*"We won this battle," Willie told him, grabbing Mark's jacket with his good arm. "We have won this battle, Mark. Do you realize what this means? Do you know what this means to us?"*

*Mark and I looked at each other and then at Willie again. We were bewildered. And Willie smiled at us with tears in his eyes now.*

*"It means we haven't lost the war yet!"*

*Believe me, faithfully yours, Juliana-Alma Bournes, a soldier in the fight for independence…and may God help and forgive me, a murderer.*

*29 December*

*Willie and Mark have sent me home. Willie told me that it was too dangerous, not just for me, but for them because they felt they must protect me when in battle and it made it even more dangerous for them. I didn't want to leave them. Yet, their wounds had been attended to, and Mark refused to stay in the infirmary. He could walk on his leg once the wound was cauterized. And Willie's shoulder hurt, but it was not a serious wound. I cleaned and cared for their wounds for two days, and cooked potatoes in an old pot over the fire to feed them, until they told me that I had to leave. We were so close to Willow Wood, to the warmth of our home and the gentle caring of our mother. But they would not come with me. My time in the army was at an end, but theirs was just beginning. They would see it through until we won this war.*

*Before I left the camp, a few of the men who lived and worked in Bucks County and knew us before enlisting, would study me.*

*One of them, a man named Jenkins, asked Willie who I was and Willie told him that I was a cousin from our mother's side of the family. It was a lie to hide my identity.*

*"I saw him shoot," Jenkins said after looking at me a long time. "He's a good shot, that one. Two Hessians he brought down. Saved your brother Mark, he did."*

*Willie looked at me when Mr. Jenkins said it, but neither of us felt proud. I had taken two lives. I, a girl and a Quaker.*

*"He could have been shot himself, but he looked sharp and thought quick," Mr. Jenkins said again. "You're a good man."*

*When Mr. Jenkins walked away, Mark's mouth twitched as though he would smile, but Willie was very serious. "Thou art going home, Juliana-Alma. Today you will return. The man is right. You could have been killed."*

*"But I wasn't. I wasn't even wounded as both of you were."*

*"Thou art going home, sister. I shan't have thy blood on my hands. Nay, I will not have thy death on my conscience and I shan't lie about who you are any longer."*

*Willie told Mark to leave with me, but Mark said that he signed up as a soldier in the Continental Army and a soldier he will remain until the war is over. "It will be hard enough to face our father, but I won't do it with a wound. I won't look as though I am going home with my tail between my legs because I am hurt."*

*I didn't want to leave them and look a coward either. Then Willie put his arm around my shoulders and said, "Thou art my sister and I cannot see you killed. If you won't go home for me, do it for Mother. Please, sister, do not make this war even more difficult for her."*

*I knew I had no choice.*

*Mother stood just outside the door of the house when she saw me coming across the field. Her hands were covered in her apron and her sweet face and red hair looked even more beautiful to me than it had before I left. I didn't know what she would say or how she would receive me, but I knew that I wanted to be home with her after all and I began to run toward her. She took me in her arms and held me close as though she would never let me go.*

*Mother is a great believer in Holy Conversation and deep affection, and she has always ruled our house not with rods and punishment, but with kind words and high expectations.*

*There was no recrimination in her words when she said to me, "My daughter, you did what you felt you had to do. Now thou art welcome home." And then she inquired very slowly with her eyes closed, "Thy brothers?"*

*I could not tell her they had been injured. They were recovering and I couldn't allow her to worry. I told her they were well and they had sent me home to her. She embraced me again, and I breathed in the smell of spice from her clothing. I made up my mind then that I would never tell her of the two lives I took on the holiest of all days.*

174

*Believe me, faithfully yours, Juliana-Alma.*

*4 January 1777*

*There was another surprise battle. It was in Princeton this time. And General Washington's men won again. O, that I could have been there, for the thrill of it filled me again when I heard.*

*Believe me, faithfully yours, Juliana-Alma*

*5 January 1777*

*Jonathan came home today. I watched from my bedroom window as he came across the field making tracks in the snow. He was not alone. He was with the boy who had stayed with us in the battle of Trenton, the boy named Elias Smythe. They walked one behind the other; Jonathan in front, and Elias behind. I saw that they were carrying something between them. Then I realized they were carrying a person. A man. A brother. Mark.*

*Mother walked out to the field to meet them, her shawl across her shoulders, her hair covered by her lacy white cap. She walked so stiffly and strangely I would not have known her except for the shock of red hair that had fallen down her back. My brother Jerome followed her and stood behind her. Jonathan spoke to her, his eyes down.*

*Then I saw her fall to her knees in the snow. I saw her pull her shawl to her mouth with both hands so that she could silence the scream that would have come from her if she did not muffle it. I could not move. I could not move. I wanted to run to her, but I could not.*

*Believe me. Juliana-Alma*

*7 January*

*On the day that Jonathan brought Mark home to us, he told us that Willie was badly injured and had been taken to Hicks Tannery in Four Ends Lane to the new military hospital there. "He's bad, Mistress," Jonathan said, looking down, unable to meet my mother's eyes.*

*When my other brothers took Mark's body from Jonathan and Elias, Mother asked Jonathan to hitch the mare to our carriage. By then I had come out of my bedroom and walked to her, to touch her, to comfort her, but she pushed me away gently.*

*"There is nothing we can do for Mark now. I will grieve later for my boy, but now we must go to Hick's and see about Willie. Get blankets, clothing and food and bandages; put them in the carriage."*

*Elias came into the house with me and helped me to gather everything Mother wanted and carry it out to the carriage. Then he turned to me and asked, "Will thou forgive me? Will thou forgive me for bringing him home like that? Or will thou always think of this sad moment when thou thinks of me?"*

*I did not understand what he was asking. I could only stare at him, trying to understand.*

*"Miss Juliana-Alma, do not blame me for being the bearer of thy dead brother. I helped Jonathan so that you would know that I admired and respected him…and William…and you."*

*I could not speak so deep was my sadness, but I nodded, trying to let him know that I held no ill will against him for being the conveyer of great sadness and grief. He touched my cheek in a strange way. I think I may never forget that touch and the look in his eyes.*

*But there was no time for further talk. Mother, Selma and I climbed into the carriage and left quickly for Four Ends Lane, stopping twice at neighbors' asking for more blankets and supplies for the hospital.*

*The military hospital at Hick's is a frightful place. When we arrived, there were men everywhere, some were moaning and some were screaming in pain. Others just lie quietly waiting for death to come for them.*

*We found Willie against a wall. He was surrounded by other men, all of them badly injured. His shoulder was still bandaged from his earlier wound, but now his stomach was covered in blood. There was not even a blanket to cover him. He stared at the ceiling of the tannery, very quiet, unmoving.*

*Mother knelt beside his cot and I did the same on the other side. Selma took one of the blankets she carried and covered him quickly. Mother pressed her hand against his forehead and he turned his head to look at her. His face was so terribly white, his lips were gray.*

*"Mother" he said so softly we could barely hear him. Each breath he took was raspy. "Mother…Mark," he started to say, but Mother hushed him and told him to stay calm. "He tried to save me," Willie insisted upon telling our Mother, "but I was already hit three times. He covered me with his own body so that I would not be…"*

*Mother took in a jagged breath, but continued to smile at Willie. I put my head down on the edge of the cot and started to cry. I could not bear it. I could not bear to see Willie dying. I could not be strong like our Mother. I could not smile to reassure him as she was doing.*

*Mother stroked Willie's hair and prayed, "The Lord is my Shepherd, I shall not want…"*

*Selma prayed with her, but I could not speak. I could not pray. I could not lift my head to watch my brother die. Willie tried to pray with Mother, but his voice was so weak. I heard him whisper, "He maketh me to lie down…" It did* not sound like *Willie*. "*He restoreth my soul…*" It was a strange voice, a hollow, strained voice muffled by the noise from his chest, as though each breath he took caused him great effort. And then he stopped, any strength he had was gone.

Mother continued to recite the psalm she had taught us as children when we were just beginning to speak. Her gentle voice continued alone, "*Surely goodness and mercy shall follow me all the days of my life, and I will dwell in the House of the Lord forever.*"

Willie closed his eyes, grabbed Mother's hand tightly in his own, and said, "*Tell Papa I am sorry.*" Then all sound from him stopped.

Father walked into the building. His eyes were frantic as he searched for Willie. Someone had told him when he was in the shop in Newtown and he ran all the way to Hick's from there. He was too late. Too late to hear Willie say he was sorry. Too late to tell Willie that he forgave him.

He walked to where we knelt beside Willie, and Mother looked up at him but didn't utter a sound. Papa's shoulders dropped forward, his hat fell to the floor, and his head hung low against his chest. After a long moment, he reached down and picked Willie up in his arms, kissing Willie's cheek as he did, and carried him outside. We followed him.

Snow had just begun to fall. Selma grabbed what supplies we had left in the carriage and took them into the building while Papa placed his son on the seat of the wagon securing his body so that it wouldn't slump forward. Papa looked back at us, waiting for Mother to jump up onto the seat, but she shook her head. "*I am staying to help today,*" she said. "*I shall be home as soon as I can to bury my sons, but today I stay to help keep other mothers' sons alive. Selma will go with you and care for Willie and Mark until I return.*"

Papa looked at me then and I told him I was also staying to help the soldiers I had fought side by side with just a week before. Papa said nothing, climbed into the carriage and pulled Willie's head onto his lap and drove away with Selma seated at the back of the carriage.

We worked very hard. We cleaned wounds, we comforted the dying, and we assisted the doctors in whatever way we could. We were ordered to take clothing off the dead soldiers so that the uniforms or clothing, socks and boots could be given to the living soldiers. The bodies of the dead were placed in quickly constructed coffins that men in Four Lanes were making in their barns, and these were loaded onto a wagon, then brought down the road to an open field where they were buried.

I took the food Mother had brought and filled a large black cauldron that *was over a fire pit just outside the building with vegetables, deer meat and water. While the food cooked, I tended to those men who were outside the hospital. I took poultices made of old bread, bran and oatmeal which had been soaked in Mother's herbs and placed them on shoulders, arms and legs.*

*I worked steadily while tending to the food in the cauldron.*

*A soldier walked over to me and told me to hold his gun while he put more wood on the fire for me. I held the gun with one hand and stirred the food with the other. A man sitting against the building with paper in his hand called to me.*

*"Turn toward me a minute, Miss," he said.*

*I looked over in his direction. He started to sketch on the paper, looking up at me once, and then down again at the paper. A young soldier sitting next to him leaned over to peek at the paper, then looked back at me.*

*"Why, he's drawing your image, Miss. That's her, ain't it?" he asked the man beside him.*

*The man with the paper and pencil nodded but kept sketching. Then he stood and handed me the paper. It was of a young woman, holding a gun and a spoon, standing near a cauldron.*

*"Surely my skirt isn't this tattered," I said to him. "And you have given me long hair. My hair is chopped short under my cap."*

*He patted my cheek. "Aye, but the clothing represents the sad and tattered life that has suddenly become yours, my young Miss. When first I saw you days ago at the battle in Trenton, fighting beside your brothers, you were a boy. Aye, do not look surprised," he told me, "I recognize you. I am an artist and I study faces. Today I imagine your hair as it was before that Christmas day—the way it will be again one day—and I drew it here."*

*I looked again at the picture. How could he have known who I was?*

*As though he knew what I was thinking, he said to me, "The color of that hair is unmistakable. I wish I could paint it."*

*I touched the ragged ends of my hair and felt my face heat up as though it was on fire.*

*I asked him if I could keep the sketch. He looked very sad then; very weary. "Yes, you may," he said. "Keep it for posterity so that your children and their children will know that you fought bravely and fiercely in an important battle in this war. You aren't the first woman to do so, and you won't be the last, but in this moment in time, you bear the mark of a woman who fights for a new nation."*

*Believe me, faithfully yours, Juliana-Alma*

# *Sixteen*

Lillian put the pages of her manuscript down after reading it to Ann in the infusion room. Ann had listened attentively, saying nothing.

"Well?" Lillian asked.

"It's pretty good," Ann said. "I've never been a student of history, but I find it fascinating, and not just because she's our ancestor. I didn't know how important Bucks County was in the Revolution. Did you?"

"Not until I started the research for this chapter," Lillian admitted.

A voice intruded upon them from the other side of a curtain which separated the infusion chairs. "Neither did I."

Lillian and Ann looked at each other. Lillian grimaced, and walked over to the curtain and pulled it aside a little. "Oh my God, I'm so sorry. Were we bothering you? I thought I was reading quietly. I didn't even know you were in there."

A woman of about seventy years of age sat in the chair. An intravenous line dripped chemo into her left arm and she was covered with a soft, colorful afghan. Her hair was a silvery gray, cut short and stylish. She was pale, but her eye makeup was put on with an expert hand and she wore pearls over her dark blue turtleneck.

"Don't apologize. I loved it. It's a fascinating story. Is it a book you're reading to your friend?"

Lillian smiled. "Not yet."

"Oh? Are you writing this story?"

"I am," Lillian told her. "But it wasn't for anyone's ears at this point. I just finished this chapter last night."

The woman thought it over a moment, then said, "Pull the curtain open and let me meet your friend."

Lillian did as she was told and said, "This is my cousin Ann."

The woman introduced herself to them then and studied Ann's face. Millicent, dressed now in a crisp white coat over black trousers and a cream colored blouse, came over and started to unhook Ann from the IV that was attached to the port in her chest. Like Dr. Meg, Millicent shared all the duties with the nurses—all equal in caring for their patients, no task too small, too unimportant.

"How are you doing?" the physician's assistant asked Ann. Ann was as fond of Millicent as she was of Meg Raphael. Although not at Ann's chemo treatments every week, she was solicitous of her patients and made certain she saw them at least once a week, and if she didn't, she'd call them to make sure each one was doing well, not feeling ill, and if they were, she would come personally to the house to see why and write out a prescription for something—whatever she thought was best—to ease their nausea or discomfort. She cared about their psyche as much as she did about their health. To Millicent, the quality of life had more to do than just not feeling ill.

In fact, she persuaded Ann to join a fundraising committee for an event that would raise money for the hospital. At first, Ann resisted, thinking she wouldn't feel up to it, but Millicent insisted, and Ann complied and started to enjoy the activities and meetings. It kept her mind off her treatments, made her feel as though she was doing something worthwhile for the place that was offering help to her.

"I'm good, thanks," Ann replied, touching Millicent's soft brown hand in affection. "The time went quickly today." She stood up from the lounge chair with Millicent's assistance, got her sea legs after sitting so long, and then walked over to her neighbor.

"It was nice meeting you. I am sorry if we bothered you."

The woman's eyes filled with tears then. She reached out and took Ann's hand.

"You're so young," she whispered. "Much too young."

Ann patted her shoulder gently.

"I'm fine. Don't be upset over me. You have your own worries."

The woman grabbed for a tissue from the box on a table next to the chair. "Today's my first day of chemo," she said, dabbing at her eyes and nose.

"Then I guess we'll see you tomorrow," Ann said. "Will you be here at the same time?"

The woman nodded, and Ann touched her hand. "Okay, then it's a date."

"Will you read more of the story?" she asked, looking at Lillian.

"Do you want me to?"

"I enjoyed it thoroughly. It helped me pass the time."

"Okay, then I'll read more of it to both of you tomorrow, but it will only be half of a chapter. I'm not quite finished with that one yet."

"But can't you tell us what happened to that family after their sons were killed?" the woman asked.

Lillian considered a long minute, not sure if she should give away the rest of the story. Then she said, "Their father drowned in the river in the April thaw that year. There were rumors that he had committed suicide; apparently he had lost his faith after losing his sons. But Germaine denied it and Juliana-Alma protected his memory the best way that she could. The story didn't end all that badly. Juliana married Elias Smythe who came directly to Willow Wood when the war was over to ask her to marry him, and he took over the land. They had five children; the youngest was a girl, who inherited the land." Lillian looked over at Ann, "Our great-great-great grandmother, Josepha."

Ann and Lillian left with a flurry of goodbyes, and walked to the car in silence. Finally, Ann said, "Looks like you've got a lot of writing to do if you're going to have something new to read to us every day. You're going to have to keep your nose to the grindstone, lady."

Lillian groaned, unlocking the car with the remote, "I hate you, cousin. You do know that, right?"

They laughed as they got into the car.

Lillian suddenly felt lighter, happier than she had in a long time. She was writing, which was the love of her life, and she was just a day away from the other love of her life coming to visit her. She didn't dread Dan's and his family's visit now. She didn't dread writing the book anymore, either. There was only one dread she still had to conquer.

She looked over at Ann who was peaked and pale from the infusion, but sitting straight up, looking better and healthier than she had just a few weeks earlier. Maybe she wouldn't have to dread that anymore either.

∽

Lillian put the vase of flowers on the dresser in the guest room, plumped up the pillows, and smoothed the bedspread. She tried to picture the elegant, cosmopolitan Louise in the quaint antique-filled room. No match there, but at least it would be comfortable for her.

She heard the car coming up the driveway. Here we go, she thought. Then she heard the screen on the kitchen door squeak open and then slam shut, and she knew the kids had gone out to wait in the driveway. They were curious about these new guests, and they'd pestered her with questions about who they were, how did she know them, what were they like, would they play badminton with them?

Lillian knew she should run down the stairs to greet the New York arrivals, but instead she stood at the guest room window and looked down to watch the car approach and stop. Jessica was the first to get out of the car. Her dark brown curly hair was pulled up in a clip and she wore jeans and a white tee shirt. Lillian hadn't seen her in a year, and she was amazed at how much more mature Jessica looked. Louise and Dan stepped out of the car at the same time, and Lillian's heart leapt when she saw him. It always did.

She bounded down the front stairs, and burst through the front door. Dan was already introducing himself to Suzy and Philip, touching Suzy's head with his large left hand, while shaking Philip's with his right. He didn't bend down to them, but instead, stood up straight and tall and addressed Philip like a peer. "It's great to meet you, Phil, after hearing so much about you from Lillian."

Lillian threw herself into Louise's arms. "I'm so glad you're here," she said to this woman who was her best friend in the whole world.

"Could you live any farther in the sticks?" Louise asked, but returned the embrace with her usual warmth.

Jessica demanded Lillian's attention then. "Hey, what about me?" and without letting go of Louise, Lillian reached out and pulled Jessica into the embrace. "My people...my wonderful people," she said, kissing Jessica's forehead.

"I loovvve this place," Jessica said, looking up at the old stone building. "It's so gorgeous...it's so...I don't know...old, you know, but *nice* old."

Lillian laughed and let go of them. Dan was standing to the side watching, still stroking Suzy's hair with one hand and holding Philip's shoulder with the other.

She smiled at him. "You found us," she said.

"I found you," he agreed, opening his arms to her then. She moved into them, putting her arms around his waist. "I'll always find you," he whispered into her ear before kissing her lips.

Lillian let her head drop back and looked up into his face. "You like my little brats?" she asked, indicating Suzy and Philip.

Suzy giggled and Philip smiled. "She always calls us that," Suzy said. "She calls us brats because she really loves us but doesn't want to admit it."

Lillian and Dan were still looking into each other's eyes, but they laughed at what Suzy said. "She's way beyond her years in psychoanalysis," Lillian informed him.

"I'd say she's got your number," Dan said.

Jessica walked over to Suzy and squatted down in front of her. "I like your shirt," the teenager told the little girl. "I'm crazy about princesses," she added, pointing to the princess dressed in pink on Suzy's shirt.

That was all she had to say. Suzy had a new Best Friend Forever at that very instant, and she took Jessica's hand. "Come to my room. Wait 'til you see what I have—all princesses, all the time, or that's what Lilly says."

"Can I say hello to your brother first?" Jessica asked her.

"No, he doesn't like girls. Just ignore him," Suzy said pulling Jessica into the house. But Jessica smiled brightly at the boy, who blushed a deep red at receiving her attention. "Mommy," Suzy called out as she passed Ann just coming out of the house, "this is my new bbf, Jessica, and she likes princesses. I'm taking her to my room."

"Do you mind?" Ann called to Jessica, but they were already halfway up the steps.

"I'll be fine," Jessica called back, already disappearing around the corner of the staircase.

Ann joined the others in the driveway. She immediately held out her hand to Dan's sister. "You must be Louise," she said.

Louise took Ann's hand and leaned in for a quick kiss on the cheek. "I am, and I'm very, very happy to meet you, Ann. Thank you for putting up with us this weekend. There are only three of us, but we are like a circus when we pile in like this."

"I'll love it!"

Dan and Lillian let go of each other and turned toward Ann. "This is Dan," Lillian said to her cousin.

"I figured as much," Ann said smiling and taking his hand.

"Thanks for the invitation," he said. "Your home is beautiful."

"Come in and see more of it," she invited, taking Louise's arm and leading them inside. Dan put his arm around Lillian and she looked up at him again and allowed him to place a kiss on the tip of her nose.

They cooked dinner on the gas grill and ate in the gazebo.

Suzy was glued to Jessica's side, and the teenager was very patient with her, agreeing to polish Suzy's fingernails, toenails, and to fixing her hair just like Jessica's was styled—which meant no style at all. They played with Barbie dolls during the meal. Lillian and Jessica exchanged several warm glances, and Lillian thanked the girl with her eyes.

Dan promised to throw the football around with Philip after they finished eating, and he kept his word. "Want to join us?" he asked Louise.

"Not on your life," she answered, wiggling her perfectly manicured fingers in the air.

"You?" he asked looking at Lillian.

"I'm a girly girl, too…I just don't look like it," she said with a smile.

"Oh, you look like it," he said before grabbing the football from Philip and throwing it across the yard with a shout to the boy to "go long."

Philip ran and jumped up, catching the ball in midair. The ladies cheered from the gazebo.

"This is so good for Philip," Ann said, her eyes glued to her son. "I'm afraid we really are a little too girly around here for a boy."

"Daddy missed out on having a boy," Jessica said, pulling a frilly top over Barbie's head and covering the doll's ample bust. "This is good for him too."

Lillian moved from her chair to sit closer to Jessica and she put her arm around her. "I haven't seen you in more than a year, kiddo. I've missed you. You're taller…and a little curvier, too."

Jessica blushed, but didn't let on that she was embarrassed. "I am. You should see me in a bikini."

"Your father lets you wear a bikini?" Lillian kidded with her.

"He doesn't know."

"That's the way, Jess. What he doesn't know won't kill him."

Ann was watching them closely. A smile played on her lips. Lillian said to Ann, "She's a good kid, this one…head on straight, no baggage, smart and sassy."

Ann nodded, "I can see that."

"She borrowed my Louis Vuitton heels last week," Louise said, not smiling, but Lillian knew her well enough to know that Louise was secretly delighted that her teenaged niece thought her shoes were cool enough to borrow.

"Those shoes are bangin'," Jessica said, her eyes widening. "She won't give them to me though."

"No I won't."

"What size do you wear, Jessica?" Ann asked.

"Eight and a half, why?"

"I have a pair of Manolo's that you can have. They hurt my feet."

"Are you *serious*?" Jessica said, putting the Barbie down on the table, her eyes wide. "Wait...*seriously*?"

"I am," Ann assured her. "I've had them a few years, but never wore them."

"Story?"

"Urban."

"Color?"

"Pale pink satin d'Orsay. I have Jimmy Choo Lolitas, too. Can't wear them, so they're yours if they fit."

"OHMYGOD!!"

"Wait a minute," Lillian said holding up her hand. "Wait just one minute here. How come you didn't offer them to me, Ann, old cousin, old pal? How come I didn't even know you have Manolos or Choos?"

Ann shrugged. "You're not the Manolo Blahnik type."

Lillian turned her head to look at Jessica in disbelief, but Jessica nodded and pressed her lips together. "You're not...you just aren't, Lillian. Face it," she agreed with Ann. "And even if you were—*too late*! She gave them to *me*."

Ann explained to Lillian where they were in her closet and told her to go up with Jessica to get them so Jessica could try them on.

"Oh, they'll fit," Jessica said, moving quickly from the gazebo, pulling Lillian with her. "I'll make them fit!"

Lillian and Jessica left the gazebo, with Lillian asking no one in particular, "What's a Manolo type? Why am I not a Manolo type?"

Louise took the abandoned Barbie doll and smiled down at Suzy, who looked completely abandoned and crestfallen when Jessica left her. "I love Barbie. Can I play with you for awhile?"

Ann was so grateful she almost cried. *What nice people they all are. What good people.*

One of Philip's friends from a few doors away came into the yard and Philip looked at Dan, not knowing what to do. "It's okay, buddy...you go ahead and play football with your friend. I'll get myself a drink. We'll finish our game tomorrow."

He walked to the gazebo and took a long drink of lemonade. "I'm really out of shape." Then looking at Ann, he said, "What a great piece of property you have here."

Ann stood up. "Would you like to walk up the canal path a little? I'll tell you about its history."

"Let's go," he said, holding his hand out to her.

They walked to the edge of the property, over the foot bridge and onto the soft towpath. Ann told him the story of the canal, the boat captains and the mule drivers who worked from before dawn until long after sundown, the famous Pennsylvania artists who made a living painting the canal in the early part of the twentieth century. He listened attentively, asked questions, and was captivated by the history of the canal and the historic county.

"We have ancestors that fought in the Revolution," Ann said. "They were Quakers. The Irish Catholic ancestors came later with the boat captains on the canal." Ann continued proudly, "Lillian's been doing a lot of research"

"She told me about Juliana-Alma…fascinating story."

They walked in silence for a while. The leaves were still lush and green and the river flowed quietly on one side of them, the canal on the other side.

"Dan, I know that Lillian went to stay with you during the summer when she left here. I gather she confides everything in you. I can't imagine what kind of person you must think I am because of what I did. Were you angry?"

"On the contrary, it made me very sad."

"Sad for her?"

"Sad for you, Ann. Sad for your beautiful children. And yes, sad for Lillian. But it also made me hopeful."

Ann cocked her head, unsure of what he meant.

"Hopeful for Lillian…that by helping you, she can help herself. I have to tell you, I knew she was very upset because she offered to marry me. Ten years I've been asking her to marry me. Ten years she's said no. Then she turns up, sobbing, which I've never seen her do before, and she tells me to get the license."

"Then why didn't you jump at it?"

"I wanted to, Ann. Oh, how I wanted to, but it wouldn't have been the right thing to do. She had to come back here to face her demons—as I always say. She hates when I say it; she tells me it's cliché.

"Demons, are we?" she asked, knowing that it wasn't what he meant at all, but couldn't help tease him a little.

"Angels are more like it," he said. "When I get her to agree to marry me, Ann, I want all of her—mind, body, and soul."

"This may not be the way, Dan. I'm just adding more difficulty."

"I don't know about that," he said, sitting down on the path to look out at the river and pulling her down with him. He picked up some pebbles and started to throw them into the water. "I think this is just the way to do it. I have a gut feeling Lillian is going to come out a restored person. She's better already. I've never seen her quite this relaxed, and dare I even say it, contented. I knew she'd be good with your kids…she's always been great with Jessica, although she loves to say she hates kids. She's such a paradox. She's all the good things she doesn't think she is. I think she's going to learn what she's really made of by being here with you."

"And if I die?" Ann asked quietly, staring out at the river.

"And if you do?" he asked her.

She gave him a sideways look. "First, thanks for not saying, 'Oh, you won't die.' You're just about the only person who hasn't said that to me. Secondly, if I die, will Lillian take the kids? If she does, will she resent it? Will you?"

He thought a long time before answering her.

"Ann, you want me to predict the future, and I refuse to even try. So let me just say this. I think Lillian loves them; I *know* she does. When we were in New York, whenever we passed a little girl Suzy's age, Lillian had a sweet story to tell me about Suzy. If we passed a boy Philip's age, she did the same thing—only she worries about him more than she does Suzy. She didn't even know she was doing it. Every child reminded her of them and she couldn't wait to tell me what they do and what they say and how they are. She cares about them. I can't see her deserting them."

He shuffled over onto his hip to face Ann, stretching his khaki-covered legs straight out. "Will she resent it? Probably she will at times. Don't all parents resent their kids sometimes? Will I? I'm honestly not sure, Ann. I'd like to think that I've evolved enough to be a good, loving, kind, compassionate, unselfish guy—if there is such a thing. Yet, I know that I've waited so long for the love of my life to finally settle down with me that maybe I will resent having to share her. But it won't be with just your kids. I'll resent sharing her with Louise, Jessica, and I imagine your brother will be in that mix too."

Ann was so moved by his honesty that her eyes welled up.

He misunderstood. "I'm just trying to be honest…"

"No," she said, silencing him. "I know you are and I'm grateful for it. Honesty is the one thing I need more than anything else right now when talking about the future. Everyone is always telling me that they don't have a crystal ball, but can I tell you something?"

He reached out and took her hand in his and the warmth from his palm surged through her, making her feel brave and protected.

"Tell me anything" he said sincerely.

"I think I saw into the future just now. I like what I see. You *are* a good, decent, kind and compassionate man. Thank you, Dan. If anyone can make my cousin happy, it's you. She's got to marry you."

"From your lips to God's ears," he said.

He pulled her to her feet gently.

Lillian approached them on the towpath. "Hey, you two; what kind of conspiracy are you up to?"

"Shall we tell her?" Ann asked, pursing her lips.

"Nah, let her suffer," he said, still holding Ann's hand in his as they walked side by side toward Lillian.

"Your turn," Ann said to Lillian. "But I warn you…I tired him out." Ann walked away from them, but before she did she whispered to Lillian, "This is one sexy and wonderful man."

Dan laughed and Lillian shook her head. They looked at each other, not touching, just taking in each other's presence.

Lillian searched his eyes, and the answer she was looking for was there.

"I love you," he affirmed vocally.

She placed her hand on his chest. "I know and I love that you love me. Did she tire you out too much for a kiss?"

"Never," he told her, pulling her close to him and covering her mouth with his. "Got any good hiding places we could escape to?" he asked her.

She did.

❧

The weekend went by too quickly. They took boats out on the river on Saturday morning, played cards on Saturday night, cooked, baked, ate, and cooked again. They hit all the historical sites they had time for and shopped in the local, quaint shops.

They caught lightning bugs in the evenings, and grabbed flashlights to play manhunt in the dark—all of them, adults included. All except Louise, who watched from the gazebo and then whispered in Suzy's or Philip's ear when she knew where the others were hiding.

Jessica never complained that she was bored. She never complained about Suzy's possessiveness. She teamed up with the little girl and Philip when the group played Monopoly, and by the second night Suzy left her mother's room and slept in a sleeping bag next to her own bed where Jessica was sleeping. The Manolos and Choos were excellent payment for babysitting.

And then it was Monday morning.

Lillian got up early so that she could make the coffee and sit in the den with Dan for a little while before everyone else woke up. She brought two coffee mugs into the room and nudged him awake. He groaned and let his legs fall off the edge of the couch, making room for her under his blanket. They snuggled there silently for a while.

"Don't go," she said into his neck.

"I wish," he answered

"This place is going to be so empty and lonely when the three of you leave."

"My heart is going to be empty without the four of you."

She nuzzled against his hairy chest. "Do you like them, Dan?"

"I like them," he answered. "I like them a lot."

"You still need to meet Joey," she told him.

"I got a feeling I'm going to like him, too, if he's anything like you and Ann."

"He's a good person, Dan. He's going to be a great man." She laughed out loud, "I guess he is a man…but he seems like a kid to me."

Dan didn't answer, but squeezed her shoulder pulling her a little closer.

"Don't go," she said again.

"Come visit New York," he urged her. "You love the city in the autumn."

"I will. Ann can spare me for a few days. She's so well now, Dan. If you had only seen her six weeks ago, you wouldn't think she is the same person. She could barely walk across the room, and now she's like her old self again. I can't believe how well she is. I think she's going to be okay, Dan."

"Have you been working?" he asked.

"On the book? Yes, for hours at a time. But I'm not freelancing. I couldn't commit to traveling. I need to work from here to help Ann."

"How about editing? You can do that from here. I can email the manuscripts to you."

"Edit someone else's work? What about my book?"

"It's an income and you could edit in the morning and write your book the rest of the day."

She sat up straight. "Hey, that's not a bad idea. You're not as dumb as you look."

He rolled his eyes. "Now you realize that?"

"I like it. When will you send me the first manuscript?"

"First I have to send you a contract."

"You don't trust me?" she asked, pretending to be wounded.

"I don't own the company. I'll email it tomorrow."

She kissed him. "You are brilliant, Danny boy, aren't you?"

# Seventeen

"Come with me," Lillian said to Ann one morning. "I want to look for something. Do we have a shovel or a rake?"

Ann laughed, "You know we do. I use it in the garden all the time."

"Right," Lillian said, as though she really hadn't noticed.

She had worked on the book until the early hours of the morning. Ann heard Lillian enter her bedroom just an hour before it was time to wake the kids for school. Yet she was up by ten and her eyes were bright with excitement. "You won't believe this," she said as she pulled Ann from the kitchen and into the back yard.

They walked into the garage, which had at one time been the carriage house, and Lillian said, "Go get the shovel."

Lillian walked to the far end of the building where their grandfather used to store lawn furniture. She pushed some old furniture toward the walls and cleared a space in the center of the area.

"What are we looking for?"

"I finished one of the journals last night—Selina's journal. Apparently, right before the Civil War, Selina's grandfather and father were involved in the Underground Railroad."

"This place was on the Underground Railroad?" Ann asked, shocked. "I never heard that. Wouldn't we have heard that?"

Lillian shrugged, taking the shovel from Ann. She tapped on the wooden floor boards. "I'm looking for a hollow sound. The hiding place was in here somewhere, under the floor. In the journal it said it was near the center beam to the right."

"Oh, Lillian, this floor must have been replaced years ago.     They wouldn't still be the same boards."

"They look like they are...why wouldn't they be? The floor under where we park the cars has been cemented, but this area is still just wood—old wood. If we never had termites, then why wouldn't the wood be the same?"

Ann shrugged and leaned against a half wall. "Imagine," she said, "our ancestors walked and talked and worked right here in this building all those years ago. I never really thought of it before…I mean, just to think…"

"And slaves hid beneath its floor."

Lillian kept tapping on the boards, starting at the center and moving first one way and then the next. She looked up suddenly, "Did that sound different?"

Ann made a face. "I don't know…I wasn't paying attention."

"Oh, for heaven's sake, Annie, get over here and listen."

Lillian tapped the shovel in several places and then they both noticed that there was a different sound—a hollow sound—in one spot. She continued to tap to the left, and the hollow sound continued.

She moved to the right and the sound changed. They searched for a trap door, but all the boards were solid. "I need a saw."

Ann said, "You'll cut your hand off…no, you can't cut a hole in the floor of the garage."

"Really, you sound like you're talking to Suzie," Lillian said. "Get me a saw. There has to be a saw in here somewhere. Granddad kept all his tools in here."

Together they walked into their grandfather's workroom and looked for a saw. "Okay, here's a hand saw," Ann said, pulling one down from a peg where her grandfather kept his tools above a scarred and well-used work table. "But how do you get it through the wood to begin with?"

"Good question," Lillian said looking around. She found the drill case. There was no bit on the drill, so they searched the drawers of the table until they found a little white box where each drill bit lay in its own section.

She took the largest one out and attached it to the drill.

They walked back to the spot where the shovel was and Lillian got on her knees and started to drill into the wood. The bit was dull but eventually it penetrated the hard board; once it did, it sank quickly. She pulled it out and stuck the tip of the handsaw into the hole and started to push and pull. Within seconds her arms began to ache. Just as she sat back on her heels to rest a minute, she heard a loud whizzing sound behind her.

"Of course, an electric saw would work, too, I suppose," Ann said, smiling at Lillian as she turned it on and off a few times for affect.

"Give me that," Lillian said.

"Promise me you'll be careful," Ann said pulling it back a little, away from Lillian's reach.

"Yes, mother, I'll be careful."

Ann held out plastic goggles to her, "But you never thought of wearing these, did you? See you weren't going to be careful."

Lillian gave Ann a warning glance and grabbed the goggles, which were almost impossible to see through because of their age. They were yellowed and there were scratches across the lenses. "I *will* cut my hand off with these stupid things blurring my vision."

Within a few seconds of holding the saw to the floor boards, the blade sank through, surprising both of them.

Lillian continued to saw through the wood, trying to stay in a straight line, but with difficulty. Then she stopped, sat back again, rubbing first one knee and then the other.

"Hey, Lilly, what are we going to do with the hole in the floor when you've finished cutting it up?"

Lillian rolled her eyes. "Annie, for heaven's sake!"

She continued to cut a square, stopping to rest her knees now and again.

Her body felt strange from the vibration of the saw and she tried to shake out the sensation.

She put the saw down, placed her fist on the floor to push herself up to a standing position, and when she was almost up, but still leaning against the boards, there was the slightest sound of a crack, and suddenly the uneven square she'd just cut caved in, taking her with it.

Ann screamed when Lillian disappeared into the hole. "Lillian!" She ran to the edge. Lillian was lying on broken floor boards and dirt about six feet down, within a perfectly square room with walls made of flagstones and bricks. "Lilly, are you all right?" There was barely enough light from the garage window to see down to where Lillian was.

Lillian gingerly stretched out her legs and then her arms. She winced when she put out her right arm. She grabbed it with her left. "Uh, oh, I think I sprained my arm or something."

"Is it broken?"

"I don't know…I don't think so…just sore. It's just the wrist. I must have landed on it. "Damn" she swore trying to get up. "My hip hurts, too."

"Wait, I'll get a ladder and come down to help you. Lie still."

Ann ran over to the ladder that was hanging from pegs in the garage wall. She had a hard time getting it down and had to stand on a pail to reach up high enough to pull it down. When she got back to the hole, Lillian was sitting with her knees pulled up, her wrist in her left hand.

"Oh my God," Lillian said looking around. "Oh my God, Annie, get down here and see this."

Ann placed the ladder on the floor and pushed the bottom carefully into the hole until it reached the dirt floor. She moved her leg around it and started to climb down. When she reached the ground, she turned quickly to Lillian and helped her cousin to her feet. Lillian was staring at one of the walls and Ann looked to see what had caught her attention.

There was a mural painted on one of the walls. It was of the canal, and standing on a canal boat were three people, a young African-American man and two women.

Beside the canal, standing next to a willow tree, there was a young white woman in a white dress holding a green and yellow shawl around her shoulders. Her brown hair was tied up in a blue ribbon.

"Who do you think they are?" Ann asked as they moved closer to look at the mural.

"The people on the boat are escaping slaves. Their names are Morris, Thessie, and Ruth."

Ann looked down and saw something shining on the dirt beneath the pieces of wood that had fallen with Lillian's weight. She bent to pick it up and when she did, she found a few more things…a button, several pieces of glass, a pencil. In the corner were a pair of wire rimmed eye glasses, the lenses missing.

The tiny room was surprisingly unspoiled except for a few cobwebs and the remnants of insects.

"Breathe it in," Lillian said, her fingers tracing over the images on the wall. "You are standing in a place that is filled with historical presence, Annie." She searched the wall very carefully and then said, "Ah, ha! Here it is…"

"Here what is?"

"Mos Adamson…a name. No date, though."

"Who is that?"

"The painter. It's a long story. Let's get out of this hole and you can wrap my wrist up while I tell you. Then we need to dig around the willow tree to look for a plaque—a headstone for a dead body."

"Ew. You're full of mystery today, lady," Ann said, helping Lillian up the ladder.

When they reached the top and stood in the garage again, she pulled the ladder up. "We've got to do something about that hole, though. The kids could fall into it."

Lillian led the way out of the garage, "They won't fall into it."

"You did," Ann reminded her. "It's an accident waiting to happen." She put away the saw and the drill while Lillian waited.

"Okay, we'll cover it up somehow, but first we need to take photographs of it."

When they got to the house, Ann took an ace bandage out of the cabinet where she kept all the first aid items. "Shouldn't you go to the Emergency Room for an x-ray?" She asked, looking at Lillian's wrist. It was beginning to swell.

"Nah, I'm fine. I can move it all around. I'll put ice on it."

Ann wrapped the wrist, put a bag of frozen peas on it, handed Lillian two Advil and poured them each a glass of iced tea.

"Okay, what's the story? We have four hours before the kids come home."

Lillian leaned on the table, the bag of peas balanced on her wrist, and started telling the story. "Sean Ginley was a canal boat captain who married Hannah Hewlett whose family owned Willow Wood. She was an only child, and she was almost thirty by the time they married. There are love letters in the chest from Sean to Hannah that he mailed from almost every town along the canal route from Easton to Bristol, wooing her until she agreed to marry him. Her mother was dead by then, but her father still farmed the land and he had built a special stable for the mule teams that worked on the canal. Once they did get married, Sean continued to work the canal, and actually purchased another boat. He hired an older boy to captain the second boat and he and the two mule drivers lived together off season in the old slave cabin that was still on the farm. Sean and Hannah had two daughters, Corinne and Selina.

"It seems that Sean had a little trouble with alcohol, and his father-in-law made him 'take the pledge' as they called it. When he did, he and his father-in-law became very close, and the older man took him into the other family business that he ran on Willow Wood...the slave hiding business."

"I'm proud of them. I feel proud that our home was used for good purposes like that," Ann said, leaning back in her chair.

"Sean would hide the runaways in the empty coal hold in the boat on his way back up the canal from Bristol to Easton, where they would rendezvous with another 'conductor' who would take the runaways further north. He didn't always stop here, of course, because during the canal season time was money. They moved steadily, tying up near whatever lock they were close to, but occasionally, when the slave chasers were suspicious and started investigating the canal workers, he had to hide the escaping slaves here—in the carriage house—in that hole that his father-in-law built for that purpose."

Ann leaned forward on the table. "Wow, this is really interesting."

"Okay, so the girls grew up but they didn't know anything about the secret room or what their grandfather and father did until Corinne was sixteen. She was out on the porch late at night and saw a young man sneak out of the carriage house and go down to the river. Panicked, she told her parents, who then had to explain what was going on. The young man she saw was around her own age. His name was Morris and he was escaping with his mother and his aunt.

"They were from a plantation in South Carolina. Morris was a house slave, and an artist and musician. He used to entertain the slave master and his family and guests by playing the piano. His mother worked in the kitchen on the plantation and his aunt was the personal maid of the women of the plantation. They were escaping because the master was going to sell Morris, and they wanted to remain together. Apparently, his mother just couldn't bear the thought of his being sent away from her protection… whatever protection she could give him.

"The owner of the plantation had some gambling debts, and Morris wasn't a kid anymore, he was growing very tall and strong and became quite valuable, so …"

Lillian shrugged, as though they'd heard this story a hundred times.

Ann shook her head. "Yet another sad story out of Willow Wood."

"Wait, you ain't heard nothing yet," Lillian told her. "While they were hiding out in that tiny little secret room, Sean was on the canal and Hannah was called away to help deliver a baby. She left instructions that Corinne was to bring food and water to the people who were hiding in the carriage house, which the girl did. Being curious and outgoing, she made friends with them. She started visiting them at night when her mother and sister were asleep. The mother of the boy, Thessie, gave Corinne a basket that she had woven from—and get this, Annie—the wetland grasses in South Carolina."

"The basket we found!"

"Yep. In the middle of the night, Morris would leave the hole and go to the river to get air and bathe. He couldn't stand being cooped up in that tiny room so he took advantage of the dark of night to leave it. Corinne would meet him and they'd go to the river together to talk. He told her about his music, but mostly he talked about how much he loved art and how he wanted to be a painter. One night as they were talking, she kissed him, and before you know it, they were in each other's arms, and…well…you know."

"Oh, God…" Ann said.

"Oh, God, is right, because one of Sean's mule drivers who was tied up in New Hope and decided to come home for the night found them on the banks of the river and went after Morris. He must have thought that Corinne was being raped. They fought, and Morris ended up drowning the guy."

Ann's eyes widened even more. "What happened?"

"Morris dragged him out of the river and to the canal and threw him in. Poor Corinne had grown up with this kid, and she was in a state of shock. She couldn't tell anyone because then they'd know about her father being a conductor and the secret hiding place, so she kept her mouth shut. Everyone assumed the mule driver had been drinking and fell into the canal, hit his head and drowned. She let them believe it, but according to Selina's journal, Corinne got very quiet, very withdrawn. Her family thought it was because of the mule driver's death and the shock of it and all."

"What happened to Morris and the women?"

"Morris just disappeared. Sean took the women north on his next trip, promising them that if he found Morris, he'd send him to them, but he never found him."

"Okay, so go on."

"The summer grew into winter, and Corinne took to staying in the house a lot, mostly in her room. Then one night in late March her sister heard her moaning in her bed. Selina got up to see what was wrong and found Corinne writhing in pain, then suddenly she opened her legs and pushed until her face turned purple."

"A baby?" Ann breathed.

"A baby…right there on the bed…but it wasn't breathing. Corinne begged Selina not to awaken their mother. Sean was away on his first trip of the season on the canal. They got dressed and wrapped the baby in the bed covers, carried it down to the willow tree. Corinne took off her shawl and wrapped the baby, sheets and all in it and they buried the baby there in a shallow grave. The next morning, Selina went down to dig a deeper whole, but the baby was gone—no sheets, no shawl, no baby, just an open hole and a lot of paw prints all around it. When she told Corinne, the poor thing thought dogs or a fox dug up the body of her baby and ate it. She was inconsolable. Selina didn't know what to do, but apparently she still didn't tell their mother. If Corinne was sixteen, Selina would have been fourteen, so she was just a kid."

Ann shook her head and sighed. "What a tragic story."

"Not done," Lillian said, leaning back in her chair. "The next night, Sean tied up his canal boat near Willow Wood and decided to come home. He noticed the carriage house door was open and he went over to close it. He found Corinne hanging from a beam there. Her mother and sister didn't even know she had left her bed."

"Oh, God, Lillian, she hanged herself?"

"Yes, right there in our garage…or what is our garage now."

They were both quiet a long time, thinking the story over. Then Lillian said, "Okay, so here's the rest. The night they buried the baby, a local man who was African-American and worked as a lock tender up in New Hope was walking along the tow path with his dog on his way to work. The locks opened about four in the morning then, so it must have been around that time. His dog stood stock still for a second, as though it heard something, and then it started sniffing the ground and crossed the bridge—our bridge—and led the man to the willow tree where it started scratching the earth. The man watched as the dog put his nose down into where it was digging and pulled up a corner of a sheet. The mound of dirt was making noise. He did not find a dead baby but one that was very much alive and crying.

"The sheets must have kept the dirt from smothering the baby," Ann said, "although I'm sure there wouldn't have been much more time before the baby did suffocate."

Lillian shrugged, as though that wasn't important. "The baby was not dragged away by dogs or foxes. Instead, he was taken in by this man and his wife, who had eight children of their own. They never said anything to anyone until, many years later, when he came to Willow Wood to tell Selina the story. He gave Selina, who was married with grown children of her own by then, the shawl. By that time, the boy, whom he had named Moses but shortened it to Mos, had gone to New York and became an artist—just like his father—his birth father, I mean. He was very successful. And get this: he painted murals on the walls of homes owned by wealthy people in New York."

"Corinne didn't have to kill herself after all," Ann said.

"No…or maybe yes. Think about all that was going on in her mind…loving Morris…the dead mule driver…the baby…the shame of it all…the secrets she had to keep …"

Ann shook her head, mulling it over. "Do you think the mural in our garage was done by Corinne's son?"

"It was, Ann. The old man who found the baby asked Selina if she could write to the artist and tell him the story of his birth. The old man and his wife had told Moses—or Mos—the story from when he found the baby, but they couldn't answer all the questions that Mos had about how he came to be buried alive. Apparently it was destroying him. He couldn't paint, he was suffering from depression. Imagine, Annie, first he finds out that his parents really aren't his parents at all, and then he finds out that he was left to die in a grave. It was driving him insane."

"Did she write to him?" Ann asked.

"I guess so, because I found a letter from Mos Adamson tucked in Selina's journal. It was obviously in answer to her letter."

Lillian ran into the library and came out with the letter for Ann to read. "It's beautiful…read it."

Ann unfolded the yellowed pages. It was four pages back and front, and the handwriting was clear and strong and looked as though it was written by an educated and artistic man.

> *10 June 1881*
>
> *New York City*
>
> *Dear Mrs. Deitz,*
>
> *I cannot thank you enough for your letter which I received one week ago. I have read it every day, three and four times each day, trying to absorb all that you told me about the circumstances of my birth. Although not easy for me to read, it has answered some important questions for me, questions that have plagued me about my birth.*
>
> *I know that writing your letter must have cost you dearly and brought back to you unhappy memories that you would otherwise have left buried with your sister. Your kindness in telling me the story is deeply appreciated; the cruel truth about my conception and birth is something that you could not avoid telling me.*
>
> *It pleases me to know that my father, the escaping slave from South Carolina, was an artist. Somehow, it allows me to feel attached to him in a way*

that I have never felt attached to anyone. The fact that he was never found gives me hope that perhaps one day I will be able to find him, or that by some happenstance he may enter my life. The door to that possibility is not closed as I once thought it might be, and for that I am grateful. I will be ever searching the face of every strange Negro man who enters my life to see if there is a resemblance.

The fact that I will never meet or know your sister, the woman who gave birth to me, gives me sorrow, I will confess. Yet, there is a sort of comfort in knowing that she and Morris, the slave, were friends. I would like to believe what you tell me in your letter that your sister loved him as you seem to think she did. I am grateful that before she died, she shared some of that with you, and confessed about the murder of the mule driver and that she was not raped. Of course, as you said, we will never know for certain all the facts of the night I was conceived. I will have to live with those questions.

I am very happy that the return of the shawl in which my father, Samuel, found me wrapped in the grave near the tree has given you comfort. At first I didn't want him to give it to you.

I wondered should I keep it as it was the only thing I had of a mother I would never know. After reading your letter, I feel that we did the right thing by returning it to you for it is a part of a woman you did know and it brings comfort to you.

I have one request of you, Mrs. Deitz, and if you will grant this I promise I will never annoy or even contact you again. As my father told you during his visit, I can no longer concentrate on my work. Painting has become almost impossible for me since finding out about my birth. I never had any reason to believe that Samuel and Jane Adamson were not my real parents, since they raised me with their own ten children as though there was no difference. It was only until I asked them a year ago why it is that I have green eyes when they and all of my siblings, or who I believed were my brothers and sisters, were much darker skinned and had dark eyes that they told me the truth.

I cannot explain to you why this affected my work so profoundly. My father believes it is because of the shock. It does not matter why; what matters is that I must paint. I have to work. I live to work. I have studied at the National Academy of Design with much success, and fought hard for the right to do so, and now it is all for naught.

I want to come to Willow Wood, to lower myself into the hole in your carriage house, and paint a mural on the wall down there where Morris, Thessie and Ruth hid during those long weeks. I am being called to do this. I *believe I will be healed if I have the chance to sit in the secret room and paint the people who I have learned are my family. I know that it must sound strange, especially since no one will ever see it, yet I know it is something I must do. Will you allow it? I will sleep there, in the hole, and be no bother to you and yours. Of that I promise. I want nothing more from you but the permission to paint a mural.*

*Finally, you ask me in your letter if I can ever forgive you for being complicit in burying me on the banks of the Delaware Canal; you ask if I can forgive your sin. Whether or not you agree to my request, I want you to know that I hold no ill feelings toward you. I don't believe that there was a sin committed. As you say in your letter, you and your sister believed me to be dead at birth, and you did what it was that you had to do to protect your sister. I do not hate you, as you beg me not to in your letter, nor do I hate the woman who gave birth to me. You say in your letter that on that night, she said to you that she wanted to bury me there under the willow tree for if no one else would weep for me, the tree would. That tells me in a strange way that she did indeed care. There is comfort in that for me.*

*I look forward to your reply regarding my request.*

*Until then, I remain, faithfully yours,*

*Mos Adamson*

"Wow," Ann said looking up from the letter.

"Wow," Lillian agreed.

"He wrote so beautifully. Even his handwriting was artistic."

Lillian nodded and reached over to take the letter from Ann.

"Lilly, will you put all of this in the book?"

"How could I not? It's an important story in Willow Wood's history, Ann. I also think that we need to contact the local historical society or a museum to let them know about this mural in our garage. It should be taken out of there if it can be—brick by brick—and reassembled and placed somewhere that it can be seen. The Mercer Museum, maybe. I can't believe no one ever looked for it before we did."

Ann remembered something Lillian had said earlier. "What was that about a plaque near the tree?"

"That's right! In Selina's journal she mentions that after her sister killed herself, she told the whole story to their parents. Their father, Sean Ginley, made a plaque of pewter and engraved the words, "Child of Corinne, 20 March 1859," and placed it at the base of the willow tree."

"But Mos wasn't buried there...the body was missing, they thought dogs had taken it."

Lillian just shrugged. "I don't know, Annie. He was a man in mourning. Maybe it gave him comfort to think that he marked the place where his daughter wanted her child to be buried."

"Lillian, I don't want to try to dig it up and find it," Ann said. "Chances are, it's been gone for years, but I don't care if it's there or not; it should be left undisturbed if it is.

She looked out through the window toward the willow tree. "Even though the spot is not officially a grave, it's hallowed ground. Please respect my wishes on this and don't try to find it."

Lillian was disappointed, but she couldn't deny that Ann had a point. The plaque was not searched for.

# *Eighteen*

Ann sat in the wing chair near the fireplace reading the recently finished chapter in Lillian's book about Hannah and Sean Ginley and their daughters. When she was finished, she placed it on her lap and stared into the fire. The log was starting to burn out but she was too weary to get up to put another one on the fire. The story made her deeply sad, and she wondered how many more tragic stories were attached to this house, how many broken hearts lived in it, how many wounded people had inhabited its rooms during its two hundred year history?

She started to remember her own family. Her grandmother and grandfather seemed perfectly happy in their later years, but they couldn't always have been that way. Not with Aunt Regina the way she was. They had to know that she was psychotic, and it must have been a rollercoaster ride living with that. When Ann was a child, none of them—not her grandparents nor her mother—ever seemed to be overly concerned, but now, looking back, she realized that they were always tied up in knots when Aunt Regina was around. Her mother adored the ground her sister walked on, but Ann remembered little comments her mother would make to her father that confused her then but made sense now that Ann knew how mentally ill Regina really was.

It made Ann angry; none of them did anything to keep Lillian safe from her mother. As an adult, Ann tried often to understand why her mother didn't report Regina to the authorities and ask for custody of Lillian.

Why didn't her grandparents? But there really wasn't any clear answer. They just didn't. Ann had asked her mother about it once, not long after Aunt Regina had killed herself, and her mother just shrugged.

"She was my sister and I loved her, and I knew that she loved Lillian. It wasn't as if she did the things she did deliberately; she did them because she couldn't help it, she was very ill."

"No, that's not a good enough answer," Ann had insisted. "Just because Aunt Regina didn't mean it didn't make it any less painful for Lillian."

Ann remembered that her mother had looked very sad when Ann said this, and Ann knew that her mother didn't have any further excuses. "I loved my sister. It wasn't her fault she was the way she was, Annie. It would have destroyed her if I took her child away from her. I just couldn't do it."

"Were you afraid of her?" Ann remembered asking her mother.

And her mother just shook her head and stared into space, "I was afraid *for* her."

Ann had let it go then, unable to bear the guilt she saw in her own mother's eyes and knowing that it was too late anyway, what had been done couldn't be undone.

And the truth was that Ann remembered Aunt Regina as being very kind—especially to her and to Joey—when she returned from her years in the hospital.

She was still remarkably beautiful, with thick dark hair tinged with red highlights and eyes greener even than Lillian's. She was taller than the other women in the family, with an hourglass figure and a long swan-like neck. She had beautiful hands, too, Ann recalled. When she was nice, she was wonderful. Ann loved her aunt when she was a little girl, but she knew now that her parents must have been careful to keep her away from Regina when she was in a manic state and in the throes of schizophrenia—except for that one terrible night.

Ann looked up at the staircase that led to the bedrooms and remembered standing at the top of those stairs, just thirteen years old. She remembered the horrifying argument that was taking place below, in the room she sat in now, not long after Joey was born and a day or so after her mother and Lillian returned from Europe.

She knew that Lillian had been in an accident that night and was in the hospital. She remembered how hard her mother cried when she got the phone call, and later that her parents had actually argued over the accident, but made Ann leave the room so that she couldn't hear what they were saying.

Late that night when Ann was in bed she was awakened by banging and loud voices in the living room where she sat now. She had opened her bedroom door and heard her aunt demand to see the baby.

"Not tonight," Ann's mother had said, sounding calm, using a soft voice. "Come back tomorrow, Reggie. He's sound asleep, and you know what it's like when they wake up. He'll never get back to sleep, and I'm exhausted. I still have jet lag..."

"You lying bitch," Regina had screamed at Ann's mother. "That's *not* your fucking baby. I want him now! You give him to me right now or so help me God I'll kill you, your daughter, and that bastard you're hiding. I'll burn this house down."

Ann remembered feeling sick to her stomach with fear. She had never heard Aunt Regina talk this way before. She had never heard anyone speak this way. She remembered that her skin felt prickly all over from her scalp down her arms and back. She closed her door and sat on the edge of the bed, the same bed that Suzie slept in now, while the arguing continued in the room beneath her. Even through the closed door, she could hear her aunt get louder and berate her mother in a screeching angry voice.

"I swear to God, Helen, I'll kill you with my bare hands. I want that baby now!"

Ann couldn't understand why her aunt was so frantic about seeing Joey.

Then Ann heard her father's footsteps move past her door and into the nursery.

She couldn't believe he was going to bring Joey to her aunt when she was so crazed. Ann jumped off the bed and opened her door. He was holding the baby in his arms. He stopped when he saw Ann and shook his head slowly. "Go back to bed," he said in a whisper. "And stay there, Annie. Don't come downstairs. Do you hear me?"

She had closed the door, but as soon as she heard him descend the stairs, she opened it again so she could hear what was being said.

"Give that to me," Regina shrieked so loud that it vibrated the floor beneath Ann's feet. It scared her more than she'd ever been scared before. She crept to the staircase and peeked down into the living room. Her body was trembling uncontrollably.

Regina was moving across the room, and Ann noticed that her aunt had on a fur coat but no shoes or stockings. Ann's father put his hand out to block her while moving his body sideways to keep the baby from Regina's reach. Ann's mother stood on the other side of the room, her hands to her mouth.

"Now, you listen to me, Regina, and you listen good," Ann's father had said in a quiet but dangerous voice. "This is my baby...*my* son. If you ever come to this house again in a mood like this, if you ever threaten to touch my son, my wife, or my daughter again, I will have you committed permanently. They'll put you away for a very long time. Do you hear me?"

"Go to hell," Aunt Regina had screamed, and lunged toward him again.

He held the baby from her reach with one arm, and with the other he grabbed her fur collar and pulled her up off her toes and close to his face. "Okay," he said, still very quiet. "Then I'll kill you and tell them it was self-defense. I'd be doing the entire family a huge favor—especially your sweet abused daughter and that milksop of a husband you're married to."

Aunt Regina had laughed at him. It was shrill and unnatural. She said, "I'm not afraid of you. You couldn't do it. You don't have the guts."

"Oh couldn't I? Don't try me." He pushed Aunt Regina away from him and she fell to the floor. Ann could see then that all Aunt Regina was wearing under the coat was a nightgown. "Now go home and take your medicine. Leave us alone. And leave your daughter alone. I pray to God that she survives the beating you gave her tonight. But I'm warning you, Regina, if she lives, it will be the last one you'll ever give her. I'll see to that."

Ann never heard anything else that happened because she vomited right there in the hallway at the top of the steps. They all looked up at her, and then her mother quickly skirted around her sister, who was still on the floor, to get to Ann. "Oh darling," she had crooned to Ann, putting her arm around her when she reached the top of the stairs. "Come into the bathroom…"

Aunt Regina must have left then because the house was silent as Ann's mother washed her face and helped her out of her pajamas and into clean ones.

"I'm so sorry," she kept saying to Ann. "I'm so sorry you heard all of that. How horrible…how horrible," she kept saying, trying not to cry. "How much did you hear…never mind…never mind. Your aunt is ill, darling, you have to understand that she's just very ill. It will be all right tomorrow. You'll see."

"She scared me, Mom," Ann remembered saying to her mother.

"I know she did, baby. But she's just not herself. Don't hate her, Annie, please just put this all out of your head. She was not herself."

With that, Ann's father had come into the bathroom and took Ann into his arms as though she, too, were still an infant and he carried her to bed.

"Where's my little brother?" Ann asked him.

"He's fine. He's in his crib. You should have listened to me and stayed in your room," he told Ann, placing her on the bed and pulling the blanket up to her chin.

His face was white except for two bright red patches on his cheeks. His hands were trembling when he smoothed her hair from her forehead.

"Daddy, what you said to Aunt Reg…"

"None of that is any of your concern, Annie. It was just family having a terrible argument." He knelt next to her bed and held her hand to his lips. "I don't want you to think of it again. Do you hear me? I wouldn't hurt a fly, princess. You have to believe me. But I'll always protect my own, no matter who is threatening them. That's what dads do. If you ever feel threatened or frightened of Aunt Regina—or anyone else for that matter—you tell me immediately. Do you understand?"

Ann shook her head no because she didn't understand a word of what he was saying or a thing that happened that night. He kissed her forehead and then her cheek and she thought he was going to cry.

"I'm sorry I disobeyed you, Daddy," she said to him, hoping she wasn't the reason his eyes were filled with tears.

"I am, too. I wish you never had to hear any of that. But it's over now. It won't happen again. That's a promise."

"Is Lillian going to die?" she asked her father, remembering then what he had said to Regina.

He covered his eyes with his hands for a moment and said, "Pray for her, honey. She had a bad accident and we need to pray for her. Can you do that?" Ann nodded and he asked, "Do you think you can go to sleep after all of this?"

Ann agreed to try and her father left the room. She heard her mother crying in their bedroom and her father's soothing voice. She fell asleep to the hum of her father's voice through the wall.

She didn't see Aunt Regina again for two years, and it was many years after that before she saw Lillian again, when Joey was about nine. Ann believed then that the reason for the absences was because Ann's parents took her and her baby brother to live in Florida near their grandparents a few months after Lillian's accident. At that time she didn't know that Aunt Regina was in an institution being treated for mental illness or that Regina had fractured Lillian's skull that night. She also knew, now that she was a mother, that a parent *would* do anything to protect a child…anything…even kill to protect that child.

Lillian walked into the room, intruding on Ann's unpleasant memory. Lillian tried to act as though she wasn't eager to hear what Ann had to say about the chapter she'd just read. Ann allowed her to sweat for a minute, then smiled and said, "It's good. It's really good."

"Yeah?" Lillian was pleased and fell back on the couch and pulled her legs up. "I've never finished anything of my own volition before. I always wrote what others wanted me to write, but I could never seem to discipline myself enough to write my own stuff."

"You're making up for lost time now. I can't wait to read the next chapter and the one after that."

"Neither can I," Lillian said, laughing at herself. "It's as if it's writing itself."

Lillian sighed wistfully. "These women are talking to me, telling me their stories, whispering in my ear. Do you notice that there's a pattern here? Breast cancer, insanity, unrequited, love…passion, sadness…it all went on in this house before, didn't it?"

"I was just thinking the same thing," Ann said.

"If these walls could talk…" they both said at the same time, and then laughed.

Ann winced and moved around in the chair to get more comfortable.

"What's the matter?" Lillian asked her.

"I don't know. I must have wrenched my back because it hurts now and again, especially if I'm leaning on it. I must have moved the wrong way when I was sleeping or something."

Lillian looked up at the coffered ceiling. "I miss New York. I promised Dan I'd go weeks ago. Can you spare me if I leave tomorrow and come back on Monday?"

Ann didn't hesitate. "Yes, I can spare you. I hardly see you anyway these days now that you're holed up in that room editing all morning and then writing for hours and hours until the middle of the night. Besides Millicent and Father Murray have me working on that fundraiser for the hospital and I'll be spending a lot of time on that in the next few days. It's next weekend and I'm swamped. So go—get out of my way."

Lillian put her hand up to her eyes dramatically, "I've become a burden to my wealthy cousin—the old maid relative who doesn't have a decent job and just mooches off her. I knew it would come to this."

"Oh, shut up, you idiot. I'm going to bed, and you better be on the way to the train station when I get up in the morning. Do you hear me?"

"Loud and clear."

"Kiss that beautiful man Dan for me," Ann threw over her shoulder as she started up the stairs.

"Oh, I'll do more than *kiss* him," Lillian said.

"And that is more than I need to know, thank you," Ann said turning the corner and disappearing down the second story hallway.

❧

Louise was away on business, and it was Jessica's mother's weekend to have Jessica, so Lillian and Dan had the apartment to themselves. They spent one day in the museums, going to a matinee, and eating at Dan's new favorite restaurant. The next day they spent in their pajamas, reading the paper, eating Brie and apples, and making love. The third day they walked in Central Park for hours.

"I just realized something…you haven't asked me to marry you this weekend," she said.

"Should I have?" he asked.

"I've grown accustomed to your asking. I knew something was off all weekend." She looked sideways at him as they walked beside the pond. "Why haven't you?"

He shrugged. "I don't know. Will you marry me?"

"No way," she said huffing. "I don't want to have to remind you to ask me, for crying out loud."

"Maybe I'll remember next time," he said, smiling, "but I really would love you to marry me…"

She dismissed the conversation as though it had no meaning. "Hey, maybe I'll bring Ann and the kids next time. We can bring Suze and Phil to see The Lion King. And then we could take one of these carriage rides. Oh, Dan, they'd have a blast, wouldn't they?"

She didn't notice the wounded look in his eyes; she was too excited about the adventure she was planning for her cousins. She didn't hear him sigh or notice him shake his head with a sad grin. "Do you think we can do it soon?"

Within two weeks, Dan had pulled some strings and purchased the tickets for the show and made reservations at the New York Palace Hotel for all of them. They took the train in, much to Suzy's and Philip's delight, and Dan met them at Penn Station.

They walked all the way to the hotel to check in, and Dan and Lillian were greatly amused at the way the children's eyes were three times bigger than normal when they looked around the elegant hotel lobby. Ann was all smiles, and Lillian teased her for bringing more luggage than she'd ever need for a year let alone a weekend. "The doormen think you're moving in," Lillian said, handing three suitcases to the doorman while Dan handed him the rest.

"One never knows what you'll need when you have two kids," Ann said. "I didn't want to run short. And one of those suitcases holds all the meds and vitamins I take."

They were walking toward the elevator when one of the employees, a young man dressed in a dark suit and crisp white shirt, offered to walk with them. "Have you been here before?" he asked them.

"No, never," Suzy answered.

"Well, welcome to the New York Palace. We're happy you're here. Where are you from?"

"Bucks County, Pennsylvania," Philip said.

Ann began to explain, "That's right outside of..."

"Philadelphia..." the young man answered for her. "I know it well; I'm also from Bucks County. My parents and sister and her family still live there."

"Really?" Ann said, delighted. "What a coincidence!"

"It is," he agreed, holding the elevator door open for them, and then stepping inside it himself. "Are you here for the weekend?"

Suzy filled him in on all they were planning to do, and he pretended to be very interested in all of it until the elevator stopped at their floor.

He held the door open again. "George the bellman will be waiting for you in your suite by now. He'll show you everything you need. Enjoy your weekend. If there's anything I can do, just call down to the front office and ask for Ed Garfield."

They settled into the suite, then left quickly to grab some lunch before going to the theater to see the matinee. By the time they returned to the room, they were loaded down with a CD of the sound track, two copies of the program, four playbills, and a puppet for each of the kids. The adults were exhausted; the kids were wired. In the corner of the room there was a tray filled with fresh fruit, cookies, juice boxes, a bottle of champagne, a tiny chocolate cake that said "welcome" on it, and roses in a silver vase. The card read, "From your fellow Bucks Countian, Ed."

The kids grabbed for the cookies and ignored Ann's protests that they still had to eat dinner. She gave up, and flopped down in the chair by the window, which overlooked St. Patrick's Cathedral. "This is so nice," she said. "I wish I wasn't so tired."

"I knew you'd love this," Lillian said. "I told Dan that when I was here a few weeks ago."

Ann looked at Dan, who was sprawled across the bed eating cookies with the kids. "You're just as bad as they are," she said.

"Never met a cookie I didn't like," he told her, winking at Suzy.

The kids put the television on and the adults relaxed for awhile before Dan said, "I better get home to change for dinner. Our reservations at The Palm are for seven."

Lillian walked him to the door and gave him a quick kiss. "Thanks for all of this," she said to him. He smiled, but didn't answer her.

She closed the door and went into the bathroom to run the shower. "I'll shower first, then you can go in, all right?" she said.

Lillian quickly showered and pulled on her underclothes, then put on the luxurious terry robe provided by the hotel. She left the bathroom to find Ann sound asleep in the chair, so she went back in and finished applying her makeup and dried her hair.

She pulled a thin blue silk dress over her head and donned a black sweater trimmed at the edges with tiny sequins. She told the kids to get dressed, helped Suzy wash up and put on a frilly dress, while Philip wiped at his face and just about wet his hands and declared himself washed. She made him change his shirt, and told him he had to wear his good shoes to dinner and not his sneakers. Then she went over to Ann's chair and touched her cousin's shoulder gently.

"Time to get up, Annie, if you want to be ready for dinner on time."

It seemed to take Ann a long time to focus. She sat up quickly, but winced and sat back again, grabbing her back.

"Lilly, do you think I could skip dinner?" she asked. "My back is killing me from all the walking."

"It was all those damn suitcases," Lillian said. "Why don't you take a long hot bath and then get into bed. Dan and I will take care of the kids. You take a break."

Ann was relieved that she didn't have to go out. She called the kids over to her.

"I expect you both to behave tonight and remember your manners. Lilly and Dan are taking you to a really nice restaurant, and I don't want you to embarrass me." She fussed at Suzy's hair and straightened Philip's collar. "You promise to be good?"

"I promise," Suzy said quickly.

But Philip studied his mother. "You okay, Mom?" he asked her.

She smiled up at him. "I'm fine. I'm just tired, sweetheart."

"Do you want me to stay here with you?" he asked her. "Maybe you shouldn't be alone?"

"No, I don't. I want you to go with Lilly, and I want you to be good but have a good time. Okay?"

He nodded solemnly, then kissed her cheek and lingered near her, glancing at her several times. Lillian's cell phone chimed alerting her to a text message.

"Let's go," Lilly called from the doorway. "Dan's downstairs in the lobby."

The children each had a plate of spaghetti and Lillian shared her chicken cutlet with them. Dan offered a piece of his steak to Philip who devoured it and left nothing on his plate, much to the delight of the waiter who made a fuss over both kids. After huge sundaes made especially for them, Suzy said to Lillian, "I'm so full I think I'm going to explode."

Dan and Lillian decided to take a long walk in the cool autumn night to exercise away their heavy meal. They wound up at Central Park where Dan picked the prettiest white carriage lined with red velvet and pulled by a white horse.

Suzy's eyes were wide and she sighed deeply. "It's just like a princess carriage," she murmured. In truth, it was a little beat up but to Suzy it was out of a fairytale. The driver helped her up into it, then gave Philip a nudge onto the seat across from her and covered them both with a white fake fur cover. Dan helped Lillian into the carriage and pulled himself up to sit beside Philip.

The driver snapped the reins and off they went with the sounds of the horse's hooves clip-clopping on the pavement. The carriage moved into the park and Suzy sat back and let out another deep, satisfied sigh. "This is heaven," she said. "Just heaven, Lilly."

Dan and Lillian exchanged smiles. She mouthed "Thank you" to him.

Philip said, "My mom would have loved this, Lilly. I wish she was here. She really would love this. Look at the lights down there."

"That would be Wollman Rink," said the driver. "Just opened a few days ago for the season." He pulled the horse off the path and closer to the wall. "Take a quick peek before I get into trouble for doing this."

They all peeked over the wall, and there below them the rink was lit up and skaters circled the ice. They could hear shouting and laughter and giggled at the people who were falling down and remarked with great admiration about those who were doing tricks.

"Do you guys skate?" Dan asked them.

"I do, but she falls all the time," Philip answered for himself and his sister.

"Well, maybe Lillian can bring you back when you have a little more time and we'll go skating here. Or if you come at Christmas, we can skate at Rockefeller Center where the big Christmas tree is. Would you like that?"

"When? When can we come back? Lilly, when can we do it?" Suzy demanded to know.

"Soon, I promise," Lilly answered.

The horse moved on again and Suzy leaned her head against Lillian's arm. "I'm so happy," she said. "I want to live in New York City."

"Well, it would be okay, but only if Mom wanted it, too," Philip reflected.

"Can we live with you, Dan?" Suzy wanted to know.

Lillian looked at him, waiting for the answer, and there was a strained smile on his face. Lillian answered for him, thinking he was stumped. "There really isn't enough room in Dan's apartment. You'll see tomorrow when we go there. Dan lives with Louise—remember Louise, Dan's sister?—and Jessica. There's not enough room for us, too. We'd have to get our own apartment, I guess, but we'd visit Dan and he'd visit us all the time."

Dan's face was even more constricted now, and she couldn't figure out what was bothering him. She smiled but he didn't return the smile, just looked away into the distance before pointing out The Plaza Hotel to the kids, reminding them that it was the hotel where Kevin McAllister stayed in Home Alone II. And, of course, Eloise.

"Can we stay there?" Philip wanted to know.

Dan nodded, "Sure, the next time you come."

❧

Ann never heard Lillian and the kids come back into the room that night. After they left her alone in the suite, she eventually pulled herself out of the chair and ran a bath. The steam covered the mirrors by the time she lowered herself into the marble tub. The water felt wonderful and she closed her eyes and took a deep breath. Her back hurt when she inhaled and she reached around to rub it. She couldn't imagine what she had done to it. After the bath, she took a pain killer and within an hour it knocked her out, but before falling asleep she made a mental note to wake up early to go to Mass at the cathedral.

She had started going back to church in recent weeks, thanks to the influence of her friend Father Murray, and going into the beautiful cathedral appealed to her.

She decided she wouldn't take the children this Sunday. She wanted to attend Mass alone and in peace. She'd get a good night's sleep and have more energy in the morning. She was just so exhausted.

She did awaken early. Suzy was in the bed next to her. Philip was on the sofa bed, buried under sheets and a blanket, and Lillian was in the bed in the other room of the suite.

Ann went into the bathroom, got dressed without waking anyone, and left a note telling them where she was in case they woke up before she returned from the cathedral. She bumped into the hotel manager they had met the day before as she got off the elevator.

"Good morning," he said, smiling brightly at her.

"Good morning, and thank you for all the wonderful goodies you sent up. We loved them."

"I'm happy you enjoyed them. Do you have a lot planned for today?" he asked, holding the heavy metal door open for her.

"We do, although yesterday was enough to last a year. I was exhausted last night. But we made such wonderful memories; the kids will never forget it."

He laughed, "New York will do that to you—exhaust you and make you happy at the same time. But you must have had a good night's sleep because you look beautiful today!"

"What a nice thing to say. If you weren't young enough to be my son, I'd kiss you. Thank you, Ed Garfield. You just made my whole day."

He smiled, "Have a good one, and if you need anything..."

"I know, call Ed Garfield," she said laughing.

Ann walked a block to the entrance of the Cathedral, sidled into one of the pews and knelt to pray. She felt burdened, although she didn't know why. She couldn't concentrate on her prayers, so she said a Hail Mary and sat back in the pew. Mass started and she was amazed by the beauty of the music and the deep resonant voices of the soloist. She'd heard years before that members of the choir at St. Patrick's were often entertainers, many from the casts of Broadway shows. She closed her eyes to listen, not praying along as she was supposed to, just listening.

She let the music and the hum of the praying congregation pour over her and found a kind of comfort she hadn't felt in a very long time. The burden she walked into the cathedral with seemed to lift. She let it all carry her away and even as she heard the people around her stand and sit and kneel, she just remained in the same spot, eyes closed, just listening.

She thanked God for allowing her to be there, for giving her some extra time, for giving her the strength to seek out help from Dr. Raphael. She knew the treatment she was undergoing wouldn't buy her life back, but she also knew that it had bought her a few more months, and she suddenly realized just how grateful she was to have those few months. They were a gift; and, although she didn't know why, she realized that at some point during these months she had begun to accept what was to come.

She never thought she would receive a miracle. In fact, she really hadn't asked for one for herself. The only miracle she had asked for was that her children would be safe and loved after she died. That miracle had been given to her. There was no doubt in her mind any longer that Lillian loved her children and would take care of them exactly as Ann would want.

Sitting in the hard wooden pew, surrounded by the hum of the prayers, the aroma of the burning wax candles, she thanked God for this miracle she had been given. The burden she had been feeling when she entered the Cathedral a few minutes earlier was gone completely now. She could see into the future with her mind's eye—Lillian and the kids, happy, contented, together. It was as though a key had turned in a lock and Ann was let out...freed from a dark oppressive vault. The beautiful liturgical music enveloped her, warmed her, and encased her with light, even though her eyes were closed. She sighed and smiled. She was so happy at that very moment that she thought her body could float above the pew.

And it was then that she knew with absolute certainty why her back was so painful.

∾

Louise had prepared Sunday dinner for all of them in the apartment. Lillian seemed as excited about them being there as Dan and Louise did. Ann was impressed by the tasteful décor of the apartment and its size, and Lillian praised Louise for her exquisite taste. Louise was an accomplished hostess and Dan a gracious host. Lillian helped them serve and Ann could see that she was very comfortable with this brother and sister and acted like she'd lived there with them for years.

They chatted constantly over the meal, no uncomfortable or awkward silences, as though they had all been friends for years. Suzy was disappointed that Jessica wasn't there, but Dan explained that she was on a school trip and wouldn't be home before they left. Louise took it upon herself to entertain the little girl, putting an apron on Suzy and allowing her to help clear the table and put the dishes in the dishwasher.

The kids were filled with stories about the day before, telling Louise every detail of what they did, almost reenacting the Lion King for her. They told her about going to dinner and then walking to Central Park and taking a horse-drawn carriage ride through the park. They hogged the conversation, but they were having such a good time and it didn't seem to bother Louise or Dan, so Ann let them chatter on.

They were all disappointed when it was time to leave Louise to go back to the hotel. Ann thanked Louise and hugged her. "Have you lost some weight?" Louise asked when they parted. "You feel a little thinner to me."

"No," Ann told her. "I wish," she joked and looked away from Lillian who heard the exchange and now perused Ann critically.

They walked back to the hotel, the children skipping ahead in the cold autumn air. Dan pointed out some nice restaurants, a park, and the United Nations. When they reached the hotel, Dan begged off from going up to the suite, explaining that he had a manuscript to go over before an acquisition meeting in the morning. He kissed Ann and Suzy and shook hands with Philip, ruffling the boy's hair afterward.

"You go on up," Lillian told Ann. "I just want to say goodnight to Dan."

When they were alone, she took his hand and asked him to sit with her on one of the sofas in the elegant lobby.

"What's wrong this weekend?" she asked him.

"Wrong?"

"You haven't been yourself, Dan. Are you angry with me for some reason?"

"Not at all." She waited for him to say more. He sighed and crossed his ankle over his knee. "Things are different, aren't they?" he asked, looking away from her.

"How?"

He shrugged. "I can't put my finger on it."

"Different how?" she persisted.

"I don't know...I just feel like you're...different."

"Different good or different bad?"

"Lillian, you're being difficult now."

"Make up your mind. Am I different or difficult?" She was becoming defensive, and she knew it.

She was afraid but didn't know why.

"Our situation is different, babe," he explained, trying to sound reasonable. "I just have to get used to...to sharing you, I guess. You just seem so wrapped up with Ann and the kids and I feel a little..."

"Abandoned?" she prodded. "Jealous?"

"Well, now I just feel stupid," he answered, annoyed, flicking a thread from his navy pant leg.

"You don't like that I'm not so dependent on you anymore..."

"You? Dependent on me? When was that?"

"You know what I mean. I've always been this wounded woman. You always had to take care of my psyche. Now I'm busy taking care of someone else."

He didn't answer her.

"You sent me back to them, Dan. Remember? You said I needed to go back and take care of business. That's what I've done."

"You're right, Lillian. And when you're right, you're right." He stood up and straightened his slacks and shirt. "And I've got to go."

"No...no, no, no...we aren't finished here," she said, grabbing his hand.

He leaned over and kissed her cheek. "Yes, yes, yes we are. I'll email you during the week—or you email me."

"Dan..."

He blew her a kiss and turned away. She watched him leave the hotel lobby and disappear into the crowd on the sidewalk outside. She suddenly understood the meaning of the expression *my heart sank*.

She stormed into the suite where Ann sat reading a book while the kids watched television in the other room.

"I don't believe him," she said, pulling off her sweater. "I just don't believe that man."

"Did you argue?" Ann asked her.

"Did we argue? No, I don't think we did. I don't know what we did, but it was weird. He's weird suddenly. What's up with him?"

Ann looked down at her book and didn't answer.

"I mean, he was really nice all weekend, but just that—nice."

"He's always nice," Ann said.

"I don't like him this way. He's scaring me."

"Scaring you?"

"Yes, scaring me."

"How, Lilly?"

"Because he was acting like he isn't…I don't think he…" she sat down on the bed feeling as though the strength in her legs suddenly left them. She looked at Ann. "I don't think he loves me anymore, Annie. I don't think he's in love with me."

Ann thought for a moment, then asked, "If that's true, if you were to find out that it's true, how would you feel?"

"Empty…alone. He's always been there. His love was always a sure thing. God damn it, Ann. I don't know what to think."

"Did you tell him you love him?"

"No. How could I when he was acting so weird?"

"Do you ever tell him, Lilly?"

Lillian looked at her cousin and shrugged. "Sure…I guess I do. I mean, I do love him. I love him with all of my heart, Ann. He's the love of my life. I haven't looked at another man in ten years."

"Yet you won't marry him?"

"Well, no, I wasn't ready."

"For ten years?"

"I wasn't ready, Ann. I couldn't do it. And now I can't because…" she stopped herself from finishing the sentence.

"Because you have to take care of me and the kids."

"Well, yes, I guess that's it. Look, I asked him to marry me during the summer and he said not until I went back to Bucks County and handled things with you."

"I wouldn't have married you then, either," Ann told her.

"Why not?"

"You were different then."

"Oh for God's sake," Lillian said, jumping off the bed. She looked through the window onto the busy Manhattan street. "That's the word he used. I'm *different*. But here's the rub: he's acting like he doesn't like me now…now that I'm not the way I used to be. I guess he liked me wounded

218

and unbalanced and cold and selfish and…"

"You weren't any of those things, Lillian. And above anyone else in the world, Dan knows it."

"What does he want, then?"

Ann shrugged. "You'll figure it out. Give him a little time. Give yourself a little time, and it will come to you. He's such a good man, Lilly. He'd never hurt you. Not in a million years. But no one wants to be hurt either."

"I hurt him?"

"You'll figure it out," Ann said again.

∾

| | |
|---|---|
| From: | Dan Paulsen [dpaulsen1@msn.com] |
| To: | Lillian Phelan [lpfreelncrwrtr@aol.com] |
| Subject: | Next two weeks |
| Sent: | 10/18 12:03 A.M. |

I forgot to tell you that I'll be going to Europe to interview an expatriate about a book he's writing. It's a little controversial, so I'm not sure we want to acquire it. I thought I'd make a little vacation out of the trip. I haven't been to Europe in years. I'll email you when I get back.

| | |
|---|---|
| From: | Lillian Phelan [lpfreelncrwrtr@aol.com] |
| To: | Dan Paulsen [dpaulsen1@msn.com] |
| Subject: RE: | Next two weeks |
| Sent: | 10/19 10:30 A.M. |

Danny boy, don't go without me. I need you. I love you. Let me come with you and we can be married in Europe. I hate the way you're acting toward me. Whatever I've done, I'm sorry. Please, Danny, please. I'm frantic with worry. Tell me everything is all right between us.
[HIGHLIGHT…DELETE]
Okay. Have a good time. I'll miss you.

# Nineteen

"Lilly, I'd like to go to Florida to see my parents," Ann said a few days after their trip to New York. They were standing in the driveway waiting for the school bus.

"Alone?" Lillian asked her.

"No, I'd like to take the kids and I'd love it if you came, too."

"What about school?"

"I'll take them out for a couple of days. I know they just started, but I have this longing to see my mother and father. We can get the school work from their teachers and make sure they keep up. Daddy will love doing homework with them."

"And what about your infusions?"

Before Ann could answer, a black convertible BMW turned into the driveway. It was an unusually warm October day and the top was down. Dr. Meg's blond hair blew around her face. She came to a stop near them. She was dressed in her gym clothes.

"Hi, Meg!" Ann said, genuinely happy to see her doctor-turned-friend.

"I'm here to find out why you haven't been to the gym in the last week," Meg said.

"I'm having trouble with my back," Ann told her doctor. "I'm giving it a rest."

Meg opened the door of her car and immediately started to probe Ann's back with her fingers.

"Stop...it's nothing," Ann protested.

"Where does it hurt?"

"There," Ann said, stiffening a little, "where you're pushing."

Meg frowned. "I wonder if it's a kidney stone."

"No, it's not that painful. Really, it's muscular...just stop pushing on me."

Lillian looked at Meg who was still frowning and probing. "Maybe you should get an x-ray before we go to Florida."

220

"Florida?" Meg asked, interested.

"Yes," Ann answered, "I want to see my parents."

Meg leaned back against her car, crossed her arms, and studied Ann's face for a long time.

"Are you trying to read my mind again?" Ann asked. She turned to Lillian. "She's always trying to read my mind."

"You okay?" Meg asked quietly.

"I have a backache, Dr. Raphael. And that's all I have. And I want to visit with my parents—I haven't seen them in over a year."

"Okay, my husband will fly you down."

"What?" Lillian asked, "Fly us down?"

"He' a pilot–we have our own plane. When do you want to go?"

"Seriously? Your own plane? Your own pilot?" Lillian continued in disbelief. "What have I done wrong in my life? How come I don't have a plane?"

Meg ignored her. "When do you want to leave and come back? He'll take care of it."

The bus pulled up to the driveway, and Meg jumped into her car. Her own kids would be arriving home in a few minutes.

"Thursday," Ann said as Meg started the car and began to go into reverse. "And I'd like to come back on Monday–this way the kids will only lose three days of school."

"You got it. I'll have him check his schedule, but I think it will be fine. You'll leave from the Northeast Philadelphia Airport. I'll call you later to confirm it." She waited until Philip and Suzy were with their mother and Lillian before pulling out of the driveway with a shout, "Love ya!"

They waved to her as she tore out, going about 70 miles an hour.

Ann and Lillian looked at each other. "Well, that's it, I guess," Ann said laughing.

"What, Mom?" Philip asked her.

"Want to go on another adventure? Want to go see Grammy and Pops?"

"Florida?" he asked.

"Florida," she answered.

"Yay! But what about school?"

"I'll worry about that. We're probably going to leave on Thursday."

Suzy put her arm around Lillian's hips and looked up into her face. "You too, Lilly?"

She smiled and Suzy smiled back. Lillian noticed that two of the teeth she lost during the summer were being replaced by second teeth. Her uneven smile was charming. "Yeah, Suzy Q, me, too."

❧

Meg's husband, John Raphael, was sweet and sociable, as was his copilot, Sam, a friend he'd known for years and who was co-owner of the plane. He allowed Philip and then Suzy to sit in the cockpit for a little while, and they were all offered the soda and snacks that he had stocked up on before taking off. The flight was smooth, and they landed on time.

Ann's father met them at the air strip in Florida, which wasn't far from his retirement community.

Ann flew into his arms when she saw him, and Lillian's throat tightened. Uncle Tim she thought. My Uncle Tim. She hadn't seen him in years, but she'd know him immediately…same tall slender build, same thick brown hair, a little grayer at the temples, but still a rich coffee color. The same blue eyes—Ann's eyes—and the same gentle smile. He had tears in his eyes when he let Ann go. "My girl, my beautiful girl," he whispered, kissing her again and pulling her close once more.

The kids demanded his attention, and he gave it to them, picking Suzy up over his head and giving her a bear hug, then grabbing at Philip's head and pulling him against his hip. He kissed the top of the boy's head. "I can't believe how big you are—both of you. Phil, you're a football player if I ever saw one. You tryin' out for the Eagles this year?" he teased, tickling Philip at his waist.

Then he looked up over their heads at Lillian. She continued to stand away, feeling the outsider. Tim held his arms out to her. "Get over here, doll baby," he said. He had always called her by that name…doll baby. It was his special name for her, but until this moment, she'd forgotten. Hearing it made her chest constrict to know that he hadn't forgotten.

"Uncle Tim," she said as she moved into his embrace. "I have missed you so much."

"And we missed you, baby doll. You look exactly the same as the last time I saw you."

"I don't. I'm old and fat now."

"You're gorgeous. You look so much like my Helen did at your age, it's almost shocking." He ran his long, thin fingers over her red hair. "I can't

222

believe you're here."

He hugged her again, then put his other arm around Ann and led them toward the luggage, which John Raphael had placed near Tim's car. They thanked John and confirmed the time on Monday when he'd take them back to Philadelphia.

Lillian was impressed by the house. It had three bedrooms as well as a den over the garage, and it was on a beautifully landscaped golf course. The beach was a short drive away, and they could get to Marco Island in less than an hour. The assisted living and nursing facility where Aunt Helen was being cared for was within walking distance since it was a part of the community. "From independence to skilled nursing," Tim said about the community as he carried Lillian's suitcase to the room where she would sleep. "It's a great place."

She looked out the window of the guest room toward the golf course. "It's beautiful," she said. "I'm so glad you're happy here."

"I miss the northeast, don't get me wrong. I miss the seasons and I even miss snow, although I don't miss shoveling it, but I imagine that eventually I'll be able to get away and visit Annie and the kids. Not just now, though. She still needs me here every day," he said, meaning his wife. "I was torn to pieces when I knew Ann was sick and I couldn't go to help her. The two most important women in my life, and I had to choose between them."

Lillian touched his shoulder. "Ann would not have wanted you to leave Aunt Helen. She'd have a fit if you did."

"She's got you now," he said. "What a relief for me...and for Joey." He looked away when he said his son's name.

"I met him, you know," she said quietly, sitting beside her uncle on the edge of the bed. "He's a wonderful young man. He's a lot like his dad."

Tim reached over and took her hand and squeezed it. "He was the greatest gift I ever received. The most generous gift anyone could have ever given us. And what you just said was the second."

They sat silently for a long while. Had anyone ever told Lillian that this is the way this first meeting would have gone, she'd have scoffed. She always believed it would have been a nightmare—awkward...painful...heart rending—not sweet and loving as it turned out to be. She had separated herself from her most beloved family members for nothing; she exiled herself for no reason. What a waste, she thought, putting her head down on his shoulder. What a freakin' waste.

"Ann wants to go see Helen. You up to it?" he asked his niece.

"No, Uncle Tim, I don't think I am. It's going to kill me to see her, I think."

"It's tough," he agreed. "You know others with Alzheimer's?"

"I wrote an article about it for a healthcare publication about two years ago. I had to visit several facilities when I was writing it, so I know what you face every day."

"It's tough," he said again.

"I'm going to let Ann and the kids go with you first. Maybe I'll take a walk over later or tomorrow."

He nodded and stood up. His hand was on the doorknob when she called, "Uncle Tim…"

He stopped and looked back at her.

"I love you. I always have—ever since I was a little girl. You were my hero."

He looked very sad when he said "I don't know how you could, baby doll."

"Excuse me?"

"I just don't, Lilly. How could you ever forgive me for not protecting you—for not taking you away from your mother? And then, on top of that, to take away your precious child…"

"Oh, no, Uncle Tim, you can't think that. Listen to me. I have wondered why no one ever took me away from my parents. I've never been one hundred percent sure you all knew what she was like until recently when I read something my grandmother wrote, but even so, it's just the way it was. I blame her—my mother. She was the abuser. No one else. Even Daddy was abused, so I don't hold him responsible. He did what he could to protect me."

"We were going to take you away from her, Lilly. You were about ten, and we found some ugly bruises on your back and shoulder when you came for a sleepover. We went to your grandparents and told them what we planned to do."

He sat on the bed again and put his hands between his legs. "They were agreeable but they warned us that she would never forgive us…never forgive Helen…and she would hound us every day for the rest of our lives. She'd never let you go easily, and we knew they were right. Your aunt just couldn't bear the thought of losing her sister's love. I never really understood that love—that protectiveness Helen felt for Regina. I guess she was raised to protect her sister. The three of them, your aunt and grandparents, lived their lives around Regina's bouts of insanity. So we abandoned the whole idea. I don't have too many regrets in my life, but I will regret that decision until I die."

He stood to leave. Lillian stood at the same time and faced her uncle. "I want you know that never once—not a single time in my whole life—not even when I was wasted in college—and they say that's when the truth will out—did I ever resent you and Aunt Helen for raising Joey. Imagine, Uncle Tim, what his life would have been like if you hadn't taken him as your own. Imagine what my life would have been like…"

"She beat you to a bloody pulp anyway…" he started, his eyes angry.

"I was able to get away from her, to go to college, make a life for myself. I could not have done any of that if I kept the baby. You raised him, you protected him, you gave him everything I couldn't—and I don't mean financially, I mean psychologically, emotionally, spiritually. He's wonderful because of what you—we—did all those years ago. Please, please, don't ever feel that way, Uncle Tim. Joey is your son. He is my cousin…and if I'm lucky, he'll be my friend."

Lillian could see how grateful he was when she finished speaking. The relief in his eyes touched her heart. She realized that during all the years she was afraid to meet her aunt and uncle again for fear that they would resent her because she was their son's mother, they were fearful that she hated them for taking Joey as their own. Once again, Lillian wondered at the waste and the foolishness of building those thick high walls around herself, walls that kept her away from those who really did love her.

❦

Ann and the kids walked into the sunny solarium where her mother sat on a brightly colored upholstered wicker chair. There was only one other person in there, who was being read to by a volunteer. Tim led the little procession deeper into the room to stand in front of Helen.

She was dressed in khaki linen slacks and a long-sleeved turquoise top. Gold and turquoise earrings dangled from her ear lobes, and she had on a gold bangle bracelet and wore khaki espadrilles on her narrow feet. Ann looked at the delicate skin on the inside of her ankles, colored dark purple by spider veins. Her hair was completely white, cut to her chin, and carefully styled. There were very few wrinkles on her thin face, although a

225

hint of jowls accented each side of her jaw. Except for her white hair and sagging breasts, she looked younger than she should. She stared out through the glass walls at the nursing home's lushly landscaped courtyard without noticing their arrival.

"Helen," Tim said, leaning near her face. "Helen, I've brought you some company."

She looked at him with recognition, but both he and Ann knew that although Helen recognized him, it was more as a nice man who visited every day, and not as the man she had lived with and loved for forty-five years.

"Hello," she said to him, her lips turning up into a small smile.

"I've got some friends here," he repeated.

Suzy stood behind her mother, a little afraid of the older woman. Philip stepped up and said, "Hi, Grammy."

Helen's smile faded, and then she took Philip's hand in hers. "Well, hello, there. Aren't you a nice little boy? What's your name?"

"I'm Philip," he said, as though he really was meeting her for the first time, even though he had been the light of her life before she sank deeper into dementia. Helen had been in the delivery room the day he was born, rocked him in her arms when he had colic, fed him bottles, played in the pool with him, and baked cookies with him. "It's nice to meet you," he added, well trained at this point.

Ann filled up with grief. It grabbed at her heart and caused her physical pain.

She stepped up to her mother's chair. "Hi, Mom," she whispered. Helen's eyes met hers, but Ann could see that they were empty, as if no one lived behind them.

"Who are you?" Helen asked her. "Are you this nice boy's mother?"

Ann nodded, holding back a sob with all the strength she had. "I am. I came to see you all the way from Pennsylvania. Are you feeling well?" It all seemed so trite, so contrived.

"Who's the little girl?" Helen asked, peeking around Ann.

"She's my daughter, Suzy."

"She's very pretty. Come here, child. Let me see you," Helen said, holding out her hand to the little girl. Suzy moved from behind her mother, but she clung to Ann's arm.

Ann whispered to her, "Don't be afraid, darling. She's still your Grammy." Ann leaned down and kissed Suzy's head. "Let her touch you,

Suz," she whispered.

Suzy reached out with one arm, while still clutching her mother. "Hi, Grammy," she said.

"You're a nice girl. What a pretty dress you're wearing. Blue is my favorite color, you know. I like blue a lot. Do you like blue? I wear blue dresses, too."

Suzy nodded.

"Do you like to color in coloring books?" Helen asked her granddaughter. "There's some over there. Do you want to color with me? I have crayons."

"I like to color," Suzy said, cautiously. She looked in the direction her grandmother pointed.

Suzy walked over to an end table that held magazines and a few coloring books. She carried a coloring book back to her grandmother who took four crayons out of the pocket of her slacks. Tim pulled a snack table over to them and together they selected a page in the coloring book and started to color.

Ann sat in one of the wicker chairs and watched her mother and daughter. They were connecting on a level Ann couldn't reach.

She and her father chatted, and Tim talked to Philip about guy things—football, soccer, hockey—until Philip said, "I'm thirsty, Mom."

"Me too," Suzy said, looking away from her coloring book.

"Okay," Tim said, "Come with me. I'll take you to the café and we'll get a nice drink." He looked at Ann. "You want to come?"

She shook her head. "I'll stay here with Mom a little while. If you want, you can take them back to the house. I'd just like to visit with her alone for a few minutes."

He patted her shoulder, took Philip's hand, and said, "Come on, Suzy."

"Are you leaving?" Helen asked the little girl. Suzy put her hand on her grandmother's shoulder. "Yes, but I'll come back tomorrow. We can color some more then. Okay, Grammy? You finish your picture now, and then we'll do another picture tomorrow."

Ann smiled at her daughter. Suzy was parroting what Ann herself would say whenever she had to stop doing something with Suzy to answer the phone or cook dinner.

Tim took them out of the room. Ann sat looking at her mother who continued to color in the book.

"Mommy," she said.

She waited a few long seconds before repeating, "Mommy."

Helen looked up at her. Blank eyes; no recognition.

"Mommy, please come back. Please come back just for a minute. I need you." She swallowed hard, trying to control the emotion that was strangling her. "I'm dying and I need my mother," she whispered.

She said all of this quietly, calmly. She didn't want to upset her mother. She didn't want to say it at all, but she couldn't stop herself. The words tumbled out of her. The longing she had for the woman her mother had been was powerful.

She crossed the room and knelt in front of the older woman. She placed her cheek on Helen's knee. "I don't think I've got any more chances, Mom. I'm scared...I'm really scared," and she broke down now.

She sensed the slightest of movements from her mother, and then she felt her mother's hand on her head, stroking her hair.

"Woe, woe, baby..." Helen sang the words almost in a whisper. Ann knew the little sing-song well. Helen sang it to every baby she had ever held. It was a song of her own creation. "...Momma's little baby...woe, woe, baby...Momma loves her baby." Helen continued to stroke Ann's head.

Ann grabbed her mother's other hand and placed her lips on it, her tears fell in heavy drops on the women's slacks leaving dark rings on the fabric. "Mommy...mommy....mommy," she chanted, kissing her mother's hand. "Help me, please help me. Help me not to be fearful of what's coming."

Ann continued to cry and to grasp her mother's frail hand, holding onto the woman who had given her life and wishing that this beloved woman could prolong that life now.

"Don't be afraid, honey," her mother said then. "Don't be sad."

Ann looked up into her mother's face, thinking that maybe Helen was aware of who she was, but she knew immediately that Helen didn't know. She was just comforting a sad and crying stranger.

"I love you, Mommy," Ann said, kissing both of her mother's hands now and then holding them to her cheeks. "We're going to be together again someday, Mom. I know we will. When that happens, you'll know who I am and we'll both be happy again—we'll be like we used to be. We'll laugh together like we used to. We'll sing Billy Joel and Elton John songs...and the Four Seasons—remember the Four Seasons?—you loved the Four Seasons. And we'll dance the Mashed Potatoes. Listen to me, Mommy. I'm going first, but I'll be there when you're ready to come. I'll be waiting for you. You'll know me, then… I know you will…you'll know me again…"

"Yes, honey, that's right. You come back tomorrow and visit. I like visitors. That man… I don't remember his name…but he comes every day and he'll bring you back again tomorrow."

Ann pulled a wad of tissues from her pocket and wiped her face and nose. She nodded at Helen and stood up. She stroked her mother's white hair. Helen picked up a crayon and started coloring in the book again.

∽

After lunch, they decided to take the kids to the community pool. Tomorrow they'd drive to the beach or to Naples, but today, they'd relax in the sun and let the kids splash around in the pool. Children were allowed between the hours of two and four, when most of the residents of the retirement community went inside to nap or prepare dinner.

"I look like a beached whale," said Lillian, pulling her cover up close around her bathing suit, "an albino whale."

Ann chuckled. "You better put sun screen on or you'll burn to a crisp."

They were surprised to find that there were still quite a few grey heads sitting around the pool when they got there. Some of the men were playing chess, and a few clusters of women were playing bridge.

No one seemed to notice them at first. Lillian put Suzy's swimmies on her arms, while Philip kicked off his flip-flops next to a lounge chair and jumped into the water. Ann laid her towel on another chair and sat down on it. Her size zero blue bathing suit looked a little big on her when she took off her cover up. Lillian rolled her eyes but said nothing, pulling at the swimmies.

Lillian backed up, away from Suzy, while giving her niece and nephew some rules of the pool, feeling behind her the entire time for her lounge chair. She backed up too far, slipped and went down on the concrete deck, pulling the chair over with her.

Her long, untanned legs went in two different directions, while the chair flipped over on top of her.

Ann gasped and jumped up to help her.

"Son of a bitch," Lillian said, grabbing and groping the air. Ann righted the chair and helped Lillian off the concrete. There was a wide scrape on Lillian's buttocks and thigh. One flip-flop was still on her foot, the other had flown into the bushes beyond them.

"Don't make a scene," Lillian whispered to her cousin when she noticed laughter starting to bubble up in Ann.

"Too late for that," Ann said, laughing out loud.

"Will you stop it," Lillian hissed between clenched teeth, mortified when she realized everyone around the pool was staring at them.

"I can't help it," Ann said, laughing harder now, while trying to get Lillian settled.

Lillian pushed her away. "I'm fine now. Leave me alone."

Ann sat back down on her chair, choking back laughter, holding a rolled towel to her mouth. Lillian put her towel on the chair and sat down more gracefully this time. But when the chair had flipped over, the back stop must have unseated itself from the groove and when Lillian placed her weight against the back of the chair, it fell all the way back and the very top hit the concrete with a loud thud.

"Jesus Christ!" she shouted this time, grabbing at the air for balance as she fell back.

All of the gray heads around the pool, all of the wide-brimmed hats and the wrinkled flabby bodies turned in her direction to see what was going on.

Ann let out a belly laugh.

"Stop it," Lillian hissed at Ann, but Ann was convulsed in a laughing fit, gagging and tearing up with the strain of trying not to laugh. She turned on her side to pull her towel over her mouth and muffle gasps of laughter.

Suzy just stood staring at them, wondering if she should laugh, and if so, at what exactly. Philip swam away from their side of the pool, removing himself from the laughing hyena and the swearing crazy person on the pool deck.

"Ann, you're a goddamned sadist," Lillian said. She pulled the back of the chair into place and made sure it was locked in place this time. Her finger was bleeding and she held it to her lips. "My ass is scraped raw and my finger got pinched in the chair, and you're in hysterics."

"I'm sorry," Ann managed to get out, but the slapstick scene kept replaying in her mind and she couldn't stop laughing. What made it even funnier was Lillian's cantankerous reaction.

"Stop...it...now!" Lillian hissed. "Everyone is looking at us."

Lillian looked across the pool. An elderly man without a shirt and a tight fitting Speedo bathing suit winked at her.

"Oh, this is nice...now you have dirty old men winking at me. Thank you...thank you very much," but between Ann's contagious laugh and the fact that now she could see the comedy in it all, Lillian was having trouble not laughing at herself.

She threw Suzy's rolled-up towel at her cousin, but she laughed when she did it. "Stop, you idiot" she said.

Ann straightened and cleared her throat. "Oh, God, I needed that laugh," she said. She wiped tears from her eyes with the corner of the towel.

"Oh, well, anytime you need a good laugh, I'll just fall on my ass for you, legs up in the air. I didn't even get a wax before we came. Can you imagine what they all saw?" She shivered thinking about it.

"That's not helping!" Ann choked again.

"Don't start again," Lillian warned. "Please."

Ann took a deep breath. Suzy jumped into the pool to join Philip and everything was quiet again. They sat silently for a long while.

"How much more do you have to do before you finish the book?" Ann asked Lillian.

"I don't know…I have some more research in Doylestown to do…I guess about three or four more chapters. Then I have to edit it and clean it up before I send it to…" She chose not to say Dan's name. She hadn't heard from him in days. He didn't respond to any of her emails, even though she knew he had his laptop with him in Europe. "Why?" she asked Ann.

Ann shrugged and moved her head from side to side to loosen her neck. "I don't know. Just wondering…I hope I get to read the ending."

"Of course you'll get to read the ending. It's only going to be about two or three months before it's completely finished. Maybe sooner."

Ann smiled into the air, but said nothing. Then after about ten minutes, she said, "Lilly…"

"What?"

"Thanks for the laugh."

"Shut up."

❧

That evening, right after dinner, Lillian went for a walk to give Ann and Tim time alone. She took the sidewalk in front of his house and meandered from one stretch to another, admiring the houses and the golf course behind them. She stopped when she saw a large building where she knew her aunt was living. She started to go in another direction, then stopped, turned back, and walked directly into the lobby.

A middle-aged woman with honey-colored curly hair sat behind a beautiful cherry wood desk and smiled brightly. "May I help you?"

Lillian hesitated and then said. "My aunt…Helen Stuart…I think she's in this building."

"Yes, she is," said the woman. "Now let me call up to her floor and see where she is. Just one minute."

She already had the phone at her ear and she was punching numbers on the dial. Lillian saw a gallery of photos in a case and walked over to look. They were of couples, men playing golf, women playing golf, families. She saw her aunt and uncle in one of the photos. She'd seen the same photo earlier in the day on Uncle Tim's wall.

"You can go up," the woman with the honey-colored hair said. "She's napping, but they said you can go into her room." She motioned to the grand staircase in the center of the lobby. "Stairs or elevator?"

Lillian smiled. "I can handle the stairs, I think."

"Okay, then go up two flights. The nurse's station is at the top."

They showed Lillian into Helen's room. It was dark in the room because the blinds were closed. "I hate to wake her," Lillian said to the nurse.

"It's okay. We prefer that they don't sleep too long at this time of day because then they don't sleep at night."

Lillian nodded and took in the room before waking her aunt. It was pleasant enough, decorated with Aunt Helen's own things which Lillian recognized. The walls were covered with framed photographs. Helen and Tim's wedding photo hung on a large wall and beside it a photo of them with their wedding party. Lillian's mother stood smiling beside Helen, the long satin folds of their gowns pressed together.

There were photos of Ann as a child, then of Ann holding Joey when he was an infant. Lillian could see what Joey looked like at every age—on a tricycle, beside a two wheeler, in his soccer jersey, in his swim suit and cap when he was on the swim team in high school…his prom photo and graduation photo. There were photos of Ann, too, and of course, Philip and Suzy.

Lillian picked up Ann's wedding photo to look more closely. She was so young. And her groom was smiling from ear to ear. There were several photos of Lillian as well, one in her carriage when she was about a year old, another sitting on Aunt Helen's lap on the gazebo when she was a toddler.

There was a photo of Lillian with her mother and father dressed in winter coats at Willow Wood, and still another with her grandparents and another with Ann when they were young. One photo was of Lillian's mother and aunt alone when they were teenagers, their cheeks touching, both smiling.

A large overstuffed chair was in one corner of the room, facing the window, which Lillian assumed looked out at the golf course like most of the other windows did at the back of the building. The room smelled of Ivory soap.

She moved closer to the bed and watched her aunt sleeping. Seeing that beloved face made her want to cry and smile all at the same time. It hadn't changed much at all. Her hair wasn't the stunning auburn of her youth, but the rest of her looked so youthful, so peaceful.

Helen must have sensed that Lillian was standing there, because her eyes opened and she pushed herself up on one arm. It took her a long moment to focus, but when she did, her face lit up and her mouth opened wide.

"Our Lillian," she said, her voice still shaky from sleep. "Our Lilly is here. Oh, come to me, come give me a kiss."

Lillian was confused. They had all told her Aunt Helen didn't know anyone in the family, but here she was calling Lillian by name.

She leaned over and Helen took her face in both her hands and kissed her cheeks, first one, then the other, then the first one again. It was her trademark kiss, and it brought Lillian back to childhood.

"Aunt Helen," Lillian breathed. "Aunt Helen, you know me?"

"Of course, I do, you silly." Helen pushed her legs off the side of the bed, and patted the mattress for Lillian to sit down.

"Have you seen my Annie?" Helen asked her.

"I have, and Suzy and Philip, too."

"Your Uncle Tim?" Helen asked, looking a little strained now.

"Uncle Tim, too. He's wonderful—you're wonderful. Look how young and svelte you are," she said, indicating her aunt's figure.

"I keep myself nice, don't I?"

Lillian nodded, smiling and holding back tears. "Yes, you always did."

"And your mother? How is my beautiful sister? Has she been behaving? Poor dear, she gets herself so upset sometimes."

Lillian looked deeply into her aunt's eyes. They were the same eyes, yet they weren't. "She's fine," she decided to answer.

"You got my letters about Joey?" Helen asked, tightening her grip on

Lillian's hand. "You read them, don't you?"

"Every one of them, Aunt Helen, over and over again. I put them away, then take them out to read them when I'm sad or lonesome. I keep every letter. Thank you for sending them to me."

"He placed second in the swim meet last week, and first the week before."

Lillian realized that her aunt was in a different year, a different era of her children's lives, but it was all right. She knew who Lillian was and Lillian was thrilled.

"He's quite an athlete, I know; and so handsome."

"Oh, he is," agreed Helen. "All the girls call the house at all hours asking for him. When I was a girl, we didn't call the boy's house at all, we waited for them to call us, you know. But not anymore."

Helen took Lillian's face in her hands again. "Oh, look at you. You're more beautiful than you ever were. Reggie must be so proud of you. I didn't ask about your father. Is he well? He had a broken arm the last time I saw him, it seems to me."

Lillian reassured her aunt, "It's all better now."

Helen gripped her hand so tightly that Lillian wanted to wince. "I want to tell you I'm sorry…but I can't for the life of me remember why. Why do I have this feeling that I owe you an apology? Maybe it's not you…maybe it's your mother. Maybe I owe her an apology?"

"No, Aunt Helen, no one. You don't owe any of us an apology. You're so good. You've always been so good to us."

"You look like me," she said, her eyes shining.

"So I've been told, and I'm happy that I do."

"You always did look like me. It made Reggie mad as hell when people said it. And when you called on the telephone, Tim would say that you sound just like me too."

"Yes, I think I do."

"What did your mother do with her red shoes? Those red high heels of hers? They'd look beautiful on you. Do you know the ones I'm talking about?"

"I do, Aunt Helen. They were her favorites. They had round toes and were fire engine red patent leather, right?"

"Yes, yes, that's right. Did she give them to you?"

Lillian couldn't hold back her tears any longer. "No," she choked out, "no, she's probably still wearing them. She always said she'd wear them right into heaven. I remember she actually slept in them one night—under the covers—when she was in her nightgown. She loved those damned red shoes." What Lillian didn't say was that it was when her mother was in a manic state that she loved the shoes the most. She also didn't mention how much the heel of those shoes hurt when they made contact with Lillian's back.

"She did, honey. She got them the day you were born, did you know that?"

Lillian shook her head no.

"She was shopping before she went into labor, she wanted to get some new clothes to wear when she didn't have to wear maternity clothes anymore. She said the red shoes would always remind her of the happiest day of her life...the day you were born. She said that you'd grow up and leave her, but she'd always have the shoes to remind her of your birth."

Lillian stood up to get a tissue from the box on Helen's dresser. She blew her nose and wiped her eyes, working hard to compose herself. When she turned back, Helen was staring at her. "Regina!" she said to Lillian. "Regina, where did you come from?"

"No, it's still me, Aunt Helen. It's Lillian."

Helen looked confused and anxious now. "I don't know who you are...you're not my sister, are you?"

Lillian didn't answer her.

"Go get my sister, please. I want my sister. I have to tell her that I'm sorry I left her there. Those boys wouldn't have hurt her if I'd stayed with her. But I was so mad."

"She isn't here," Lillian said, touching her aunt, but Helen pulled away from her hand. She reached over and pushed the button for the nurse to come in. Within seconds, the nurse arrived.

"What's the matter, Miss Helen?" the nurse asked, her voice calm and sweet. "Are you okay?"

"Get my sister," Helen demanded.

The nurse looked at Lillian and smiled gently. "Okay, dear, I'll go call her. You sit in the chair and relax until she comes."

The nurse led Helen to the chair overlooking the golf course. Looking at Lillian, the nurse said, "I think we better leave her. She's getting agitated."

Lillian asked if she could kiss Helen goodbye, but the nurse advised against it and led her out of the room. "She gets this way sometimes. She calls for her sister every day. They must have been very close."

Lillian looked back at the closed door of her aunt's room.

"Yes, they were. They were very close," Lillian said.

❧

When they returned to Bucks County, Ann went to the gym every day, but her back wasn't much better.

"Maybe you need a chiropractor," Lillian suggested.

But Ann didn't answer her. She continued to take her vitamins, drink her shake, and when Lillian wasn't looking, sneak pain killers. When Lillian came home from the supermarket one day a week after their trip to Florida, she noticed a car in the driveway and found Ann entertaining two men in the living room. They were talking softly when Lillian entered the room.

"I'm sorry, I didn't mean to interrupt. Ann, do you want me to get everyone a drink—tea, coffee, a soda?"

"Come in, Lilly. This is Daryl Worthington, my attorney, and his associate, Ben Johnston."

Lillian shook their hands. She recognized one of them and said, "Starbucks, right?"

He nodded, "That's right…every morning. I think we were on the same schedule."

"We need you," Ann said. "I have some things to discuss with you and Daryl and Ben. I have to put you on the spot right now."

Lillian sat down in a chair opposite to the lawyers. "Oh?"

"Will you be Philip and Suzy's legal guardian when I die?" Ann couldn't have been more matter-of-fact when she asked. "If you will, I shall sign the house over to you. It's completely paid for. You raise the kids here, or sell it and move somewhere else with them, it's up to you. If you don't want to raise the children, the house you used to live in on State Street in Newtown will be yours—again, free and clear. No mortgage, but we have put in some tax protection for you on both houses. You can sell it, live in it, it's yours to do with as you wish."

Lillian sat back in her chair. "I get a house whether or not I take your kids?"

Ann nodded, the lawyers nodded, and then Lillian nodded.

"I can't believe you're asking me this after all these months. They are as much my kids now as they are yours, Ann. I love them."

"And Dan?" Ann asked her, cocking her head to one side.

"I don't know that Dan is even in the picture anymore, but if he loves me, he'll love the kids."

"You'll sign papers to that effect?" Daryl Worthington asked.

"Give me the pen," she answered without blinking.

They conducted business and the two men left just in time for the school bus to arrive.

"What will you do with the house in Newtown now that I've agreed to take the kids?" Lillian asked Ann as they watched the kids run up the driveway towards them.

"I'll sell it and put the money in an account for you," Ann answered.

"You don't need to do that. I'd take the kids even if you were a pauper. I'd live on that park bench with them if I had to. Put the money in a trust for the children. We'll have to educate them."

"I won't be around to educate them, Lilly."

"Come on, Ann, the new drugs are working…"

"Lillian, my liver is failing. The tumors are almost gone, but the liver is shutting down."

Lillian's mouth dropped open. It felt as though cold fingers were wrapping around her lungs. "You've been going for tests again?"

"Be quiet, the kids are coming," Ann said, stepping into the cold late October air to greet her children. "How about some ice cream?" she called to them.

"Today? In the middle of the week?" Philip asked surprised.

"Today? In the middle of the week!"

Ann turned to wave to Lillian while she pressed the unlock button on her car remote.

"We'll be back in about an hour," she called, ushering the kids into her car. She didn't invite Lillian to come with them.

# Twenty

"I don't know that I want to know or write anything else about Willow Wood today," Lillian announced one cold November afternoon. She plopped down on the couch and looked at Ann who was sitting in her chair near the fire.

"More sad stories?" Ann asked, knowing that Lillian had been at the book all morning. "Is Willow Wood jinxed, do you think? So many sad stories…so much death and illness and unhappiness here…starting with the Revolution when the sons of this house were killed during the Battle of Princeton. How many mothers who lived in this house had to bury their children? It's not right. It's just not the order of things for a parent to have to bury a child. Yet it happened over and over again."

Lillian took the role of optimist for a change. "Yes, but there were happy times in this house and on this farm, too, Annie. People die, Ann. People die before their time in everyone's family, and probably in every ancient house that has survived the American Revolution and the Civil War and all the wars before and after. Life is that way, fair or not. Yet, in between those awful times, there's laughter, and marriages, and babies born who are loved and wanted. In this house, Annie, people celebrated anniversaries, graduations, holidays and birthdays. Even from my own troubled childhood, this house holds warm and happy memories for me."

Ann said, "So you've become a philosopher, have you?"

Lillian laughed. "I don't know about that! But I'm learning more about life from reading those letters and journals than I ever learned in college. A house that survives that kind of trouble and sadness is simply a house that has sheltered life…with all the good and all the bad."

She studied the flames of the late afternoon fire. "This house has a soul simply because of all the souls that have lived and died in it, who have cried and laughed inside its walls, including our own grandparents and parents."

Ann stood up and leaned against the stone fireplace. "Are Germaine and Juliana-Alma, and Willie and Mark, and Hannah and Sean and Selina and the poor, poor Corinne here with us, do you think? Are their spirits in this room?"

"No! No ghosts…I don't like ghosts at all," Lillian said with a shiver.

"Are there ghosts, do you think?" Ann wanted to know. "Father Murray has convinced me that there is an afterlife and I believe in heaven these days. I'm certainly saying enough rosaries to get me into it. I'm okay with dying if that's where I'd go…I want to go to heaven. But I wonder, Lillian, do we kind of stay around when we have unfinished business…if things aren't settled before we die…if we are afraid to leave our children…do we linger here on earth and not have peace in that life?"

Lillian looked down at her hands, but tried to answer lightly. "You're asking me…as though I, the heathen of all heathens, know the answer to that question?"

"You aren't a heathen. You're as Catholic as I am. You pretend to be a heathen, but you aren't. You went to Catholic schools just as I did, you received First Holy Communion and Confirmation, and went to Mass every Sunday and a Catholic college. Tell me what you believe, Lilly. Do you believe in ghosts?"

"No," Lillian answered. "I don't."

"Why not?"

Lillian closed her eyes and sighed deeply. "I don't want to be haunted, I guess."

"If you thought that your mother's spirit was right here in this room, it wouldn't help you…comfort you?"

Lillian grimaced. "Oh my God, Ann! Help me? I'd duck waiting for the next blow."

"Be serious," Ann told her.

"I don't know, Ann," Lillian said, sighing. "I don't want my mother here in this room because I want her to be at peace. She certainly didn't have any peace here on earth. If I want to think of it at all, I would want to believe that she made amends with God somehow and is happily settled on her own personal fluffy white cloud, eating chocolate-covered strawberries and drinking champagne."

Ann sat down again, still troubled. Lillian walked over and placed her hand on Ann's back. "Listen, kiddo," she said, "I don't know what you want to hear, what kind of answer you're searching for, but I'll tell you that you're right, I do believe that there is a heaven. I believe in all three persons of the Trinity, and the—what's it called?...*intercession*...of the Blessed Mother. I had a professor in college say that God wants us to be with Him. I think I believe that. But all of this happens in time—in *God's time*, not ours—we don't make those decisions, only He does."

Ann put her face in her hands, and Lillian knelt next to her cousin, her lips near her Ann's ear. "Annie, let me take over any unfinished business you have. Give that unfinished business to me if and when you have to, and I promise you I will not let you down. I will take care of them, Annie. I will. Don't be afraid...of anything. God will take care of us. These aren't just empty words, Ann."

Lillian pulled Ann's hands from her face to look in her eyes. "It's not that I think God wills us to be sick and die, but for whatever reason it happens. We're all here on this earth for a reason, and when we fulfill whatever job we have to do, we leave. Sometimes it's for a year, sometimes 30 years, sometimes 80 or 90...whatever it takes. But I think He's with us through it all. So be at peace if you can. And I will, too. We've got to, Annie. We have to trust in Him, I guess. God's got our back, right?" Lillian pushed gently at Ann for a response. "Okay?"

Ann leaned her forehead against Lillian's. "Okay."

"Okay. Now I'll go back to being a heathen. And don't haunt me...please," Lillian said smiling, trying to lighten the mood between them. "I'm such a scaredy cat, you know, I'd just flip out. No apparitions in my bedroom or anything like that. Don't move my things around to let me know you're there. And for God's sake, Annie, don't make noises in the middle of the night. I will have a nervous breakdown."

Ann smiled a little now, then shrugged, teasing, suggesting it was a possibility.

Lillian pointed at her. "I swear, Ann, I'll have you exorcised. I mean it! I will."

∞

Two days later, Lillian decided that she really did want to finish the story of Willow Wood. She reached down into the blanket chest and pulled out more papers. She found a clipping from the Bucks County Intelligencer that was dated in the late fifties. According to the date on the masthead, her mother would have been around seventeen. The paper was cut so that the article remained attached to the masthead, but the rest of the page had been cut away to form an upside down L.

The envelope it was in was marked *Regina* in Lillian's grandfather's handwriting. She found it toward the bottom of the chest, as though someone deliberately tried to bury it. When she saw her mother's name, she wanted to push the envelope back into the chest and keep looking for other history about Willow Wood, history that had nothing to do with her mother, but her grandfather's handwriting made her stop.

She brushed her thumb over her mother's name, then turned the envelope over and opened it.

### FIVE MEN ARRESTED IN RAPE AND BEATING OF SEVENTEEN YEAR OLD GIRL

*Makefield…Five men from Bucks County have been arrested in the rape and beating of a seventeen year old girl from a well-respected family in Makefield. She was walking along the deserted canal towpath when they came out of the woodlands and attacked her. Janice Aldrich, who was walking her dog early the next morning, found the young woman lying at the bottom of the empty canal where she was left for dead, and ran to the nearest house to call the police. The young woman, who was unconscious at the time and whose identity is being kept undisclosed because she is a minor, was brought to Doylestown Hospital and survived. She was released five days later. She was able to identify three of her attackers.*

Lillian's pulse raced through her body; she felt it in her neck and heart and even in her thumbs where she held them against the paper. Nothing had ever been said to her about this incident. *My mother… raped?* She wondered why no one had told her that her mother had been attacked when she was only seventeen.

She remembered now that once when she was a teenager and acting wild and rebellious, she stormed out of her house after an argument with her father, walked to Willow Wood, but didn't go in. She didn't want to upset her aunt. Her parents found her on the canal towpath later that night. She was alone when they found her, and her mother fell to her knees sobbing and thanking God over and over that Lillian was all right. She made Lillian promise she'd never go there alone again…no matter how angry she was at her parents. Her mother had taken Lillian's face in her hands gently and begged, "Please, Lillian, don't do it again. No matter what we do to you to make you mad, please don't come here alone ever again. Promise me, darling, please promise me." It took an hour for Lillian and her father to calm her mother down.

Now, Lillian sat completely still, holding the article between her fingers. Would it have been easier to forgive her mother if she had known that her mother had been brutally raped and almost killed? She honestly didn't know. But now she understood better why her grandparents and aunt had always been so protective of Regina. It made sense now, if anything could make sense about the calamity that was her mother.

The next article, this one in two pieces and stapled together, reported on the beginning of the trial. Several more articles—all of which named her mother now, since more than a year had passed and Regina was no longer a minor—narrated the ongoing results of the trial.

It recounted the testimony of the woman who found Regina, the policemen's testimony, Regina's own testimony, Regina's sister's testimony that they had been walking together, but because of an argument, Helen had left her sister alone on the towpath.

The last article, dated a year and a half later than the first one, reported that three of the men, all nineteen years of age at this point, were convicted and sent to prison for ten years for battery and attempted murder.

Two more were found not guilty and released. None of the men's names were familiar to Lillian, not even the last names, yet all were from Bucks County where she had grown up.

Three of them had been identified by her mother because she knew them well; they went to high school with her. The other two, who were released, were strangers to Regina, boys from another school district. They were released because there was no evidence that they assisted in the crime.

What this meant to Lillian was that after the trials were finally over, two of the kids who had attacked her mother were set free to live and work in the area.

Her mother must have seen them in stores, the library, even in the store where she worked as an adult. And if not them, then certainly their parents, maybe sisters or brothers.

Lillian felt sick to her stomach and her hands started to tremble. A compassion for Regina—the person she was so used to hating—washed over her.

She wondered why her grandfather saved these articles. What for? They were terrible reminders of what had happened to her mother. She wondered, also, if Regina had been mentally ill before this incident, or if this trauma had brought on her paranoid schizophrenia. Did one of the attackers have a crush on her and did she verbally assault him during one of her "moods"? Did she call them nasty names? Make fun of them? Turn her vitriolic tongue on them in front of their friends at school? Did they want to put the beautiful, brilliant, and venomous Regina Stuart in her place? Or did *that* Regina Stuart spring up as a result of the attack?

*It doesn't matter*, Lillian thought now. There was no one to ask anymore. She wondered if her father had known; was that why he was also so protective of Regina? He must have known. Why else would he have put up with her for all those years? She knew they had been high school sweethearts. Did he love her because of the attack or in spite of it?

This article explained what Aunt Helen meant when Lillian was with her in Florida—the reason for Helen's apologies and even her protection all the years before that. She felt guilty for leaving her sister alone that night on the towpath. She blamed herself for what happened to Regina.

Lillian found one loose-leaf page in the envelope, and on it were three questions, again in her grandfather's handwriting: *Why didn't Regina come straight home when Helen left her on the towpath? Did she intend to meet those boys? How much praying do I have to do to keep myself from killing each one of them with my bare hands? My Regina. My girl.*

Lillian wanted to feel something after reading these articles. She wanted to feel angry in behalf of her mother…she wanted to feel protective of her as everyone else in Regina's life had. She wanted to hate those five men who had done that awful thing and made her mother the tyrant that she had turned into. Yet…*nothing*…she felt nothing. The compassion she had felt moments before left her as quickly as it had come.

The same resentful anger toward her mother was still there…inside her. Any sadness she felt was for her poor tormented grandfather who had to live with the knowledge that his daughter was beaten and raped and he wasn't around to protect her. He and his wife and their other daughter spent the rest of their lives protecting Regina, trying to make up for what had happened, but their love never made up for that one disastrous violent moment. Regina spent the rest of her life taking it out on those who loved her most.

*I'm sorry*, she thought. *I'm sorry it happened. But goddamn it, I had nothing to do with it. Why did I have to be punished my whole life for what happened to her? Why didn't anyone protect me the way they protected her?*

Guilt flooded through her then. *What sort of person am I? How can I read this and be so cold?*

Lillian took the articles and her grandfather's loose-leaf sheet and put them back into the envelope. She buried it in the chest where her grandfather had buried it many years before.

# Twenty-one

The days turned colder as Thanksgiving approached. Ann had stopped going to the gym, the protein shakes were done with, the pain medications increased. Lillian noticed that Ann's skin was waxy and sallow, but Ann covered it up with makeup.

She still took care of the kids, but she was sleeping in the afternoons again, and Lillian had to take over the breakfast detail during the week. Philip didn't seem to notice the change, and Suzy was oblivious to it. Ann still wore the wig, even though her hair had begun to grow in, so nothing seemed different where the children were concerned.

Monica took the kids after school a lot, and Lillian wondered if Ann had confided in Monica about her medical condition. To repay Monica, Lillian invited her kids to the movies on a few Saturday afternoons.

Dan and Lillian were emailing again, but their communications were strained. Ann advised Lillian to go to New York and have it out, but Lillian didn't want to leave her and the kids.

"You're a coward," Ann said to her. "I'm fine for now, so don't use me as an excuse."

Lillian ignored her, continued to edit manuscripts for Dan and send them back to him, but they spoke very little on the phone. It had been a month since she'd seen him. She longed to tell him what she'd found out about her mother, but it just didn't seem the right time with their relationship so strained.

Then a week before Thanksgiving, Ann didn't come down for breakfast, not even to kiss the kids goodbye before they left for the bus. Lillian went up to check on her, and found her sleeping soundly. When she didn't come down for lunch, Lillian awakened her. Ann wore a soft cap on her head when she slept at night, not just to cover her scalp, which had tufts of hair growing out of it in spots, but to keep her head warm now that the nights were colder. It was askew on her head, and Lillian reached over to straighten it. Ann was groggy, confused, and complained of being dizzy and sick to her stomach.

Lillian called Meg's office. "Bring her to the ER. I'll meet you there."

Ann didn't want to go, but Lillian insisted. There was a long wait in the ER, and Lillian called Monica to ask her to get the kids after school. "Keep things as normal as possible for them. I don't want them to be frightened."

Monica agreed and Lillian closed her phone at the same time the hospital personnel called Ann's name. She was examined by a Physician's Assistant, then by a nurse, then the ER doctor. They asked her all the same questions, took her pulse, her blood pressure, took blood, put her on IV fluids, patted her shoulder reassuringly, but told her nothing.

"I'm going to kill someone," Lillian said to Ann when they were alone in the room.

Meg walked in at that moment and said, "You're not allowed to kill anyone in the Emergency Room. It's too messy, and we're always too busy to clean up the mess." She was in scrubs and wasn't wearing makeup or jewelry.

Lillian chuckled, "Okay, I'll control myself."

"What's up with you?" Meg asked Ann.

"You're the doctor; you tell me."

Meg examined Ann's belly, felt her back, her neck, and listened to her heart and stomach with her stethoscope. When she was finished, she leaned on the rails of the hospital bed.

"We're waiting for the blood test results, so I won't know much until they come back."

"I want to go home, Meg," Ann told her, very seriously. "You know that, right?"

Meg nodded slowly. The PA stuck his head into the bay, "Dr. Raphael..."

She patted Ann's hand and said, "I'll be right back."

From where Lillian stood, she could see Meg looking at the chart. Meg sat down on a rolling chair as she pulled up the pages one by one and read them slowly. She raked her fingers through her hair and flung the chart on the desk in anger. Lillian said to Ann, "I have to pee...I'll be right back."

"Go pee," Ann said.

Lillian went directly to the desk where Meg sat. The doctor's shoulders drooped; her face was paler than it had been. "And?" Lillian demanded.

"She's in end stage, Lillian."

Lillian knew it wasn't good news, but she didn't expect this. "What the

246

hell does that mean?" But she knew what it meant. She'd educated herself months before.

"Her poor little body just can't take anymore. Lillian, you have to face this now. You're going to have to be a rock in the next few weeks."

"Weeks?" Lillian asked alarmed, feeling her stomach turn.

"Weeks...maybe days. I don't know; no one does. She and I have talked about when this time came, and she wants hospice at home. Nurses will come to the house every day to care for her when she gets worse, but the bulk of the work will be on your shoulders. We can put her in a nursing home, in hospice, if you'd rather do that, but it isn't what she wants. She wants to be with the kids as long as she can. It won't be easy, Lilly. And the kids will have to know. I think Ann realizes that."

Lillian felt the blood drain from her head. She grabbed for the edge of the desk. Meg jumped up and took Lillian in her arms. "Sit," she said.

"I feel ill," Lillian said.

"Are you going to throw up?"

"No, not like that, just dizzy and...ill."

"I know the feeling. I've gone through this with patients a hundred times, but I feel sick every time. Today is worse, though. I guess that's why they advise us in med school that it's not a good idea to make friends with patients."

Lillian straightened up and took a deep breath. "What's next?"

"I send her home with you. When it's time, I'll order the hospice nurses, a hospital bed, and whatever else you need. As I said, I don't know how long."

Lillian took another deep breath, feeling as though she couldn't get enough oxygen into her lungs. Then she looked at the doctor she'd come to trust and respect and said, "Let's do it."

"You won't be alone," Meg said, hugging her. "I promise I won't desert either one of you and neither will Millicent. We're going to be here for you both."

❦

Ann was feeling better when they arrived home and even helped Lillian prepare dinner as they waited for Monica to bring the kids home. Lillian had offered to go to Monica's to pick them up.

"I don't think so," Ann said.

"Why?"

Ann sighed. "Because Monica lives in your old house."

"In Newtown? Mrs. Snyder's? I thought you told me…"

"No, the one you lived in with your parents. There's a McMansion development around it now with new roads, so the address is different. I thought she lived in one of the McMansions the first time I went there, until I pulled up in front of it and knew it had been your parents' home."

"Why didn't you tell me?"

Ann shrugged. "I don't know. I was afraid it would upset you, I guess. I know how you react when I broach the subject of your childhood or your parents. And you can't stand Monica, so I figured it would make it even worse."

Lillian tried to act nonchalant as she took food from the refrigerator for dinner, but her hands were trembling. It had been a long day. "I can stand Monica," she said. Then, "What does it look like?"

"It's still very stately and elegant. It has different colored siding on it now—it's white instead of red—and it's been renovated inside. Monica had some walls knocked down and a huge gourmet kitchen put in. There's an addition on the back of the house which is the family room. But the dining room and living room look almost the same—same fireplace and mantel. When I was there I kept looking at it and remembering the beautiful wooden soldier nut crackers your mother collected and how she would line them up among pine boughs and holly on the mantel. I pictured the way she decorated the house during the holidays. She was so creative, Lillian. Remember how tall the Christmas trees in your house always were, and the gorgeous glass ornaments she collected… "

Lillian slammed the food on the counter. "You're right; I don't want to talk about it."

They heard the Lexus in the driveway, and waited in silence until the children bounced into the house, kissed their mother and ran upstairs to change out of their school clothes. Monica came in after them, looking less coiffed and glamorous than usual. "Well?" she asked.

Ann answered her. "Well, it was just a little dizzy spell. I'm feeling better."

"Lillian?" Monica asked, not believing Ann.

"A little dizzy spell; you heard the lady."

Monica wasn't fooled, but she wasn't going to intrude either. "I'm here…every day, any day, any time of day, for anything. Please tell me you hear me and you will call me."

"We hear you and we will call you," Ann promised, reaching over to kiss her friend on the cheek.

Monica grabbed Ann closer in a tight embrace. Her eyes were wet when she pulled back.

"Don't cry," Ann told her. She didn't tell her why she shouldn't cry or that everything would be all right. She just smiled a small, sad smile. "Go…your family is waiting for you."

Monica left quickly without saying goodnight and ran toward her car. Lillian watched from the kitchen window and saw Monica cover her face once she was inside the Lexus.

They all ate dinner together, although Ann could eat very little, and then the children went into the library to do their homework.

Lillian started to clear the table in silence, and when she reached over Ann for the second time, picking up two dirty plates, Ann grabbed her arm in a fierce grip. She looked up at Lillian's face, her eyes overflowing for the first time that day. "End stage. It's such a scary expression, isn't it?"

Lillian nodded, frozen in place, the plates still in her hands. Then she put them down on the table and pulled Ann into her arms. She held this beloved "little" cousin and neither of them spoke for a long time. Ann composed herself, took the dish towel Lillian offered her and wiped her face, then left the kitchen to lie down on the couch and watch TV with her children just as she did every night after dinner.

Lillian went to bed when everyone else did, which wasn't usual. Normally she wrote another chapter of her book at night when the house was quiet, but that night writing about history seemed much too trivial.

At two-thirty in the morning she was still wide awake. She opened her cell phone and dialed Dan. His voice was heavy with sleep when he answered, but she smiled with relief when he answered, "Hey, Darling." At least he was still calling her his darling.

"She's in end stage," she said.

There was a long silence, and then he said, "I'll see you in a few hours." She could tell he was getting out of bed, ready to get dressed and drive to Pennsylvania.

"No, don't," Lillian protested. "She wants everything to be as normal for the kids as possible for as long as possible. But I was wondering if," she stopped for a long moment and he waited for her, "next week is Thanksgiving and I'd like to make it really special. Joey is coming home for it. Danny, I need you, too. I've never needed you more than I do now. I need you and Louise and Jessica. I need to sit next to you and breathe you in and touch you and have you touch me, and I'm not saying this in a selfish way, because I know this isn't about me, it's about my cousin and her precious little guys, but it *is* about me, too, damn it, and anything about me involves you because I love you, Danny, I love you more than life itself…" Lillian took in a deep breath after finishing her long, drawn out admission.

"We'll be there. We'll arrive on Wednesday, unless you want us sooner."

"Wednesday," she managed to choke out.

"Wednesday, darling—it's only a few days away. Hang tight. Be strong, Lillian. You *are* strong or you wouldn't be there with them now. Right?"

"I don't know if that's true. I really haven't been tested yet, Dan. I'm so afraid that I'll fail—that I'll screw up."

"You won't. *We* won't. We'll get through this together. I promise you, Lillian."

# Twenty-two

They arrived as promised and about five minutes before Joey arrived. The quiet house suddenly became a center of activity—suitcases, boxes of food covered with aluminum foil, bags of fruit, desserts in high square white boxes—and Lillian in the middle of it all directing traffic. Ann sat in a chair and watched with a smile. She accepted all the kisses from the new arrivals.

Joey squatted down beside her chair, studying her carefully. "I'm good," she said to him before he even asked. "I'm so glad you're home." She touched the hair on his forehead. "I'm so happy you're here, Joey."

He didn't accept her first statement, but he didn't have a chance to say anything because Philip ran to him, knocking him over, overturning a lamp. Ann laughed, Lillian threw her hands up in the air, and Joey wrestled with the boy on the floor. Suzy had already taken custody of Jessica, who was prepared this time with lots of princess books and stickers and a new box of crayons.

Dinner that night was pizza and hoagies. Dan and Joey offered to go to the pizza place to pick them up. Lillian was a little anxious about this first meeting between the two, but when they arrived back, they were laughing and joking with each other and it made her feel...she wasn't sure how to express it even to herself...*light* was the only word she could think of. A kind of thrill went through her ribcage when she saw them together.

Lillian invited Dan to sleep in her room since she usually slept on the floor of Ann's room now in case Ann needed her, while the girls slept in Suzy's room, with Louise in the bed and the girls on air beds on the floor. Joey slept in the guest room, which was really his room. Ann needed her privacy.

When everyone was settled, Dan put on his jacket and held Lillian's out to her.

"Where are we going?" she asked, slipping her arms into the jacket.

"Just out back. I want five minutes with you alone."

They slipped out the kitchen door and walked toward the gazebo. The moon was unobstructed by clouds and shone on the river ahead of them. They walked ankle deep in fallen leaves.

As soon as they reached the gazebo, Dan took her in his arms and kissed her. She was giddy with relief. "Oh, God, Dan, that feels so good," she said. "I've been so upset about you...about us."

He kissed her again, deepening the kiss this time, his mouth hungry for hers, his hands pulling her closer.

"What happened to us last month?" she asked when they parted.

"You became the woman I wanted you to be and it scared the hell out of me."

"How did I become that woman? What's different about me?"

He smiled down at her, the moonlight just falling on his face enough for her to see it. "You know how to show love now," he answered, nuzzling her neck, making her weak in the knees.

"Well, then, why did you pull away from me? Why did it scare you?"

"Because you couldn't show me. You showered it on the kids and Ann, but you still kept me at arm's length. I was so afraid that after all these years—all this time that I believed that you loved me but just couldn't express it—I was wrong. I was afraid that I'd deluded myself."

"And now?"

"Let me see...oh yes, 'I need you, Dan. I love you more than life itself.' That's what you said on the phone." Dan pressed his nose against hers. "Bingo!"

She pushed at his chest annoyed. "I've told you that I love you before that."

"No, Lillian. It was always a 'Sort of...yeah, I guess I love you' attitude. You never said the words."

"It had something to do with my needing you, too. You have to confess that you felt that I didn't need you as much now that I had Ann and the kids and I was taking care of them competently. Well, sort of competently."

"Yes, I confess it. I need to be needed by you, and I'm not ashamed of it. But I also need to be loved by you."

She got serious then. "I signed papers the other day agreeing to be the kids' guardian."

"And?"

"And how do you feel about that?"

"They're sweet kids, Lil. They need us. I might feel a pang now and again about having to share you—but I have to share you anyway. I've always had to share you with your work, your wanderlust, and with my sister and daughter. I've had to share you with all your baggage. But you've almost moved beyond that, I think."

"Almost, Dan? I'm not sure what you mean."

"You haven't quite learned how to forgive, and that worries me."

"I have always forgiven you when we argued…"

"You know what I mean…*who* I mean."

She pulled away from him and leaned on the gazebo's rail to look out at the dark, wintery river. "Yeah, well, that's not going to happen, Dan."

"She was your mother, Lillian. She was sick, you told me that yourself."

Lillian thought about the newspaper article she had come across in the chest and played with telling him, but decided against it. She didn't want her mother intruding on this moment. The hell with her. She ruined enough of my life. I refuse to make excuses for her no matter what she went through, Lillian thought.

"Dan," Lillian said turning to him. "Will you marry me?"

"Why?"

She huffed, genuinely annoyed now. "Oh come on, Dan…"

"No, I want to know why you are asking me to marry you."

"Because I love you. Because I need you. Because you're so freakin' sexy that I can't keep my hands off you when you're near me. Because I love your daughter. Because I love your sister. Because I'm…"

"Because you're afraid to raise Philip and Suzy alone?" he offered.

She screwed up her face. "God, no. I can raise them with my eyes closed now. Since when does a woman need a man to raise kids?"

"Since the beginning of time."

"Anyway, let me finish what I was saying. I want to marry you because I feel worthy…worthy of such a good man…worthy of being loved…because I'm worthy to be your wife. It wouldn't have been any good when I didn't feel that way, but now I do. Now I'm ready. And by the way, I think you're worthy of me, too."

He reached out for her again and she went to him. "Name the date," he said kissing her hair.

"I think we might want to wait a little. I can't do anything until Ann…"

"I know…"

"You don't mind waiting a little longer?"

"It's funny," he said "I feel like a young man tonight—like a kid realizing for the first time that he's desperately in love and he can't wait to get married. After waiting for you to be ready all this time, I'm suddenly very impatient. I gotta have you..."

He reached into his jacket pocket, saying, "I'll tell you what, maybe this will keep me patient." He handed her a ring box. "Maybe when I look at it on your finger, it will remind me that there's light at the end of the tunnel."

Lillian opened it, but a cloud passed over the moon. They laughed before she said, "It actually shines in the dark. Look at it. Oh, Dan, a diamond engagement ring for a woman like me? It always seemed so wrong for me..." She looked up at him, half smiling, "Didn't it?"

"Never to me," he said, taking the ring from the box and holding it out, suggesting that he put it on her finger.

"All right, if it fits, then I know it's not so wrong for me," she said splaying the fingers of her left hand out to him and closing her eyes.

It fit.

# Twenty-three

The turkey cooking in the oven filled the house with a homey, stomach-rumbling aroma. Dan and Lillian had gotten up early to prepare the Thanksgiving "guest of honor." He cleaned the bird while she prepared the stuffing. They put it in the top of the double oven and within an hour, one by one, the inhabitants of the old stone house started to drift down into the kitchen.

Louise was first, holding Suzy's hand. "It smells great in here," she said. "What a way to wake up."

Lillian poured Louise coffee and then picked Suzy up in her arms to kiss her. "Happy Thanksgiving, Suzy Q," she said, giving Suzy a butterfly kiss with her eyelash, and offering her cheek for one in return.

"Are we having turkey for breakfast?" Suzy wanted to know.

"Silly girl," Lillian said, putting her down on a chair at the table. "No, we're having lots of gooey sweet things for breakfast—just the kind of stuff your mother doesn't want you to have usually, but it's a holiday so we'll get away with it." Lillian placed an icing-covered cinnamon sticky bun in front of Suzy and a cup of hot chocolate piled high with whipped cream. The little girl threw her head back in ecstasy.

Next came Philip, no slippers on his feet. Lillian pointed down at his bare feet, and he turned with a sigh to climb the back stairs again for his slippers and robe.

Then Joey came down—in flannel pajama pants and a tee shirt but no robe and no shoes—and Lillian pointed to his bare feet. "What?" he asked, shrugging.

"Your sister doesn't allow any of us to walk around in our bare feet, so get some slippers on."

He bumped into Jessica on her way down. She was wearing suede Uggs. "Smart girl," he said gloomily.

Jessica entered the kitchen and put her arms around her father's waist. She was still having trouble opening her eyes. "It's so early," she said.

"What's that smell?"

Dan kissed her forehead. "Turkey in one oven and sticky buns in the other."

"Mmmmm," she said. She scooted Suzy over to share the kitchen chair with the little girl.

By the time the boys came back down, everyone was grabbing at the platter of buns and pieces of the coffee cake Louise had brought from a New York bakery. Lillian put on a second pot of coffee and heated more milk for hot chocolate. It seemed to her that everyone was talking at the same time, but she found herself taking great pleasure in it. Once again she realized that she had deprived herself of so much during the last twenty-two years.

She slipped out of the kitchen unnoticed to check on Ann. Ann was just getting out of the shower when Lillian entered her room. They talked through the bathroom door, which Ann had left ajar.

"It is pandemonium downstairs," Lillian told her.

"I can hear that," Ann answered. "I love it."

"I have something to show you," Lillian said, looking down at her finger.

She heard Ann move around the bathroom, more hurried now, and then Ann opened the door wider. She was wearing a terry robe and a towel wrapped around her head. "What?" she asked.

Lillian held out her hand, feeling ridiculously like a young girl showing off her friendship ring.

Ann's eyes opened wide and she let out a squeal. "Lilly! Oh my God, Lilly, it's gorgeous!"

"It fits," Lillian said, beaming.

"I guess so," Ann said, taking the extended finger in her hand and moving it this way and that to get a better look at the sparkling diamond. "It's so you!"

Lillian was surprised. "It is? Really?"

"Well, yeah, it's so elegant and understated...yet it's so...*huge*..." she said laughing. "It's set in platinum, of course?" Ann said.

"Of course, I guess. I don't know. I didn't ask him."

"It is, I can tell." Ann sat down on her bed. "I'm so happy. If I wasn't so weak I'd do a jig."

Their eyes met, and Ann could see a worried look cross over Lillian's face.

"Hey. Stop…" Ann said.

"Stop what?"

"Feeling guilty because you just got engaged while I'm sick."

"Dan's a good man," Lillian started to say, but Ann waved her hand.

"*I told you* that months ago. I know it, and I am truly, truly happy—for you, for the kids, for Jessica, and for myself. And this is the one thing I didn't manipulate. It happened just as it should have, without my interference."

Lillian frowned and started to rub Ann's back and shoulders through the robe to dry her. "Don't kid yourself. Your mark is all over this engagement!"

Father Murray joined them for dessert. He was dressed in casual clothes, a gray sweater and jeans. He, Joey, Jessica and Dan played scrabble on the game table, while Philip and Suzy wrote their Christmas letters to Santa in front of the fireplace and Ann lounged in her chair with a cup of tea. Lillian and Louise shared the couch, their feet up on the coffee table, while they drank Benedictine and Brandy from snifters.

"Mom, I'm putting an ATV on my list for Santa, okay?" Philip asked.

Ann sat up in her chair. "Absolutely no ATVs under any circumstances. Cross that off your list because you're not getting one. You'll kill yourself, and Santa knows that."

"My friends have ATVs" he protested, but she gave him one of her "mother-looks" as Lillian called them. He sighed and Lillian saw him moving his pencil in a line across the page, then write something else.

Louise asked Lillian, "Did you live here growing up?"

"Near here, two towns over," she answered, staring into the fire. "We lived in an old frame farmhouse on what was then a deserted road."

She sipped the smooth amber liquid and continued. "My mother loved this old poem—I don't even know who wrote it—that went: Whenever I walk to Suffern along the Erie tracks I go by a poor old farmhouse with its shutters broken and black. I must have passed it a hundred times, but I always stop for a minute…to look at the house… the tragic house…"

"The house with nobody in it," Ann joined in.

The cousins smiled at each other. Lillian continued then. "So, when my parents were still newlyweds, my mother found a tragic house, a house with nobody in it, with its shutters broken and black, and they bought it. Every day that Daddy wasn't working at his job, he worked at fixing the house up."

"Your mother worked just as hard," Ann reminded Lillian. "She had this natural talent for interior decorating, and they renovated every room themselves. Aunt Regina was the most talented, artistic woman I ever knew. Once the house was finished, she started in the gardens. The house was on all the garden tours in the region when we were kids."

"Is that what her career was?" Jessica asked from the scrabble table.

Lillian didn't answer, so Ann said, "No, my mother started an interior decorating shop hoping Aunt Regina would go in with her and they could work together. My mother was talented, but she always said her sister was much more so. But Aunt Regina didn't want to partner with my mother."

"She worked in a department store, in the curtain department," Lillian added.

"Why?" Jessica asked.

Dan frowned at his daughter, "You're being intrusive, Jess."

"It's all right, Dan," Lillian said. "My mother was schizophrenic. I think she knew that if she worked with her sister it would ruin their relationship. And she did love her sister."

Ann finished her tea and put the cup on the table next to her. "My mother's shop became very popular and it was bought by a large decorating firm from New York. My mother worked for them then. Right after Joey was born, my parents decided to move to Florida near where our grandparents had moved, and Mom opened a shop down there. We used to come up and stay in this house for a few weeks during the summer."

"I remember one year when I was about five we had a cookout and Aunt Regina and Uncle Tony came," Joey said. "Aunt Regina bought me a brand new red and black two wheeler bike. It was my first one. She was wearing jeans and sneakers, and she actually taught me how to ride it by holding the seat and running alongside while I pedaled. By the end of the afternoon, I was riding alone up and down the driveway, then up the towpath along the canal. She walked for hours with me, up the towpath and back again."

Ann leaned her head against the back of the chair. She was wearing black jeans and a mohair sweater the color of bubble gum, and Lillian thought she looked beautiful—young and healthy despite her illness. "I remember that, Joey," Ann said. "She gave me a silver Tiffany bangle bracelet during that visit with a heart dangling from it. I wore it for years."

"I fell on the towpath and Aunt Regina ran to me," Joey continued. "Her hands were shaking and she started to cry because she was afraid I had gotten hurt. I just skinned my knee, but you'd think I'd broken my neck. We had to walk the bike back home. I was crying, so to distract me, she told me stories about when she was a little girl living along the canal, and then stories about Lillian when she was little. She told me Lillian was the most beautiful girl who ever walked the earth and the smartest, too. Then she told me that I had the best mother in the world..."

Lillian turned from the couch to look at him sharply, but he smiled, and said pointedly "...so I guess you're right, Lillian, she really did love my mother."

Lillian stood up. "Does anyone want another slice of cake or pie?'

They all groaned that they were too full. Ann was starting to doze in the chair and Louise had closed her eyes, too. Lillian walked over to the scrabble players. "I'm just going to throw the dessert dishes into the dishwasher."

"I'll help," Dan said, but Joey pushed him back down into his chair saying, "No, I will. I need to move around and I haven't helped at all today."

He threw his letter tiles back into the pouch and followed Lillian into the kitchen grabbing dishes from the dining room table as he went.

She took the clean dinner dishes out of the dishwasher and stacked them on the counter, while Joey rinsed the dessert plates.

"I'm really happy for you, Lilly," he said. "I like Dan a lot."

"Thank you," she smiled at him. "He's a good guy." She hesitated for a moment, then added, "And thank you for telling me what my mother said about me, Joe."

They worked in silence then until the first load of dishes was put away and the second load was in the dishwasher. She handed him the dish towel so he could dry his hands before going back to the living room. She stood at the sink, wiping it out.

When he was finished, he stood behind her, put one arm around her and kissed the back of her head. She looked up and could see herself and Joey reflected in the window over the sink. His arm, strong and muscular, crossed in front of her. There was something about the embrace—the spontaneous act of affection—that touched her deeply. Her throat tightened with emotion.

He kissed the side of her head this time and whispered, "You are a good, good person, Lilly. Thank you for what you're doing for Ann, thank you for...everything."

She reached up and touched his arm, unable to speak, hoping that he would know she was grateful to him, too…that she loved him.

Joey let her go and left the kitchen just as Father Murray came in. "As much as I hate to, I've got to get going. I have six o'clock Mass in the morning."

"I'll walk you to your car."

He protested, but she grabbed Ann's oversized sweater from the pantry and preceded him out of the house.

"Congratulations," he said to her, indicating the ring. "Where will the wedding be?"

She laughed then. "Why? You want to marry us?"

"Is Dan Catholic?"

"Yes, but neither one of us is a practicing Catholic as you know. However, we practice *other* things, if you know what I mean." Her smile was devilish.

"Oh, I know what you mean all right, you harlot." he chuckled. "I'll marry you, but you have to go to confession and communion and you have to promise to be celibate until your wedding day."

"Yeah, right…we'll talk…" They both laughed again.

He turned serious then, "She's dying now, isn't she?"

"Did Meg tell you?"

"No, I saw it in her face tonight. I know the look. I'm sick over it."

"No miracles for our Annie, Father?"

They were approaching his car at the end of the line of cars in the driveway. "Miracles happen in all different forms, Lillian. I think Ann has had a miracle—several—and you're one of them. She has the comfort of knowing that Philip and Suzy are loved and will be taken care of by a person she trusts and loves."

"What is today—Love Lillian Day? I've been getting accolades since last night and the truth is I don't deserve them. Go back to your rectory and pray for us, Father, 'cause there are bigger and better miracles needed here than me."

"I'll come every day now to bring her Holy Communion. Have you been saying the Rosary with her, Lilly?"

"No. I know she says it every day, but I don't participate. I wouldn't even know how…even if I wanted to. And don't try to guilt me into it. Praying isn't one of my things."

He looked sad…defeated…and it made her feel guilty after all.

"Oh, all right, I'll try; there's always hope for me," she said. She leaned up to kiss his cheek. "Happy Thanksgiving, Padre."

He smiled and got into his car.

∾

Ann had gone to bed before everyone else, but after an hour she needed a second pain pill and found that she didn't have any in her bedroom. She put a scarf around her head, slipped into her robe, and walked down the back staircase, hoping no one would see her. The television was on but there weren't any voices coming from the living room. She found the vial of medicine, put a pill in her mouth and drank some water. She started back up the stairs but was curious as to why it was so quiet in the other room.

Ann peeked around the kitchen door into the living room. They were all asleep. She saw Lillian sound asleep in a chair and Dan sleeping in another chair beside her. Louise was lying on the couch, snoring ever so lightly, and Jessica was on the floor with Suzy's head resting on her slender hip—a pillow cushioning Suzy's head. Joey and Philip were asleep on the love seat, Philip's head slumped against the young man's shoulder. Someone had thrown a blanket over Jessica and Suzy, so she assumed they were the first to fall asleep.

She studied all of them for a long time, allowing her eyes to fall on each face. She knew she should be sad—she would be missing from this homey scene—yet she wasn't...not at that moment...not even when she thought *behold your precious children's new family, Annie.*

# Twenty-four

True to his word, Father Murray came every day to spend time with Ann. They spent a lot of that time laughing together, especially when Lillian gave the priest a hard time. Millicent came every day to check on Ann, and Dr. Meg came at least every other day. She listened to Ann's lungs and did her "doctor thing" as Lillian called it, but mostly she just spent time with her friend, who also happened to be a patient.

Monica stopped by frequently, and Lillian was even beginning to like Monica, albeit grudgingly. She still couldn't stand the up-talk, and actually said to Monica one day, "Are you telling me or asking me?" To which Monica answered, laughing, "You're so sassy, Lillian, but you do make me laugh."

"Stop with the up-talking already…" Lillian said in exasperation.

But Monica didn't. Instead she accentuated it good naturedly, winking at Ann, who enjoyed the good-humored altercations between her cousin and her friend.

Ann made a list of the Christmas gifts Lillian had to buy for the kids. She explained that each child's gifts from Santa were wrapped in different wrapping paper. "Something pink and princess for Suzy's gifts and something in reindeer or snowmen for Philip. But none of the gifts we buy them—gifts that are from us or Joey—should be wrapped in that paper. You see, that's the paper from the North Pole. Got it?"

"Got it," Lillian said. "So I can't wrap my presents for them in any gift wrap that has a princess or a reindeer."

"No, you can," Annie said, "but it just can't be in the same paper that Santa wraps their gifts in. And we should hide the presents in the attic so Philip won't find them. He gave me a hard time last year. I found him looking in my closet and in the basement. He's catching on to the Santa thing, I think."

"Well, he is a little old to be…" Lillian started, but Ann shushed her.

"Don't say it!"

A few days later Lillian took the kids to pick out the Christmas tree while Ann rested so she'd have enough energy to decorate it with them. It was lovely, and Ann had some of Lillian mother's ornaments in her own collection.

"Where did you get them?" Lillian asked her.

"My mother couldn't give them away when your mother died. She took some and gave some to me. I guess my father has the rest. Oh, and there's a box for Joey, but Dad hasn't given them to him yet. He wants Joey to settle down first. I think the nutcrackers are in Joey's box."

When Lillian just nodded, Ann said, "But they all belong to you so just say the word."

"No, that's fine. I don't need them…want them…care." Yet as she found an ornament that had belonged to her mother, she'd look at it a long time, handle it, remember.

Monica came to the house one day and asked that they participate in a cookie exchange at her house. "No thanks," Lillian said without hesitation.

"Yes, you have to," Monica insisted. "Ann can sit all night. She doesn't have to do a thing but enjoy herself. And she hasn't been out since before Thanksgiving."

"No thanks," Lillian said again.

This time Monica stamped her foot on the floor of the kitchen and slammed her keys on the table. "You *will*, Lillian, you will do this for me."

"I don't want to, Monica."

"Well…well…just…*fuck you!*" Monica said loud enough to make both Lillian and Ann turn to her in surprised silence.

Monica reddened a little. "Now you've made me mad enough to use language like yours!" she said to Lillian.

"Jeeze, okay, okay, we'll come," Lillian said. "I don't want to, though."

Monica waved her off. "You know, Lillian, sometimes we have to do what we don't want to do."

Ann started to defend Lillian, but Lillian silenced her. "All right, I get it. Don't make her mad. I don't want her using that language around me again—it's shocking! So what kind of cookies do I have to bake and how many dozen?"

∾

Lillian pulled the car up to the front of Monica's house, the house where she had lived in with her parents as a child and teenager. There were houses all around it now, and a sidewalk in front. She wouldn't have recognized the neighborhood, but she knew the house immediately. It was white, as Ann had told her, but it still had the black shutters and the lipstick red front door.

Ann looked at her from the passenger seat. "Are you going to be okay in there?"

"Lots of memories in there for me, Annie," Lillian said, feeling very tentative, very vulnerable.

Ann turned her body toward Lillian. "Look, do me a favor. If you can't handle it and you're getting upset, give me a sign and I'll tell Monica I'm tired or not feeling well and we'll leave. She'll believe me and will let us go without any fanfare."

"How soon after we get in the house can I give you the sign?" Lillian asked as she helped her cousin out of the car. "Is five minutes too soon, because so help me, if Monica up-talks once, I'm outta there."

Ann laughed. Each of them carried decorated bags filled with Ann's mother's favorite butter cookies that had been pressed out in Christmas trees and candy cane designs and decorated with glistening red and green sugar.

Monica opened the door for them. She kissed Ann's cheek and took her coat, while throwing a warning look at Lillian to say, don't start with me. She brought them into the living room, where some of the other guests had already gathered.

There were hors d'oeuvres, savory mini pies, and all sorts of desserts on the dining room table.

Ann passed on everything, but Lillian filled a small plate with hors d'oeuvres. She tried not to look around, not to see any ghosts in the corners of what had been her mother's house.

The mantel in the living room was draped with pine roping. Various sizes of red and gold candles were placed on the mantel surface. Lillian stood in the middle of the room, looking at the mantel, but instead of the candles and pine roping, she saw only her mother's wooden soldier nutcrackers. She lost her appetite and took her plate into the kitchen.

The changes that were made there were major; she wouldn't have recognized it. It was larger, with granite everywhere, stainless steel, a stone floor, and cherry wood cabinets. Mom would have liked this. She was shocked at herself for even thinking it.

They did the cookie exchange and Ann seemed to be enjoying herself so Lillian didn't give her any signs to leave. Lillian brought the trays and bags of cookies out to the car. She stood looking at the house, remembering the last time she left it. She was eighteen, carrying two suitcases and a knapsack, and had two black eyes because she was still recovering from a broken skull. Her father was putting her bedding and stereo in the trunk of his car. Her mother had already been sent to Friends Hospital in Philadelphia. Lillian left for Boston College that day and never came back; not once in twenty-two years. Not even when she moved to Newtown and knew she was fifteen minutes away. Not even a drive by.

Monica opened the door and called to her. "Lillian, I think Ann wants to leave."

Lillian hurried up the path and moved past Monica to where Ann was sitting. Ann was suddenly very pale and sitting very still in the chair next to the fireplace.

"Her coat is upstairs in the bedroom. Shall I get it?" Monica asked her.

"No, I'll get it. You go sit with her, chat with her as though nothing is wrong so the others don't realize she's sick…which bedroom?"

"The one at the top of the stairs to the right," Monica told her.

Lillian walked up the stairs and looked around at the hallway. This part of the house was almost exactly as it had been, even the color on the walls and the door trim were close to the colors her mother had used when she decorated the house. The oak doors were still stained dark. It unnerved Lillian.

She knew the bedroom Monica had indicated was the master bedroom—her parents' bedroom. She stepped into it and saw the coats piled up on the king size bed.

And as if all the years had just melted away, she saw her mother and father on the bed and herself running from the doorway and jumping into the middle, while they both laughed. They pretended to be surprised, but Lillian knew they weren't. Her father chucked her gently under her chin and called her an imp, while her mother picked up the covers to give Lillian room to snuggle under them. She was about Suzy's age then, with long red curls and uneven teeth just like Suzy's.

Her mother's silk nightgown smelled like roses. Her mother always had rose scented sachets in her dresser drawers and all her lingerie smelled like roses. Lillian snuggled closer to her mother under the covers, and her mother pulled her even closer.

"Come close, Lilly doll, come close, I'll keep you warm, baby."

Her mother took her fingertip and ran it, barely touching, along Lillian's top lip and under her chin, "Now, don't laugh...you're not allowed to laugh." But Lillian couldn't hold her laughter in because it tickled so much. She'd rub the spots and then begged her mother, "Do it again, Mommy!" Her father said he might as well get up and make the coffee, and he leaned over Lillian to kiss her mother on the lips and her mother clung to him, laughing. Then he kissed Lillian on the forehead. "My girls," he said. "My beautiful ladies."

Lillian had to lean on the door jamb for a moment now. The memory was so strong...so sweet. She could actually smell the roses mixed with her mother's Chanel No. 5, could feel her mother's soft white skin against her cheek.

She pulled herself into the now, and walked to Monica's bed, searching for Ann's coat and her own. When she found them, she left the room, and her eyes glanced at the closed door of what had been her own bedroom when she was growing up.

She heard the ghost voices now—the yelling...the shrieking...the crash of things being thrown against walls. She closed her eyes. A familiar nausea crept up into her throat, then the chest-tightening fear she had lived with for almost all of her childhood. Names: *fat whore, tramp, ingrate, bad girl*—that was the one that she hated most of all...*bad girl... you bad, bad girl...I hate you...I wish I never had you...you're hideous...I'm ashamed of you...your bastard...you're disgusting.*

Lillian fell against the wall to steady herself. Give me a good memory, for Christ's sake. And it came to her. She had wanted a blue velvet dress for her birthday when she was twelve but her mother had said they couldn't afford it.

It was tea length, trimmed with silver, and the first "big girl" dress she'd ever wanted. It cost two hundred dollars, and it was in the window of the store where her mother was employed.

"We can't afford that, you idiot. You're such a stupid, selfish girl it will be a wonder if you get anything."

On the morning of her birthday, when she opened her door to go to the bathroom, a large unwrapped white box fell in and onto her foot. She sat on the floor, right there in the doorway, and opened the box. It was the blue velvet dress with the satin trim. Under it was a package with pantyhose—her first pair. She squealed in delight and her parents were laughing even before they burst out of their bedroom where they'd been peeking through a crack in their door.

"Happy birthday, precious. Happy birthday my darling, darling baby." They made a "Lillian sandwich" with Lillian between her parents as they hugged her at the same time. Her mother was in a good mood, a loving mood.

Her mother reached down and took Lillian's chin and pulled her face up to look at her. "The day you were born was the happiest day of my life. I love you, baby girl."

# Twenty-five

Ann was failing. She wanted to wait until after Christmas to tell the kids, but she realized that she couldn't wait much longer. It was happening faster than she expected.

Meg wanted to order the hospice nurses now and a hospital bed. Ann was having trouble getting in and out of her bed to get to the bathroom, and Meg suggested a commode.

"Not until I explain to the kids," Ann said.

Lillian had started to sleep on the air bed in Ann's room every night so she could help if Ann needed her. One night Ann called to her and Lillian jumped up, still foggy from sleep. "It's Suzy…she's coughing," Ann said. "Go see what's wrong. She's been coughing for an hour."

Lillian listened. Suzy sounded croupy.

Lillian went to her room, and felt her head. She was burning with fever.

"I don't feel good, Lilly," she said, then coughed hard, the sound hollow and deep.

Lillian picked her up in her arms and brought the little girl into Ann's room. "What do I do?" she asked Ann.

"Call her pediatrician. They have a service. He'll call back."

Lillian placed Suzy on the bed next to her mother and grabbed the phone. Ann rolled onto her side and stroked Suzy's cheek. She told Lillian the telephone number—she had it committed to memory. Lillian explained to the service and hung up. Within ten minutes the phone rang. The pediatrician gave Lillian instructions: sit in the bathroom with the shower running, or use a cool air humidifier in her room if you have one, give her a dose of child strength acetaminophen or ibuprofen, and call the office in the morning to make an appointment. If she didn't improve tonight, go to the emergency room.

Lillian got the humidifier and set it up in Ann's room. To be safe, she also ran the shower and took Suzy in her arms and sat on the toilet while the room filled up with steam. She gave Suzy the medicine. Suzy relaxed and wrapped her legs around Lillian and put her cheek on Lillian's shoulder. Lillian rocked back and forth on the toilet, crooning softly, rubbing the little girl's back and wincing every time the child "barked" with the miserable sounding cough.

After about an hour, when Suzy was quieter, Ann shuffled to the bathroom door.

"She sounds better," she said to Lillian.

"Her fever is down, too."

Suzy was sound asleep now, with one cheek on Lillian's shoulder and the other turned up. Her cheeks were flushed red, and she slept with her mouth open, but her breathing wasn't as noisy and labored and she felt cooler.

"Put her in the bed with me," Ann said.

"Are you all right?"

"I have to use the bathroom, and I need a pain pill."

Lillian put Suzy on Ann's bed and covered her. She felt her head and face again, satisfied that the child was cooler. She checked the humidifier and then went back to the bathroom door and knocked gently.

"Annie, you okay?"

The door opened, and Ann came out. Lillian started to help her, but she shrugged Lillian off. "Leave me alone," she snapped.

Lillian backed away. "What's the matter with you?"

"Nothing, just get out of my way," Ann said, a sob catching in her throat.

"What did I do, Annie?" Lillian asked, reaching out to the sick woman, who slapped her hands away again.

"Ann!"

"I can't stand you," Ann said. "I hate you. I hate that you have to take care of me. I hate that you have to take care of my babies because I can't anymore. I hate you...I goddamned hate..." before she could finish, she lost her balance and started to go down. Lillian grabbed her and they fell to the floor together, Lillian cushioning Ann's fall. Ann started to sob, and clutched at Lillian fiercely, burying her head in Lillian's lap. "I'm sorry...I didn't mean it...I'm so sorry...oh, dear God, Lilly, I'm so sorry..."

Just as Lillian had held and rocked Suzy in her arms a few minutes earlier, she did the same with Ann now. And just as she had with Suzy, she crooned soothingly, stroking Ann's tufts of hair and bald spots.

Lillian dug deep into her memory. Aunt Helen always sang something to them when they were children. She tried to remember…she struggled…what was it…and then she suddenly knew it. She rocked her dying cousin with the words to the song.

"Woe, woe, baby…" she began to sing-song in a whisper, still rocking and stroking Ann, "Woe, woe, baby" there on the floor of what had been their grandmother's bedroom many, many years before. Ann's body stopped writhing. "I don't hate you, Lilly," she said.

"I know," Lillian answered. "I know you don't, Annie."

Ann quieted; her head was still in Lillian's lap. Then she fell asleep in Lillian's arms.

❧

Ann was sitting in the living room when Philip and Suzy came home from school four days later. The hospital bed had been delivered and was in her bedroom, the commode beside it. Lillian met the kids in the driveway and told them their mom was in the living room and wanted to see them.

Suzy ran ahead and Philip took his time. Lillian put her hand on his shoulder. She knew that he knew. Lillian had guessed weeks before that Philip was all too knowledgeable about it.

But as long as it wasn't actually spoken about, he could pretend it wasn't happening. Lillian dreaded the conversation that was about to take place.

Suzy threw her backpack on a kitchen chair and ran in to see her mother. "Hi, Mommy!"

"Hi, baby. How are you feeling? It was your first day back to school after being sick, were you okay?"

"I'm all better," Suzy told her, bouncing onto the couch after kissing her mother. "We had art today."

"You did? Did you paint something for me?"

"Yes, but it's still at school. Mrs. Janice had to hang the pictures up to dry. I can bring it home next week. It's a Christmas tree."

"I see," Ann said, looking closely at Suzy for any signs of being flushed or feverish. Philip came in and ambled over to Ann's chair. He put his hand on hers when he kissed her cheek.

"Let me kiss you back," she said before he pulled away, and he offered his cheek to her. She pressed her lips to his cheek, which was still cold from the air outside. He stood near the fireplace when she let him go.

"We have to talk, guys," she started.

Lillian stood in the kitchen, her back against the wall next to the doorway, listening.

"I'm not feeling too well lately. I guess you've noticed."

"You're dying," Philip said.

Ann cleared her throat before answering him. "I'm pretty sick, yes."

Suzy stopped moving and looked with round eyes at her mother.

"What does that mean?"

"It means she's going to heaven, Suz. She'll take care of us from heaven, but Lilly will take care of us here," Philip told his sister, very matter-of-fact, very mature.

Suzy looked at her brother. "But where will Mommy be?"

"I told you, she'll be in heaven."

Ann looked at her son. "Philip, how do you know all this?"

He shrugged.

"Did someone tell you?"

"I knew you were sick, Mom. I'm not stupid. And Lilly was watching TV with us a few weeks ago and there was a commercial about a lady who had cancer and a hospital was able to make her better, and Lilly threw her coffee cup at the wall. It smashed all over. She told us it was an accident, but I saw her do it. I knew she was crying when she cleaned it up. I kinda knew before that, but then I was sure."

"She made such a mess," Suzy said, remembering the incident, and waving her hand in the air. "I told her you wouldn't like that she broke the cup and got coffee all over the wall, and she told me she knew, so we shouldn't tell you. I didn't tell because I didn't want her to get into trouble."

Ann smiled. So did Lillian standing in the kitchen; her eyes filled with tears.

"I will always, always love you, Philip and Suzy. And you'll see me again one day—it will take a long time, but that's okay. That's the way I want it. In the meantime, you're right, Philip, I will be taking care of you from heaven while Lilly takes care of you here on earth. You'll be loved and protected, and very happy. You'll also have Joey, and Dan and Jessica and your new Aunt Louise. Lilly will bring you down to see Pops every year and maybe Pops will be able to come up to see you sometime soon."

Ann's voice trembled now; she was having a hard time holding it together. Lillian didn't know what to do, whether she should go in to help or stay out of Ann's way. Ann called out for Lillian.

She went into the room, took Philip's hand, and led him over to sit on the couch where Suzy was. She sat down between them, their hands in both of hers.

"I love you guys, too," she said to them, "just like you were my own kids."

"Will you have more kids when you marry Dan?" Philip wanted to know.

"I doubt it," she said. "We have the two of you and Jessica. You're all we want. You're all we need. You fill up our lives with joy."

She looked up at Ann who was looking at her with a grateful, watery smile.

"Where will we live?" he asked then.

"Here," Lillian answered, "in this house. But we'll also have an apartment in New York City. You'll go to school here in Bucks County, but we'll able to go to New York and go skating in Central Park and Rockefeller Center and to shows and museums. And then there's Madison Square Garden for basketball and hockey games. You can be Philadelphia sports fans and New York sports fans. We'll have the best of both worlds." She saw him look at his mother, and she added quietly, "As best as it can be."

"Are you going to die today?" Suzy asked her mother.

Ann smiled. "No, baby, not today. I'm going to live as long as I can, but I'm probably going to be staying in my room a lot. I'm more comfortable in bed these days. And there may be some nurses coming in to help Lillian take care of me. I don't want that to frighten you."

"It won't. Can I help take care of you?"

"Sure. You can bring me tea and cookies every afternoon when you get home from school."

"I'll go get some now," Suzy declared, jumping from the couch and running into the kitchen. They heard her rummaging in the cookie box, and Lillian said, "I better help with the tea."

Ann nodded. Philip got up and walked over to Ann's chair. He sat down on the floor and leaned his head on her leg. "I love you, Mom."

"I love you, too, handsome."

"I don't know what to say," he told her, his eyes filling with tears when he looked up at her.

"You just said it all, Philip. Never stop loving me, okay?"

He pulled himself to his knees and put his head on her lap and cried hard for a long time.

# Twenty-six

There was more laughter than sadness in Ann's bedroom in the next couple of weeks. Suzy, Philip and Lillian put another Christmas tree up in her room and a DVD player so they could watch Christmas movies and their usual nightly shows with her before they went to bed. Sometimes she was awake, sometimes not, but the noise didn't bother her.

Between a wise-cracking nurse named May and Lillian, along with constant visits from Meg and Father Murray who argued warmly about whether or not he was trying to convert Lillian, Ann was kept entertained every day, all day, unless she was sleeping.

The school knew about Ann now, and food poured into the house from mothers of kids in Suzy and Philip's classes. More food came from parishioners at Father Murray's church. Lillian didn't have to cook for weeks, and there was more food than they could eat. She froze much of it, deciding to use it for Christmas dinner.

Joey came home a week before Christmas to stay until mid-January when classes started again and he had to return to Boston. They had decided to put Santa's presents under Ann's tree instead of in the living room so she could watch them being opened on Christmas morning.

"Take them to the children's mass on Christmas Eve," Ann told Lillian and Joey. "Father Murray said it will be perfect for them...festive. It starts at nine in the evening, so by the time it's over, the kids will be tired and ready for bed."

"Dan's coming that day," Lillian told her.

"Then you can all go with them. It will make it special for them."

"Oh, yeah, real special when the roof caves in on top of us when I walk in!" Lillian said in a huff.

Ann laughed. "Believe me, half the people at Mass on Christmas haven't been there since the Christmas before—no, I'm wrong—since Palm Sunday. Catholics love getting free stuff."

"You're such a cynic," Lillian scolded, laughing.

273

The Mass was beautiful. The children were all called up onto the altar to watch as the priest put the figure of the Christ Child in the manger.

The children's choir sang beautifully. Even Louise was impressed, and Jessica held Suzy's hand through the whole Mass. None of them received Communion except Philip and Jessica, the only ones in the group who were in good standing with the Church. Suzy was still too young and wouldn't celebrate her First Holy Communion for a year yet.

When Mass was over at around ten o'clock, Father Murray asked everyone to kneel and be very, very quiet, because someone special was going to pay a visit to the Christ Child in the manger. They weren't allowed to call out or leave their pews. Everyone knelt and the Church lights dimmed. Suddenly a rolling murmur went through the congregation starting at the back. Santa Claus walked quietly down the middle aisle, and walked straight to the manger, took off his red cap, and knelt before the image of the baby. The Church became silent. The choir hummed "Away in the Manger."

Santa stood, bowed to the altar, and left through a side door of the church.

"The Mass is ended. Go in peace," Father Murray said. "Merry Christmas, everyone. I think you'd better get home fast. Obviously, Santa is in the neighborhood!"

The noise level rose about ten decibels then, and everyone followed Father Murray in the recessional before the last hymn was sung. Lillian could hear his laughter outside before they reached him. "You sound like Santa," she said, kissing him. He shook Dan's hand and kissed Jessica and Louise. He picked up Suzy in his arms. "Well, were you good?" he asked Philip. "Will Santa be stopping at your house tonight?"

Suzy answered for both of them. "Absolutely…we've been very good."

Father Murray kissed her cheek and put her down. He looked at Lillian. "I can't come in the morning, but would you mind if I stopped by tomorrow afternoon? Would I be intruding?"

She laughed, "Since when? You always turn up without asking…"

Dan shook the priest's hand. "We'll look forward to it. You owe us another game of scrabble. You won three in a row on Thanksgiving."

"Pour a beer at one o'clock—I'll be there before it's warm," Father Murray told them.

No one thought the children would quiet down enough to sleep. They were wired when they got home. But they quickly changed into their

Christmas pajamas and rushed into Ann's room to tell her all about Santa Claus visiting the Christ Child in the church. One of the hospice nurses, a Jewish woman who was particularly fond of Ann, had offered to stay with Ann while everyone went to Mass.

She had put Ann's wig on her and a little light makeup, and had helped her to dress in a red sweater over her nightgown. The back of the hospital bed was raised all the way up. Ann was receiving her pain killers through an IV in her arm now, and she had the ability to push the button whenever she needed it.

Lillian could tell that she hadn't pushed the button because her eyes were bright and she wasn't sleepy or groggy.

Everyone brought chairs into Ann's room and Lillian poured eggnog. She held two containers—one with Bourbon and one without. Joey read the Night Before Christmas and Lillian told the kids, "Okay, that's it. Bed ... or Santa will not come."

They kissed Ann goodnight and ran into the guest room. Because it was Christmas Eve, Ann suggested that they should sleep in the same room. This way they could find their presents together in the morning. "Whoever gets up first will wake the other one—it happens every year."

Joey made them promise to wake him up, too. Jessica asked if she could sleep in the guest room with them so she could also wake up to find the presents. Dan agreed but only if they all went to bed at the same time.

Joey and Jessica laughed, but since there was a TV in the room, they agreed. Joey told Jessica to sleep in the bed and he'd sleep on the floor with the kids. It took twenty minutes to get them all settled in and quiet, but Lillian was shocked to find that the little ones fell asleep immediately. The older kids were watching "National Lampoon's Christmas Vacation" on a cable station.

Lillian helped Dan carry all of Jessica's gifts from the trunk of his car to put them under the tree in the living room where the adults' gifts were. Louise was in bed, and Ann was sound asleep, her pain now relieved by the morphine drip.

Dan and Lillian went into her room once they knew everyone was asleep. She fell across the bed exhausted, and he did the same. "Have you noticed that since we're engaged, we haven't made love?" she asked. "Like, what's that about? I'm still sexy, right?"

He smiled and nodded, "Sexiest." Then he nuzzled her neck. "When we're married, it will be better than it ever was. It'll be sanctified then."

She chuckled. "Listen to you. You've been talking to Father Murray again," she said.

"Are we going to ask him to marry us?"

"I don't know, Dan. We'd have to go through too much to get married in the Church. I like him very much, but you're divorced, and we'd have to start going back to church, and..." she pretended to shiver, "confession...oh, good God..."

"I think I'd like that. And my first wife got an annulment a few years after our divorce, so we can be married in the Church. We have to raise the kids Catholic anyway—you promised Ann—and Jessica attends Mass. Why not go back into the fold? There's been something missing in my life for a long time."

"It was me," she said, putting her leg over him.

"It was," he admitted. "But it's more. Can we talk to him about it?"

She sighed. "Let's think about it. Tonight I have to get some sleep because I have a feeling those kids are going to be up before dawn. I hope you remembered to bring your tools, because we have a lot of things that have to be put together in the morning—princess mansions, princess coaches, mini kitchen appliances, stuff for Philip..."

"I remembered, and I'm up for the task."

"Listen to us, we sound like an old married couple already." She slipped off the bed and kissed his lips.

"Where are you going?" he asked.

"I have to sleep in Ann's room. I don't leave her alone at night."

❧

Lillian could barely get to the surface of wakefulness when the kids came bounding into the room looking for their gifts. Suzy gasped when she saw them under Ann's tree. Two mounds were piled high and sprawled halfway across the room. One mound was bright pink in a princess motif; the other was blue and white and covered in snowmen.

"Philip, he left them in here! Santa was in Mommy's room," she squealed, but Philip had already found them and threw himself on the packages he knew were his. Joey and Jessica followed them into the room, and Dan walked in behind them, fully dressed and carrying a mug of coffee.

Lillian looked over at Dan from her bed on the floor. She was surprised to find that the back of Ann's bed was up and her cousin had tied a long

Christmas scarf around her head. She was smiling, but looked tired and pale. "How long have you been awake?" Lillian asked her.

"About an hour," she answered. "I was waiting for them."

After opening each package, Philip would bring it to Ann's bed to show her, and Ann would act surprised and amazed that Santa knew exactly what he wanted, and that there were even some surprise gifts that weren't on his list.

Lillian knew that Ann was hoping they'd get through this one more Christmas with Philip believing in the magic of Santa, or if not believing completely, still wondering if it could be true.

Suzy tore through her gifts like a tornado—ripping the wrapping paper off one, opening it, screaming out loud what it was, and throwing it aside to get to the next box. Her gifts were opened long before Philip finished opening his.

When he was showing Ann his last wrapped present, she said to him, "Look out the window, honey. I thought I heard Santa out in the back after he put all of these gifts in here. He made a lot of noise."

Philip studied her while she said this, but before he could walk over to the window—and before Dan could grab Suzy, who had heard the exchange—Suzy jumped up and ran to the window Ann had indicated. "Philip, it's a…"

Joey bolted over the pile of gifts and reached her just in time to put his hand over her mouth. He put his lips near her ear, whispering to be quiet and let it be a surprise. Philip left his mother's bed and walked tentatively to the window.

When he got there and looked down, he grabbed the sill with both hands, and looked back into the room directly at his mother.

"You said…" he started, but stopped when she shrugged.

"What? What's down there?" she pretended not to know.

He thought very carefully for a moment, looked back through the window and then back at her. "If I tell you, will you let me keep it?"

Ann exchanged a quick glance with Dan. "Well," she said, pretending to think it over, "I suppose if it's something that Santa brought to you, it will be okay. He wouldn't bring you anything that he didn't think you could handle and act responsible when using."

Suzy was wiggling against Joey's hand now, trying to get free to announce to everyone in the room what Santa had left for Philip, but Joey held tight, laughing.

Lillian was perplexed. She had purchased all the gifts, wrapped them, and put them under the tree.

By the way Dan and Ann were looking at each other, she knew Dan had something to do with what was down in the yard and she could tell that Joey was in on it too.

"What is it, Philip?" she asked getting off her air mattress to see. But the little boy dashed out of the room with Dan, Joey and Suzy following. Dan yelled out to the boy, "Put shoes on, Phil, and your jacket."

Lillian went to the window. There below her was a red, silver and black mini all terrain vehicle, complete with a matching helmet and a huge red ribbon and bow. She looked over at Ann in surprise. "No ATV's!" she mimicked. "Absolutely no ATVs under any circumstances. Cross that off your list because you're not getting one—you'll kill yourself."

"A mother has the privilege to change her mind, you know—especially at Christmas—and especially when her cousin is engaged to a very persuasive gentleman who has a partner in crime who happens to be her own brother, and who have promised on their lives to teach, train, and enforce rules that will keep that mother's son safe and sound…and happy."

Louise had come into the room now and was looking down at the lawn with Lillian. Philip was in his pajamas, boots, and jacket sitting on the seat of the mini ATV with his helmet on. Joey and Dan were on each side of him, showing him the controls and acting as excited as Philip was.

Louise clucked. "Men are really just waiting for the opportunity to devolve back into childhood, aren't they?"

Lillian and Ann laughed, and Ann said, "Dan cooked it all up. They picked it out and bought it during Thanksgiving weekend and then sneaked out to Monica's early this morning. She had been hiding it. She had to hide it from her own kids in fear that they would think it was theirs."

"How come I wasn't in on this caper?" Lillian asked.

Ann didn't answer, and Lillian understood that Ann had to have something of her own to give to her little boy this Christmas

Suzy would be enthralled with her Princess Mansion and the Coach once Dan put them together, but Philip needed this to be his special Christmas—he was hurting more, fearing more, and knew more.

The entire crew spent Christmas Day in their night clothes—except Dan who had been dressed by four thirty that morning to get the ATV in the yard before the kids woke up. By late morning, the pink mansion was up, the coach was put together, the mini kitchen was working, and all the computer games had been figured out.

Breakfast was eaten, then Christmas dinner, then sandwiches in the late evening.

But the sound of the ATV was heard all day in the yard of Willow Wood—until dark, when Lillian went out and took the key out of the ignition, letting all three "boys" know that it was over for the night.

Earlier that morning, when all the gifts had been opened, Ann had asked Lillian to leave her window open just a little. She wanted to hear them when they were outside.

She lie in her bed and listened to the motor of the ATV moving over Willow Wood's land. She heard her son's laughter and her daughter's delighted squeals when Suzy was allowed to ride on it.

She heard her brother calling out to his nephew, giving instructions. She heard the men's laughing voices when the wheels of the ATV got stuck and when Philip pushed on the pedal too soon, covering Joey and Dan with dirt and mud. She laughed, too.

She drifted in and out of sleep all day, always with the same gentle, satisfied and contented smile on her lips.

# Twenty-seven

Lillian knew something was wrong when she went into Ann around nine o'clock that evening. Ann's breathing was shallow and her face was drawn and gray.

"Are you in pain?" Lillian asked her.

Ann nodded. Lillian saw that the morphine drip control had slipped off the bed. Lillian grabbed it and hit the button. It would only allow the dosage prescribed within the time allotted, so Lillian was worried that it wasn't going to ease Ann's pain.

Within a few seconds, though, she saw Ann's face relax as the morphine took affect, but before Ann fell asleep again, she took Lillian's hand. "I've changed my mind," she said through dry lips. "I want to go to the hospital."

"I won't let the morphine drip fall off the bed again. I'm going to attach it to the bed. I won't let it happen again."

Ann shook her head. "No...listen to me." Her eyes were closing already, her eyelids too heavy to keep open, but she continued through slow painful breaths. "I don't want to die here in the house. I was wrong. The kids will never get over it. They'll have to relive it every time they come upstairs. It won't be a home anymore; it'll be a place of death. And it will ruin Christmas for them every year." She tried to run her tongue over her lips. "I want them to remember the way I was this morning."

Lillian just stood looking down at Ann, unable to move for the moment.

"Call Meg," Ann said to her before surrendering to the effects of the drug. "Get her to make the arrangements for the hospital tonight."

Lillian lifted the phone and dialed Dr. Meg's cell phone. Meg's voice was high in spirits when she answered, "Merry Christmas!" Lillian could hear laughter and voices in the background.

"I wouldn't bother you on Christmas, but..." Lillian started.

"It's all right. Just tell me," Meg said, her voice serious immediately.

Lillian explained what Ann had just told her, then leaned her head on the wall and cradled the phone closer to her face. "She's slipping away, Meg. She was alert this morning, but now...oh, God, Meg, she's slipping away..."

"I'll take care of everything. I'll be over in a few minutes. Can you get the kids out of the house? I don't want them to see the ambulance take her away."

Lillian thought a moment, and then said, "Yes, I'll call Monica."

Monica told her to bring the kids over immediately. They would pretend that it was another Christmas surprise and they'd have a sleepover.

Monica told her to let the kids bring a couple of their own new toys, and she had Christmas presents for them also. Mothers are always thinking, Lillian thought.

"Lillian," Monica said before they hung up, "you know I'll take good care of them, right? And you know that I care deeply about Ann and you. I'll be here for you whenever and however you need me."

Lillian couldn't speak for a moment. She'd been so judgmental and snotty to this kind-hearted friend. "You're the best, Monica," she managed to choke out and hung up.

Lillian leaned over Ann, kissed her brow, and whispered, "I'm taking care of everything, Annie. Sleep now."

She pulled herself together and went back to the living room with the brightest smile she could muster.

"Guess what?" she said, too loudly, too brightly. Tone it down, she told herself, or they'll catch on. "I was just talking to Monica and she asked me if you guys would like to go over there for a sleepover." She's got some surprises there for you, too."

Suzy jumped up from her mansion where she was playing with Jessica. "Can we go? Can Jessica come?"

Jessica groaned and fell back on the floor, acting exhausted. "I'm beat, Suzy. Can I stay here while you go play with your other friends?"

The rest of the room was silent—all of the adults were staring at Lillian, knowing something was seriously wrong. Joey stood up so quickly his chair tipped back and onto the floor. Lillian lifted her hand slightly to silence him. Philip just looked up at her, studying her face.

Suzy asked again "Can we go?"

"You sure can." Lillian looked at Dan, whose face had turned pale and whose eyes were bright with tears. "Could you bring the guys over to Monica's for me?"

"Sure, I'd be happy to. Come on guys, you can stay in your pjs." He made himself busy getting their jackets and shoes and helping them dress. Jessica helped him, too young herself to realize that something was wrong. She packed the toys they wanted to bring with them—arguing with Suzy that the mansion was too big, but she could bring the new Barbie doll and some of the doll's clothes and the Princess Coach.

Philip asked Lillian then, "Can I kiss mommy goodnight?"

Lillian looked around the room at all the solemn, fearful faces. Joey nodded to her, his eyes filled with tears. "Yes, let them," he said.

"Okay, but you have to be really quiet because she's sleeping, okay?"

The children started up the stairs and Joey and Lillian followed. When they went into the room, Joey picked up Suzy so she could reach her mother's cheek without climbing onto the bed. Ann stirred a little.

Then Philip put his hand over Ann's on the bed, and whispered to her, "We're just going to our friends' house, Mom. We'll be back in the morning. You just sleep. And thanks for letting Santa bring me the ATV."

Lillian saw the slightest movement of Ann's head as though she had heard and was gathering every ounce of strength to respond. Her eyelids fluttered, but she couldn't open them. Her lips curled up into a smile, though. Philip kissed her hand. "Merry Christmas, Mom. I love you," he said leaving the bedside and walking out of the room.

Joey handed Suzy to Lillian. He rushed into Ann's bathroom and closed the door behind him. Lillian heard a sob muffled only a little by the closed door. As she led the children out of the room, she heard Ann's breathing become labored again.

Lillian took them back downstairs, trying to be chatty, reminding them to remember their manners at Monica's, and then Dan shepherded them out of the house.

Meg walked in seconds later, before Lillian could explain what was going on to Louise. "There's an ambulance on the way, but they won't have their sirens going."

Meg rushed up the stairs to Ann's room while Lillian explained to Louise and Jessica what was happening. Jessica started to cry and Louise put her arms around the girl to comfort her.

Joey was sitting next to Ann's bed when Meg entered. He was holding Ann's hand with one of his, stroking her fingers with his other hand. Tears fell from his face and nose onto the edge of the bed. He didn't stand up when the doctor came in; he didn't acknowledge her at all.

He just sat looking at his sister's face. Ann's face was very peaceful. There was no labored breathing. There was no sound at all.

Meg placed her stethoscope on Ann's chest for several long minutes. She straightened up and looked at the young man holding his sister's hand. She said very gently. "I'm sorry...I'm so sorry."

Lillian was in the doorway when Meg said it. She walked in and went directly to Joey. She put her hand on his back.

He stiffened at first, but she leaned down and placed her lips on the top of his head. He kissed Ann's fingers and gently laid her hand back onto the bed. Then Joey turned on his chair, put his arms around Lillian's waist, placed his cheek on her stomach, and gave over to the kind of sobs that only a young man with a shattered heart can produce.

His beloved big sister was finally at peace, but the world would be less sweeter.

Lillian held him against her, but looked at Ann's face from over Joey's head.

*Annie...Annie...Annie.*

Lillian would grieve...she would mourn...she would cry...but for now, she would comfort her son.

# Twenty-eight

Lillian sat on the gazebo in the late March chill, wrapped in a plaid throw she'd grabbed from the couch in the living room.

The river was gray, and it was high and moved swiftly because of the mountain thaw that fed into it miles north. They'd had a rainy winter and she wondered if the river would overflow this spring. She didn't worry about Willow Wood. In all its years, with all the floods that had plagued Bucks County along the Delaware, Willow Wood had never been flooded. The Native Americans were right, she thought, remembering the story of how the property had been selected more than two hundred and forty years before.

The kids wouldn't be home from school for an hour yet, and she breathed in the fresh spring air, willing herself to relax. She'd been working on her book all day. She finished it an hour before. Her back ached from sitting long hours at her keyboard. She hadn't moved for five hours, and she was paying for it now. But the book was finished.

She regretted that Ann had not had the chance to read the ending. She would have liked it. She had loved the history of it all. Lillian should have worked harder—should have put in longer hours—so that she could have finished it before Ann died.

Ann would have been delighted, too, with the news Larry, the handyman, brought to Lillian just a few weeks after Ann's death. His hunch had been right. The blanket chest was even older than he had originally thought. It was pre-Revolutionary, and it was built in Newtown, probably by Willie Bournes, the young Quaker who defied his parents and went to war with George Washington.

He'd built only six pieces of furniture in his young life, and all were in the same style as the chest. Lillian always called it a treasure chest, now the chest itself proved to be a treasure. She would have loved to share all of that with Ann.

It still grabbed at Lillian's throat when she thought about Ann.

Three months to the day. She and Dan had put off any thoughts of a wedding until they knew that Philip was ready. Philip had been acting out, doing things that were uncharacteristic for him. He'd been quiet and morose at times before Ann's death, but his behavior since her death was unusual for him. He'd taken to teasing his sister until she cried. He had even punched her once when she was annoying him. Twice Lillian had to take the ATV away from him because he was driving recklessly.

She even found him on the road one day, and she lost her temper. She told him that if he couldn't follow the rules, she'd sell it to someone who could. He didn't even seem to care about what she said. He just put the vehicle in the garage and went to his room.

Lillian hated herself for overreacting, but she couldn't let him run wild and possibly be hit by a car. She couldn't sleep for a few days because of the incident, berating herself for threatening him, and wondering just how to get through to him. He didn't ask to drive it again for two weeks, and when he did, he just said to Lillian, "I wouldn't mind driving my ATV again. But it's up to you, I guess."

"Are you ready to follow the rules?" she had asked him. What she had wanted to say was *yes, yes, go have fun, Philip! Please have fun again. Please laugh again.* But she knew that wouldn't be the right thing to do.

It was hard being in charge…being the boss. Ann had been so much better at it.

Suzy was easy. She cried—mostly in the open when something reminded her of Ann, but sometimes she cried all alone in her room and it broke Lillian's heart—but she recovered quickly. She asked lots of questions about heaven and death, and Lillian answered them with the help of books people had given her and talks with Father Murray.

Suzy was upset about her brother's behavior. She scolded him a few times in her usual sassy way, but he either ignored her or yelled at her loudly, warning her to leave him alone. Lillian saw the wounded look in the little girl's eyes when he did so.

Lillian brought them to a children's grief support group and to private sessions with a children's grief counselor—a middle-aged woman with a soft voice and gentle manner. Sometimes Lillian thought the counselor was helping Lillian more than the kids; she didn't see any difference in Philip.

Joey had intended to come home for spring break, but Lillian talked him into going away with some of his friends to a resort in the Caribbean. He sounded guilty, but she insisted. "You'll be working in a full time career after this semester—you need to relax and have some fun. We're good here. Come for a long weekend in April, but take this time to chill with your friends."

"All right," he finally agreed, then added, "but I miss you, Lilly."

She smiled into the phone. She had never imagined how three words could have such an impact on her heart. "I miss you, too, kiddo. And the kids miss you. But we'll be okay until April."

Joey finally agreed, then said, "I think I'll cut the vacation short, though, and visit my father for a couple of days." She thought that was a great idea.

Uncle Tim had flown up for the funeral and he looked very drawn and old when he left the day after. Lillian called him twice a week now, just as Ann had always done. She knew that the death of his daughter took the kind of toll on him from which he would never recover. He said as much. "This is the first time that I've actually been happy that Helen has Alzheimer's," he told Lillian. "She wouldn't have survived this kind of pain. Sometimes I wonder if I will. It's just too hard."

Dan came every weekend now, and he was wonderful with Philip. He was patient and took him to the store and for long walks up the towpath on the canal. He took Philip to the boys' basketball games at school and became friends with the other dads who were there with their sons. He even went out with the group for pizza after two of the last games of the season.

Philip relaxed when he was around Dan. He seemed to find comfort from Dan.

And Dan took the kids to Mass every Sunday, alone or with Jessica when she came to Bucks County with him. Lillian continued to hold out and refused to attend, but Dan seemed to enjoy it. He and Father Murray had gone out to dinner twice, and they were planning to play golf together when the weather broke. They were becoming good friends, and Dan seemed to be embracing his faith in a way that made Lillian a little envious of it.

Lillian enrolled Suzy in dancing school, which the little girl loved, and Suzy planned to play soccer in the spring. Together, Lillian and Dan kept life as normal as possible for the children.

And they brought flowers to Ann's grave at least once a week, although Lillian visited it alone more frequently during the week. She knew Ann wasn't there, but it brought her comfort to lean on the headstone and talk out loud to her cousin. She wondered if it was a macabre thing to do—Ann wasn't there—but Lillian felt comforted from her visits...stronger.

Her parents' grave wasn't far from Ann's in the same cemetery, as were her grandparents and many of her other ancestors. It was exciting when she found names on ancient headstones of some of the people she was writing about in her book. She would put flowers at her grandparents' grave sometimes, but she never went to her parents' grave. She thought of it, and her eyes would drift over in that direction, but she never did. She purposely avoided walking near the grave.

Now, sitting on the gazebo, she realized that she hadn't been there in over a week. The last time she was in the cemetery, she met Father Murray who had just conducted a funeral service. They exchanged pleasantries. He remarked that Ann's grave would start to grow grass within weeks and would look much better, and Lillian agreed and said they planned to plant some pansies and keep a tiny garden near the headstone. She thought it would be good for the children, or at least the grief counselor thought so. He agreed.

"Your parents are buried somewhere near here, aren't they?"

"Yes," she answered him, looking away.

"Maybe you could plant a garden there, too."

Lillian continued to look in the other direction.

"You know, Lilly, you have a beautiful heart."

She smiled, a little embarrassed, and then frowned at him, waved him off with a look.

"No, you do," he said again. "The Catechism of our Church speaks of the heart as a dwelling place where one is and lives, a place to where one withdraws...a place of truth."

She didn't know what to say or what he wanted from this statement, so she just started to walk away from Ann's grave, leading him through the lane of granite and marble markers.

"But yours is not a sacred heart," he said, walking beside her.

"Thanks a lot," she said laughing now.

Father Murray was serious. "St. John said, 'If anyone says I love God, but hates his brother, he is a liar. For whoever does not love a brother whom he has seen cannot love God whom he has not seen.'"

The priest took a moment before continuing. "It's damned easy to love those who love us and don't harm us. But loving those who have harmed us—forgiving them—well now that takes a sacred heart."

"My heart's good enough," Lillian said, annoyed with the priest now.

"You're getting mad at me," he said quietly.

She shrugged, walking a little faster, thinking it was time for a quick escape. She liked him better when he was light hearted and they teased each other. This was someone different.

"A few years ago in Utah there was a terrible tragedy," Father Murray said. "A man killed his pregnant girlfriend. They showed the penalty phase on a cable channel and I watched it, although it was tough to see. All of the murdered woman's relatives got up and told this man just how horrible he was and what a terrible thing he did and that they'd never forgive him. They expressed hatred. But when it was the victim's mother's turn, this woman, who you could see was grieving desperately for her daughter and the grandchild she would never know, said, 'I serve an amazing God; a God who forgives and heals and restores people. All I know is that I do forgive you, and I know that it is only through God that I am able to do that.' Think about how free she must have felt then, Lillian. What extraordinary love and peace she must have experienced."

Lillian stopped and turned on the priest. "Why are you telling me this? What the hell do you want from me? Do you want to know what I think of that woman? I think she was a fool. I don't know, maybe she was a good person, but I would have felt like the others."

He smiled at her, "I don't know if that's true about you. I think you would forgive a stranger faster than you can forgive your loved ones."

She was exasperated and started to walk again. "I'm not mad at Ann for dying if that's what you're getting at."

"No, it isn't what I'm getting at. It's the flowerless grave just a few lanes away that I'm thinking about."

"I don't know who's been sharing my business with you. Dan maybe? Ann before she died? It doesn't matter who; I don't appreciate it."

"Your mother was sick, Lillian."

"Damn you!" she blurted the words out and turned on him again. "Enough…okay? Enough!"

"You'll never be the best mother you can be to those kids until you come to terms with your own wounded heart. You have to look into your heart for the truth, and you don't do that."

She had walked several feet away from him as he said this. She kept walking until she reached her car and opened the door. Then she slammed the door closed without getting in and stormed back to him.

"You listen to me," she said, her finger pointing at him. "I *can* be a good mother to them because I know better than anyone what a bad mother is. They will never be hurt, physically or emotionally, so screw you if you think I can't do this right. And forgiving my mother or not forgiving her will have absolutely nothing to do with it. Do you understand what I'm saying, you righteous jerk?"

"You're right, forgiving your mother won't do it all…it's yourself that you haven't forgiven, and that's what I'm worried about most."

She put her hand down. "Me?"

"You're as unforgiving of yourself as you are of your mother. You know I'm right, Lillian; you know what I'm saying. You hate her because you feel guilty about the whole terrible situation that was your mother and father and you, and because you couldn't understand them and what role you played in all of it. She created the chaos, I know that, but you feel guilt for it."

The rage she felt went to the core of her being. "Do you think you have the right to steam roll over people just because you wear that stupid collar?" She moved up to him, almost nose to nose. "You don't know jack shit. Don't bother me anymore. And don't suck up to Dan to try to get to me. We're finished; you and I are finished. You crossed a line today and we're not friends anymore. If I see your car in my driveway, I'll lock the goddamn door." She walked away but turned and walked backward, adding, "I don't want your church, I don't want your homilies, and I don't want your insipid advice about forgiveness and sacred hearts. You can shove it all right up your rosy-red Catholic ass!"

Sitting on the gazebo now she wished she *would* hear his car in the driveway. She wouldn't lock the door. The whole altercation with him made her think; it made her soul search and look into her own heart, just as he had told her to. Oh, she had been mad at him all right. She had been furious. When she got home that afternoon, she threw things and broke things, and called him every name under the sun. She cursed him, his church, his fellow priests, and then she sat down on Ann's empty bed and knew with a clarity she had never had before that he was absolutely correct.

She couldn't forgive herself. If only she'd been a good girl and not a bad girl growing up.

If only she had understood what her mother was going through, that her mother really was sick and what that meant. If only she didn't get pregnant and allow it to fracture her mother's relationship with her aunt. If only she didn't go away and never come home. If only she'd visited her mother in Friends Hospital once or twice. If only she had answered her mother's letters, in all of which Regina begged Lillian to forgive her. If only she had known about the beating and rape her mother had endured as a teenager.

If only she understood her father better. If only she didn't resent him for not protecting her, but the truth was, he stayed in a miserable marriage to protect her the best way he knew how. And the saddest truth of all was that he loved her mother; he loved the woman she was when she took her medicine. The last few years of his life were peaceful with Regina—but it infuriated Lillian. If only she had come home for her father's funeral, maybe her mother would have stayed on her meds. If only she'd come home at all…maybe her mother wouldn't have committed suicide.

Her anger, her memories, her failures, her tears and looking at them through her wounded heart, as Father Murray had called it, had exhausted her.

She pulled herself into a fetal position on Ann's bed, wishing her cousin was still alive, wishing that she could talk it all out with Ann, knowing that Ann would have understood, would have allowed her to bare her soul as she never had before.

She wanted a witness to these revelations—a witness who understood the dynamics—the dysfunction—of their family.

She fell into a deep sleep on Ann's bed. She didn't even hear the kids come home from school. She awakened to find Philip standing in his mother's bedroom doorway asking, "Lilly? Are you dead?" as though anyone who lay on that bed would die.

She had jumped up and grabbed him in her arms and he didn't struggle out of them. He allowed her to hug him.

"No, kiddo, no, I was just sleeping, buddy. I'm sorry I scared you. I had a bad day that's all. Philip, I'm so sorry you found me sleeping here."

"Just don't sleep on my mom's bed anymore, okay?" he said, pulling out of her arms gently, his eyes on hers, his face cautious and a little worried.

She agreed but after that day he seemed even more removed and uncommunicative. Now, sitting on the gazebo in the March coolness, she heard the school bus stop, and she pulled herself out of the chair and walked toward the driveway.

Suzy ran up to her, pigtails swaying. "My friend is going to be a flower girl in her cousin's wedding!" Suzy told her.

"Wow, that's cool," Lillian said opening the door of the kitchen to let them in.

"I want to be a flower girl," Suzy declared.

Philip snickered, "Yeah, well that ain't gonna happen."

"Why?" Suzy wanted to know.

"Because you're too ugly to be a flower girl," he sneered at her. "You'd ruin all the pictures."

"Philip, stop," Lillian said with a sigh. She poured milk for each of them. "Don't be mean to your sister."

"I can if I want to," he said, breaking a cookie in half with a snap and making a face at Suzy.

"Don't talk to me that way," Lillian told him leaning against the counter. "I'm getting tired of your rudeness. Enough already, okay?"

"Fuck you," he said.

The words sucked air out of the room; they all just stopped still in surprise, including Philip.

Then Lillian grabbed him by the shoulder of his shirt and brought him to his feet. "I don't believe you said that!"

"Let go of me," he said, shrugging to get out of her grip.

"You are absolutely infuriating these days, Philip. What would your mother think..." and there it was, out before she could stop it. She pictured herself reaching out to grab the words, to push them back into her mouth.

He struggled to get out of her grip. His face was bright red, "I don't care what my mother would think. My mother doesn't think at all anymore. She's dead! I hate her anyway."

Suzy screamed at him. "You shut up! You shut up! Don't say that!" She started to cry.

He grabbed his baseball bat and ran out into the back yard. Lillian ran after him, Suzy close behind her.

"Philip, where are you going? What are you doing?" Lillian called out to him.

He was running toward the canal, directly toward the willow tree.

"Philip!" Lillian shouted, truly panicked now.

He ran under the branches, where fresh pale-green leaves were just budding, and he swung the bat against the trunk of the tree. Its long flowing tendrils swayed with the impact in a slow motion dance. He hit it again. Lillian heard a crack and then saw the tree dance one way and then back again. He hit it a third time, and Lillian could do nothing but stand and watch. Suzy grabbed her hand, trembling and sobbing, her eyes wide and frightened as she watched her brother who seemed to have gone crazy.

"I hate this tree," he shouted and hit the trunk again, breaking a chunk of it off this time. "I hate this ugly, stupid tree. I...*whack*...hate this...*whack*...tree."

Lillian got it. The tree. His mother had loved the willow tree. She sat under it all summer and they had such lovely moments together there. This was the only way he knew how to punish his mother for leaving him.

The tears of that willow, which Ann had laughed at and loved, rained on the little boy now that she was gone, but the *tears* weren't fun anymore.

Philip smacked it again—twice more—and then fell to his knees, spent and sobbing. Suzy looked up at Lillian. The little girl was quiet now, not crying.

"Should you go to him?" she asked just like an adult would.

"I don't know, Suz."

They approached the tree warily, and Lillian bent over to look under the feathery branches. Philip was still sobbing.

She knelt near the tree. "We have to forgive her, Philip," Lillian said as calmly as she could. "I know you're mad at her. But she didn't want to die. We have to forgive her for getting sick and leaving us. If she had any control over it at all, she wouldn't have left you. She wouldn't have been sick. She wouldn't have died. She loved you too much. So you're going to have to forgive her. We all just have to forgive her."

"What do you know?" he screamed, looking over his shoulder, his face smeared with dirt, snot and tears. "You don't know anything!"

"My mother was sick, too, when I was little. And she died. I've been really, really mad at her for such a long time that it's made me a little sick, too. I don't want that to happen to you and Suzy."

He fell sideways against the trunk of the willow, moaning in grief. Her throat constricted with sorrow for him. It was one of the most pitiable things she'd ever seen.

"Here's my problem," Lillian said, still kneeling on the cold ground in front of him just outside the branches but close enough to speak softly and calmly. She didn't want to intrude on his space under the tree, because as mad at the tree as he was, she knew it was sacred to him, too. "I don't know how to advise you. Like, how am I supposed to be able to tell you how to forgive your mother, when I can't forgive mine and I'm a grown up?"

Suzy was hunched down, bent in half, her little hands on her thighs, tears still wet on her face. "I know how," Suzy said, a very adult look on her sweet little face. "You just close your eyes and picture mommy—you do it, too, Lillian, only you picture your own mommy—and you say out loud, 'I forgive you, Mommy. You shouldn't have gotten sick and died, but it's okay 'cause you didn't want to, and I forgive you because I love you and you loved me. That's what moms and kids do. They love and forgive no matter what.'"

Both Philip and Lillian stared at Suzy while she said this. The little girl opened her eyes again and looked back at them. "I feel better already," she said. "I forgive you, too, Philip, for being such a brat to me," Suzy added, her charming gap-toothed smile showing bright.

Philip swallowed hard and wiped his face with his sleeves, smearing dirt over it.

"Thanks," he said, meaning it. He stood up, picked up the bat again, and walked out from under the tree. He stepped to the edge of the canal, closed his eyes, told his mother he forgave her and he loved her and always would, and threw the baseball bat into the channel where once upon a time canal boat captains steered boats filled with coal…or whiskey…or escaping slaves.

When he turned back toward Lillian and Suzy, there was just a hint of a smile on his lips, the one dimple in his cheek deepening. His dirty face was streaked with tears, but it was lighter…calmer…beautiful.

*So, there it is,* Lillian thought. *You get mad, you beat the hell out of a tree—or in some circumstances yourself—you close your eyes and tell your mother that you forgive her for being sick and dying before you had the chance to tell her you loved her and you would always love her despite how angry you are at her. Then you throw all the anger, the sadness and the bitterness in the canal and leave it there once and for all.*

She'd have to tell Father Murray that this was *another* way to get a sacred heart when she called him later.

"You're brilliant," Lillian said just as the setting March sun shone brightly on all three of them. She kissed each of them on the tops of their heads and hugged them to her. "You two guys are absolutely brilliant."

They didn't understand why, but then they didn't understand things Lilly said a lot of the time, and they ignored her now just as they usually did.

"I'm hungry," Philip said, putting his arm around Lillian's hip and reaching out to take his little sister's hand. "Can we have pizza tonight…half pepperoni?"

∾

| | |
|---|---|
| From: | Lillian Phelan [lpfreelncrwrtr@aol.com] |
| To: | Dan Paulsen [dpaulsen1@msn.com] |
| Subject: | Here it is! |
| Sent: | 3/26 2:47 A.M. |
| Attachment: | The Women of Willow Wood |

Danny, what are you doing in April? Father Murray has an opening on the 20th. Suzy wants to be a flower girl. I love you, Danny boy. Let's get married.

PS: My book is finished and attached. You're going to like it. The dedication reads: *To the memory of my mother, Regina Stuart Phelan, and all the women who were bathed in the tears of the willow.*

# BOOKS BY THIS AUTHOR

### FICTION
*Holding Silk*
*Ashley Hall*
*Tears of the Willow*

### NON-FICTION
*Joshua's Ring*
*Colonial Inns and Taverns of Bucks County*
*The Delaware Canal: From Stone Coal Highway to Historic Landmark*

# ABOUT THE AUTHOR

In addition to writing novels and non-fiction histories, Marie Murphy Duess develops and conducts creative writing workshops, and gives presentations about local history based on her non-fiction titles.

She is a member of the International Women's Writing Guild, Historical Novel Society, the Independent Book Publishers Association, and The Questers Organization. She is the Vice President of Duess Consulting Services, a communications and graphic arts company.

She lives in beautiful Bucks County, Pennsylvania, with her husband, Ed.

She also shares her home with a dog who has failed dog obedience school twice, and Stoli, the cat from hell.

For more information, visit www.MarieDuess.com

# *DISCUSSION QUESTIONS*

1. Would you have given this book a different title? If so, what is your title?

2. Did you think that the historical chapters and references were distracting to the contemporary story?

3. What surprised you most about the story?

4. Were you able to identify with Lillian? Were her emotional limitations reasonable?

5. Why would Lillian have moved back to Newtown when she had so many unhappy memories of her childhood?

6. What did you think about Ann's deception? Was it acceptable in her circumstances? Would what she did make you angry if you had been Lillian?

7. Would you have done anything differently if placed in their situations?

8. Did any of the characters remind you of someone you know? If so, do you feel that you understand that person a little better now?

9. How did the way Lillian and Ann see themselves differ from how others see them?

10. What did you think of Lillian and Dan's relationship? What kind of man is Dan?

11. What do you think the priest meant when he spoke to Lillian about needing a "sacred" heart?

12. Do you agree that forgiveness is one of the most important things a person can experience to find peace?

13. Have you ever experienced knowing or living with someone with mental illness?

14. Was there any particular passage in this book that touched a nerve?

15. Was there anything different that Lillian could have done to help the children?

16. Have your views about mental illness changed after reading this book?

17. What did you learn from this story? Was there historical information in it that you had not known before?

18. Did your opinion about the book change as you read it?

19. Did your opinion about the characters change?

20. Would you have ended the book differently? If so, what would your ending have been?

21. If there was a sequel to this book, which characters would you like to know more about?

# ABOUT THE HISTORICAL PASSAGES IN

# TEARS OF THE WILLOW

*If you would like to learn more about the area in which this story takes place, please visit the following historic sites.*

## Washington Crossing Historic Park, Washington Crossing, PA

http://www.ushistory.org/washingtoncrossing

In the early winter of 1776, the Continental Army was greatly challenged. The American troops had been on the run from the British, and when they crossed the Delaware River and arrived on the frozen farmlands of Bucks County, Pennsylvania, they were weary, battered, and ailing. After arriving in Bucks County, General Washington planned two successful surprise attacks that proved to be a turning point in the Revolutionary War.

Washington Crossing Historic Park is a wonderful place to learn more about this important time in American History.

## Delaware Canal State Park

http://www.dcnr.state.pa.us/stateparks/findapark/delawarecanal

A walk along the peaceful 60-mile towpath on the Delaware Canal is a joy to be experienced at least once in your life. It is the only remaining continuously intact canal of the canal era, which took place in the early and mid-19th century.

## Friends of the Delaware Canal, New Hope, PA

http://www.fodc.org/

Visit the headquarters and museum in the historic Locktender's House at Lock 11 in New Hope, Pennsylvania, and learn more about the boat captains, mule drivers, and locktenders who helped propel the United States into the Industrial Revolution.

## Revolutionary War Burial Site, Langhorne, PA

http://www.historiclanghorne.org/

Langhorne Borough, 114 East Maple Avenue, Langhorne, PA 19047

The story of this almost forgotten burial site for Revolutionary soldiers is a must-read.

## Mercer Museum, Doylestown, PA

84 South Pine Street, Doylestown, PA 18901

http://www.mercermuseum.org

A magical museum, filled with artifacts from history.

*Bucks County is rich in history.*

*Its many historical societies and quaint boroughs keep history alive.*

*Come visit, bring the children, and learn more.*

Made in the USA
Middletown, DE
06 September 2017